About the Authors

Annie West has devoted her writing career to creating charismatic heroes who entice and enthral, and sassy heroines who capture the lives of their heroines. As a lover of unusual locations for romance, from vibrant cities to desert encampments and fairytale castles. Annie lives in eastern Australia with her hero husband, between sandy beaches and gorgeous wine country. She finds writing the perfect excuse to postpone housework. To contact her or join her newsletter, visit annie-west.com

Carole Mortimer was born in England, the youngest of three children. She began writing in 1978, and has now written over 170 books for Mills & Boon. Carole has six sons, Matthew, Joshua, Timothy, Michael, David and Peter. She says, 'I'm happily married to Peter senior; we're best friends as well as lovers, which is probably the best recipe for a successful relationship. We live in a lovely part of England.'

The day **Maggie Cox** saw the film version of *Wuthering Heights*, was the day she became hooked on romance. From that day onwards she spent a lot of time dreaming up her own romances, hoping that one day she might become published. Now that her dream is being realised, she wakes up every morning and counts her blessings. She is married to a gorgeous man, and is the mother of two wonderful sons. Her other passions in life – besides her family and reading/writing – are music and films.

The Secret Heirs

COLLECTION

Secret Heirs: His One Night Consequence

ANNIE WEST

CAROLE MORTIMER

MAGGIE COX

MILLS & BOON

First Published in Great Britain 2020
By Mills & Boon, an imprint of HarperCollins*Publishers*
1 London Bridge Street, London, SE1 9GF

SECRET HEIRS: HIS ONE NIGHT CONSEQUENCE © 2020
Harlequin Books S.A.

Forgotten Mistress, Secret Love-Child © 2009 Annie West
The Infamous Italian's Secret Baby © 2009 Carole Mortimer
Mistress, Mother...Wife? © 2011 Maggie Cox

ISBN: 978-0-263-28074-

0120

MIX
aper from
responsible sources
FSC™ C007454
www.fsc.org

This book is produced from independently certified FSC™ paper to ensure responsible forest management.

For more information visit: www.harpercollins.co.uk/green

Printed and bound in Spain
by CPI, Barcelona

FORGOTTEN MISTRESS, SECRET LOVE-CHILD

ANNIE WEST

This one's for Judy!
Hope it brings you joy.
Warm hugs and huge thanks to
Anna, Josie, Marilyn, Monique and Serena,
whose expertise made this book possible.

CHAPTER ONE

ALESSANDRO spared barely a glance for the promotional material he tossed into his out tray. His newest PA still hadn't learnt what he should see and what he had no time for. The textile manufacturing arm of the company would be represented at the upcoming trade fair. But one of his managers could handle that. It hardly needed the CEO to…

Oddio mio!

His gaze caught on a photo as a brochure landed askew, half covered by discarded papers.

Alessandro's eyes narrowed on the curve of a woman's smile, a tiny mole like a beauty spot drawing attention to a mouth that would catch any man's interest. Wide, lush, inviting.

Every muscle froze even as his pulse revved and blood roared in his ears.

That smile.

That mouth.

Yet it wasn't sexual awareness that arrested him. A tantalising wisp of almost-memory wafted behind his conscious thoughts. A taste, sweet as ripe summer cherries, rich and addictive.

Heat filled him, despite the climate-controlled air in his spacious office. A zap of something that might have been emotion stifled the breath in his lungs. Alessandro froze, telling himself not to analyse but to relax and let the sensations surface. *Willing* the recollections to come.

Like a lacy curtain in a breeze, the blankness cloaking his

memory of those missing months two years ago rippled. It shifted, parted, and then dropped back into place.

His hands clenched, white-knuckled on the edge of his glass and black marble desk. But Alessandro didn't register pain, just the infuriating, familiar sense of nothingness.

Only to himself would he acknowledge how helpless that void made him feel. How vulnerable. It didn't matter that he'd been assured those lost months contained nothing out of the ordinary. Other people remembered that time: what he'd done and said. But he, Alessandro Mattani, had no recall.

Swift as thought, he tugged the brochure from the papers. It was an advertisement for a luxury hotel. He turned it over. A luxury hotel in Melbourne.

Alessandro waited, but no spark of recognition came. He hadn't travelled to Melbourne.

Not that he could remember.

Impatience flared and he forced it down, breathing deeply. An emotional response wouldn't help. Even if the sense of loss, of missing something vital, sometimes threatened to drive him to the edge.

He flipped over the flyer again. A woman, a receptionist, smiled at a handsome couple as they checked in. The photo was professionally styled, yet despite its air-brushed gloss, there was something riveting about the receptionist's smile.

The setting was opulent, but Alessandro had grown up with luxury and barely bothered to notice. The woman, on the other hand…she intrigued him.

The more he stared, the more he felt an atavistic premonition that made his blood pump faster and prickled the skin at his nape. She was so familiar.

Had she smiled at him like that?

A tickle of awareness started low in his belly.

A tickle of…certainty.

Carefully he catalogued her features. Dark hair pulled back sleekly from a pleasant but unremarkable face. Her nose was pert, a trifle short. Her eyes were surprisingly light for her brunette colouring. Her mouth was wide.

She wasn't beautiful. She wasn't exotic enough to turn heads. And yet she had…something. A charisma the photographer had seen and capitalised on.

Alessandro traced the angle of her cheekbone, the gentle curve of her jaw, to pause on the lush promise of her lips.

There it was again. That tingle of presentiment. The intuition that she was no stranger. It drew every muscle and sinew in his body tight, as if in readiness for action.

Behind the opaque gauze of his faulty memory something shifted.

Sensation, soft as the tentative brush of those lips against his. That taste again, of sun-ripened cherries. Irresistible. The phantom caress of delicate fingers along his jaw, over his rapidly pulsing heart. The sound of feminine sighs, the aftermath of ecstasy.

Alessandro's chest heaved as if from intense physical exertion. Sweat prickled his nape and brow as his body stirred with arousal.

Impossible!

Yet instinct clamoured with a truth he couldn't ignore.

He knew her. Had met her. Held her. Made love to her.

His nostrils flared on a surge of wholly masculine possessiveness. The primitive sense of ownership, of a male scenting his mate, was unmistakeable.

He stared at the image of a stranger from the other side of the world. If he hadn't visited Melbourne, had she travelled here to Lombardia?

Frustration at those missing months simmered.

For long minutes Alessandro considered the photograph, his thumb absently caressing the curve of her cheek.

Impossible as it seemed, the certainty grew that this woman held the key to his locked memories. Could she open them? Restore what he'd lost and obliterate the sense that he was somehow less than he'd been. The gnawing hint of dissatisfaction with his world.

Alessandro reached for the phone. He intended to have answers, no matter what it took.

* * *

'Thanks, Sarah, you're a lifesaver.' Relief flooded Carys. Today everything that could go wrong had. At least this one thing, the most important, was sorted.

'No worries,' her neighbour and babysitter responded. 'Leo will be fine staying over.'

Carys knew Sarah was right, but that didn't stop the twinge of regret, sharp in her chest. When she'd taken this job at the Landford Hotel it was with the expectation she'd be home most days at a reasonable hour. Early enough to look after her son.

She didn't want Leo growing used to an absentee parent too busy with her career to spend time with him. The sort of home life Carys had taken for granted as a child.

Especially since Leo only had her.

The twinge beneath her breast intensified, catching her breath as pain ripped through her. Even after all this time she couldn't suppress the shaft of regret and longing that pierced her whenever she remembered.

She needed to toughen up. Once upon a time she'd chased her dream, but she wasn't fool enough to believe in it any more. Not after she'd learned so cruelly how futile that dream was.

'Carys? What's wrong?'

'Nothing.' Hastily she forced a smile, knowing Sarah could read her tone even over the phone. 'I owe you one.'

'You sure do. You can babysit for us next weekend. We've got plans for a night on the town, if you can mind Ashleigh.'

'Done.' She looked at her watch. She had to get back before the next crisis hit. 'Don't forget to give Leo a goodnight kiss from me.' Stupid to feel that catch in her throat because tonight she wouldn't feed him his evening meal or kiss his plump pink cheek at bedtime.

Her son was in good hands and, she told herself sternly, she was lucky to have landed a job that usually gave her regular time with him. She was grateful the management had been impressed enough to allow her reasonably family-friendly hours.

Today was the exception. The flu that ravaged the Landford's staff had hit at the worst possible time. More than a third of the staff was off sick just when there was a series of major functions.

It didn't matter that Carys had already spent more than a full day on the job. The collapse just an hour ago of David, the senior functions manager, with a soaring temperature, meant Carys had to step into that role too.

Nerves fluttered in her stomach. This was her chance to prove herself and justify David's faith in her, having taken her on despite her incomplete qualifications. He'd been a good friend and a terrific mentor. She owed him not only her position, but the hard-won self-confidence she'd slowly built since coming to Melbourne.

'I don't know what time I'll be back, Sarah. Probably in the early hours.' Steadfastly Carys refused to worry about how she'd manage the trip home. She couldn't rely on public transport at that time, and the cost of a cab was prohibitive. 'I'll see you around breakfast time, if that's OK?'

'That's fine, Carys. Don't fret. We'll see you when we see you.'

Slowly Carys replaced the phone and stretched her hunched shoulders. She'd been working at the computer and on the phone without a break for so long her body ached all over.

She glanced at the monitor before her and saw the lines of the spreadsheet she'd opened dance and jumble before her eyes. She pinched the bridge of her nose, knowing that no matter how hard she concentrated, working on the document would be a test of endurance and determination.

Sighing, she reached for her tinted reading glasses and leaned forward.

She had to finish this. Only then could she make last minute checks on the arrangements for tonight's masked ball.

Carys stood in the corner of the ballroom near the door to the kitchens, listening to the head waiter's whispered update. It was mayhem in the kitchen with more staff struck down by this virulent flu. Only a couple of the extra waitstaff had arrived to replace those who'd phoned in ill, and the chefs were barely able to cope.

Fortunately, the guests hadn't noticed anything wrong. The Landford prided itself on superb service, and the staff were doing everything to live up to that reputation.

The ballroom, all black and gold, was gracious and formally elegant. Antique chandeliers sparkled, casting a glow that set jewels scintillating among the A-list crowd. The guests looked impossibly chic as befitted one of Fashion Week's major events.

The room smelled of exclusive fragrances, hothouse flowers and money. Serious money. Celebrities, designers, buyers, the *crème de la crème* of Australian society, were here tonight and plenty of international high-flyers too.

And they were all her responsibility.

Carys' pulse thundered and she struggled to focus on her companion's words. She must concentrate if she wanted to ensure tonight was a success. Too much was at stake.

'All right. I'll see if we can get someone else from the restaurant to help out.' She nodded, dismissing him and turning to the house phone on the wall. She reached out to hit the speed dial number for the restaurant, then froze.

A tingling sensation began at the base of her spine. It burned its way up her back like the slide of hot ice on bare skin. Except her skin wasn't bare. She wore a regulation jacket and straight skirt, dark stockings and high heels.

Yet through the layers of clothing her skin sizzled, the hairs on her neck prickling.

Carys replaced the phone with stiff, unsteady fingers. She pivoted, turning to face the shifting, colourful crowd. Staff circulated with gourmet canapés and vintage champagne; groups broke and reformed.

The guests, most of them wearing exquisite handmade masks, were busy enjoying themselves or networking or showing off their finery. They wouldn't notice anyone who didn't belong in their rarefied circle.

That suited Carys. She didn't hanker for a place at a fairy-tale ball. Not since she'd given up on the whole Prince Charming fantasy.

Yet heat washed her cheeks. Her breath snagged in her throat and her pulse accelerated as instinct told her she was being watched.

Her heart was in her mouth as frantically she searched the

throng for something, someone, familiar. Someone who could make her skin tingle and her heart race as it had before, long ago.

Briefly she shut her eyes. Madness! That was in the past. A past best forgotten.

Tiredness and nerves had simply made her imagine things.

Her path and his would never cross again. He'd made certain of that. Carys' lips twisted in a grimace as familiar pain stabbed her chest.

No! Not now. She refused to let her wayward imagination distract her. People depended on her. She had a job to do.

From across the packed room he watched her.

His fingers curled, white-knuckled, around the back of a nearby chair. Blood roared in his ears as his heart thundered out of control. The shock of recognition was so strong he shut his eyes for an instant and lightning flickered across the darkness of his closed lids.

Opening them, he saw her turn to the wall phone, her movements jerky.

It was her. Not just the woman from the brochure, but more, the woman he remembered. Correction—almost remembered.

An image teased his mind. An image of her walking away from him. Her back rigid, her steps staccato bites that ate up the ground as if she couldn't get away fast enough. Bites that echoed the rapid pulse of his drumming heart as he stood rooted to the spot. She carried a case, the taxi driver ahead of her stowing another bag in his vehicle.

Finally she paused. Alessandro's heart stopped and rose in his throat. But she didn't turn around. A moment later she was in the car as it accelerated in a spurt of gravel and swooped away down the private road from his Lake Como home.

Still he stood, prey to an alien mix of sensations. Fury, relief, disappointment, disbelief.

And hurt! Pain filled the yawning chasm inside him.

Only once before in his entire life had Alessandro felt so intensely. At five, when his mother had deserted him for a life of pampered luxury with her lover.

He stirred and shook his head, banishing the misty image, belatedly aware again of the crowded ballroom.

Yet the powerful brew of emotions still stirred in his breast. *Maddona mia!* No wonder he felt vulnerable. Such feelings… Who was this woman to awake such responses in him?

Anger mingled with impatience. That mere chance had led him here. That he could so easily have missed this opportunity to learn more.

Deliberately he flexed his fingers and let go of the chair back, feeling at last the deep imprint of curved wood score his palm.

The wait was over.

He would have his answers now. Tonight.

Surreptitiously Carys slid a foot from her shoe and wriggled her toes. Soon the ball would be over. Then she could oversee the clearing away and setting up for the next day's fashion show.

She suppressed a rising yawn. Every bone in her body ached, and she wanted nothing more than to flop into bed.

She skirted the dance floor. She'd just check on—

A hand, large, warm and insistent took hers, pulling her to a halt. Quickly she summoned a serene expression, ready to deal with the guest who'd overstepped the boundaries by touching her. She hoped he wasn't intoxicated.

Carys had just pinned a small professional smile on her face when a tug of her hand made her turn.

The carefully crafted smile slid away.

For an instant Carys' heart stopped beating as she looked up at the man before her.

Unlike most of the revellers, he still wore his mask. His dark hair was cut brutally short, sculpting a beautifully shaped head. The mask shadowed his eyes, but she caught a gleam of dark fire. His mouth was a grim slash above a strong, firm chin.

Her eyes widened, staring at that chin. It couldn't be…

Then he moved and she caught the faint tang of an unfamiliar cologne. Her heart dived.

Of course it wasn't him!

A scar snaked up his brow from the edge of the mask. The

man she'd known had been as devastatingly handsome as a young god. No scars. His complexion had been golden too, olive, gilded by hours in the sun, not as pale as this stranger's.

And yet…

And yet she stupidly wished in that moment it was him. Against all logic and the need to protect herself, how badly she wanted it to be so.

Carys drew herself up straighter, fumbling for poise while her nerves screamed with disappointment.

He was tall, far taller than she, even though she wore heels. Surely as tall as… No! She wasn't going there. Wasn't playing that pathetic game any more.

'Can I help you?' The words emerged huskily, more like an intimate invitation than a cool query.

Silently she cursed the way he'd thrown her off balance just by reminding her of a time, and a man, best forgotten.

'I think you've mistaken me for someone else.' She rushed into speech again, needing to rein in wayward thoughts. Her words were clipped, though she was careful not to reveal her annoyance. If she could extricate herself without a fuss, she would.

Carys tugged her hand but his grip firmed and he drew her forward. She stumbled, surprised by his implacable hold.

Tilting her head up, she looked him in the eye. She expected him to comment on the food or the music, or demand assistance in some way.

Instead his silence unnerved her.

Her skin grew tight as the illusion grew that they stood alone, cut off from the others.

Around them conversation buzzed, music swirled, and a tinkle of feminine laughter sounded. But the man in the perfectly cut dinner jacket, with the perfectly cut jaw, said nothing. Just held her.

Heat flared under her skin as again instinct shouted a warning to beware.

His hold shifted and his thumb slid over the sensitive place between her thumb and forefinger. A spike of heat transfixed her. Her eyes widened as a tremor echoed through the secret recesses of her body.

'You need to let me go.' She lifted her chin higher, wishing she could see his eyes properly.

He inclined his head, and the breath she hadn't known she held whooshed out. See? He probably just wanted something mundane like another bottle of wine for his table.

She opened her mouth to enquire when someone bumped her, propelling her towards the hard male torso before her.

Carys heard a muffled apology but barely noticed.

Large hands grasped her upper arms. In front of her stretched an expanse of exquisitely tailored elegance, that ultra-masculine chin with just the hint of a cleft and a pair of shoulders to make any woman sit up and take notice.

Shoulders just like…

Carys bit her lip. This had to end.

This was a *stranger.* So he had shoulders to die for and a jaw that seemed achingly familiar. The gold signet ring on his finger was one she'd never seen. And, despite the similar height, he was leaner than the man she'd known.

Another couple buffeted her, talking volubly as they passed. Suddenly she found herself plastered against a hard body that seemed all heat and raw strength. Her senses whirled in a giddy riot.

She imagined she could feel each muscle of his body against hers. Beneath the expensive cologne an elusive undertone of warm male skin tickled her nostrils and she inhaled sharply. He was too familiar, like a phantom from one of the endless dreams that haunted her.

His odd silence intensified her sense of unreality.

Then his hold shifted. A hand slid down her back, poised almost possessively just above her bottom, long fingers spread. Heat roared in the pit of her belly. The heat of desire. A sensation she hadn't felt, it seemed, in a lifetime.

Her body responded to the ultra-masculine allure of his, softening, trembling—

'I need to go.' Carys jerked her head back from the muscled chest that drew her like a magnet. 'Please!'

Her mouth trembled in a wobbly grimace, and to her dismay

hot tears prickled her eyes. Part of her yearned crazily to succumb to his potent maleness.

Because he reminded her of the one man who had taught her the dangers of instant physical attraction.

She had to get out of here.

With a strength born of desperation, she wrenched herself free and stumbled back, off balance when he released her instantly.

Carys took a shaky step away, then another.

The man in the dark mask watched her, eyes unreadable, his body as still as a predator about to pounce.

Her throat squeezed tight in inexplicable panic. She opened her mouth but no sound came. Then she spun and blindly forced her way through the crowd.

Wearily Carys tucked a strand of hair behind her ear. The last of the guests had finally gone and the vast ballroom was empty but for the staff tidying up and moving furniture.

The chirrup of a house phone snagged her attention. She found herself crossing her fingers that there were no more problems. Not tonight, correction, this morning. She was running on empty.

She was still unsettled by the memory of the stranger. The man who'd seemed so familiar yet couldn't be.

'Hello?'

'Carys? Glad I caught you.' She recognised the new guy on night duty at reception. 'You've got an urgent call. I'll connect you.'

Instantly all weariness vanished at the sound of those dreaded words 'urgent call'. Carys' stomach dropped and fear filled the void. Was it Leo? An illness? An accident?

She twisted a button on her jacket, waiting breathlessly for bad news as her nerves stretched taut.

It would be tonight of all nights that something went wrong. She should have found a way to get home earlier.

The click of the new connection was loud in her ears. As was the silence that followed, a waiting silence.

'Sarah? What's wrong? What's happened?'

There was a pause in which she heard the echo of her own breathing.

Then a voice like black velvet emerged.

'Carys.'

Just one word and every hair on her body rose. It was the voice that haunted her dreams. A voice that, despite everything, still had the power to thicken her blood, turning it to warm treacle.

Her knees buckled and she found herself sitting on the edge of a table that had been moved up against the wall.

Her fingers splayed over her throat in a desperate gesture of vulnerability.

It couldn't be!

Her mouth opened and her throat worked, but no sound emerged.

'We need to meet,' said the voice of her past. 'Now.'

CHAPTER TWO

'WHO is this?' Carys' voice emerged as a raw croak.

It couldn't be.

Not here. Not now.

Not after she'd finally convinced herself she never wanted to see him again. Fate couldn't be so cruel.

Yet some wayward self-destructive impulse sent a buzz of excitement skimming along her nerves. Once she'd longed for him to make contact, to come after her, tell her he'd been wrong. Tell her…no, she wasn't so credulous as to believe in such fantasies any more.

What did he want? Her hand tightened like a claw at her throat. A premonition of danger filled her, icing her blood.

'You know who it is, Carys.' Just the way he pronounced her name with that sexy Italian accent turned the word into a caress that melted her insides.

He'd always threatened her self-control. Carys remembered murmured enticements in that dark coffee voice and how he'd persuaded her to give up everything she'd worked for just for the privilege of being with him.

Fool!

She shivered and sat up straighter, berating herself.

'Please identify yourself,' she said tersely.

It couldn't be him. He'd never follow her to Australia. He'd made that clear when she'd left with her tail between her legs.

But the memory of the stranger tonight at the ball, the masked man who'd made her think of *him,* battered at her disbelief. Wildly she shook her head, trying to clear a brain overloaded by exhaustion and stress.

Was she going mad? Seeing him, even hearing him, when she knew perfectly well he was ensconced in his oh-so-exclusive world of rich, elegant, aristocratic friends. Of high-flying business deals and blue blood and glamour.

Where people like her only provided brief amusement.

'Don't pretend not to know me, Carys. I have no time for puerile games.' He paused as if waiting for her to rush into speech. 'It's Alessandro Mattani.'

Silence throbbed as she clutched the receiver. Her heart crashed against her ribs. She would have slid to the floor if she hadn't already been sitting.

'Alessandro…'

'Mattani. I'm sure you recognise the name.' His voice was sharp as a razor.

Recognise the name! Once she'd even hoped to share it with him.

A bubble of hysterical laughter threatened to explode from her stiff lips. Carys slapped her palm across her mouth, concentrating on deep breaths. She needed oxygen.

The room spun crazily and dark spots whirled in her vision.

A clatter jerked her back to full awareness, and she looked down as if from an enormous distance to see the phone had slipped from her nerveless fingers onto the table.

Alessandro Mattani.

The man she'd loved.

The man who'd broken her heart.

A sound caught her attention and Carys looked up, suddenly aware again of her surroundings. The last of the staff were leaving and waving goodnight.

Belatedly she lifted a hand in acknowledgement.

Dazedly she looked around. The stage was set for to-morrow's fashion show. Enormous jardinières with arrangements of exotic orchids and jungle greenery had been strategically positioned as she'd instructed. The lights were dimmed and she was alone.

But for the voice on the other end of the line. The voice of her dreams.

Tentatively, as if reaching out to touch an untamed animal, Carys stretched her fingers to the phone. She lifted it, and a deep voice barked in her ear.

'Carys?'

'I'm here.'

Silence, but for the impatient hiss of indrawn breath.

'No more games. I want to see you.'

Well, bully for him. She was past the stage of worrying what Alessandro Mattani wanted.

Besides, she wasn't foolish enough to go near him again. Even now she didn't trust her hard-won defences against the man who'd only had to smile and crook his finger to get what he wanted from her. She'd surrendered her job, all her plans, even her self-respect to be with him.

Carys stiffened her spine and braced her palm on the table beside her.

'That's not possible.'

'Of course it's possible,' he bit out. 'I'm just twelve floors away.'

Twelve floors? Her heart galloped faster. Here, in Melbourne? At the Landford?

Her gaze swerved to the edge of the dance floor, instinct and disbelief warring.

'That *was* you tonight? At the ball?' If she'd been less stunned, she might have cared about how much her strained voice revealed. But she was battling shock. She had no thought to spare for pride.

He didn't answer.

Heat sparked low in her abdomen and washed through her like a flood tide. It *had* been him. He'd held her in his arms.

How often had she yearned for his embrace? Despite what she'd told herself about forgetting the past.

He'd held her and she hadn't known him?

But she had, hadn't she? Despite the new cologne, the paleness of his once-golden skin, the scar.

Fear jolted through her, stealing her breath.

He'd been hurt! How badly? Urgent questions clamoured on her tongue.

Shakily Carys gathered the tattered remnants of control. She ignored the unspoken questions, opting for the most important one.

'What do you want?' Her voice sounded stretched too thin, like beaten metal about to snap under pressure.

'I've already told you.' Impatience threaded his words. 'To see you.'

She couldn't prevent a snort of disbelief at his words. How times had changed.

Finally pride came to her rescue.

'It's late. I've had a long day and I'm going home. There's nothing more to say between us.' Tentatively she slipped her feet to the floor, waiting to see if her legs would collapse under her.

'Are you sure?' His words, soft and deep like the alpine eiderdowns they'd once shared, brushed across her senses. His voice was alive with erotic undercurrents.

She jerked upright.

Flame licked that secret needy place deep inside her, the place that had been cold and empty ever since she'd left him. The realisation drew her anger.

No, she wasn't sure. That was the hell of it.

'I'm in the presidential suite,' he said after a moment. 'I'll expect you in ten minutes.'

'You have no right to give me orders.' Belatedly she found her voice.

'You don't wish to meet me?' Incredulity coloured his tone.

Had he never had a knock-back from a woman?

Certainly not from her. She'd been putty in his elegant, powerful hands from the instant she'd fallen head over heels for him.

'The past is the past.' At the last moment she prevented herself saying his name. She didn't want the sound of it on her lips. It was too intimate, evoked too many memories.

'Perhaps so. But *I* wish to meet *you.*' His tone made it clear that he wasn't about to go down on bended knee and beg her forgiveness.

Carys rubbed her forehead. The very thought of Alessandro, darling of the jet set, commercial power-broker and hundred percent red-hot macho Italian male on his knees before any woman was ludicrous.

'You have ten minutes,' he reiterated.

'And if I don't come?'

He took his time responding. 'That's your choice, Ms Wells.' His formality in that silky smooth voice held more threat than any bluster. Or was that her imagination?

'I have personal matters to discuss. I thought you'd prefer to do that in the privacy of my suite. Of course, I can see you instead during business hours tomorrow.' He paused. 'I understand you share an office with colleagues? Presumably they won't be inconvenienced by our conversation.'

He left the sentence dangling and Carys bit her lip, imagining how her workmates would react to Alessandro and his *personal matters.*

'No doubt your manager won't mind you taking time off to deal with a private matter,' he purred in that outrageously delicious accent. 'Even though I understand you're only here on an extended probation?'

Carys' jaw dropped. He'd had her records investigated! How else could he know about her long probation period since she'd been employed without completing her qualifications?

Those employment details were supposed to be confidential.

Her defensive hackles rose as the old sense of inadequacy surfaced. Of not being good enough. Not making the grade. And more, of being cornered, facing an implacable, unstoppable force that threatened to overpower her.

Defeat tasted bitter on her tongue.

Or was that fear? Fear that, despite his initial rejection, Alessandro had come to take Leo from her.

Her shoulders tightened.

'Ten minutes,' she confirmed.

Alessandro stood at the full-length window, staring across the Yarra River to the lights of Melbourne's cityscape.

He didn't see them. Instead his brain conjured an image of blue-grey eyes, wide and apparently guileless.

He shifted as heat shot through his body straight from his groin at the memory of her soft body nestled against him.

From the moment he'd sighted her across the ballroom, he'd known. The awareness he'd experienced looking at her photo was nothing compared with tonight's instant gut-deep certainty.

This woman was his.

Alessandro tossed back the espresso his butler had brewed, feeling the shot of caffeine in his blood.

His earlier flash of memory told him they hadn't parted amicably. Hell, she'd walked out on him! No other lover had ever done that.

Yet he knew with absolute certainty there was still something between them. Something that accounted for the nagging dissatisfaction that had plagued him since the accident.

Why had they separated?

He intended to discover everything about the yawning blankness that was his memory of the months preceding his accident.

He refused to let her escape till he had answers.

From the moment he'd held her, the sense of unfinished business between them had been overwhelming. Even now he felt the low-grade hum of awareness, waiting for her.

There was more too. Not just the immediate sense of connection and possessiveness. There was an inner turmoil that surely must be long-dormant emotions.

He'd watched her, listened to her, and been dumbstruck by the intensity of his conflicting feelings.

Alessandro had harnessed all his willpower to drive himself to recover from his injuries and turn around the faltering family business. He'd blocked out everything but the need to haul the company from the brink of disaster. Everything else had been a pallid blur.

Until now no one had come close to breaking through his guarded self-possession. Not his step-mother, not the many women angling for his attention. Not his friends.

Despite his wide social circle, he was a loner like his father. The old man had isolated himself, focusing only on business after his first wife's betrayal and desertion.

As a result Alessandro had learned the Mattani way early, concealing his boyish grief and bewilderment behind a façade. Over the years that façade of calm had become reality. He'd developed the knack of repressing strong emotions, distancing himself from personal vulnerability.

Until tonight. When he'd come face to face with Carys Wells. And he'd…*felt* things. A stirring of discontent, desire, loss.

He frowned. He had no time for emotions.

Lust, yes. He was no stranger to physical desire. That was easily assuaged. But the disturbing sensations churning in his belly were unfamiliar, caused by something more complex.

A knock sounded on the door. Grateful for the interruption to his unpalatable thoughts, Alessandro put down his cup and turned as the butler crossed the foyer.

Alessandro was surprised to register his shoulders stiffening, locking as tension hardened his stance.

Since when had he, Alessandro Mattani, experienced nerves? Even when the specialists had shaken their heads over his injuries, referring to complications and a long convalescence, all he'd felt was impatience to get out of hospital. Especially when he'd learned the impact his accident, so soon after his father's death, had caused.

The commercial vultures had begun circling, ready to take advantage of the mistakes his father had made in those last months and of Alessandro's incapacity.

'Ms Wells, sir.' The butler ushered her into the sitting room.

She stood as if poised for flight, just inside the door. Once more that shock of connection smacked him square in the chest. He rocked back on his feet.

Jerkily she lifted a hand to smooth her hair, then dropped it as she caught his scrutiny.

Tension, palpable and vibrating, strung out between their locked gazes.

Carys Wells looked out of place in the opulence of

Melbourne's most exclusive hotel suite. Unless, of course, she was here to provide a personal service to the occupant. Delivering a message or bringing room service.

Alessandro's thoughts jagged on the sort of *personal* service he'd like her to provide.

It didn't matter that he knew any number of more beautiful women. Clever, high achievers who combined chic style, business savvy and an eagerness to share his bed.

Something about Carys set her apart.

Her curves would horrify the perpetually dieting women he knew in Milano. Her dark hair was severely styled, if you could call scraping it back into a bun a style. Her make-up was discreet, and she wore a sensible navy suit that no woman of his acquaintance would be seen dead in.

Yet the way her face had lit with emotion earlier hinted at a more subtle attractiveness. And those legs... The sight of her shapely calves and trim ankles in high heels and dark stockings tugged at his long-dormant libido.

Alessandro's hands flexed. He wanted to explore further, to discover if her legs were as sexy all the way up.

Instinct—or was it memory?—told him her legs were superb. Just as he knew he'd found pleasure in her neatly curved figure and her deliciously full lips.

Belatedly he dragged his gaze from the woman who'd lured him halfway around the world.

The way she sidetracked him was unprecedented. One way or another he had to get her out of his system.

'*Grazie,* Robson. That's all for tonight.'

The butler inclined his head. 'There are refreshments on the sideboard should you require them, sir, madam.' Not by so much as a flicker did he indicate he knew the woman before him to be a co-worker. Then he moved silently away towards the kitchen and the staff entrance.

'Please—' Alessandro gestured to the nearby lounge '—take a seat.'

For a moment he thought she wasn't going to accept. Finally she walked across the antique carpet to sit in a cavernous wing chair. The glow of lamps lit her face, revealing a tension around her pursed lips he hadn't noticed before. She looked tired.

Alessandro flicked a look at his watch. It was very late. He'd become accustomed to working long into the night, fuelled by caffeine and his own formidable drive.

Conscience niggled. He should have left this till tomorrow. But he'd been unable to ignore the edgy frustration that drove him relentlessly. He was so close he couldn't rest till he had answers from her.

He'd already been stymied once. Alessandro had confronted her at the ball only to find he'd been robbed of composure and even the power of speech by a shocking blast of recognition. He'd frozen, the one thought in his atrophying mind to hold her and not let her go.

The completeness of that instant of vulnerability had stunned and shamed him. *Never* had he felt at such a loss. Not in business. Definitely not in his dealings with women.

Now he was himself once more. It would not happen again. *Alessandro Mattani did not do vulnerable.*

He thrust aside the momentary doubt at his tactics and strode across to the sideboard.

'Tea, coffee?' he offered. 'Wine?'

'I don't want anything.' She sat straighter, her chin hitched high in unspoken defiance. That spark of rebellion brought colour to her cheeks and made her eyes sparkle.

Alessandro paused, watching fascinated as she transformed from drab to intriguing in an instant. Then he turned, poured himself a small measure of cognac, and took a seat opposite her.

All the while she watched him with those luminous eyes that had captivated him the moment he saw her.

What did she see? Was she cataloguing the differences in him? It surprised him to discover how much he wanted to read her thoughts. Know what she felt. Did she too experience this gnawing tension, like an ache between the ribs?

'I see you've noticed my scar.'

The wash of colour along her cheekbones intensified, but she didn't look away. Nor did she respond.

Alessandro wasn't vain enough to worry about his marred face. Besides, it was his wealth and position as much as his looks to which women responded. They might say they wanted a man of charm or kindness, but he knew how fickle they were. Neither marriage vows nor ties of blood between mother and child could hold them when they found someone who offered more wealth and prestige.

That didn't bother Alessandro. He had both in abundance. If ever he wanted a woman permanently he'd have his pick. Some time in the future. Not now.

He swirled the fine brandy in its glass, inhaling its mellow scent.

'Am I so repulsive, then?' He shot her a look that dared her to prevaricate.

Repulsive? Carys wished he were. Then maybe she could tear her gaze away. Her heart hammered. She struggled to hide her shortened breathing as she felt the tug of his potent masculine aura.

It had always been the same. But she'd prayed time and common sense would cure her of the fatal weakness.

She met his intense moss-green gaze, recognised the way his thick dark lashes shadowed his eyes. His eyelids dropped as if to hide his thoughts. The familiarity of that expression, as much as its banked heat, made her insides squirm in mixed delight and distress.

'You got me here to talk about your looks?' Carys had more sense than to answer his question.

To her horror she found him more attractive than ever. Even the scar leading from just beneath one straight black eyebrow up to his temple failed to detract from the beautiful spare lines of his leanly sculpted face.

She gripped her hands tight in her lap, alarmed to discover that, when it came to pure animal attraction, Alessandro still exerted a power she couldn't deny.

Just as well she had more sense than to succumb to it. She was cured. Surely she was.

'You keep staring at it.' He lifted the brandy to his lips. Carys watched the movement of his throat as he swallowed and her pulse tripped crazily. She'd rarely seen him in formal clothes, but they only enhanced his magnetism.

Alessandro had been an enigma, suave and sophisticated, impossibly elegant even in the most casual clothes, even *without* clothes. But at the same time there'd been something earthy and all-male about him. Something innately stronger than the varnish of wealth and centuries of good breeding.

'What are you thinking?' he asked.

Heat flared in her cheeks as Carys realised she was imagining him naked, long-limbed and strong. She tore her gaze away.

She might despise him, but she was still woman enough to respond to his sheer sex appeal.

'Nothing. I was just thinking about how you've changed.' It was only half a lie.

'Have I altered so much?' She sensed movement and turned her head to find him leaning forward, elbows on his knees.

She shrugged. 'It's been…' Just in time she stopped herself. He didn't need to know she recalled to the day how long it had been. 'A while. People change.'

'How have I changed?'

Carys wondered at the intensity of his stare. She felt it like the caress of a jade blade across her skin, smooth but potentially lethal.

'Well, there's the scar for a start.'

She closed her lips before she could blurt out questions about his health. Had he been in an accident? Or, her thudding heartbeat faltered, had it been surgery?

Sternly she told herself she didn't care.

'I'm in excellent health now.' The murmured words surprised her. How had he read her mind?

'Of course you are,' she said too quickly. 'Otherwise you wouldn't be here.' If he was ill he'd be in Italy, under the care of the country's top doctors, not summoning her to his room in the early hours to talk about…what *did* he want?

Carys' nerves spasmed in denial. There could only be one reason for his presence. Only one thing he wanted.

Her son.

Surely Alessandro's presence here meant he'd decided belatedly that he wanted Leo after all.

Alessandro didn't do things by halves. If he wanted something he'd take it all. And surely any normal Italian male would want his own son?

Fear wrapped icy fingers around her heart. If she was right, what chance did she have of stopping him?

'How else have I changed?'

Carys frowned at this fixation with his looks. The man she'd known had been careless about that, though he'd dressed with the instinctive panache of one who'd grown up amongst a chic, fashion-conscious set.

'You're paler than before. And thinner.'

When they'd met, he'd been on a skiing holiday, his olive skin burnished dark golden-brown by the alpine sun. His body was all hard-packed muscle and rangy height. Carys had looked into his dancing green eyes and sensuous smile that made her feel she was the only other person on the planet. Without a second thought she'd fallen for him like a ton of bricks.

Now he seemed pared down, but that only emphasised his spectacular bone structure. The way he moved made it clear he hadn't lost his whipcord strength and abundant energy.

He lifted the brandy to his lips again, but not before she read a wry grimace. 'I've been working long hours.'

Such long hours he'd stopped eating?

Carys looked away, silently berating herself for caring.

'Some things don't change, then.'

Those last weeks, Alessandro had used work as an excuse not to be with her. At first she'd thought there was a problem with the business, or with Alessandro assuming its control after his father's death, but her tentative questions, her attempts to understand and offer support, had been firmly rebuffed.

The company was fine. He was fine. She worried too much. He just had responsibilities to fulfil. She remembered the litany.

Methodically Alessandro had shut her out of his life, day by day and hour by hour. Till their only communication was during the brief pre-dawn hours when he'd take her with a blistering-hot passion that had threatened to consume them both.

Until she'd discovered it wasn't just business taking him away. That he'd had time for other things, other…people. How gullible she'd been, believing he'd be content with the naïve, unsophisticated woman who shared his bed…

'Being the CEO of a multi-national enterprise requires commitment.'

'I know that.' She'd given up worrying about the ridiculous hours he'd begun working. Given up trying to understand what had happened to the charming, attentive man with whom she'd fallen in love. That man had worked hard too, but he'd known how to switch off. How to enjoy being with her.

Her stomach churned. Whatever they'd once shared was over. He'd left her in no doubt she'd never live up to his exacting standards.

What was she doing here?

Her throat closed as the futility of their conversation swamped her. This could lead nowhere, achieve nothing but the reopening of painful wounds.

Carys shot to her feet. 'It's been…interesting seeing you again. But I have to go. It's late.'

The words were barely out of her mouth when he was before her, looming so close she had to tilt her head to meet his eyes. His gaze licked like flame across her skin.

Instinctively she stepped back, only to find her way blocked. Heat engulfed her as her brain processed frantic messages. Of surprise. Of anger. Of excitement.

'You can't leave yet.'

'I can and will.' She refused to play the fool for him again. 'We're finished.'

'Finished?' One straight brow quirked up, and his mouth curved in a tight, unamused smile. 'Then what about this?'

He snagged her close with one long arm so she landed hard against him. Then he lowered his head.

CHAPTER THREE

'ALESSANDRO!'

Her voice was scratchy with surprise as she said his name for the first time, making him pause. Yet the sound was familiar. He felt it deep in his bones.

She was familiar, the way her body melded to his, all feminine enticement as he pinioned her to him.

He'd tried to hold back. Go slow. Behave sensibly.

But from the moment she'd walked in everything had changed. His caution, his adherence to the niceties of social behaviour had melted away. Now he operated on raw, primal instinct that overrode logic and convention.

He held her satisfyingly close. With her breasts cushioned against his torso, her hips pressed against him. He felt anticipation surge.

When she'd arrived, looking weary yet defiant, he'd questioned his need to confront her tonight. But those doubts disintegrated as her body softened against his and he heard the tell-tale hitch in her breathing.

There might be fire in her eyes, but the way she fitted against him belied her indignation.

This was mutual.

He had no conscious recollection of her but his body remembered her. The stirring in his loins told its own tale of familiarity and desire.

He looked down into grey-blue eyes, darkening with sparks

of azure and indigo, and felt he was falling through mist, towards a bright sunny place.

He inhaled her spicy soft cinnamon fragrance and his brain cried *Yes! This is the one!*

'Alessandro!' Her voice was more determined now, like her hands pushing at his chest. Yet that underpinning note of hesitancy betrayed her.

He lifted one hand to palm her face. Her cheek was soft and pale as milk. Her eyelids fluttered and drooped then snapped wide open.

'You have no right to do this. Let me go.' Yet she'd stopped struggling, merely stood straighter and unyielding in his embrace.

'No right?' He swiped his thumb across her mouth, tugging at her lower lip, feeling its luscious pad and the moist heat of her breath against his skin.

Her mouth opened and those eyelids flickered betrayingly.

Tendrils of fire twisted and coiled through his body, unfurling and spreading as he watched her response to that simple caress.

He widened his stance, surrounding her with his thighs and pulling her closer to his pelvis.

The promise of bliss was a primitive tattoo in his blood, pounding heavier, faster, demanding action. Yet Alessandro reined in the impulse to demand more. He had to know, to understand, as well as feel.

'You give me the right when you respond to me that way.' Again he slid his thumb along her mouth, this time pressing deeper till he felt her tongue slick against his finger.

He stiffened, every muscle clamped tight at the roiling surge of need that engulfed him.

Madonna mia! How potent was this woman, that the mere touch of her tongue could splinter his control?

Surprise darkened her eyes. She felt it too.

'I'm not…doing anything,' she protested in a hoarse voice that told its own story. Suddenly she was pushing at him again, trying to lever herself away.

'Carys.' He loved the sound of her name on his tongue. Just

as he anticipated, he was addicted to the taste of her lips. 'Would you deny me? Deny this?'

Deftly he slid his hand round to cup her head, feeling the silky weight of her hair against his palm. Then he drew her close, bending to meet her lips.

She turned her head, refusing access to her mouth. His senses filled with the velvet softness of her skin, the sweet temptation of her body's perfume, as he brushed his lips below her ear.

Her restless movements stopped instantly. Arrested by the same sensations that bombarded him? Desire and heady bliss?

He slid his mouth over her neck, then up to her ear, circling the delicate lobe with his tongue.

She started in his arms as if zapped by the same jolt of energy that skewered him to the spot. Through the pounding in his ears he half heard, half felt her sigh.

'You can't deny this,' he murmured.

Her skin tasted clean and sweet, like spring flowers made of flesh. Hungrily he nuzzled the corner of her jaw, the edge of her chin, the beauty spot beside her mouth.

Bracing to pull back just a fraction, he looked down into her face.

His lips curved in a tight, satisfied smile when he saw closed eyes, lips parted invitingly, as if urging him to claim her.

Her hair had started to come down as she tried to avoid his grip. Now, looking at the long strands of wavy silk falling across his wrist, he realised it wasn't black as he'd thought in the ballroom. It was darkest brown, tinged with sparks of russet fire.

An image filled his brain, of rich dark hair spread over plump white pillows. Of his hands threading through its satiny splendour, splaying it out like a radiant sunburst.

Not just an image.

A memory!

Of Carys, lying sleepily in bed with him. Of her lazy smile, so dazzling it rivalled the brilliance of the snow-lit scene visible through the window above the bed.

The impact of that sudden recollection rocked him off balance, his arms tightening automatically around her.

For the second time in one night he'd remembered!

He'd known coming here was right.

With this woman he could unlock the closed door to the past. Restore all that was lost. Once he remembered he'd be free of this lurking awareness of something missing, of something incomplete in his life.

Then he could move on, content with his life again.

'Alessandro.' Her eyes were open now and aware. He read shock there and chagrin in the way she gnawed at her lip. 'Let me go. Please.'

He'd been taught to respect a woman's wishes. The Mattani code of honour was deeply ingrained, and he would never force himself on a woman. But it was too late to dissemble. Carys wanted this as much as he, despite her words.

Surely one kiss couldn't hurt.

'After this,' he murmured. 'I promise you'll enjoy it.' Almost as much as he intended to.

He captured her head, turned her face up to his, and slanted his mouth over hers.

Carys strained to shove him away. Desperation lent power to her tired limbs, yet she made no impact on him. If anything his wide shoulders loomed closer. He was stronger than her by far.

The knowledge should have frightened her. Yet part of her exulted. The unreformed hedonist inside her that she'd only discovered when she'd met Alessandro. The lover who'd been enraptured by his masculinity and athletic power. The heartbroken woman who'd loved and lost and secretly hoped to have her love returned.

Her struggle was as much within herself as against him.

Warm lips covered her mouth, and a judder of shocking need raked her from head to toe. It was instant, all-consuming and undeniable.

But she refused to give in to it. She pressed her palms against his shoulders and leant back as far as his encompassing arm allowed. Frantic to escape, she remembered too well how she'd always responded to him.

His kiss was unexpectedly tender, a gentle caress of firm lips along the closed line of her mouth.

His unfamiliar cologne, subtle yet masculine, tinged the air. The heat of his body warmed hers. His arms held her as if he'd never let her go.

Another illusion.

Carys tried to whip up her resolve, her scorn. But her mind fought a losing battle when her body was already capitulating.

'No!' She had to get away. Had to stand firm against him. 'I don't—'

It was too late. With the unerring instinct of a born predator, Alessandro took advantage of her momentary lapse and plunged his tongue into her open mouth.

Her breath stopped as reality splintered into fragments around her. He caressed her tongue, the inside of her cheeks. The dark world behind her closed eyelids came alive with flashes of fire. He grasped the back of her head, then tilted his own so he could delve deeper with a slow thoroughness that made her shudder in response.

Her hands on his shoulders curved, holding tight. Her panic faded. Tentatively her mouth moved with his, following the dance of desire they'd created together time and again. Carys mimicked his movements and slowly, like a sleeper waking from hibernation, felt the life force surge in her blood. Hunger gnawed her belly.

Soon she answered his demands with her own.

This felt so *right*.

His arms curved close, tugging her intimately against him. His kiss lured, delighted and provoked her into a response that escalated from tentative to eager and unashamed.

Now Carys' hands slipped from his shoulders to his neck, then up to furrow through his short, crisp hair and mould his head with desperate fingers. He was real, solid and wonderful, not the ephemeral phantom of her dreams. She needed him close, closer, to satisfy the burgeoning craving for more.

Heady, half-formed memories bombarded her. Of Alessandro pleasuring her. Of him holding her tight in his arms as if he'd never let her go. Of the instant spark of recognition and understanding that had passed between them the moment they'd met.

But these were tiny flickers, mere shadows of thought. She was absorbed in relearning the feel of Alessandro. His hair, his lips and tongue, the hot steel of his arms around her, the muscle and bone strength of his long body. His taste and scent.

Carys leaned in, glorying in the slide of achingly full breasts against his hard torso. She rose on tiptoe, seeking more, trying to get closer, to absorb herself into the wonderful luxury, the effervescent excitement of his kiss.

With a muffled groan, Alessandro lashed his other arm around her, lower, wrapping round her buttocks and lifting her off the ground.

Yes! Carys gave herself up to each exquisite sensation: of their mouths meshing, of his formidable strength enveloping her, of burning hot skin beneath her fingers as she moulded his jaw and cheeks.

Alessandro moved. She felt his thighs shift around her as he walked, and then there was something solid behind her while Alessandro pressed close. A wall? A couch? She'd lost all sense of perspective.

He tilted his hips in a slow grinding movement and desire blasted through her. His pelvis and hers were in perfect alignment, the heavy bulge in his trousers a portent of pleasure to come.

Instinctively she curved her body up to meet him. A throb began deep between her legs, an edgy neediness that strung her tight with anticipation.

'Temptress. Siren.' His muttered words were hoarse, as if squeezed out under duress.

Carys let her head loll against a hard surface and gulped oxygen into her air-starved lungs. Alessandro ravished her face and throat with burning kisses that ignited tiny explosions of pleasure through her taut body. And all the while he pushed close as if he could melt the barrier of their clothes and bring them both the bliss they craved.

One large hand slid down her hip and over her thigh, igniting tremors of fresh awareness. When his palm climbed back, her skirt bunched beneath it, riding higher and higher.

Carys opened her mouth, vaguely aware of the need to protest, but his mouth slammed into hers again, robbing her of breath and the beginnings of thought.

Once more Alessandro pleasured her, this time with a kiss so sweet yet so demanding it devoured the last of her resistance. She lolled back as he drew forth every last shred of hidden longing.

Willingly Carys complied as he lifted her leg up around his hip, and then the other. The bittersweet ache between her legs, and deeper, inside her womb, became a steady throb. Encircling him with her legs, she squeezed tight.

As if he understood, Alessandro pressed close again, pushing his erection just…there.

Yes! That was what she wanted. To have him warm the empty places in her body and her soul that had been chilled for so long.

Large hands slid under the tight, rumpled fabric of her skirt, up her thighs till they reached bare, quivering flesh.

'Stockings,' he breathed against her mouth. 'You dress to drive a man insane.'

She wasn't listening. Carys heard the low burr of his voice, felt his breath against her lips, but the words made no sense. Only the approval in his tone was real.

Haphazardly she ripped at his bow tie, desperate for his hot skin bare beneath her palms.

Long fingers slid around her thighs, stroking and teasing her sensitive skin. She jerked and squirmed, tugging at his shirt till, with a rip, it tore open.

A torrent of slurred Italian signalled his approval. But she barely noticed for heaven was in the touch of wiry hair and steamy satiny flesh under her hands. In the rapid pulse of his heart pounding against her touch.

His hands moved, and a knuckle brushed against the damp cotton of her panties.

'*Cara*,' he growled deep in his throat. 'I *knew* you wanted this as much as I do.' He insinuated probing fingers beneath the elastic of her underwear while, with his other hand, he fumbled at his belt.

Reality, hard and relentless, broke upon her in an instant of icy clarity. The heady, exquisite arousal faded as her mind kicked into gear.

Was it the greedy touch of his fingers in that most intimate of places? The practised way he undid his belt and ripped open the fastening of his trousers? The smug satisfaction in his voice?

He didn't even want *her,* an outraged voice cried in her head. He wanted 'this'. Sex. Physical satisfaction.

Presumably any woman would do. Carys was just conveniently available.

More than available. Willing. Desperate for him.

Aghast, Carys stiffened.

What had she done? She'd let her loneliness, memories of the bliss they'd once shared, lead her into self-destructive temptation.

'No! Stop.' Mortified, she shoved with all her might, wriggling to dislodge his questing fingers and unwrap her legs. 'Let me go!'

She moved so unexpectedly he didn't prevent her and even moved back a precious few centimetres, allowing her to slide her legs free. That was when she registered it was a wall behind her, as her stockinged feet hit the floor. She had to brace herself against the weakness in her knees so she didn't collapse.

He'd almost had her, up against the wall of his suite! Fully clothed!

The glorious heat they'd shared bled away as mortification and disbelief welled. After all that had happened how *could* she have been so weak?

'Carys…'

She batted his hands away, stumbling to escape and tripping over a discarded shoe.

Her self respect was in shreds. Her chest heaved with distress as she fumbled with shaky fingers to push her straight skirt down her hips. Her eyes blurred.

'Let me.'

'No!' Carys whirled to face him, arms outstretched to keep him at bay.

Even with lipstick on his jaw, and his jacket and dress shirt torn open to reveal a dusky, hair-dusted chest, he looked in command, powerful and controlled.

Sexier than any man had a right to be.

Then she saw the way his chest rose and fell, as if from

exertion. The tendons in his neck stood out and his facial muscles were drawn too tight. A flush of colour slanted across his cheeks and his nostrils flared as if he fought for oxygen.

The evidence of simple animal lust. That was all Alessandro had ever felt for her.

When would she learn? Self-disgust filled her.

Her poor tortured heart compressed as a weight as big as Flinders Street Station pushed down on her chest. Breathing was agony.

But the realisation of what she'd almost done was worse. One kiss…one kiss and she'd been scrabbling at his shirt, desperate to feel his body against hers, urging him on to take her.

Her chin crumpled and she bit her lip. She'd invited her own degradation.

Once again Alessandro had proved himself a consummate seducer. But that was no excuse. She should be able to resist him. She had to. Where was her self-respect?

'Don't touch me,' she whispered as she wriggled her hips, tugging the skirt down. She kept her eyes above his waist, not wanting to see what she'd felt pressing intimately against her, inviting her to mindless pleasure.

Involuntarily her internal muscles clenched. Her betraying body was still ready for his possession. The knowledge flattened the last remnant of her pride.

'*Va bene.* As you wish.' The feral gleam in Alessandro's eyes warned her he wouldn't be thwarted for long. 'Instead we will talk. For now.'

Fire scorched her throat and she looked away, unable to meet his dark scrutiny any longer.

Slowly Carys backed across the floor, feet sinking into the plush depth of carpet. He didn't follow her but stood, arms akimbo, as if waiting for her to come to her senses.

'We have to talk, Carys.'

Like hell they did. They'd done enough *talking* for one night. The brush of cool air on her heated skin made her frown and reach for her throat, only to discover her blouse hung open to reveal her white cotton bra.

How had that happened? Carys clutched the edges of her

blouse together with numb fingers. She shot an accusing glare across the room, but Alessandro said nothing, merely raised an eyebrow and crossed his arms over his chest as if waiting for her to come to her senses.

For all his immobility she couldn't rid herself of the notion he merely waited to pounce.

Would she have the resolve to stop him next time?

'I'm not staying here to be attacked again.'

'Attacked!' He drew himself up to his full height and stared down his long aristocratic nose at her. 'Hardly that. You were panting for my touch.'

His arrogant claim was the final straw because it was true. Her resolution had failed. She was weak and nothing could protect her from him. Nothing but bluff.

She shrugged, the movement more stiff than insouciant.

'I was curious, that's all. And,' she hurried on as he opened his mouth to reject her explanation, 'and besides, it's been a while since I…'

'You've been saving yourself, *cara?* Is that it?' His smoky voice urged her to assent and blurt out that there'd been no one since him. Wouldn't he just love that!

Fury sizzled along her veins. Glorious wrath at the man who'd taken her innocence, her love and her trust and thought he could have her again at the click of his fingers.

'No,' Carys lied. It would just feed his ego to know there'd been no one since him. She shifted her gaze.

He held her in thrall. What would it take to make him relinquish his pursuit? Desperation drove her to blurt out the first thing she could think of to stop him.

'My boyfriend and I had a disagreement and—'

'Boyfriend?' His voice thundered through the suite. 'You were missing your *boyfriend?* You can't tell me you were thinking of him just now?'

'Can't I?' Carys swung her head round and felt his dark green stare like frozen shards of crystal grazing her skin.

'I don't believe you.' But she'd sown the seed of doubt. That was obvious from his sudden pallor.

A tiny fillip of triumph rose. Maybe she could make herself safe from him after all.

'Believe what you like, Conte Mattani.'

'Don't use that title with me,' he snapped. 'I'm not some stranger.'

She said nothing, merely backed a few more steps towards the foyer.

'You don't intend to leave looking like that,' he announced in a cold, disapproving tone.

Carys felt the weight of her hair tumbling round her shoulders and knew she looked as if she'd been ravaged to within an inch of her life. She was barefoot, half undressed, her lips bruised and swollen from the intensity of their passion, and her nipples thrust shamelessly against the cotton of her bra. Anyone looking at her would know precisely what she'd been doing.

She had a choice: an ignominious flight from the presidential suite looking like a complete wanton or a cosy *tête a tête* with Alessandro Mattani.

She was across the room before he could move a step.

'Just watch me.'

Alessandro stood on the private terrace of his suite, watching the dark-clad workers scurry across the bridge and swarm the streets. Morning peak hour and he'd already been at work for several hours.

Habitually he started early and finished late. But this morning…he raked a hand through his hair as frustration filled him.

He'd slept even less than usual, bedevilled by tantalising dreams of luscious pale limbs entwined with his, of generous feminine curves and silky smooth skin, of smoky blue-grey eyes enticing him to the brink of sexual fulfilment. Each time he'd woken, sweating, gasping for breath and formidably aroused, to the realisation Carys Wells had fled rather than allow them the release they both craved.

He rubbed a hand over his freshly shaved jaw, as if to dispel the tension there.

Even in sleep she denied him.

He could barely believe she'd run. Especially after he'd felt the hunger in her, a hunger as ravening as his own. It was a wonder their clothes hadn't disintegrated around them, their passion had been so combustible.

He grasped the iron balustrade savagely. Could it have been a tactic to tease him into wanting more then leave him aching with need? What could she hope to gain?

He shook his head. No woman was that good an actress. Besides, he knew every trick in the book when it came to conniving women, and Carys hadn't played the tease. He remembered the scent of her arousal, sharp and musky.

Oh, no, Carys Wells had wanted him all right.

Why had she denied them both?

A stiff breeze blew up from the river and chilled his skin. He should have taken things slower, scoped out the situation rather than allowing his driving need free rein.

One of the first things he'd learned when he entered the commercial world was to plan carefully and unemotionally and only strike at the most opportune moment.

Last night it hadn't been his brain doing the thinking.

He'd frightened her off. Her wide eyes had been desperate as she backed to the door. For an instant he'd even suspected they shone overbright.

A ripple of regret passed through him and he frowned.

His security team assured him she'd got home safely, unaware of their surveillance or their orders to keep her safe. Yet still Alessandro felt the weight of guilt. It was his fault she'd fled.

He should have controlled himself and conquered his animal instincts. Yet he'd been unable to comprehend anything but the need to possess her.

Alessandro scrubbed his palm over his face again, grimacing. He couldn't remember ever acting with less forethought. He'd been like a starving man set before a banquet, unable to summon even a shred of restraint.

Was he always like that with her?

The question tantalised him. The frustration of not knowing ate like acid into his gut.

He was so close, and still the answers eluded him.

A discreet ringtone interrupted his thoughts and he drew his cellphone from his pocket.

It was Bruno, head of his security team, reporting on Carys' movements this morning. Alessandro froze into immobility at the report, delivered in a carefully uninflected tone.

Eventually he roused himself enough to issue a few more orders. Then he took the phone from his ear and waited for the image Bruno was sending.

There it was. A little blurry with movement, but unmistakeable. Carys Wells, in a familiar dark suit and not a hair out of place. But what held Alessandro's attention wasn't his erstwhile lover. It was the burden she carried in her arms.

Small, rounded, riveting his attention.

A baby.

Carys had a child.

The air purged from Alessandro's lungs in a hiss of disbelief. His jaw tightened so hard his head began to throb as he stared at the image before him.

Whose child? The boyfriend from whom she'd been separated? Some other man? A long-term lover or a passing stranger?

Pain roused him from his turbulent thoughts. Alessandro looked down to discover he'd grasped the railing so hard the decorative ironwork had drawn blood on the fleshy part of his palm.

Dispassionately he stared at the welling redness, then back at the picture of Carys and her child.

Only then did Alessandro recognise the emotion surging so high it threatened to choke him. Fury. Raw sizzling wrath that she'd been with another man.

It didn't matter how or why they'd separated. Every instinct screamed that Carys belonged to *him*. Could it be any clearer after the way they'd been together? The intensity of their passion made every other liaison pale into insignificance.

He'd come seeking answers. Last night he'd discovered answers weren't enough. He wanted Carys too, for as long as the attraction between them held.

Looking at her holding another man's child in her arms sent spears of flame through his chest and gut.

The sight should have cured him of his lust.

Instead he felt a burning desire to discover the identity of the man who'd fathered Carys' baby and mash him into a pulp with his bare hands.

CHAPTER FOUR

CARYS pulled her long, flapping coat tight around herself as she left the staff entrance. A cheap second-hand purchase, it helped combat Melbourne's cold, but it was a size too large, billowing out in the wind and allowing chill draughts to tease her.

A glance at the louring sky made her pick up her pace, scurrying to avoid the blur of rain already washing over the city. With luck her train would be on time and she'd get home at a reasonable hour. Two of her colleagues had returned to work today, so she didn't have to stay back.

Carys looked forward to the luxury of some quiet time with Leo then a long luxurious soak and a good night's sleep.

Resolutely she avoided the knowledge that she'd probably spend another sleepless night tossing and turning.

She'd made it through the day in a state of numb shock, working like an automaton, except when the sight of a tall dark-haired man, or an unexpected call, froze the blood in her veins.

She'd expected him to come after her. If not last night when she'd left him high and dry, then today.

He knew where she worked. He knew far too much. Why had he left her alone?

Foreboding crept through her. He was biding his time.

It could only be Leo he wanted. Her precious boy. What else would drag Alessandro here from Italy?

The realisation was like a knife at her neck. A man with Alessandro's resources could get anything he wanted.

If he wanted Leo…

Carys had no illusions that he was here for anything else. For Alessandro, last night had simply been about the chance for hot sex.

Absence from his wife must be wearing on him.

Bile rose in Carys' throat, a savage, scouring bitterness. Shame flooded her and she ducked her head.

She hadn't even remembered he was tied to another woman! The overwhelming reality of his presence had blasted Carys back to a time when she'd been his, body and soul. When she'd believed he was hers. Before he had married his blue-blooded heiress.

Carys tasted salt on her tongue as she bit her lip.

Distress filled her at how close she'd come to compounding her stupidity in an act that would shatter her principles.

She hadn't been able to meet her eyes in the mirror this morning, recalling her uninhibited response to him.

Fury, disbelief and disappointment filled her. At him for using her as a convenience to assuage his physical needs. For not being the honourable man she'd once thought him. At herself for abandoning her pride and principles in letting him sweep her into his tempestuous embrace.

Carys squared her shoulders. She'd played the fool for the last time. Besides, he'd relinquished all rights when he—

A pair of massive mirror-polished black shoes blocked the pavement before her. Carys side-stepped to skirt the man, but with one long stride he moved too, forcing her to stop.

Her gaze climbed a pair of bulky legs in pin-striped trousers so beautifully tailored they almost tamed the rampantly muscled solidity of the man. Neat shirt, dark tie, perfectly fitting jacket and a swarthy face topped by pepper and salt hair. Gold winked in the man's earlobe as he turned his head and Carys stared, sure she'd seen him before.

'*Scusa, signorina.* This way, please.'

He extended one arm, gesturing towards the kerb.

Carys turned to see a limousine with tinted windows drawn up beside her, its back door open.

Her pulse sped up to thunder in her ears. A sprawl of long masculine limbs filled her vision of the interior and her heart rate spiked. The last thing she wanted was to share such an intimate space with Alessandro Mattani.

'You've got to be kidding,' she muttered, automatically stepping back from the road.

The large Italian moved closer, shepherding her towards the vehicle. Resolutely she planted her feet on the pavement, refusing to budge.

She looked around, hoping to find the street filled with people, but the few she saw were racing for cover as big fat drops of rain spattered the pavement. There was no one to interfere if Alessandro's goon tried to manhandle her into the car.

'Why don't you get in before you both get soaked?' asked a cool voice from the back of the limo.

Outraged dignity came to her rescue. 'And if I'd prefer to get drenched than share a car with you?'

'I'd say it was very selfish of you to force Bruno to suffer the same fate just for the sake of your pride.'

Her eyes rounded. Pride? Alessandro thought this was simply about pride?

The man beside her moved, closing in beside her, and Carys darted a glance at him, wondering if she had any hope of getting away. He was built like a rugby player, all dense-packed muscle. Right now he had that grim, blank-eyed set to his face that she'd seen on the super-tough minders of the rich and famous.

'Per favore, signorina.'

Drops splattered his jacket as the rain fell faster. He didn't bat an eyelid, just watched her with the stony countenance of a man ready to deal with anything.

She'd bet five feet six of female, hampered by heels and a skirt, would be the work of a moment to overpower.

'Don't let his looks fool you, Carys,' came a laconic voice from the limo's interior. 'Bruno has a weak chest. He's just got over a bout of bronchitis. I wouldn't like him to have a relapse. And you wouldn't want that on your conscience.'

Carys blinked, catching the merest flicker of expression on the security man's face. A smile? Surely not.

Movement to one side caught her eye, and she turned to find

Alessandro had slid to the edge of the seat and was regarding her with a peculiarly unreadable expression.

'His wife would flay me alive if I brought him home with pneumonia.'

Despite her anger, Carys felt her lips twitch. Once, long ago, Alessandro's dry wit had been one of the things that had drawn her to him. She'd almost forgotten that, her memories skewed by those final, unhappy days when banter and teasing had been absent between them.

'I would have thought blackmail was more your style,' she jeered. 'Or threats, rather than an appeal to my conscience.'

Rain trickled into her collar, but she stood ramrod straight. This man was dangerous.

A shrug of those lean shoulders and he said something in Italian that made Bruno move away to give them space. Carys barely had time to register the chance for escape when Alessandro's voice curled around her, silkily smooth. 'I regret last night, Carys. It wasn't planned.'

He paused, awaiting a response that she steadfastly refused to give. If that was his idea of an apology he had a lot to learn.

Alessandro's eyes narrowed as she stood rigid under his scrutiny. Something glittered in that forest-dark gaze that sent shivers of trepidation running through her. Despite his earlier light-hearted words, his stare sizzled. She guessed his deadpan expression disguised an anger almost as great as her own. Now she looked more closely, she read tension in his shoulders and grim mouth.

Too bad. She tilted her chin up, wishing she had a long aristocratic nose like his so she could look down it.

'But if that's the way you'd prefer to do this,' he purred, 'then I can oblige.'

She'd opened her mouth to say she preferred to have nothing to do with him, when his next words forestalled her.

'I'm sure the hotel management would be interested in the security camera footage of the lobby outside the presidential suite last night, and in the lift. If they cared to check the recording they'd find it...illuminating.'

'You wouldn't!' Shock hammered her like a physical blow, sucking out her breath. That tape would show her emerging from his suite in the early hours looking like…like…

'Wouldn't I?' His stare was unnervingly blank. 'I'm sure they frown on staff providing *personal* services to guests.' His tongue dripped with hateful innuendo and Carys burned with frustration and fury. Her hands clenched around the shoulder strap of her bag.

'I wasn't providing a service, you—'

'It doesn't matter what you were doing, Carys. All that matters is how the evidence appears.' He leaned back with a smug glimmer in his eyes.

Evidence. It sounded so formal.

It *would* be formal if anyone decided to check the recording. Formal enough to get her the sack.

Her heart dived and she shivered, but not from the rain's chill. She needed this job. How else could she support Leo? Good positions were hard to find for someone with limited qualifications.

Would Alessandro make good on his threat?

Once she'd thought she'd known this man. Had trusted him. Had even believed he was falling in love with her.

What a naïve innocent she'd been.

She'd learned the hard way not to trust her judgement with him. Better to assume him capable of anything to get his own way. He'd already made a fool of her once.

He was her enemy, threatening the life she'd begun to build, her independence, even, she feared, her child.

'What do you want?' She didn't care that her voice was scratchy with distress, despite her attempt to appear calm.

'To talk. We have unfinished business.'

He didn't wait for her to assent but slid back across the wide leather seat, making space for her.

Unfinished business.

That was how he described one little boy?

Her throat closed convulsively as the fight bled out of her. She couldn't ignore Alessandro. She had to face him and hope against hope she could retain some control of the situation.

She tottered forward on numb legs and entered the limousine, her wet coat sliding along a leather seat that looked and smelled fresh from the factory.

Only the best for the Conte Mattani.

Under no circumstances would she, an ordinary single mum with not an ounce of glamour, be classed as *the best*. Alessandro had made that abundantly clear in Italy.

Her heart bumped against her ribs. Had Alessandro decided her little boy was a different matter?

The limo door shut with a quiet click and she sagged back, shutting her eyes. She was cold to the bone.

There was no escape now.

Moments later the front door closed and the vehicle accelerated. Belatedly she remembered to do up her seatbelt. A swift sideways glance told her Alessandro wasn't happy, despite having got her where he wanted her.

The proud, spare lines of his face seemed austere and forbidding silhouetted against the city streets. He looked as approachable as some ancient king, brooding over judgement.

The flicker of unease inside her magnified into a hundred fluttering wings. She was at a disadvantage to him in so many ways.

His silence reinforced that she was here at his pleasure.

Carys flicked her gaze away, not deigning to ask where they were going. Two could play the silent game. It would give her time to marshal her resources.

As she stared straight ahead, trying to control her frantic, jumbled thoughts, she found herself looking through a smoky glass privacy-screen at the back of Bruno's head.

Recognition smote her.

'He was on my street. Last night!' Carys leaned forward to make sure. There was no mistaking the bunched-muscle silhouette of the minder's neck and shoulders, or the shape of his head.

As she'd walked up the ill-lit street to her block of flats in the early hours, she'd faltered, her heart skipping as she noticed a brawny man in jeans and a leather jacket just ahead. He looked to be waiting for someone. But as she'd hesitated he'd turned to stroll away in the opposite direction.

Nevertheless, she'd scurried inside as fast as possible. Her street was peaceful by day, but the shopping strip a few blocks away had been attracting unsavoury characters at night.

'Bruno, your bodyguard. He was outside my home.'

She swung round to find Alessandro watching her steadily. His lack of response infuriated her.

'You're not even bothering to deny it!'

'Why would I?' His brow furrowed in a hint of a frown that, annoyingly, didn't detract from his handsome looks.

'You had him follow me?' Already Alessandro had pried into her personnel records. Now his stooge had been scoping out her home. He had no qualms about invading her privacy.

'Of course.' He stared coolly as if wondering what the fuss was about. 'It was late. I had to make sure you got back all right.'

His explanation took the wind out of her sails and she slumped in her seat, her mind whirling.

'You were trying to *protect* me?'

Something indefinable flickered in his eyes. 'You were out alone at an hour when you should have been safely home.'

At least he didn't mention her state of disarray. Even in a pair of shoes borrowed from the staffroom, and with her shirt buttoned again, she'd felt as if the few people she'd met on her journey took one look and knew exactly what she'd been up to in the presidential suite.

Alessandro made her sound like a teenager in need of parental guidance. Not a twenty-five-year-old woman supporting herself and her son.

Yet it wasn't indignation Carys felt rise like a tide inside her. It was warmth, a furtive spark of pleasure, that he'd cared enough to worry about her safety.

In the old days she'd been thrilled by the way he'd looked after her, showing what she'd thought was a strongly protective nature.

Until she'd discovered her mistake. What she'd seen as caring had been his way of keeping her isolated, separate from the rest of his life. It had been a deliberate tactic to ensure she didn't know how he used her.

The lush melting warmth inside her dissipated as a chill blast of reality struck right to the bone.

'I'm perfectly capable of looking after myself! I was doing it long before you turned up.' Carys wrapped her arms around the faux-leather bag on her lap and turned away.

She was proud of what she'd achieved. When she'd arrived in Australia she'd been a mess, her heart in tatters, her confidence shattered. Even her destination of Melbourne was unplanned. She'd been too distraught to do more than turn up at the airport and board the first available flight home.

Now she'd built a new life for herself and Leo. She was working hard to achieve the financial security they needed.

'Is that so?' Scepticism dripped from each syllable as he held her with a glacial green stare. 'You really think that the best neighbourhood to bring up a child?'

Her fingers, busy fiddling with the zipper on her bag, froze. Every muscle tensed.

Now they'd come to the crux of the matter.

She waited for him to accuse her of being a bad mother, to demand his rights and push his case. Yet he remained silent, only his lowered brows hinting at displeasure.

'The flat is sunny and comfortable. And affordable.' It went against the grain to hint at her lack of funds, but no doubt he knew about her precarious finances.

Despite working right up till she went into labour, Carys had used all her meagre savings in the months after Leo's birth. If it hadn't been for the money her father had sent long-distance, she wouldn't have been able to support them. When the going had got really tough, she'd even thought of moving to be with her dad. Till she imagined his horror at the idea.

Only now, with her job at the Landford, could she make ends meet, though most of her wages went on childcare and rent and there was precious little for other necessities.

'And the location? Your neighbourhood is becoming a hub for drug dealing and prostitution.'

He didn't bother to hide his disapproval. If she hadn't been wearing a thick coat, his coruscating glare would have scraped off layers of skin.

'The reports are exaggerated,' she bluffed, refusing to admit he'd tapped into her own fear. That the cosy nest she'd created for her son grew less desirable by the week.

Only days ago there'd been more syringes found in the park and another bashing in the street. Carys had decided that, despite the friends she'd made locally, she'd look for somewhere else to bring up Leo.

'If you say so.' His tone implied boredom.

Carys was puzzled. This was his opportunity to weigh in with comments about her inability to care for Leo. To make a case that she shouldn't have sole custody.

Yet Alessandro seemed totally uninterested. Had she got it wrong? Hope rose shakily in her breast.

But if he wasn't here for her little boy, what did he want from her?

Alessandro tamped down the fury he'd felt ever since receiving this morning's report. Fury that Carys should live in such a neighbourhood. That she'd hooked up with a man who obviously refused to take care of her and her child.

That he, Alessandro, had let her get under his skin enough to be concerned for her!

He cursed himself for a fool. She'd walked out on him, moved on from whatever relationship they'd had. He should do the same. Dignity and pride demanded it.

He *would,* he vowed, once he knew all he needed to about those blank months.

Yet that sense of intimate connection still hammered at him. It was stronger even than the cool logic around which he built his life.

Despite her antipathy and her child by another man, Alessandro couldn't banish the possessiveness that swamped him when he was with her. It consumed him.

Never had he experienced such feelings.

His fists tightened as his temples throbbed. Flickers of images taunted him. Whether remnants of last night's erotic dreams or snippets of memory, he didn't know.

He wanted to hate her for the unaccustomed weakness she wrought in him. Yet the bruised violet smudges under her eyes snagged his attention. It had taken more than one sleepless night to put them there.

His belly clenched as he took in her pallor and the way her worn coat dwarfed her. Last night he'd seen she was tired, but he'd been too overwhelmed by his own cataclysmic response to register what looked now like utter exhaustion.

He'd been impatient to solve the riddle that had haunted him so long. Too busy losing himself in her lush curves and feminine promise to admit the extent of her vulnerability.

That vulnerability clawed at his conscience. He should never have unleashed the beast of sexual hunger that roared into life when she was near.

'Where's this boyfriend of yours? Why doesn't he help you?' He snapped the words out, surprising himself. It wasn't his way to blurt his thoughts.

Wary eyes met his. They darkened like storm clouds and instinctively he knew she concealed something.

Carys blinked and looked away. 'I'm fine by myself. I don't need anyone to—'

'Of course you do. You shouldn't be living in this area. Not with a baby.' He spared the run-down neighbourhood the briefest of glances. It was seedy, an area of urban decline. 'He should help you.'

Her mouth remained mutinously closed.

Alessandro knew a wholly uncharacteristic desire for hot-blooded argument. He, who never let anything ruffle his equanimity! Who was a master at sublimating useless emotions and pursuing his goals with single-minded purpose.

How this woman unsettled him. The last twenty-four hours had been a roller coaster of unfamiliar feelings that made a mockery of his habitual control.

He resented that more than anything.

'Who is he, Carys? Why do you protect him?'

Because she loved him? Alessandro's mouth flattened. This should be none of his business, yet he couldn't let go.

'I'm not protecting anyone!' she muttered. 'There's no one. What I told you—'

'You said you'd argued. That's no excuse for him walking out on his child and its mother.'

Alessandro's nostrils filled with pungent distaste. His reaction to the idea of any man getting Carys pregnant was bone-deep rage. His belly cramped as he strove to master his feelings.

Who *was* this woman that she made him react so?

She stared silently, an arrested expression on her face.

'Is he someone you work with?' The words shot out through gritted teeth.

She shook her head. 'Don't be absurd.'

There was nothing absurd about it. Working side by side led too easily to intimacy. He'd had to move his PA elsewhere after she'd mistaken their working relationship for something else. He'd lost count of the female employees and business associates who'd thought work the perfect way into his bed.

Silently he cursed himself for needing to know.

'He's married? Is that it?'

Carys stared into his glowering face and struggled against a sense of unreality. He looked genuinely perplexed. Deep grooves bracketed a mouth that morphed from sensual perfection into a wrathful line.

She shook her head as if to clear it. She mustn't have heard right.

'There *is* no man in my life.' She hesitated, knowing a craven urge to avoid the truth. 'I made that up so you'd leave me alone.'

Alessandro's brow furrowed, his eyebrows disapproving black slashes that tilted down in the centre. And still he looked better than any man she knew.

'Don't deny it. Of course there's a man.'

'Are you calling me a liar?' His refusal to accept her word reopened a wound that had never healed. He hadn't believed her before. Why should things be different now? Her word wasn't good enough.

Pain mixed with Carys' fury. Her distress was all the more potent for having been suppressed so long.

'Spare me the show of innocence,' he sneered. 'You didn't get pregnant all by yourself. Or are you trying to tell me it was an immaculate conception?'

'You bastard!' Her arm shot out faster than thought. An instant later her hand snapped across his cheek as her fury finally boiled over.

Her palm tingled. Her whole arm trembled with the force of the slap. Her breath came in hard, shallow pants. She barely noticed the dangerous glint in his narrowing eyes or the way he loomed closer.

Then, out of the blue, the implication of his words sank in. Relief swamped her, making her shake as she sagged back in her seat.

He wasn't here to take Leo away.

Hysterical laughter swelled inside at her stupidity. Alessandro didn't want to take her boy. Of course he didn't! He'd made his disinterest and disapproval clear from the start. He'd left her in no doubt both she and her baby weren't good enough for him and his rarefied circle of moneyed friends.

Why had she thought he'd changed? Because part of her still foolishly ached to believe he was the fantasy man she'd fallen in love with?

Pain welled.

It felt as if Alessandro had taken her last precious fragment of hope and callously ground it underfoot, shattering a fragile part of her.

'You really are some piece of work, Alessandro Mattani.' Her voice was hoarse with distress, her throat raw with pain as if she'd swallowed broken glass. 'I should have known you hadn't changed.'

'Me, change?' Astonishment coloured his voice, at odds with his look of rigid control.

'Yes, you. You coward.' Carys pressed a palm to her stomach, trying to prevent the churn of nausea. 'Even after all this time you refuse to acknowledge your own son.'

CHAPTER FIVE

THE woman was mad.

Or conniving.

Alessandro met her glittering eyes, dark now as a thunder storm, and saw lightning flash.

Did she even notice that he'd grabbed her wrist and yanked it from his face? That he still held it in an implacable grip?

She didn't seem to notice anything except her own fury.

His cheek burned from her slap and pride demanded instant retribution. No one, man or woman, insulted Alessandro Mattani.

Yet he held himself in check. He would not resort to violence against a woman.

More importantly, he needed to know what she was up to, this mad woman with the wild accusations and glorious eyes.

'Don't be absurd. I don't have a child.' That was one thing he'd never forget, no matter how severe his injuries.

Besides, he'd always taken care not to lay himself open to paternity claims. He enjoyed short-term liaisons, but that didn't mean he took risks with his health or his family honour.

'Spare me the act, Alessandro,' she hissed. 'Others might be impressed, but I'm not. I gave up being impressed the day I left you.'

He frowned as he felt tremors rack her body and her pulse catapult into overdrive.

'You're angry because our relationship ended?'

Women never liked knowing they held a temporary place in his life. Too often they set their sights on becoming the Contessa

Mattani. But he had no illusions about matrimony. For him it would be a duty, to carry on the family name. A duty he was happy to postpone.

Her mouth opened in a short, humourless laugh. 'I wouldn't have stayed if you'd paid me,' she spat out. 'Not once I knew what you were really like.'

Such vehemence, such hatred, was new to Alessandro. The shock of it ran through him like a jolt of electricity. It felt as if he held a jumping live wire in his hand, liable to twist unpredictably at any moment and burn him to cinders.

She was unlike anything or anyone in his well-ordered life.
She fascinated him.

'What's this about a child?' *That* sort of claim was one he would never take lightly.

Her mouth twisted in a grimace. 'Forget it,' she muttered, turning her head away. Her dismissive tone would anger a less controlled man.

Carys tried to tug her hand free, but he held her easily. He had no intention of letting her take another swipe at him. Swiftly he captured her other hand, holding both effortlessly till she gave up trying to escape and subsided, chest heaving, against the back of the seat.

'I can hardly forget it.' He pulled her hands, making her turn. Studiously he ignored the way her rapid breathing emphasised the swell of her breasts. 'Tell me.'

Thick dark lashes rose to reveal silvery-blue eyes that flashed with repressed emotion. Her pulse pounded beneath his fingers and she swiped the tip of her tongue over her lips as if to moisten them.

Instantly desire flared in his belly.
Just like that.

The immediacy of his response would have stunned him if he hadn't experienced it last night. Whatever the secret of her feminine allure, he responded to it with every particle of testosterone in his body.

He watched her hesitate and kept his expression unreadable. All the while he was aware of the way her moist pink lips unconsciously invited him to plunder her mouth. His fingers tightened on her hands, as if ready to tug her close.

'There's nothing to tell.' Her look was pure belligerence. 'You have a child. But you already know that.' She paused; for the first time the heat in her expression disappeared and her eyes turned glacial, stabbing him with invisible icy shards. 'Why make me repeat what you know?'

'I want the truth. Is that too much to ask?' Finally anger exploded behind Alessandro's façade of calm. A roaring flame of wrath at this woman who turned his life inside out. He strove to resist shaking the truth out of her.

He couldn't remember ever being so irate.

But then no woman had ever dared make such accusations. Plus the frustration of not knowing his own past would drive any man wild. Alessandro abhorred that sneaking sense of powerlessness, not remembering.

Her chin lifted. 'Is it too much to ask that you stop crushing my hands?'

Instantly he released her, flexing fingers rigid with tension. He hadn't intended to hurt her. Another disturbing sign that his control was close to shattering.

'Thank you.' She paused, her gaze skating sideways. 'I promise not to slap you again. That was…unintentional.' She turned. 'We're here.' She spoke quickly, relief evident in every syllable.

Already Bruno was opening the door to the pavement. The driver stood at Alessandro's door, waiting for him to alight.

'We'll finish this discussion inside.'

'I'm not sure I want you in my home,' she countered.

'You think I *want* to be there?' Being with Carys opened a Pandora's Box of conflicting feelings he could do without.

But he needed to fill the gaps and banish once and for all the nagging sense of something missing in his life. Besides, he had to end this nonsense about fathering a child. He would not countenance such allegations.

Alessandro unfolded his legs from the car and stood up. He felt stiff, as if his muscles had cramped during the drive. He pushed his shoulders back and looked around the street. Graffiti marred the building opposite and a couple of ground-floor windows were boarded up further down the block.

Carys scurried ahead into an ugly square building, not looking back. Her shoulders were hunched and her head bent.

But she couldn't avoid him. He stepped forward.

'Signor Conte.' Bruno waited on the pavement for him.

'Yes?' Alessandro paused, his eyes on Carys.

'On the way here I received answers to the enquiries I made this morning. I didn't like to interrupt your discussion with *la signorina.*'

Bruno's careful tone snared Alessandro's attention, dragging it from his furious thoughts. He turned to meet his security chief's blank stare, sensing he wouldn't like this.

'And?'

'There's no record of a marriage. Signorina Wells is single.'

So, she hadn't bothered to marry the baby's father.

Alessandro shoved his hands deep into his pockets, refusing to examine the emotions stirring at that news.

'There's more?'

Bruno nodded. 'The birth was just over a year ago here in Melbourne.' There wasn't a hint of expression in his voice and a tickle of premonition feathered Alessandro's spine.

'What other details did you get?'

'The mother is given as Carys Antoinette Wells, receptionist, of this address.' Bruno gestured to the tired red-brick block of flats.

Alessandro waited, instinct making his skin crawl. 'And the rest?'

Bruno's eyes flickered away. He drew himself up straighter. 'The father is listed as Alessandro Leonardo Daniele Mattani of Como, Italy.'

Despite the fact that by now he'd half expected it, each word slammed into Alessandro's gut with the force of a sledgehammer.

His name. His identity.

His honour.

Damn her for using him in this way! She'd taken his name and dragged it in the mud with her petty manipulations.

What did she hope to achieve? Money? Position? A hint of respectability even though her child was born out of wedlock?

But why hadn't she come forward if she'd wanted to try screwing cash from him? Was she waiting for the most auspicious time to approach him?

As if there would ever be a good time for such a plan!

He felt his lips stretch in a grimace of distaste that bared his teeth. His nostrils flared and the blood pounded loud and fast in his ears.

'Wait here,' he barked. Without waiting for a response, he strode up the cement pavement to the eyesore of a building. A red mist hazed his vision. The need for justice, for retribution, spurred him on.

This was about far more now than curiosity. More even than the stirring of a libido that had been dormant since he'd woken in hospital twenty-two months ago.

Carys Wells had gone too far. She'd sullied his honour.

For that she would pay.

Carys had only just collected Leo from next door and put him down, still sleeping.

The rap on her door came too soon. She looked at Leo's peaceful form and felt a tug of intense protectiveness. There'd been no time to decide how to deal with Alessandro.

Who was she kidding? She'd always been putty in his hands. Even now when she almost hated him, she had no illusions about that.

She'd never be rid of him until they had this out.

Reluctantly she walked through the miniscule flat, wiping her damp hands on her skirt. Her legs shook as another tattoo of raps sounded.

The glorious surge of anger had seeped away, leaving her prey to nerves and bone-melting exhaustion.

Fumbling, she unlatched the door and swung it wide.

Alessandro stood there, vibrating with a dangerous energy that wrapped right round her, squeezing her lungs. His eyes sizzled with a fury she'd seen only once before. The day he'd told her, with arctic composure, she'd outstayed her welcome.

Yet even now his potent charisma tugged at her. She bit down hard on her lip, desperate for the strength to face him.

Wordlessly he strode past her into the small sitting room-cum-kitchen. For such a big man he still managed to avoid brushing against her which, given the size of the entry, was a feat in itself.

Her lips turned up in a grimace as she pushed the door shut. He couldn't bear to touch her now she'd called him on his behaviour. How different from last night when his hands had been all over her, marking her with his own special brand of sensual possession.

Hot shame suffused her.

'You used my name for your bastard child.'

She spun round to find him towering over her, the image of disdain. But his anger was no match for hers.

'Don't ever talk about him like that!' She ignored the blast of his disapproval and jabbed an accusing finger.

'What? You're telling me you married after all?'

'No! Why would I go looking for a husband after my child's father had already rejected us?'

Alessandro leaned forward, using his superior height to intimidate her. 'For the same reason you perjured yourself, listing me as the father on the birth certificate. To try to claim some measure of respectability. Or financial support.'

The irony of his accusation hit her full force. If she'd expected support of any kind from Alessandro she'd been grossly mistaken.

She might have harboured a fatal weakness for this overbearing, arrogant, gorgeous man, but, where her son was concerned, she refused to be bullied. She stuck her hands on her hips and stared back, glare for glare.

'It was for Leo. He has a right to know who his father is.'

'Have you no shame?' Alessandro's dark green eyes sliced right through her self-possession.

'Only about the fact that I was once foolish enough to…' She stopped herself in time. She would not lay herself open to derision by admitting the feelings she'd once held for him. 'To believe in you.'

But she sensed he wasn't listening. He was absorbed in his own thoughts.

'Leo? You called him—'

'Leonardo. After your father.' She hesitated, aware now of her sentimental folly in choosing a family name for her son. She'd wanted to give him a link to his paternal family, even though that family had roundly rejected him.

Had she secretly thought one day Alessandro might be pleased to have the baby named after the father he'd lost? How misguided she'd been. He looked as she imagined some aristocrat of old must have when confronted with a troublesome serf.

'You dared to—'

'I'm not ashamed of what I did,' she bit out between clenched teeth. 'Live with it, Alessandro!'

A muffled wail sounded. Immediately Carys spun round and hurried to the bedroom she shared with Leo. She refused to stay and be reviled by Alessandro Mattani of all men.

Moments later Leo was in her arms, a warm cuddly bundle smelling of baby powder and sunshine and little boy. Carys held him against her and shut her eyes, feeling the serenity and joy she always experienced holding him.

'Mumum!' He reached up and patted her face.

Carys nuzzled his soft cheek then held him away. 'Hello, sweetie. Did you have a good day?'

His face split in a broad smile. 'Mum!' Then something over her shoulder caught his attention and he stared, his grin fading.

The skin on her neck prickled as she sensed Alessandro's presence in the room. She didn't have to turn to know he stood behind her.

She froze.

For so long she'd daydreamed about him coming to find her and Leo. He'd admit he'd been wrong and be devastated by the pain he'd caused. Carys would even find it in her heart to forgive him once she realised his true feelings for her and changed his ways. He'd take one look at Leo and his heart would melt like hers had when she'd first seen her son.

But that would never be.

There was no warmth in his heart for either of them.

Apprehension trickled like hot ice down her backbone. She couldn't bear it if he took out his anger on Leo. She cuddled her son tighter, but he leaned sideways, craning to keep Alessandro in view.

'Mumum!'

'No, darling. Not mummy.' For a split second she knew a hysterical urge to tell him it was daddy. But she wouldn't invite Alessandro's wrath.

She turned, shoulders braced and chin up, holding her baby close. If Alessandro dared make one more disparaging remark—

But she needn't have worried. All trace of arrogance and anger had vanished. Instead her tormentor stood curiously still, arms loose at his sides. His brows were knitted and he stared at Leo as if he'd never seen a baby before.

Instinctively Carys cuddled her son nearer. She smoothed back his glossy dark hair, almost long enough to be cut. But Leo paid her no heed. He was busy gazing up at the man who refused to be called his father.

She remembered how Alessandro's collar-length hair had once been like sable under her hands, just like Leo's. Their eyes were the same too. Though Leo's reminded her of a cheeky pixie's, with their twinkle, and Alessandro's showed no warmth at all. They might have been made of rock crystal.

She watched Alessandro's hands clench. The tendons in his neck stretched taut.

And still he stared at Leo.

A shiver raced down her spine.

'How old is he?' Alessandro's voice was curiously husky.

'He had his first birthday six weeks ago.'

'He was born early?'

'No. He went to full term.' Why all the questions?

Leo's sudden movement took her by surprise. He wriggled in her arms and lunged forward with all his weight as if trying to swim across the gap between himself and Alessandro.

'Mumum!' His hands opened and closed as if trying to grasp the big man before him. But Alessandro didn't move.

Carys felt her heart spasm at the sight of her little boy reaching for his father. He was doomed to disappointment.

Alessandro would never acknowledge him.

Would never love him. Or her.

Finally, after all this time, she shrugged off the last tarnished remnants of hope. The ache in her throat nearly choked her, but she felt freer than she had in almost two years. Surely, in time, the wounds would heal.

Meanwhile she had to protect Leo from the pain of knowing his dad didn't want him. She'd make up for the lack of a father, she decided fiercely. Leo would never want for love or encouragement or kindness. Not like she had.

Her arms tightened and he wailed, turning accusing eyes on her. 'Mum!'

'Yes, sweetheart. I'm sorry. Are you hungry? Are you ready for something to eat?' She took a step towards the door, studiously ignoring the tall man, standing as if riveted to the spot. 'Let's get you some food, shall we?'

It seemed a lifetime before Alessandro moved. Finally he stepped aside. 'After you.'

Carys didn't deign to respond.

She'd made it to the kitchen, Leo clamped safely on her hip, when a deep voice halted her in her tracks.

'Tell me how you came to be pregnant.'

He had to be kidding!

She whirled round to find him only a metre away, his eyes glued to her son. The intensity of his gaze unnerved her and she stroked her palm protectively over Leo's cheek.

'Oh, come *on*, Alessandro!' Her lips were stiff with fury. 'I don't know what sort of game you're playing, but I've had enough. This stops now.'

Dark green eyes lifted to pinion hers. Banked heat flared in that hooded gaze. Instantly a coil of reaction twisted in the pit of her stomach. Fear and something else she refused to name.

'No, Carys.' His words fell like blows, slow and heavy. 'It's just starting.'

Abruptly he turned to pace the room, but not before she read the bleak emptiness in his eyes.

'Because as far as I know for certain, we met for the first time last night.'

CHAPTER SIX

'So THAT'S it? We met in the Alps, where you had a job in a ski resort. We had an affair and I invited you back to my home.' Alessandro kept his voice neutral, as emotionless as if he were reading a company report rather than repeating the most astonishing thing he'd heard in years.

The whole idea was absurd.

He'd never invited any woman to share his home. The only woman he could imagine living there was the woman he'd one day make his wife. A woman he hadn't yet met.

He'd spent his adult years ensuring the women he dated understood he wasn't interested in deep, meaningful relationships. That was just female-speak for snaring a rich man gullible enough to believe she wanted him for his character and personality!

'We lived together, but it didn't work out, and you came back to Australia,' he continued, watching her avoid his gaze. 'You discovered you were pregnant and you called my home repeatedly, eventually spoke to my stepmother and as a result, believed I wanted nothing further to do with you?'

'That's about the size of it.'

Her offhand response fuelled the remnants of his earlier temper. Didn't she realise how vital this was?

Alessandro's fists clenched tight. He abhorred the need to share the fact of his memory loss with a stranger. Even a stranger with whom he'd once been intimate.

He'd been brought up never to show vulnerability, never to feel it. No wonder his discomfort now was marrow deep. His certainties, his sense of order, his grasp of the situation were far too shaky for a man accustomed to taking charge.

Still Carys didn't look at him but busied herself feeding the tot in the high chair. Was it his imagination or was she taking far too long fussing with cloths and dishes?

Alessandro kept his eyes on her, rather than her son. Meeting those big green eyes so like his own made him uneasy. And the way the boy kept staring at him, surely that wasn't normal.

The child wasn't his. He'd *know* if he had a son.

He'd always been careful about contraception. He would have children at the appropriate time, when he'd found a suitable bride. She'd be clever, chic, at home in his world, sexy. She wouldn't bore him after two weeks as most females did.

The harsh overhead light caught rich colour as Carys bent her head and the child tugged a lock of burnished hair loose from her prim bun.

Something snagged in Alessandro's chest, looking at her. And her son.

No!

He refused to feel anything except annoyance that her story didn't trigger any memories. It was all still an infuriating blank.

She turned and lifted the baby high in her arms, her prim white blouse dragging taut with the movement.

Something plunged in the pit of Alessandro's belly and heat spread in his lower body.

At least one thing was explained: his sense of possessiveness when he looked at Carys. She'd been his and, if her story was true, they'd shared a relationship unlike his usual liaisons. He'd desired her enough, trusted her enough, to install her in his own home.

Incredible! Yet it would be easy to check.

Had he planned to keep her as a long-term mistress? The idea fascinated him.

Watching the tight material of her skirt mould her thighs, the thin cotton of her blouse stretch over her breasts, the idea didn't seem quite as absurd as it should.

If it weren't for the baby, he'd be tempted to take up right now where they'd left off last night.

Sudden pain slashed behind his eyes and through his temple as he struggled to remember. The headache he'd fought in the car hovered. He was well now. Recovered. Only occasionally did the pain recur, a reminder of the past.

'Are you all right?' Smoky eyes held his. He dropped his hand from his temple and stretched his legs in front of him, shifting his weight on the lumpy sofa.

'Perfectly.' He paused, following the movement of a chubby little starfish hand that patted her breast then tugged at one of her buttons. A moment later she caught the baby's hand in hers.

Alessandro raised his eyes. Her cheeks were delicately flushed, her lips barely parted.

'You haven't told me why we split up.'

The colour in her cheeks intensified. But not, he'd swear, with sexual awareness. Her nostrils pinched, and her lips firmed.

'I don't want to talk about this. There's no point.'

'Humour me,' he murmured, leaning forward.

He wanted his pound of flesh. But what choice did she have? He looked as immovable as Uluru. Instinctively she knew he wouldn't leave till his curiosity was satisfied.

Carys believed him about his missing memory. He looked so uncomfortable she knew it was a truth he didn't want to share. She'd heard of such amnesia from her medico eldest brother. And it explained so much that had puzzled her. Like why Alessandro had come round the globe to find her.

What other reason could he have for going to such lengths? Especially since he'd dumped her so unceremoniously.

She bit her lip, glad she was the only one to remember every ignominious detail of that scene.

'You don't remember *anything?*' Pointless to ask, given his patent lack of knowledge about her, about them. Yet it seemed impossible she'd been wiped totally from his memory.

Once they'd been close. Not just physically intimate, but close as soulmates, or so it had seemed.

How could all that just disappear completely?

Because what they'd shared was far less important to Alessandro than it had been to her?

'My memory stops several months before my father's death.' His words were terse. She guessed he viewed amnesia as a weakness he should be able to master. 'I don't remember meeting you.' His tone implied he still doubted what she'd told him. 'Those months are blank. I don't even remember driving before the accident. Just waking up in hospital.'

Slowly Carys lowered herself into the rocking chair. She let Leo stand on her thighs while she held his hands. It was a game he loved, marching on the spot.

Besides, it gave her a chance to rest her shaky legs. The shock of Alessandro's revelations was a stunning blow. She still felt faintly nauseous and her limbs trembled, thinking of him injured seriously enough to cause amnesia.

'You didn't tell me how the accident happened.' She paused, wondering if her concern was too obvious. But she had to know. She avoided staring at the scar reaching up to his temple. Instead she fixed her attention on a spot over his shoulder.

His shrug was fluid and easy.

'I was driving to Milan. The car skidded in the wet when I swerved to avoid a driver on the wrong side of the road.'

On the way to the office, then. Of course. He preferred to drive himself, claiming it helped him sort out his priorities for the day's business. From the rough timeline he'd mentioned, it must have happened soon after she left.

Had she thought, even for an instant, that her departure would disrupt his precious business schedule?

Her ridiculous naivety still stunned her.

'And you're all right?' Her heart pounded, imagining the scene. Carys swallowed hard on a jagged splinter of regret and fear. 'No other after-effects? No pain?'

No matter what she told herself, she hadn't completely severed her feelings for this man. She should despise him for the way he'd treated her, yet her conflicting emotions weren't so straightforward.

Carys refused to meet his intent gaze, choosing instead to watch Leo as he babbled to her.

'I'm perfectly healthy.'

Alessandro paused so long she looked up. He stared straight into her eyes as if reading her hunger for every detail. Her need for reassurance. Eventually he continued, his clipped words indicating how little he cared to dwell on his injuries.

'I was lucky. I had lacerations and a couple of fractures.'

At her hissed indrawn breath he shrugged. 'I mended quickly. I was only in hospital a few weeks. The main concern was my memory loss.' Darkening eyes bored into hers. 'But the specialists say there's nothing I can do about that except let nature take its course. There's no other brain damage.'

Carys slumped back, only now acknowledging the full depth of her fears. Relief warred with a sense of unreality.

'I see.' This strange, constrained conversation didn't seem real given the past they shared. But it gave Carys a little time to work through the implications of his news.

He mightn't remember her, but last night in his suite he'd seduced her with a combustible passion that had sheared straight through every defence she'd painstakingly erected in the last two years.

How had he done that if he couldn't even recall her?

Was he such an awesome lover he could make any woman feel the heady, mind-blowing certainty that she wanted nothing more than Alessandro Mattani, unbridled and consummately masculine? Were the intimacies she'd shared with him and always thought so special, the wondrous sensations, something he shared with countless women?

Her weakness mortified her.

'And your wife?' Carys failed to keep the bitterness from her voice as she choked out the word. 'I assume she's not with you?'

'Wife?' The single syllable slashed through the heavy atmosphere in the room. 'You're not saying I have a wife?'

Did she imagine it or had he paled? His lazy sprawl morphed into stark rigidity as he sat up, staring.

Carys hesitated. 'You were single when I left, but you were

seeing someone else, planning to marry her. Principessa Carlotta.' She couldn't prevent distaste colouring her voice.

Of course Alessandro would only marry one of his own, a rich, privileged aristocrat.

Carys swallowed bile as memories surged. Of how she'd obstinately disregarded his stepmother's warnings about Alessandro's intentions. And about her true, temporary place in his world. Of how she'd foolishly pinned her belief and hopes on the tender passionate words he whispered in her ear. On the rapture of being with him, being loved by him.

No! Having sex with him. The love had been all on her side.

'You seem to imply I did more than just *see* her.' His tone was outraged; his eyes flashed a furious warning. 'And that I did so while you and I were…together.'

If the cap fits, buddy. 'So you did.' Deliberately she turned away to focus on Leo, happily jouncing on her knees.

'You're mistaken.' Alessandro didn't raise his voice, but his whisper was lethally quiet, an unmistakeable warning. 'I would never stoop to such despicable behaviour.' Green eyes clashed with hers. They were so vibrant with indignation she expected to see sparks shoot from their depths.

'I was there, remember.' Carys took a slow breath, forcing down the rabid, useless jealousy that even now clawed to the surface. She concentrated on keeping her voice even. 'And unlike you I have perfect recall.'

Silence. His stare would have stripped paint at twenty paces. It scoured her mercilessly.

Yet Carys refused to back down. He might believe he was incapable of such behaviour, but if his memory ever returned he was doomed to disillusionment.

'I don't need to remember to know the truth, Carys.' He leaned forward, all semblance of relaxation gone. His voice echoed an unshakeable certainty. 'No matter what you think you understand about that time, I would never betray one lover with another. Never have two lovers at the same time. It wouldn't be honourable.'

Not honourable!

Carys suppressed an anguished laugh.

Was it honourable to have a lover share his bed but exclude her from the rest of his life because she wasn't good enough for his aristocratic friends? To use her for temporary sex while he courted another woman?

Whatever had gone wrong between Alessandro and the *principessa* to prevent the marriage, that was exactly what he'd been up to.

Carys had simply been convenient, gullible, expendable.

She swung her head away, refusing to look at him. Even now the pain was too raw. A cold, leaden lump rose in her throat, but she refused to reveal her vulnerability.

She drew a slow breath. 'When I tried to contact you about the pregnancy, your stepmother said you were preparing for your wedding. She made it clear you had no time to spare for an ex-mistress.'

'Livia said that?' His astonished tone drew her unwilling gaze. His eyebrows jammed together in a V of puzzlement. 'I can't believe it.'

No. That was the problem. He hadn't believed her before either. Her word meant nothing against his suspicions. The reminder stiffened her backbone.

'Frankly, Alessandro, I don't care what you believe.'

'It's true Livia is fond of Carlotta,' he murmured as if to himself. 'And that she wants me to marry. But arranging a wedding? It never went that far.'

How convenient his loss of memory was.

Carys had confirmation of the betrothal from another source too. But most convincing of all had been the sight of Alessandro with the glamorous, blue-blooded Carlotta. Even now the recollection stabbed, sharp as a twisting stiletto in her abdomen, making her hunch involuntarily.

The princess had stared up at him with exactly the same besotted expression Carys knew she herself had worn since the day he'd swept her off her feet and into his bed. Alessandro had kept the other woman close, his arm protectively around her as if she were made of delicate porcelain. He'd gazed into her eyes, utterly absorbed in their intimate conversation as if she were the only woman in the world.

As if he didn't have a convenient lover waiting obediently at home for him.

Carys blinked to banish the heat glazing the back of her eyes. Resolutely she focused instead on Livia's dismissive words when Carys had rung to tell Alessandro about her pregnancy.

Alessandro will do what is necessary to provide for the child if it's his. But don't expect him to contact you in person. Her tone had made it clear Carys was too socially inferior to warrant anything more than a settlement engineered by his formidable legal team. *The past is the past. And questions about your, shall we say…extra-curricular activities raise suspicions about the identity of the child's father.*

That slur, above all, had been hard to swallow.

How furious Alessandro's stepmother would have been if she'd known Carys hadn't accepted her word. Instead she'd left numerous messages on Alessandro's private phone and sent emails, even a hand-written letter. She'd been so desperate for personal contact.

Only after months of deliberate, deafening silence had she finally accepted he wanted nothing to do with either her or her unborn child. Then she'd determined to turn her back on the past and start afresh, not even considering a legal bid to win child support. Leo was better off without a father like that.

Yet now it seemed Alessandro hadn't known about her pregnancy.

Her breath jammed in her throat. All this time he hadn't known!

He hadn't rejected Leo at all.

Nor was he married.

Her head spun, trying to take in the implications, her emotions a whirling jumble. Once she might have believed that would change everything.

Now she knew better.

One glance at Alessandro confirmed it. He was absorbed in his thoughts, totally oblivious to the little boy perched on her lap, twisting around time and again to try catching the attention of the big man who so effortlessly dominated their flat.

Alessandro had no interest in her either. She was nothing but a source of information.

Or an easy lay.

A shudder passed through her as memories of last night's passion stirred. Carys stiffened her resolve.

She looked into her baby's excited green gaze. He twinkled back at her mischievously as he nattered away in a language all his own. *He* was the important thing in her life. Not ancient dreams of happily ever after with the wrong man.

Whether Alessandro had known about the pregnancy or not didn't matter. What mattered was that the grand passion they'd shared had been a cheap affair, not a love on which to build a future. And he couldn't have made it clearer he had no interest in Leo.

Bridges burned. End of story.

Carys ignored the ache welling deep inside at the finality of it all and summoned a wobbly smile for Leo.

'Time for a bath, young man.' She gathered him close and stood on creaky legs. Suddenly she felt old beyond her years. Old with grief for what her son would never have, and with a stupid, obstinate hurt at being rejected again. After a lifetime of not measuring up, not being quite good enough, it was stupid to feel so wounded, but there it was.

'Why did I tell you to leave my home? You still haven't told me.'

She looked across to see Alessandro on his feet, hands jammed deep in his trouser pockets. He stood as far from her as he could while remaining in the same room.

Didn't that say it all?

'I'd decided to go anyway.' She lifted her chin. After learning about Alessandro and Carlotta the scales had fallen from her eyes. Carys knew she had to get as far away from him as she could. 'But you accused me of having an affair, of betraying your trust.'

The irony should have been laughable. But Carys had never felt less like laughing. She jiggled Leo higher in her weary arms and straightened her back.

'An affair? With whom?' His brows furrowed and his features took on a remote, hawk-like cast. Condemnation radiated from him.

'With Stefano Manzoni. He's—'

'I know who he is.' If anything, Alessandro's scowl deepened. His jaw set like stone and a pulse worked in his temple.

'Nice company you keep,' he said after a moment, his voice coolly disapproving.

Talk about double standards!

Carys jerked her chin higher. 'I thought he *was* nice. At first.' Until he wouldn't take no for an answer. He was another macho Italian male who couldn't cope with rejection. Though, to be fair, she'd never felt unsafe with Alessandro. 'I would have thought that as your Princess Carlotta's cousin he'd be utterly respectable.'

'She's not *my* Carlotta.' The words emerged through taut lips.

'Whatever.' Carys hunched stiff shoulders. 'Now, it's time for me to bathe Leo.' Her composure was in tatters and her limbs trembled with exhaustion. She felt like a wrung-out dishrag. 'I'd appreciate it if you'd go now.' She couldn't take any more.

Alessandro's appearance had dredged up emotions she thought she'd vanquished. Emotions that threatened to undo her. She needed desperately to be alone.

All she had left was the torn remnants of her pride, and Carys refused to collapse in a heap while he was here.

Head high, she walked on unsteady legs towards the front door, intending to show him out.

Leo's sudden sideways dive out of her arms took her completely unawares. One minute she was holding him. The next he was plunging headlong towards the floor when his bid to throw himself at Alessandro failed.

'Leo!'

Belatedly Carys grabbed for him, her weariness banished as adrenaline pumped hard and fast through her bloodstream, but her reactions were too slow.

'It's all right. I've got him.' How Alessandro got there so fast she didn't know, but he scooped Leo up in his arms just before he hit the floor.

Her heart catapulted against her ribs, slowing only when she saw he had the baby safe in his large hands. Relief shook her so hard her legs wobbled.

He held Leo awkwardly, at a distance from himself.

As if he couldn't bear to touch him? Or as a man would who'd never had experience with babies?

Carys hesitated, trying to decide which. In that moment Leo latched onto Alessandro's suit-clad arm, plucking at the fabric as if trying to climb closer. Green eyes met green, and Leo frowned, his chubby face puckering as he regarded the unsmiling man before him.

Finally, like the sun emerging from behind a cloud, Leo smiled. His whole face lit up. His hands thumped on Alessandro's arm and he crowed with delight.

Terrific! Her son had developed a soft spot for a man who never wanted to see him.

Obstinately Carys shied from dwelling on the sight of her son in his father's arms. It would be the only time. It was foolish to feel even a jot of sentimentality over the image of the tall, strong man holding her precious baby so ineptly yet so securely.

Carys hurried forward, arms outstretched.

'I'll take him.'

Alessandro didn't even turn his head. He was busy regarding Leo, not even flinching when the child's rhythmic thumps against his arm became real whacks as he grew impatient with the adult's lack of response.

'Alessandro?' Her voice was husky. The intensity of his stare as he looked down at his son made something flip over in her stomach. Anxiety walked its fingers down her spine.

'I'll arrange for the necessary tests to be done as soon as possible. Someone will ring you tomorrow with the details.'

'Tests?'

He didn't even turn at the sound of her voice, but he did lift Leo a little closer, winning himself a gurgle of approval and a spate of excited Leo-speak.

Carys watched Leo lean up, patting both hands over Alessandro's square, scrupulously shaved jaw. A squiggle of emotion unsettled her, seeing her little boy with the man she'd once loved.

If only circumstances had been different.

No! It was better she knew what sort of man Alessandro was and that in his eyes she could never measure up.

'DNA tests, of course.' He flashed an assessing look from slitted eyes. 'You can't expect me to take your word this is my son.'

Her stomach went into freefall.

She'd fought so hard to have Alessandro acknowledge his son before giving up in despair. Yet now she felt fear at his sudden interest. Fear at what this might mean.

Leo was hers. But if Alessandro decided he wanted him…

She found refuge in stormy anger. 'Distrust must be your middle name, Alessandro.'

The idea of him seeking independent scientific proof was a slap in the face.

Especially as he'd been her only lover.

His distrust tainted what they'd shared, reducing it to something tawdry. Her skin crawled as she met his glittering gaze and felt the weight of his doubt.

His fiery green stare scorched her. 'Better distrustful than gullible.'

CHAPTER SEVEN

THREE days later Carys received a summons to the presidential suite. David, her manager, relayed the news with a quizzical look that made the blood rise hot in her cheeks.

'Moving in exalted circles, Carys,' he murmured. 'Don't hurry back.'

She was aware of the other staff, watching surreptitiously as she pushed her chair back and stood up.

Carys had been a bundle of nerves for the past few days, ever since Alessandro had pulled strings to have the DNA tests taken in the privacy of her flat. Another reminder, if she'd needed it, of his enormous wealth. His ability to get what he wanted.

The technician had been friendly, talkative despite the marked silence between Carys and Alessandro. She'd seemed oblivious to the atmosphere laden with unspoken challenges and questions. Or maybe the woman was used to the high-octane emotions such circumstances engendered. After all, there'd be no need for mouth swabs and scientific proof if there was trust between a couple.

If a man believed his lover.

Sucking in her breath, Carys straightened her shoulders and took her time walking to the lift.

Alessandro must have received advice from the pathology company. Surely that was why she'd been summoned. No doubt he'd paid for the privilege of getting an ultra-fast turnaround on the lab results.

Her stomach cramped in anxiety.

What would he do now that he knew Leo was his?

The question had haunted her for days so that even when she finally slept, stress dreams plagued her. She woke feeling even more tired than when she went to bed.

The butler was waiting at the door for her, his smile friendly but impersonal.

Had he seen her desperate flight from the suite several days ago? Carys kept her chin high as she forced an answering smile to her lips and walked in.

The lush quiet of the suite engulfed her. Its understated opulence showcased fine furnishings and every modern convenience provided just for one man. It had been designed for the mega-wealthy, the vastly important.

No wonder she felt wretchedly small and nervous as she approached the silent man who dominated the room.

He might fit in here, but she didn't. Carys was completely, unalterably ordinary. Not by any stretch of the imagination could she be considered special. She'd faced that long ago, before Alessandro had tempted her for a brief, crazy time to believe in miracles.

'Carys.' The sound of his deep, slightly husky voice rippled like a sensual caress across her skin. Her reaction, her physical weakness for him, made her hackles rise.

'Alessandro.' She nodded. 'You demanded my presence?'

His head tilted slightly as he watched her, his look assessing but his face unreadable.

'I *requested* your presence.'

'Ah, but when the request comes from the presidential suite we staff tend to jump.' For some reason she found safety in emphasising the huge gulf between them. As if she could magically erase the memory of the madness that had gripped them last time she was here.

Her gaze flickered to the plump lounges, the wall where he'd held her and caressed her and almost…

'Please, take a seat.'

To her surprise, he gestured to an upright chair in front of an antique desk. Carys shot him a startled glance but complied. Better this than the intimacy of the sofas.

It was only as she sat that she noticed the papers spread across the desk. 'You've had the test results, then.'

'I have.'

Carys could read nothing in his voice or in his face. Was he disappointed, angry, excited to discover he had a son? Or, she thought with a sinking sensation, didn't he feel anything at all?

'Coffee, Robson. Or—' Alessandro paused to catch her eye '—would you prefer tea?'

'Nothing, thank you.' The idea of swallowing anything made her stomach curdle.

'That will be all, Robson.' Alessandro waited till the butler left before he turned to her again.

Instead of taking a chair, he lounged, arms crossed, against the desk. He was near enough for her to register his cologne. Her nerves reacted with a shimmy of excitement that made her grit her teeth in annoyance. She wished he'd move away. Far enough that she wasn't plagued by remnants of the physical attraction that had been so strong between them.

'What is it you want, Alessandro?' After days of silence from him, now he expected her jump to do his bidding. It infuriated her.

'We have arrangements to make. And you need to sign this.' He waved a hand towards the paper on the desk then reached into his jacket pocket, eyes still holding hers. 'You can use this when you've read it.'

Casually he laid a gold fountain pen on the desk beside a wad of papers.

Carys turned to face the desk. Not lab results after all. A quick look showed her long numbered paragraphs. Dense type-script. Pages and pages of legalese.

Her heart sank. Just the sort of document she hated. She couldn't deal with this while Alessandro stood so close.

A flutter of panic flared in her breast and she reached out one clammy hand to flick through the wad. The last page had space for her signature and Alessandro's.

As the pages settled again, she tried to concentrate on the first paragraph, but one of the lines kept jumping sideways so she lost her place.

Damn. Had she brought her glasses? She fumbled in her jacket pocket, aware of Alessandro's silent scrutiny.

'What is it you want me to sign?'

His eyes blazed green fire as he watched her from his superior height. Did she imagine a hint of tension around his mouth? A faint tightness between his brows?

'A prenuptial agreement.'

'*A what?*' Carys' reading glasses slid from numb fingers as she swung round to face him.

The sober light in his eyes told her she wasn't hearing things.

'An agreement setting out both parties' entitlements—'

'I know what a prenuptial agreement is.' She dragged in a deep breath to fill her suddenly constricted lungs, her pulse racing jaggedly. 'We don't need one. It's for people who plan to marry.'

He smiled then. Not a grin. Not even a real smile. Just a brief quirk of the lips that might have signalled amusement or impatience or even annoyance.

And still his eyes bored into her like lasers.

'We need it, Carys.' His words were crisp, clear and unmistakeable. 'Because we're getting married.'

He reached out and stroked a finger down her cheek. Fire streaked across her skin and blasted through her hard won calm. 'It's the only possible course of action. You must have known we'd marry once I discovered the child is mine.'

For an eternity the words hung between them. She stared up at him, lush mouth sagging, bright eyes stunned. Then, like the flick of a switch, animation returned.

'*The child* has a name, damn you!'

Carys jerked from his touch, catapulting from the chair and almost knocking it over in her haste. She stood defiant and furious, feet planted squarely and chest heaving.

'Don't you *ever* talk about Leo again as if he were some…some commodity!'

Madonna mia! With her eyes flashing and high colour in her softly-rounded cheeks, energy radiating from her in angry waves, she was stunning. More than pretty. Or beautiful. Something far more profound.

Enough almost to distract him from the important business of securing his child.

Alessandro felt the drag of attraction in his belly, his limbs, his mind. It was the possessive hunger he'd felt for days but mixed with another sensation so deep-seated it rocked him where he stood.

In that moment the careful logic that dictated his decision to marry faded. This was no longer about simple logic. The force that drove him was purely visceral.

She would be his. He would accept no other alternative.

He would have Carys *and* his son. A wave of hot pleasure suffused him.

'Of course he's not a commodity. He's Leonardo.' Alessandro inclined his head, savouring the name. 'Leo Mattani.'

An image of intelligent jade eyes, handsome dark hair and a small determined chin surfaced. His son.

His son!

Satisfaction and pride welled in his chest and—

'No! Leo Wells, not Leo Mattani. And that won't change. Marriage is a preposterous idea, so you can forget it.' Carys took a step closer, her chin rising.

Once more a blast of white-hot hunger shot through him.

What a woman she was! So fiercely protective and proud.

And as a lover…? Alessandro inhaled sharply, breathing in her skin's warm cinnamon scent. He looked forward to rediscovering the passion they'd shared. It must have been spectacular for him to take the unprecedented step of inviting her to live with him.

But first, most important, he would secure his son.

A twist of deep-seated memory skewered Alessandro, ripping a familiar hole through his belly. Of the feckless way his own mother had abandoned her '*caro Sandro*' without a backward glance. How selfish greed had triumphed over the supposedly unbreakable bonds of maternal love. She'd put her own salacious desires and hunger for wealth above her son.

Despite Carys' fiery attitude and her protectiveness, Alessandro knew the frailty of maternal love. The fickleness of women.

He would safeguard his son. Shield him and ensure he never wanted for anything.

The terms of the prenuptial agreement, with its hefty allowance for Carys while she stayed with him and his son, would ensure stability in Leo's life.

Alessandro's legal team had worked night and day to make it watertight. The obscene amount of money Alessandro had allocated to buy his wife would keep her just where he wanted her. Where Leo needed her.

With Alessandro.

'My son will grow up as Leo Mattani. That is not open to debate.' Alessandro waved his hand dismissively, his expression remote. 'Any other alternative is unthinkable.'

'Unthinkable?' Carys planted her hands on her hips as she stared into the proud, arrogant face of the man she'd once loved. 'He's been Leo Wells since he was born and he's been just fine, thank you very much.'

'Just fine?' Alessandro shook his head abruptly, voice deepening and nostrils flaring with disapproval, the epitome of masculine scorn. 'You think it fine that my son is born illegitimate?'

For a moment Carys stared helplessly into his dark, heated gaze, reading indignation and outrage.

In a perfect world Leo would have been born into a loving family with parents who were permanently committed to each other. But that hadn't been an option.

'There are worse things in the world,' she said quietly, wrapping her arms round her torso as old pain tore through her. The pain of lacerated dreams.

She'd done everything she could to ensure Alessandro had known about her pregnancy. But even if he'd known, even if he'd proposed marriage, nothing could change the fact that he wasn't a man she could trust with her heart. Or that she'd never fit into his world.

Silence hung between them as he stared down at her.

'And you think my son will continue to be *just fine* growing up in a run-down tenement among thieves and pimps?' One haughty eyebrow rose to a lofty height and Carys felt the weight of his disapproval push down on her.

'You're exaggerating,' she countered, ignoring a twinge of guilt that she hadn't been able to find somewhere better. 'It's not that bad. Besides, I'm planning to move.'

'Really? And how will you find better premises on your wage?'

His supercilious tone made Carys bite her lip in frustration. It didn't matter that her salary was the best she could get with her qualifications or that she worked hard for the money she earned. In the long term her prospects were good for promotion. But in the meantime...

'I will provide for Leo. I always have.'

For a moment Alessandro's gaze seemed to soften. 'It must have been difficult, managing on your own.'

Carys shrugged. She didn't dwell on that. On the fact that her siblings and father, scattered as they were around the globe, hadn't found time to visit when Leo was born, or afterwards. They'd sent gifts instead. A money box from her advertising executive sister in Perth. A set of children's books Leo couldn't read for years from her physicist brother in New Zealand. An oversized fluffy rabbit from her brother at a medical outpost in New Guinea. And from her dad in Canada money to secure the bond on her flat.

They meant well and they cared in their distant, uninvolved way. But how she'd longed for one of them to make the effort to be with her when she'd felt so alone. When depression had vied with excitement and determination as she struggled on her own.

Defiantly Carys met the eyes of the one person who'd had the right to be at her side when Leo came into the world.

But that time was past.

'I'm used to managing alone.' Years younger than her siblings, the late child of parents engrossed in demanding careers, she'd virtually brought herself up. 'Leo and I are OK.'

'OK isn't enough for my son. He deserves more.'

Carys compressed her lips, fighting the urge to agree. The doting mother in her wanted Leo to have the best opportunities.

The sort of opportunities a working single mum couldn't provide.

'What Leo needs is love and a secure, nurturing environment. I give him that.' She defied him to disagree.

'Of course he does. And we'll provide it. Together.'

Had Alessandro stepped closer? His eyes mesmerised and his persuasive dark coffee tone made the impossible sound almost sensible.

Carys gave herself a mental shake.

'There's no question of *together*. What we had is over.'

It died two years ago, when you betrayed me with another woman then accused me of being unfaithful. She didn't say it out loud. There was no point in revisiting the past. Carys had to focus on the future, on what was best for Leo.

'It will never be over, Carys.' His voice dropped to a caress, like the stroke of velvet on bare, shivery skin. 'We have a child together.'

She clasped her hands before her, horrified to find them shaking. His words conjured images that were too vivid, too enticing, of what it had been like when they'd been lovers.

'But that's no reason for marriage! You'll have access to him, see him as he grows.' It was a father's right. Besides, despite the emotional turmoil it would cause her to see Alessandro regularly, it was a relief that Leo would grow up knowing his father. Every boy deserved—

'*Access?*' The word shot out like bullet. 'You think that's what I want? What my son needs?'

This time it wasn't her imagination. Alessandro obliterated the space between them with a single stride. He loomed above her like an impregnable mountain citadel. Unmoving and unforgiving. Utterly forbidding.

She trembled at the impact of his powerful presence. Energy radiated from him. A dangerous undercurrent of power.

'You have strange ideas about fatherhood. I've already missed the first year of my son's life. I don't intend to miss any more.' His clipped words revealed gleaming white teeth as they bit out each word. Involuntarily Carys shrank a little.

'I just meant—'

'I know what you meant.' He paused, scrutinising her as if she came from another planet. 'Leo is my son. My flesh, my blood. I refuse to be a part-time visitor in his life while he grows up on the other side of the world.'

'But marriage!' Her tongue stuck to the roof of her mouth on the word. 'The idea is absurd.'

Alessandro's eyes darkened. His face stiffened and his lips thinned. 'I assumed you'd prefer that to the alternative.'

'Alternative?' Carys' voice was a cracked whisper as foreboding slammed into her. That look in his eyes…

'A legal battle for custody.'

CHAPTER EIGHT

CARYS' fingers twisted into knots as he said the words she'd been dreading. She swallowed convulsively, forcing down fear. 'I'm his mother. Any court would give me custody.'

'You're sure, Carys?' An infinitesimal shake of his dark head accompanied the words, as if he pitied her naivety. 'You have a good lawyer? As good as my legal team?'

Plus the Mattani millions to back them up. The words were unspoken, but Carys heard them nonetheless.

'You wouldn't…' Her voice petered out as she met his unblinking stare. He would. He'd do what it took to get Leo.

Jerkily she swung away, frantic for breathing space. For time to marshal her jumbled thoughts. Her chest cramped so she could barely breathe and her head pounded as tension crawled up her spine and wrapped clammy fingers around her temples.

He was wrong. He must be! No court would take a child from his mother.

And yet…Carys stumbled to a stop in front of a massive window commanding a view of the city. Alessandro's wealth and power were far beyond anything she or her family, if they were so inclined, could gather. He lived in a world of stratospherically rich, privileged and well-connected families. The normal rules didn't apply to them.

Did she dare take Alessandro on? She should have nothing to worry about. She was a good mother. Leo was thriving.

Yet the poisonous seed of doubt grew.

The thought of their cramped flat in a run-down neighbourhood, the best she could provide on her meagre wage, haunted her. Would that be held against her? Contrasted to the vast resources of the Mattani family?

There were so many ways Alessandro could get what he wanted, even without gaining sole custody. What if he refused to return Leo after a visit? If he kept him in Italy?

Carys didn't have the resources to go there and demand her son back. She didn't have the power to force Alessandro's hand. She'd be at his mercy. Who knew what delays Alessandro could throw up to stop her seeing Leo while their lawyers slogged it out?

A shiver rippled through her and she lifted a hand to her throbbing temple. This was the stuff of nightmares.

The man she'd loved wouldn't have threatened her like this, no matter how they'd parted. He'd never have robbed her of her baby.

But that man was gone. The realisation felt like someone had carved a part out of her heart. Alessandro had no memory of the happiness they'd once shared. To him she was merely a stranger who had what he wanted.

She longed to hold Leo, safe and warm in her arms. Hide away from Alessandro and his demands.

But there was no hiding.

'My preference is to keep this between us, Carys.' His deep voice came from just behind her, making her jump. 'I wouldn't *choose* a court battle. That would be a last resort.'

He expected her to be grateful for that? Hurt and fear coalesced in a surge of desperate anger till her body hummed with the effort of containing it.

'Well, that's a comfort! I feel so much better now.'

Long fingers grasped her shoulder, their heat branding through her clothes. She resisted but his grip firmed and she turned.

Was that compassion in his gaze?

She blinked and the illusion disappeared. Alessandro's face was angular, hard, powerful. He would never back down.

'You come swanning into our lives and think you can run roughshod over everyone.' Her words tumbled out so fast they slurred. 'As if only you know best.' Carys drew herself up to her full height. 'Your demands are outrageous. You've got no right—'

'I have the right of a father.' His cool words stopped her tirade. 'Remember that, Carys. You are no longer the only one with a say in how our son is brought up.'

Our son. The words were a douche of cold water dousing her indignation. Reminding her how vulnerable she was.

'I offer you marriage, Carys. Position, wealth, a life of ease. And—' he paused '—a home for our son. He will grow up with both parents. In a secure, stable home. What objection can you have to that?'

'But we don't care for each other. How can we—?'

'We have the best possible reason to marry. To bring up our child. That's something worthwhile and enduring.' The words sank into the silence between them as his touch warmed her shoulder. She wanted to pull away, but his intense gaze pinioned her. 'There is no better reason to wed.'

Except love. The futile little voice rang in her ears.

Carys ignored it. She'd given up believing in seductive fantasies of romance two years ago.

Yet she couldn't douse her dismay at the matter-of-fact way Alessandro spoke of marriage for the sake of their child. Perhaps the aristocracy were accustomed to convenient marriages, brokered for family or business reasons.

How could she marry a man she didn't love? A man who'd betrayed her trust?

Her lips twisted ruefully. Look where her fantasies of love had got her!

'Unless…' His fingers tightened then dropped away. His head jerked up and he regarded her down the length of his aristocratic nose, his look coldly accusing. 'Unless you've become attached to someone here?'

Carys hesitated, tempted to grab at the excuse. But she couldn't lie. Once already she'd tried to deflect Alessandro's interest by pretending to have a boyfriend, but she hadn't been able to maintain the pretence.

She shook her head, shifting back a pace and turning her head away. He was too close for comfort.

Did he know how distracting he was, standing in her personal space, radiating energy like a human generator? The hairs on her arms prickled just being so near him.

'Good, then there's no reason to refuse.'

'But what if…?' Carys bit her tongue, furious that she'd begun to blurt out her wayward thoughts. Furious she was even listening to his bizarre reasoning. She must be mad.

'What if…?' His whisper made her shiver and stiffen as the warmth of his breath caressed her cheek.

For three heartbeats, for four, Carys remained silent. Then unwillingly she continued. 'What if one day you meet someone you…care for? Someone you want to marry?'

Even now, cured of the love she'd felt for Alessandro, the thought of him with someone else squeezed her insides into a tortured knot of distress.

'That won't happen.' Certainty throbbed in his words and she turned, curiosity stirring at his instantaneous response.

'You can't know that.'

Alessandro's beautiful, sensuous mouth kicked up at the corner in a mirthless smile that made a mockery of the heat she'd imagined in his eyes moments before.

'I know it absolutely.' His gaze held hers till her chest tightened and she remembered to breathe. And still his expression of weary cynicism didn't change. 'Romantic love is a fallacy invented for the gullible. Only a fool would consider himself in love, much less marry for it.'

Carys felt her eyes widen, staring up at the man she'd once believed she'd known. He'd been considerate, witty, urbane and, above all, passionate. The sort of lover a woman dreamed about. A lover who tempted a woman to believe in the most outrageously wonderful happily ever afters.

She'd always understood he kept something of himself back. She'd sensed his deep-seated reserve despite the intimacies they shared. A sense of aloneness she'd never quite breached. An aloneness that intensified after his father died and Alessandro withdrew, devoting himself to business. Yet it shocked her to discover the hardened kernel of scepticism behind his charming exterior.

It made him seem so *empty*.

Had he always been like that? Or was this the result of the trauma he'd been through?

Distress and unwilling compassion burgeoned for this man who seemed to have so much, yet apparently felt so little.

Absurdly she wanted to reach out to him.

And what? Comfort him? Show him compassion? Love?

No! She reeled back, stunned at the depth of feelings he engendered even now.

Her hand, half raised as if to reach out to him, dropped noiselessly to her side.

'Marriage is a duty,' he continued, oblivious to her reaction. 'There was never any question of me marrying for love.' His scornful tone almost made her wince, recalling how blithely she'd believed he was falling in love with her as she'd fallen for him.

Acidly she wondered how he'd class his interest in other women. Even if he were married, there would be other women. Alessandro was a man who enjoyed sex. He wouldn't stay celibate just because he'd married a woman he didn't love. He'd have no qualms about pursuing someone who took his fancy. After all, she'd been his bit on the side, hadn't she?

'I believe in marriage for life.' His words cut through her stark thoughts. 'Once married there would be no divorce.'

'A life sentence, in fact.'

'You would not find it so hard, believe me, Carys.' A hint of mellow honey edged his words and Carys shut her eyes, fighting the insidious weakness in her bones. He was talking about money, luxury, position, that was all. Not anything important, like the emotions he so despised.

'You're not worried I might fall for someone else and want a divorce?' The words tumbled out in self-defence.

Taut silence reigned as his displeasure vibrated on the air between them.

'There will be no divorce.' His words were adamant, his tone rough-edged. 'As for believing yourself in love…'

Abruptly he stepped in front of her and lifted her chin with his hand. She felt herself fall into the shaded depths of his green gaze. Heat sparked in her abdomen as he leaned closer. A thrill of excitement skimmed down her backbone.

No! She wasn't making a fool of herself like that again. If he thought he could seduce her into falling for him all over again, he had another thing coming.

Furiously she jerked out of his hold. 'Don't worry,' her voice was icy with disdain. 'There's no danger of me falling in love with *anyone.*'

Once bitten, now cured for life!

His eyes blazed with curiosity. Then those heavy lids dropped, hiding his expression.

'Good. Then we have an understanding.'

'Now, just a minute! I didn't say I—'

'I'll leave you to read the agreement.' He gestured to the papers on the desk as he turned away, obviously eager to go. 'There are arrangements to be made.' He paused, spearing her with a look. 'Consider well what I've said, Carys. I'll be back soon for your answer.'

She hadn't meant to, but finally Carys was drawn to the elegant regency desk with its fateful document. The thickly worded pages taunted her, evidence of Alessandro's superior position, of his lawyers and his precious money.

She wasn't really considering marriage. Was she? Fear swooped through her stomach and her damp hands clenched.

Alessandro couldn't force her to marry.

He was gambling that a judge would give him custody. More, he was probably bluffing about court action. He wouldn't...

The memory of eyes flashing like jade daggers in the sun pulled her up short.

He would. To get his son, of course he would.

How had she ever imagined Alessandro would settle for part-time fatherhood?

Stiffly she raised a hand and drew the papers towards her. She settled her glasses on her nose and began reading.

By the third page panic welled. It had taken twenty minutes of desperate concentration and still some of the text eluded her.

She was exhausted after so many sleepless nights and emotionally drained. Even at the best of times her dyslexia made reading solid text like this a challenge. But now…she bit her lip, fighting down angry tears of frustration.

Leo's future was at stake and she didn't have the skills to ensure he was protected! What sort of mother was she?

The old, jeering voice in her head told her she was a failure, and for a moment she was tempted to believe it.

She slammed her palms on the table and pushed her chair away. It wasn't a matter of skills or intelligence. It was simply a disability, exacerbated by tiredness and stress.

Besides—it suddenly hit her—the prenup wasn't about Leo. It was about her rights and Alessandro's.

She flicked to the end and found a section, mercifully short, that declared she would get nothing, either in cash or interest in Alessandro's fortune, in the case of divorce. Relief filled her. That was the heart of it. All the rest was legal bumph of conditions and counter-conditions.

Still, caution warned she should have a lawyer read this before she signed.

Hell! Caution warned her to run a mile rather than consider marrying Alessandro Mattani! Even in a convenient marriage where they'd be virtual strangers, he had the power to turn her world on its head.

But this wasn't about her. This was about Leo. Leo who had the right to both his parents. Who didn't deserve to be fought over in a tug-of-love battle. Whom she loved so much she couldn't bear the risk of Alessandro taking him from her.

Carys blinked glazing hot eyes and straightened her spine.

She didn't have a lawyer to check the document, but that didn't matter. She didn't have a choice.

Heart heavy, fingers tense, she picked up Alessandro's custom-made pen and turned to the final page.

Carys Antoinette Wells. Such a pompous document deserved her full name. But instead of writing with a flourish, her hand shook so much it looked like the signature of an inexperienced teenager, pretending to be someone else.

The pen clattered to the desk. Carys got slowly to her feet, stiff like an old woman, her heart leaden.

A muffled sound drew Alessandro's attention. He lifted his head, all too ready for a distraction from paperwork.

These last days Alessandro had found it extraordinarily difficult to give business his full attention. To be expected since he'd just discovered he had a son and was in the process of acquiring a wife.

A renegade spurt of pleasure shot through him. At the thought of Leo. And, more surprisingly, at the idea of Carys, soon to be his wife.

His lips twisted in self-mockery. Two years of celibacy had honed his libido to a razor-sharp edge. That explained the anticipation surging in his blood. Even the freshly recovered memory, visited again and again, of her lying in his bed, dark russet hair spread in sensual abandon, seized his muscles in potent sexual excitement.

Since the accident his sex drive had been dormant. At first he hadn't given it a thought. All his physical and mental strength had been directed to recovery. Then there were the gruelling hours he'd put in day after day, month after month, to turn around the family company that had careened towards disaster.

Yet as the months passed, he'd realised something fundamental had altered. Despite the temptations around him, he barely found the energy to take out a pretty girl, much less summon the enthusiasm to have one in his bed.

He'd always been a discriminating but active lover. Twenty-two months of celibacy was unheard of.

Was it any wonder he fretted over those lost months, as if something in that time had reduced his drive? Somehow weakened his very masculinity?

Not even to himself had he admitted anxiety that the change in him might be permanent.

Now though, there was no doubt everything was in working order. There was a permanent ache in his groin as he fought to stifle the lustful desires Carys provoked.

His lips stretched taut in a smile of hungry anticipation.

The sound came again. A whimper, drawing Alessandro's attention. He turned to find Leo stirring in his mother's arms. She'd refused to let the cabin crew take the boy but had stretched out on her bed with the tot in her arms. They'd looked so comfortable together Alessandro saw no reason to object.

Now the little one was fidgeting and twisting in his mother's loose embrace.

Alessandro watched his son's vigorous movements and felt again the cataclysmic surge of wonder that had overcome him when he'd held the boy in his arms. The idea that he had a child still stunned him.

Green eyes caught green and Leo stopped his restless jigging.

'Ba,' Leo said solemnly. 'Ba, ba, ba.'

Alessandro put his laptop aside. 'No. It's papa.'

'Baba!' One small arm stretched towards him and pride flared. His son was intelligent, that was obvious.

Alessandro stood, scooped the boy off the bed and held him carefully in both arms. An only child himself, Alessandro had virtually no experience with young children. But he'd learn fast, for his son's sake.

He'd been brought up by nannies and tutors, following a strict regimen designed to ensure he grew early into self-reliance and emotional independence. Alessandro didn't intend to spoil his son, but he'd ensure Leo spent time with his father—a luxury Alessandro had rarely enjoyed.

He lifted his son higher, registering the elusive scent he'd noticed before, of baby, sunshine and talc. He inhaled deeply and found himself staring into a small bright face.

'I'm Papa,' he murmured, brushing dark hair back from his son's forehead. It was silky and warm under his palm.

'Baba!' Leo's grin was infectious and Alessandro's lips tilted in an answering curve.

'Come. It's time to get better acquainted.' He turned towards his seat but paused as he caught sight of Carys. She lay on her side, arms outstretched invitingly.

In sleep she looked serene, gentle, tempting.

What was it about her that tempted him when so many

beauties hadn't? That turned him on so that just standing looking down at her, he was hard as granite with wanting. Desire was a slow unmistakeable throb in his blood.

She was the mother of his child, and that was a definite turn on. The thought of her body swelling and ripening with his baby was intensely erotic and satisfying.

But he'd lusted after her before he knew about Leo. When she was a stranger in a photograph.

Why was she different?

Because she challenged him and provoked him and got under his skin till he wanted to kiss her into submission?

Or because of something they'd shared?

Something about Carys Wells made him hanker to believe she was different.

Different! Ha!

She'd admitted she had left him because he'd found out about her with another man. Stefano Manzoni. The very shark who'd been circling, aiming to take a fatal bite out of Alessandro's company after Leonardo Mattani's death. That added insult to injury.

The idea of Carys with Stefano made Alessandro sick to the stomach. Had the affair been consummated? Fury pounded through him at the images his mind conjured.

He'd make absolutely sure from now on that Carys had no time to think of looking at another man.

Then there was the way she'd pored over the prenup in Melbourne. Proof, if he'd needed any, that she was just like the rest. She'd been so absorbed, she hadn't heard him enter then leave again.

Of course she'd signed without any further demur. As soon as she'd read the size of the outrageously large allowance he'd grant her while she lived with him and Leo, she'd been hooked. Just as he'd intended.

The generosity of that allowance had caused a stir with his advisers, but Alessandro knew what he was doing. He'd make sure Leo had the stability of a mother who stayed. Alessandro's son wouldn't be left, abandoned, as he had been.

No. Despite her strange allure, Carys wasn't different.

And yet…there would be compensations.

He looked from her abandoned sprawl and enticingly sensual lips to the chubby face of the son in his arms.

He'd made the right decision.

Carys didn't know whether to be relieved or astonished that Alessandro didn't take them to his home in the hills above Lake Como. She'd loved the spare elegance of his modern architect-designed house, built to catch every view with spectacular windows and an innovative design.

Now though, he drove his snarling, low-slung car to the massive family villa. *The villa to which she'd never been invited during her months living with him.*

She hadn't been good enough for his family.

The knowledge stuck like a jagged block of ice in her chest as he turned into a wide gravel drive. Her breathing slowed as trepidation filled her.

They passed lawns and garden beds, artfully planted shrubberies, and emerged before a spectacular view of the lake. To the left the villa rose serenely, like a sugar-encrusted period fantasy. To the right stretched Lake Como: indigo water rimmed by small towns and sunlit slopes.

Beside her sat Alessandro in silent magnificence. Six feet two of brooding Italian male. His straight brows and thinned lips made it clear how he felt about bringing her to the family mansion. Clearly she wasn't the sort of bride he'd have chosen in other circumstances.

The knowledge ate at her like acid. She hadn't been good enough before. Now only Leo's presence in the back seat elevated her enough to enter the Mattani inner sanctum.

Carys sensed old doubts circling, the belief that she really was second best, not able to live up to her family's exacting standards, let alone Alessandro's.

The sight of the villa, redolent with generations of power and wealth, only reinforced the sinking sense of inadequacy she'd striven all her life to overcome.

'Your home is very imposing,' she murmured as she shoved

the traitorous thoughts away. She would *not* go down that track. Only tiredness made her think that way.

Plus nerves about what lay ahead.

'You think so?' Alessandro shrugged. 'I've always thought it overdone, as if trying too hard to impress.' He waved towards one end of the villa, thickly encrusted with pillars, balconies, decorative arched windows and even what looked from this angle like a turret.

'I hadn't thought about it like that.' She scanned the pale silvery-pink façade, taking in every quaint architectural device, every ostentatious finish. Alessandro was right. Yet with its mellow stone bathed in morning sun it was beautiful. 'Now you mention it, it's rather like an ageing showgirl, a little overdone, a little too obvious. But appealing anyway.'

A shout of laughter made her turn. Alessandro leaned back in his seat. He grinned as he met her startled gaze. That grin brought back crazy, wonderful memories. Her heart jumped then began pounding against her ribcage as heat sizzled, a long slow burn, right to her heart.

'You've hit the nail on the head. I'd never have described it that way, but you're absolutely right.' His gaze met hers and a shock wave hit her at the glint of approval and pleasure in his eyes. 'Just don't let Livia hear you say that. It's her pride and joy.'

'Livia?' The surge of jubilation Carys had felt in the unexpected shared moment ebbed. 'Is your stepmother here?'

'She no longer lives here. She spends her time in Milan or Rome. But you'll see her. She'll give you advice on what's expected of you. Fill you in on the social background you need to know.'

And you can't? The thought remained unspoken.

Of course he couldn't. Alessandro would be too busy with business or with other interests to spare time for his new fiancée. Swiftly Carys thrust aside the idea of his 'other interests' and schooled her face into a calm façade.

'Is that necessary?' She met his steady look then turned away to fumble with her seat belt. 'I'm sure she's busy.'

And she never liked me anyway.

Spending time teaching the ropes to a gauche plebeian whose sense of style began and ended with chain-store bargains would be hell for Livia. And worse for Carys.

'Not too busy to assist my bride.' His cool tone reinforced what Carys already knew, that this would be a duty for the older woman, not a pleasure.

'I'll look forward to it,' Carys said through gritted teeth and turned away, only to find her door already open. A man in a butler's uniform bowed, waiting for her to step out.

'*Grazie,*' she murmured, dredging up her rusty Italian.

He smiled and bowed deeper. 'Welcome, madam. It's a pleasure to have you here.'

Delight warmed her as she realised she could understand his clear, precise Italian. It had been almost two years since she'd spoken it, but she had an ear for languages. Perhaps because she'd spent so many years honing her memory and learning by heart at school. She'd discovered that was the best way to avoid revising with reams of written notes.

Hesitantly she tried out a little more Italian as she got out of the car. She was gratified when Paulo, the butler, encouraged her faltering attempts. Soon he was telling her about the comforts of the villa awaiting her, including a lavish morning tea, and she was responding.

Carys let him usher her from the car, only to pull up short at the sight of Alessandro waiting for her.

He held Leo, still slumbering, in his arms. For a moment the sight of her son, flushed with sleep and hair tousled, snuggled up against the wide shoulder of his magnificent, handsome father, made her heart falter in its rhythm.

Then Alessandro spoke, fortunately in a voice pitched only for her ears. 'If you've finished practising your charm on my staff we can go in.'

Confused, Carys met his searing dark scrutiny.

'Now we're marrying, you need to forget about winning other men's smiles.' His grim tone made it clear he wasn't joking. 'My wife needs to be above reproach.'

'You think I was *flirting?*' Amazement coloured her voice.

She could scarcely credit it. Alessandro sounded almost… jealous.

The idea was preposterous. But the glitter of disapproval in his eyes intrigued her.

She imagined things. Alessandro had wanted her sexually in Melbourne only because she was convenient and shamingly willing. But that was past. Now he saw her solely as Leo's mother. He hadn't touched her since he'd discovered his son. Clearly he wanted her for Leo not himself.

Carys thanked her lucky stars for that. It gave her distance. Safety. For if he ever decided to seduce her again, she wasn't sure she had the strength to resist.

'I think it's time we went in and settled our son,' he said, ignoring her blurted question. He breached the distance between them, consuming her personal space till she found it almost impossible to draw a steady breath. 'You'll be tired after the journey and you need rest before this afternoon.'

'This afternoon?' Bemused, Carys shook her head.

'Livia has arranged a designer to fit you for your wedding dress.' His lips curved up in a tight smile that could have signalled either pleasure or stoic acceptance. 'We marry at the end of the week.'

CHAPTER NINE

FOUR hours later Carys waited, palms damp with trepidation, for the haute couture designer who'd been brought in to produce her wedding gown.

The fact that Alessandro's name could procure a top designer to dress her in such a short time only reinforced his enormous wealth and the huge gulf between them. Carys had never had anything made to order in her life.

The few high-fashion gurus she'd met while working had been condescending creatures. Perhaps because they took one look at her: average height, average face, unfashionably rounded figure, and knew she was no clothes horse.

At least this one already knew the worst. Alessandro had insisted on having her measurements taken in Melbourne and sent through to Milan, with a rather unflattering photo.

Carys glanced at her watch. Maybe the designer wouldn't show. Maybe they'd decided the challenge of passing her off as anything approaching chic was too hard.

She grimaced as she paced the salon, wishing the appointment was somewhere less imposing. The luxurious formality of the reception rooms stifled. Carefully she avoided the gilt-edged antique mirrors and stiff, silk-upholstered chairs. She felt like an ugly duckling, plucked out of her comfortable little pond and plonked in a palace.

If only she'd been allowed to buy a ready-made dress.

Despite her nerves, her lips twitched as she remembered Alessandro's look of astonishment when she suggested it. Only a big formal wedding would do for the Conte Mattani and his bride. No quick civil ceremony was permitted.

So now she had to face a temperamental artiste, no doubt disappointed the bride wouldn't live up to their designs. Carys stood straighter, preparing for the worst.

A knock sounded on the massive double doors and Paulo's voice introduced her visitor. Carys felt her jaw lock as his words rolled over her. Her body stiffened with disbelief.

Impossible as it seemed, the worst was even more horrendous than she could have anticipated.

Her stomach went into a freefall of shock.

How could Livia have done it? How could she have chosen this designer of all people? She must have known—

'Signorina Wells?' The softly spoken words finally penetrated. Reluctantly, stiffly, Carys turned.

The woman before her was just as she remembered. Slim, elegant, huge dark eyes in a gorgeous elfin face. Dressed with a casual grace and a fortune in pearls that accentuated her delicate appeal.

Was it any wonder Alessandro had planned to marry her?

Pain, razor sharp and vicious, sheared through Carys. She grabbed the back of a nearby chair rather than double up in anguish. Desperate tension crawled up her spine as she strove to school her expression.

'Principessa Carlotta.' The words were rusty, thick, the product of a throat aching with distress.

Did they really expect her to submit to this woman's ministrations?

'Carlotta, please.' Her smile was warm, her husky voice appealing. Carys registered surprise that she seemed so approachable. So apparently ready to befriend the woman Alessandro had chosen over her.

Carys knew if their places were reversed she couldn't behave so blithely.

'Forgive me.' The other woman stopped a few paces away, her smile disappearing as concern etched her brow. 'But are you all right? You look very pale.'

Carys wasn't surprised. It felt as if all her blood had drained away. She clamped her hand tighter around the chair back, summoning the strength she needed to stay upright.

'I'm…' What? Surprised to find my husband's ex-lover here? *Or was she still his lover?*

The thought smashed through her rigid self-control and Carys found her knees crumpling. Abruptly she sat, grateful to discover an antique sofa behind her.

'You're unwell. I'll call for assistance.'

'No!' Carys cringed at the idea of a fuss. She couldn't believe her own weakness. She'd faced this years ago. It was just the shock of meeting her rival face to face. 'It's jet lag,' she murmured. 'We only arrived a few hours ago.'

Despite her exhaustion, she hadn't been able to sleep in the vast gold-on-cream bedroom suite she'd been given. She'd felt out of place and on edge, her mind whirring.

'Forgive me, *signorina*, but I think it's more than that.' Dark eyes scrutinised her carefully. It was clear the princess was an astute woman.

Carys released the breath she'd been holding. She couldn't play this charade. She'd never been good at dissembling. She'd rather face facts, however unpalatable.

'Won't you sit down?' Her voice sounded choked.

After a moment the princess took a chair opposite, every movement a study in fluid grace and elegance.

Carys felt like a country bumpkin in her presence. Carefully she locked her hands in her lap to stop them shaking, then drew another sustaining breath.

'The truth is it was a shock to see you.' She paused, watching the other woman tilt her head in curiosity. 'I saw you once with Alessandro, two years ago.'

Pride screamed at her to stop there, to retain her dignity. But despite the craven impulse to keep quiet, Carys refused to play games of innuendo and unspoken secrets. She wasn't that sophisticated. If her blunt unrefined ways didn't fit her husband's milieu, then so be it. If she was going to live here she had to face this.

'I was Alessandro's lover,' she said, her voice stretched thin like fine wire. 'But then I discovered he was planning to marry you.'

There. It was in the open. No hiding from the truth now.

The other woman's mouth sagged and her eyes widened. There was shock in her expression and the taut lines of her neck. Now, this close, Carys wondered if she'd been unwell. She seemed almost gaunt, suddenly fragile rather than chic.

'It was you? I thought there was someone, but Alessandro never said.'

'No.' Bitterness filled her mouth. 'Alessandro kept me very much to himself.'

'But you've got it wrong.' The other woman leaned forward, one thin hand stretched out.

'No, *principessa*. I know exactly how it was.'

'Please. You must call me Carlotta!' There was such tension in her small frame and wide eyes Carys didn't demur. 'And Alessandro and I were *not* planning to marry.'

What? Carys sat bolt upright in her seat, torn from welling self-pity in an instant.

'Nor were we lovers,' Carlotta said. 'Ah, I can see from your expression that's what you thought. But we were never more than friends.'

Carys remained silent. 'Friends' was often a euphemism for something more. Was Carlotta trying to gull her? What reason could she have?

'You must believe me, *signorina*—'

'Carys,' she said abruptly. Formality seemed absurd now.

'Carys.' Carlotta gave her a faltering smile. 'There was no marriage plan, except as a notion put forward between our families. Alessandro's stepmother and my father resurrected the idea. It had been discussed years ago when we were just teenagers, but it never came to anything. Alessandro and I...' She shrugged. 'We grew up together, but there was never that special spark between us. You know?'

Carys knew. The spark Alessandro ignited in her had blazed

like wildfire, instantaneous and all-consuming, incinerating everything in its path. Her doubts, her natural reticence, every defence she had. Oh, but it had been glorious. Heat drenched her chilled body, just remembering.

She looked into the other woman's earnest face. Could it really be true?

'But Livia told me…'

Carlotta nodded. 'Livia promoted the match. She and my family thought a marriage would be in all our interests.'

Something about her diffident tone caught Carys' attention. 'Interests?'

The other woman shrugged one shoulder. 'Business. You know how bad things were after Alessandro's father died. It was touch and go whether Alessandro would lose the company.'

No. Carys hadn't known. She'd guessed things were grim. Had tried to offer support, but the more she'd tried the more he'd turned from her, isolating himself.

'There was talk of a merger, saving Alessandro's company and boosting my family's.' She paused and looked down at her hands. 'Plus I'd been through a difficult time and they thought marriage to Alessandro would save me from myself.'

'I'm sorry. I don't understand.' This was beyond Carys.

Carlotta raised her head and met her gaze squarely. 'I was recovering from anorexia nervosa.' Her liquid dark eyes dared Carys to condemn her, but Carys felt only horror that anyone, much less this beautiful woman, should be struck down by the insidious condition.

'Two years ago I was barely out of hospital. With my family's help, and with Alessandro's, I was just beginning to find my confidence. To go out and even think of starting work again.' She shook her head. 'It took Alessandro's strength and persistence to force me out into society. Even at that worst of times for him, he found time to help me. If it hadn't been for him beside me those first few times, even my parents' support wouldn't have got me out the door.'

'I saw you with him,' Carys found herself saying, 'at a hotel in town. You wore full-length gold. You looked like a fairy princess.' And Carys had never felt more an outsider, standing in the shadows looking in at the glittering world she'd never be part of. At the man she'd lost.

'I remember that night.' Carlotta nodded. 'The gown had to be altered so much. But the full length and long sleeves hid the worst of my condition.'

'I'd never have guessed. You were breathtaking.' Carys sank back in her chair, her head reeling as she digested Carlotta's news.

Was that why Alessandro had seemed so protective? Because he was worried about Carlotta's health? But why had he never said anything to Carys?

'You don't believe me.'

Carys looked up to find Carlotta watching her. 'I do. I just…Livia deliberately let me believe…' The older woman had told her baldly that Alessandro was engaged to marry someone of his own social circle. That he was simply with Carys as a final fling before settling down. She'd even dropped by unannounced with a box of printers' samples for him. It had been full of wedding invitations.

'Livia wanted the marriage quite badly. At one stage it looked as if the company might go under. Which, if you forgive me saying, would impact on her own wealth.'

Livia as a desperate woman? The idea hadn't occurred to Carys. She seemed so assured, so regal, so in control. But perhaps if her position was threatened…

'I heard about the engagement elsewhere too,' Carys said slowly. At the time the evidence seemed insurmountable, especially when Alessandro had refused to explain, merely stating baldly he would never behave so badly and accusing *her* of infidelity! 'I met your cousin, Stefano Manzoni.'

'You know Stefano?'

'Not know, precisely. He took me for coffee and drove me home.' Carys refrained from adding Stefano had viewed her disillusionment with Alessandro as an invitation to sexual dalliance. For all his charm and flattery he'd had more arms than an octopus.

'Ah, Stefano had hopes of that merger. When it became clear it wouldn't happen, he spent a lot of energy aiming for a hostile takeover. But he didn't succeed. He was no match for Alessandro.'

The pride in Carlotta's voice made Carys watch her carefully, but she read no sign of possessiveness. No hint of intimacy in the way she spoke of Alessandro.

'I'm sorry my friendship with Alessandro hurt you. If I'd known—'

'It wasn't you.' Carys leaned forward at the other woman's obvious distress, instinctively accepting what she said as true. It was far more likely that Livia, jealous of her position and eager to shore up the family wealth, had gone all out to scare off an upstart foreigner.

And how little effort it had taken! Carys had been her own worst enemy, only too ready to believe her. The knowledge made her stomach churn in self-disgust and regret.

Alessandro had grown unapproachable, shunning her attempts to comfort him, but if Carlotta was right, he'd never betrayed Carys!

Excitement buzzed through her veins. A crazy delight that he had been loyal to her, though he hadn't loved her. That meant so much.

It meant that though all personal feelings were at an end between them, Carys was marrying a man she could respect.

'But now everything is right between you both,' Carlotta said with such a sweet smile Carys didn't have the heart to disabuse her. 'I'm glad. Alessandro deserves happiness.' She stood, and for the first time Carys noticed the large portfolio resting against her chair. 'And now perhaps we can discuss your gown. I have ideas I hope you'll approve.'

Alessandro replaced the phone with careful precision, a scowl dragging at his brow. The sound of Livia, so rarely flustered, still gabbling her excuses, rang in his ears.

He wasn't in the mood for excuses.

While in Australia he'd been unable to contact his stepmother in person. Frustration had built with each passing day till he'd simply left news that he was bringing home his fiancée and requesting she start the wedding preparations.

It still galled him to discover he'd lived with Carys Wells prior to his accident but hadn't been told about her after his coma. That Livia had kept it from him and told his staff not to refer to the woman who'd been his lover.

As if he needed protecting from his past!

He shot to his feet and paced the room.

Livia's explanations didn't alleviate his thwarted fury at being kept in the dark. It didn't matter that Livia thought Carys on the make, out to snare a wealthy man. Or that Carys had already walked out of his life. Or even that the doctors had said it was best if he were left to recover his memory without prompting.

He should have been told.

Livia's talk of a possible match at the time with Carlotta meant nothing. Alessandro knew without being told what had prompted that— Livia searching for an easy way to shore up the family finances. As if he and Carlotta would ever make a match of it. And, more to the point, as if he'd abrogate his responsibility to salvage the company by buying his way out of trouble with his wife's money!

He rubbed his jaw, realising he now had an explanation for Carys' belief he'd two-timed her with Carlotta. Livia had no doubt blown their friendship out of all proportion.

For a moment he considered enlightening Carys, proving he was innocent of her accusations. But she wouldn't believe him. The distrust flashing in her eyes was too easy to read.

He turned and strode back across the room, unable to ignore any longer Livia's most important revelation.

She'd hinted the affair had been a casual fling, because he'd kept Carys to himself and refused social invitations.

But that only stirred his curiosity. There had been plenty of lovers in his life, yet he'd never been reluctant to take them out publicly. That was one of the functions they performed— company at the many social events he attended.

His skin prickled with preternatural awareness as he remembered Livia saying while Carys was in residence he'd shunned the social whirl, preferring to stay home with his lover. Such behaviour was unprecedented.

And the only reason he could fathom was unthinkable.

That he'd been totally absorbed by her, unwilling to share her with others.

His ability to fixate on what interested him had been one of the keys to his business success. And though he hid it well, his possessive streak was well developed. He hadn't liked to share his toys as a child, and as an adult what he had he held on to.

If he'd felt...attached to Carys, he'd have kept her to himself rather than parade her before the sharks ready to pursue an attractive woman.

If he'd felt attached.

Alessandro shook his head. He didn't do serious relationships. Didn't believe in romantic love. It should be impossible.

Should be.

Yet that frisson of instinct told its own story.

He scrubbed his hand across his jaw, knowing a moment's unfamiliar hesitation.

There were too many unanswered questions, and Carys alone held the key to every answer.

Even his fiancée's relationship with her family puzzled him. Not one of them would attend the wedding. That wasn't like any family he knew.

The woman was an enigma as well as a temptation.

He turned on his heel and strode to the door.

He found her in the grand salon, leaning into the corner of one of the uncomfortable antique sofas Livia had installed.

In her crumpled aqua skirt and matching beaded top, her hair in a ponytail, Carys was a breath of fresh air in the stuffy, formal room.

He walked closer.

She didn't move. Her head rested on one arm as if she'd leaned sideways and fallen instantly asleep. One beaded sandal dangled precariously from her toes. The other lay discarded and his gaze moved to her slim, bare foot, pale and shapely and ridiculously enticing with its painted pink toenails.

A tremor of heat ricocheted through his belly as he followed the lissom curve of her ankle to her calf, her knee and, where her skirt had rucked up, to her thigh.

He remembered the feel of her supple legs encasing him as he thrust her back against the wall of his suite at the Landford. The musky scent of her arousal. The sound of her whimpering mews for more. The sheer erotic blaze of glory that had been him and Carys, on the verge of consummating this…need between them.

Just the echo of that memory had him hard and wanting and ready, feet planted wide and breathing constricted.

Yet instinctively he resisted.

Livia's news made him pause.

It *couldn't* be true that Carys had become so important to him before his accident. He, who'd learnt early not to trust in love or the fidelity of the female sex!

No. There was some other explanation behind his relationship with Carys.

And for the way she made him feel now.

Protective. It was ludicrous. This was the woman he'd told to leave because she'd been with another man. And yet…

Alessandro shook his head, adrift on a sea of turbulent, unfamiliar emotions. He was used to his life proceeding in the pattern he designed. Emotions had no place there. Or they hadn't before Carys.

His shoulders cramped as he fought the tug of feelings, weaknesses, he preferred not to acknowledge.

Despite a few hours' sleep on the long flight from Melbourne, dark smudges were still visible beneath her eyes.

Unwilling concern twisted in his belly.

This woman got to him as no other!

Without giving himself time to think, he bent and scooped Carys into his arms, ignoring the sense of familiarity that rose and crested, like a wave of warmth, as he tucked her close to his torso. Clearly he'd carried her before.

His body knew hers, only too intimately.

He turned for the door. She'd rest better in her own bed. He'd leave her there and then look in on Leo.

Alessandro lengthened his stride as he headed for the main staircase. That time alone with Leo on the flight had whetted his appetite for his son's company. He found the boy more fascinating than any other child of his acquaintance.

Alessandro had reached the top of the stairs when Carys woke. Her lips parted in a sleepy smile, and heat doused him. Eyes as bright as stars met his and instantly desire exploded into life, tightening his groin, tensing every muscle. In that moment he veered automatically towards the master suite rather than the rooms where she'd been installed.

An afternoon of pleasure, rediscovering her feminine delights beckoned. He quickened his pace.

Then the misty soft smile disappeared, and alarm filled her eyes. Her mouth tightened and she jerked as if trying to wriggle out of his hold.

The heat in his belly fizzed out as quickly as it had ignited. He slammed to a stop. No other woman had ever looked at him in such horror.

'What are you doing?' It was an accusatory gasp. Automatically Alessandro lifted his chin, unaccustomed to such a tone.

'Carrying you to bed. You need rest.'

If anything her tension increased. He felt her stiffen. Her eyes blazed.

'No! I need to see to Leo. He—'

'Our son—' Alessandro paused, savouring the words '—is being looked after by a very capable and pleasant carer.' Carys opened her mouth, to object no doubt. He overrode her. 'In the longer term we will look for a more permanent carer to help with him, but for now be assured he's in safe hands.'

She drew in a deep breath and Alessandro wished he weren't so aware of the soft inviting press of her breast against his chest. It was the most refined torment.

'I can walk from here.'

'But we're almost there.' He stepped forward again, this time towards her guest bedroom. Still he felt her tension. She was stiff as a board, rigid with…anxiety? Distress?

Concern twisted in his belly, a flare of regret for what had happened this afternoon.

'I'm sorry you weren't warned it would be Carlotta coming to discuss your wedding gown today.' He said it slowly, unused to apologising. He'd always prided himself on behaving honourably. 'I only just found out myself.'

It had been Livia's little surprise to confront Carys with the woman she believed had been her rival.

Even now Alessandro found it hard to believe Livia had done anything so crass. He mightn't trust Carys, might have been betrayed by her, but his behaviour and his family's must always be above reproach.

From now on Alessandro would have his personal staff oversee all the wedding arrangements. His stepmother could attend and kiss the bride, but he no longer trusted her with anything more.

'It's all right,' Carys said quickly. 'We had a…useful discussion.' For a moment her gaze clung to his, then she turned her head abruptly, as if dismissing him.

Clearly she didn't accept his apology.

Alessandro registered a curious feeling of emptiness, as if something inside his chest shrivelled. An instant later he put the nonsensical notion from his mind. Resentment stirred at having his word doubted.

'She will do an excellent job,' he said tersely. 'Carlotta is one of Italy's most talented new designers.'

'I'm sure she is,' his bride-to-be said in a hollow voice. 'Her ideas are very clever.'

She sounded as enthusiastic as a woman being measured for her shroud. The idea slashed at his pride.

And this the woman he'd wanted to take to his room and ravish! It shamed him that even now he craved her.

He pushed open her bedroom door and quickly lowered her to the bed, stepping back as if her very touch contaminated.

Separate rooms until after the wedding were preferable after all. Carys needed time to accustom herself to marriage. And he needed space to master these unwanted feelings.

'I'll leave you now to rest.'

Alessandro spun round without waiting for a response and strode from the room.

He didn't see the longing or the anguish in her eyes as she watched him go.

CHAPTER TEN

CARYS drew a deep breath and paused before stepping into the church. The clamour of photographers and sightseers unsettled her, another reminder that she was marrying one of Italy's richest, most eligible men.

Only the presence of Alessandro's security staff kept the eager throng back.

She wished now she'd accepted Alessandro's suggestion that one of his cousins escort her down the aisle.

Foolishly she'd kept alive the faint hope her father would come to give her away. It wasn't a romantic match, but this marriage was for keeps. For Leo's sake. And because once wed she knew Alessandro would never relinquish his wife.

This ceremony would change her life for ever.

Her lips tightened as she smoothed shaky fingers over rich silk skirts. Even after all these years the pain of her dad's rebuff was as strong as ever.

All those missed school plays and speech days where her performances and athletic awards failed to measure up to parental expectations of academic brilliance. She should have realised he wouldn't come, just as her siblings had perfectly sound reasons for not attending, even with Alessandro's offer of free travel. They'd been too busy, promising to visit sometime in the future when life was less hectic.

'Are you ready, *signorina*?' Bruno's familiar husky voice interrupted her reverie. 'Is anything wrong?'

Everything!

She was marrying the man she'd once adored. Not for love, but in a bloodless marriage to keep her son. She had no friends here to support her. She was out of her depth, marrying into an aristocratic world she'd never fit into.

Worst of all, she suspected that despite all that had gone before, she might still…care for Alessandro.

Being with him had awoken so many memories.

More, Carlotta's news that he'd never betrayed Carys, hadn't been unfaithful, had opened the floodgates to emotions she thought she'd eradicated.

He might not love her, but he was essentially the same man she'd fallen for years ago. More impatient, more ruthless, yet just as charismatic and intriguing. And not the lying cheat she'd believed when she'd left him.

Guilt plagued her that she'd believed the worst of him. Her own insecurities had made her too ready to doubt.

Regret gave way to longing, and she found herself wishing this marriage was for real. For love, not expediency.

No! Alessandro wasn't looking for love.

And nor was she.

'*Signorina?*' Bruno stepped close, his tone concerned.

'Sorry, Bruno.' Carys directed a wobbly smile at the body-guard. 'I'm just…gathering myself. It's a little overwhelming.'

'It will be all right, *signorina*. You'll see. The *conte* will take care of you.'

As he'd taken care of all the wedding arrangements, with a ruthless efficiency that brooked no delay. She was merely an item to be checked off his list.

Acquired: one wife, ditto mother for my son.

Carys repressed a hysterical giggle and lifted her bouquet. The rich scent of orange blossom filled her nostrils, and she swayed, stupidly unsettled by the evocative perfume.

'So he will, Bruno. Thank you.'

She was stronger than this. She didn't do self-pity.

This was for Leo. She had to focus on that. Pushing back her shoulders, she stepped through the door Bruno held open.

Music swelled, the sound of murmuring voices faded, and she was aware of a sea of faces turned towards her. She let her gaze trawl the congregation rather than look down the aisle to where Alessandro stood, waiting to make her his wife.

Pain constricted her chest and she faltered, but curious stares prompted her to move on. They were all strangers, friends of Alessandro. No doubt assessing the bride to see if she lived up to expectations.

Carys lifted her chin, knowing at least she was dressed the part. Carlotta had done a superb job creating a stylish gown that made Carys look feminine and almost elegant.

In grey silk so pale it almost passed for cream, the dress was closely fitted from neck to hips, turning her curves into an almost hourglass figure. From there it flared into lush folds and a rippling train studded with azure beads like hundreds of flashing stars. Long, fitted sleeves and a high collar gave it a severe, almost medieval style, belied by the deep, slit neckline, embroidered with azure sapphires.

The effect was austere yet sumptuous. It was the most flattering, gorgeous thing Carys had ever owned.

She heard whispers as she passed, saw the envy in female eyes, and a tiny thrill of pleasure skimmed her spine.

Now she noticed smiles, one or two familiar faces. And suddenly, there were Alessandro's three female cousins, whom she'd met only two days ago. Accompanied by their husbands and their brood of handsome children. All smiled broadly, nodding encouragement.

They'd chosen pews on the bride's side of the church. Warmth invaded her chilled body at the thoughtfulness of the gesture. It made her feel she wasn't quite so alone.

Then came Carlotta, beaming and gorgeous in ruby red, delight in her dark eyes. And Leo, clapping excitedly and calling to her from his carer's arms. Carys leaned over and gave him a quick cuddle, gaining strength from the flood of love that rose within her.

The buzz of whispered conversation began again and she straightened, feeling the curious stares stabbing into her back. She turned and there was Livia, her fixed smile cool.

This was the woman who'd tried to keep Alessandro and Carys apart. How would she react if she knew that, despite this charade, they were virtually strangers? That the ceremony was a cruel parody of the dreams Carys had once cherished?

Momentary pleasure faded as reality slammed into Carys. It obliterated her tentative poise and transfixed her with a knife-blade of regret through the chest.

Finally she couldn't ignore any longer the tall man looming before her. Impatience radiated from every superbly tailored inch.

Her fingers clenched on the bouquet as she fought the impulse to run pell-mell back up the aisle and away to freedom. Blood rushed in her ears and her body tensed for flight.

Then he extended one powerful arm, his hand outstretched towards her. She felt his regard like a lick of flame on her face and her body. Her skin prickled in response.

There was no escape. He sucked the air from her lungs and shattered the remnants of her defiant courage.

Like an automaton she stepped forward, letting Alessandro capture her hand. Feeling in that moment the inevitable thrill of energy his touch always evoked.

Yet even that couldn't thaw the chill around her heart.

If only they were marrying for any other reason. If this was about caring instead of custody.

Desolation swept her. If only Alessandro remembered the past, remembered even a little of what they'd shared. But he didn't. Probably never would. Only she recalled the glory as well as the pain, the companionship and the ecstasy and the sense of belonging that had made their relationship unique.

What good were such memories when she couldn't share them? They might as well be figments of her imagination, torturing rather than comforting. She'd never again experience that closeness with the man she was about to marry.

'Carys.' The word feathered across her nerves like the stroke of his hand. His sexy accent invested the name with undercurrents that made her tremble. He turned her towards him and inevitably her eyes lifted to his face.

Her breath caught in astonishment as she met his deep green gaze. Its intensity scorched.

She tried to draw breath, but the incendiary flare in his eyes arrested her. Instead her breathing shallowed, became rapid and unsteady. Her knees trembled and tattered hope rose at what she read in his face.

Alessandro's expression almost made her believe…

The priest spoke and instantly, like a curtain descending to hide a stage, Alessandro's face became blank, wiped of all expression. No heat, no vibrancy, no emotion.

Had she imagined it? Wanted so much to believe he felt something, anything for her that she'd invented that look of fixation and wonder?

Looking now into shadowed dark eyes, Carys felt that tiny seed of hope shrivel in her breast.

The past was the past. What they'd once shared was dead.

In its place she gave herself in a farce of marriage.

Carys tasted the ashes of old dreams on her tongue as she turned to face the priest. Instinct screamed that she was making a terrible, terrible mistake.

But, for the sake of her son, she'd go through with it.

Hours later, drooping with fatigue, face stiff from pinning on a smile, Carys was too weary to object when Alessandro swept her off her feet and into his arms in front of their guests.

'There's no need for pantomime,' she whispered, attempting to ignore the insidious melting sensation as his arms closed round her. 'My legs work perfectly.'

'No pantomime, *wife*,' he murmured as he carried her from the enormous marquee and across the lawn to the sound of applause. 'In Italy men carry their brides across the threshold.'

Carys eyed the hundred metres between them and the villa and kept her lips closed. If Alessandro wanted to indulge in a show of machismo, she had little chance of dissuading him. She'd just have to pretend being held in his arms didn't evoke a cascade of tingling awareness she couldn't control.

She stiffened in his hold.

'You could try smiling,' he said under his breath. 'People expect a bride to look happy.'

Carys bared her teeth in what she guessed was more of a grimace than a smile of joy. The strain of acting the happy bride had taken its toll, shredding her frayed nerves.

'I'm a hotel management trainee, not an actress.'

Not for anything would she let him guess how deeply his embrace affected her. How that terrible gnawing sensation ate once more at her belly, and how her arms ached with the effort not to lift them around his neck so she could sink against the broad cushion of his chest.

'Little viper.' There was no heat in the look he gave her. But there was…something.

Her heart raced faster.

'You can put me down now. We've crossed the threshold.'

He didn't answer, just made for the sweeping central staircase and climbed it with a speed that belied the burden he carried.

Dimly Carys was aware of more applause and laughter from the few staff gathered in the foyer.

But nothing could distract her from the look on Alessandro's face. The determined set of his jaw and the hooded, unreadable expression in his eyes. He was so *focused*.

'Alessandro?'

He didn't answer as he reached the top of the staircase and plunged down a wide hallway.

'My room is to the left.' Was that her voice? That wisp of sound? Her hands clenched together so hard the pulse throbbed through her palms like a beaten drum. Her chest hollowed with an emotion that should have been trepidation.

Ahead wide double doors stood open. Alessandro strode through them then paused to kick them shut with a thud that reverberated right through her.

Slowly the sound died away to echoing silence. A silence taut with rising tension.

Still he held her.

She felt the rise and fall of his chest against her, surely more pronounced than when he'd climbed the stairs.

Did she imagine the shift of those long-fingered hands? The tightening of his embrace, drawing her more firmly against his powerful torso? Heat radiated from him, seeped into her flesh and bones, melting the tightness of her tensed muscles.

Craven, she turned her head, unable to meet his stare. Afraid he might see in her face traces of the crazy yearning that still plagued her. The yearning for *him*. No matter what she'd told herself, she'd never been able to obliterate it.

But she had to hide it.

Her breath hitched audibly as she saw the wide bed that took up one end of the vast room. Canopied in emerald green silk, perfectly centred between French doors that gave on to a balcony overlooking the lake, it took her breath away.

A long garland of roses was strung across the bed head, and rich velvety petals, like a shower of cream and blush and crimson, lay scattered across the sheets.

It looked like nothing so much as…

'Our wedding bed.' Alessandro's deep voice was resonant with an inflection she could almost swear was satisfaction.

Except she knew he had no desire for intimacy. No desire for her. This union was pragmatic, necessary. A legality.

Carys opened her mouth, but no words came. She drew a difficult breath, suddenly aware of how the tight silken bodice cupped her breasts and of the delicate scratch of her new bra's hand-made lace against peaking nipples.

Hot embarrassment flooded her. And more heat that wasn't embarrassment, creating an unsettling, pooling sensation way down low in her womb.

She shifted in his hold, praying he wouldn't notice her traitorous body's reaction to him.

'Your cousins have been busy,' she said in a scratchy, unfamiliar voice. Now she understood the presence of the other women in the house this morning, whispering and laughing over some secret as they made their way upstairs.

She felt the shrug of powerful shoulders. 'Another tradition. It's supposed to bring luck to a marriage. Blessings and, who knows, maybe even fertility.'

Carys wriggled, now desperate to escape. She couldn't keep up this façade of composure. Not when she felt his heart thudding against her, the warm tickle of his breath in her hair and the heat of his hands cradling her.

He made her want things she shouldn't. Things that could never be.

'The union is already fertile. We have Leo. We don't—'

Her words died as, instead of releasing her, Alessandro carried her to the bridal bed. A moment later she was sprawled across the mattress, the rich, sensual perfume of damask roses rising from the petals crushed beneath her.

Automatically she struggled against the encumbering long skirts and the veil dragging her down.

Then she looked up and froze. The expression of feral hunger in Alessandro's face made her heart hammer in her chest. Adrenaline spiked her bloodstream.

She told herself it was from fear. But she didn't believe it.

'You wouldn't condemn Leo to being an only child, would you?'

Alessandro looked down at the woman who was now incontrovertibly *his* and felt a satisfaction such as he'd never experienced.

It outstripped the pleasure of finally wresting the family company back to a secure footing. Even the recollection of his first major business coup, the difficult and astoundingly successful acquisition of a rival manufacturing firm, couldn't match the exultant surge of pleasure that shot through him as he looked down at his woman.

His wife.

It wasn't supposed to be like this. It was supposed to be convenient, sensible, a considered option to safeguard the interests of his son. But right now only his own interests were at the fore of Alessandro's mind.

This week had been a test of endurance such as he'd never known. Time and again he'd reined in the impulse to reach for her and make her his, assuage the physical hunger and, more, the edgy sensation that she could fill the nameless void at the core of his world.

When she'd walked down the aisle, an ice-cool, delicious vision of femininity, his temperature had soared and his libido had leapt into urgent life. It had taken all his resolve to stand and wait, not to throw her over his shoulder and abduct her to some-place private.

Laid out before him like a delicacy awaiting his approval, Carys stoked a fire in his blood for which he knew there could be only one solution.

Sex. Hot and satisfying.

Alessandro drew a slow breath, inhaling the scent of flowers and woman that had haunted him all afternoon.

Damn it. Carlotta had done her job too well. That dress em-phasised every sultry line and curve of the woman he'd married. It had driven him crazy from the moment he saw her.

His gaze skimmed the perfect swell of her breasts, hidden yet accentuated by the shadowy V of a neckline that had dragged his attention back again and again. With those scintillating blue stones on the bodice drawing his gaze, he'd spent half the recep-tion ogling his new wife instead of speaking to guests.

When they'd danced he'd put his hands around a waist that was surely too tiny for a woman who'd given birth, and felt a powerful surge of possessiveness overwhelm him.

It didn't matter that he couldn't recall the past between them. It was the present that mattered. Not even his doubts about her trust-worthiness impinged on his thinking. Right now nothing mattered more than slaking his desperate lust for his brand new wife.

The self-imposed wait was over at last.

He lifted a hand to his tie and tugged it undone.

'Alessandro!'

His eyes had a glazed look: too intense, too febrile. As if the cool, utterly controlled man she knew had been replaced by a being only half tame. His scar complemented his lawless air. He looked dangerous, rapacious. He'd turned from magnate to pirate in the blink of an eye.

A delicious shiver shot through her, even as she tried to be sensible.

Sleeping with Alessandro would solve nothing. Not when his heart wasn't engaged. Experience proved she was too vulnerable to him, too hungry for more.

But it's not sleep he wants, purred a demon voice inside her head.

She watched in fascination and dawning horror as his bow tie slid from his neck to the floor. Dark olive fingers flicked open his shirt.

Carys scrabbled backwards on the bed, hampered by the long veil underneath her and the voluminous skirts.

'What do you think you're doing? This wasn't part of our bargain.' If only her voice was strident rather than breathless. Instead it sounded like an invitation.

'Our bargain was marriage, *piccolina.* You're my woman now.' His voice had dropped to a throaty growl that should have warned but instead thrilled her.

She squeezed her eyes shut, seeking the strength she needed.

A dip in the mattress had her eyes popping open to discover Alessandro kneeling astride her thighs, pinning her wide skirt to the bed.

His glittering gaze raked her as if there was no exquisite gown covering her. As if she was his for the taking.

A shiver of pure carnal anticipation ripped through Carys, making a mockery of all her logical protests.

The truth was that, stripped of the varnish of urbane sophistication, Alessandro held an even more potent allure. His untrammelled machismo sent her hormones into overdrive.

'Alessandro.' Her voice was a telltale husky quiver, but she pressed on. 'You don't really want this.'

Or me. Her throat closed convulsively before she could blurt that out.

He'd turned away from her totally once he had discovered Leo. The completeness of his withdrawal, from hot pursuit to cold distance in the blink of an eye, had left her in no doubt she'd been a convenience, easy to use and easy to discard. Of no intrinsic value.

Hot, familiar pain suffused her and she dropped her eyes. She fought against a lifetime's experience of rejection, telling herself she *was* important.

'Not want this?' His words were sharp as the crack of a gun firing. His nimble fingers paused from reefing his shirt undone. 'What are you talking about?'

'You want to make it appear as if we're a real married couple, for the benefit of the guests,' she said in a low, cramped voice, her eyes fixed on his hands rather than his face. 'But carrying me all the way up here did the trick. There's no need to continue the charade.'

'Trick? Charade?' He spoke softly, yet the words throbbed with outrage. 'We are *really* married. You are *really* my wife. And I am now your husband. The *only* man in your life. Remember that.'

'There are no other men in my life.' She wished he'd move. Being caged by his long, lithe, hot body was doing terrible things to her pulse. It throbbed deep between her legs, in the place that suddenly felt so empty and needy. Her lovely dress felt too constricting, the bodice cramping her breath. If only he'd move away.

'And there will be no others from now on. Remember that.'

'I don't need a man in my life.' All she needed was Leo.

'Then you should not have married me, Carys.'

The finality of his tone penetrated, yanking her gaze back to his. Her mouth dried as she looked into his proud, severe, gorgeous face. Clear intent was etched in every angle and curve as well as in the glint of green fire in his deep-set eyes.

'I will not be used as a convenience, Alessandro. We might have married for our son's sake, but you can't have me on tap.' Her jaw ached with tension and she fought to keep her words calm, despite the emotions jangling through her.

'Convenience!' His eyes flared wide. 'You think *this* is convenient?' He snatched her hand up and pressed it, palm down, against his groin.

A massive erection throbbed against her touch. Hot and powerful, it filled her hand. Carys gulped at the memory of all that power unleashed inside her. Need spiralled deep within and she clenched her thighs against the moist proof that he still turned her on as no man ever had.

She tried to pull back, but he wouldn't let her.

Her pulse rocketed as he loomed over her, an autocratic, sexy captor, trapping her with his superior strength. And more, with the raw promise of pleasure in his eyes.

Heat exploded in her belly. The heat of sexual excitement.

She shouldn't want him, but she did. Badly. Despite pride. Despite everything.

'From the moment I saw your photo I've been hard.' He shook his head and she saw a fleeting glimpse of confusion in his eyes. It almost matched her own disbelief at the revelation. He'd wanted her? Not just seen her as a source of information for the memory he'd lost?

Could it be true? Part of her needed to believe that he'd wanted her, even if only on the most superficial level. That she was special to him.

'Hungry for a woman I didn't even know! And in Melbourne…' His eyes flickered half closed as he tilted his body, pushing right into her hold with a jerky thrust that ended in a low masculine groan of need.

The sound aroused her terribly. Memories swamped her of Alessandro gasping out his desire and his pleasure as they melded together in passion. She squirmed beneath him, fruitlessly trying to ease the wanton ache in her womb.

'Do you know what it did to me, letting you go?'

Dumbly she shook her head. He'd seemed so controlled. Yet now, looking into a face drawn tight with barely bridled hunger, a face of pain, Carys began to doubt her certainty.

'For the first time in two years I wanted a woman, but it was obvious you weren't ready. You were exhausted and overwhelmed by the changes in your life.'

He leaned forward, braced on one hand above her, the other hand still clasping her to him. Part of her revelled in his dominance, even as she fought to clear her mind. 'I thought you needed time, Carys. That's why I pulled back.'

For the first time in two years? Her brain stuck on that statement.

She couldn't have heard right. Alessandro was a virile man who revelled in physical pleasure. When all else had bled away, and their relationship grew empty, he'd still been a passionate lover, almost ferocious in his need for her. And in his need to give her equal pleasure.

A shudder of pure longing rippled through her.

'Don't soft soap me, Alessandro. I don't care how many lovers you've had since we were together,' she lied. 'So you don't have to pretend to—'

'Celibacy?' His mouth twisted in derision. 'And what if it's true? What if there's been no one since you?'

Her mind boggled at the idea of Alessandro celibate without her, only feeling desire when he saw her again.

As if his subconscious had kept him for her alone.

No! That was nonsense. The inane imaginings of a woman who'd once been too much in love.

'You can't mean it.'

'You know,' he growled, 'I'm getting tired of you telling me what it is I mean or feel.'

CHAPTER ELEVEN

WITHOUT warning he moved back. Carys was free, her skirts no longer pinned beneath his knees, her hand no longer pressed against that most intimate part of him.

She was relieved. Of course she was. She drew a long, shaky breath. In a minute she'd move and—

Her skirts bunched as strong hands slipped up from her ankles over silk-stockinged calves and knees. By the time Carys collected her stunned thoughts his fingers had reached her thighs, pausing to circle the tops of the stockings Carlotta had insisted she wear with her new underwear and glamorous gown.

Dumbfounded, Carys stared up over a froth of silk to Alessandro's stern face. He was looking down to where his hands played with her suspender straps. Her breath jammed in her lungs at the incredibly erotic sensations his feather-light caresses evoked.

She leaned up, intending to push him away, but it was too late. Already he'd thrust the fabric higher, baring her to his gaze. She felt a waft of air as, with a single tug, he ripped the delicate fabric of her panties away.

The look on his face stopped her instantaneous move to cover herself. Heat sizzled in her blood at the way he stared. Hungry. Possessive. Intense.

The air thickened, making breathing difficult. All she heard was the throb of her pulse, heavy and quick.

The soft wool of Alessandro's trousers brushed her thighs as he knelt between her legs, pushing them wider. Desire exploded as her blood rushed faster in her shaking limbs.

She needed to resist the lure of his seduction. But now, faced with the reality of Alessandro, rampant with desire, her longings obliterated every sensible reason for resistance.

All she could think of was that he hadn't betrayed her. Hadn't taken another lover when they were together, and, if he were serious, not even since they'd parted.

What she'd felt for him hadn't died. It had only been dormant. Even her heartache hadn't killed it off.

'The only thing that would stop me now is if you said you didn't want this.' He lifted his head and pinioned her with his gaze.

She lay supine before the blaze of power she read there, stunned by the immensity of the feelings rising within her.

'Can you tell me you don't want this?'

On the words one long finger slid unerringly through moist folds of skin where she was most vulnerable and sensitive.

Carys shook at the riot of sensations radiating out from his intimate caress. She felt so vibrantly alive. So needy.

Hands in tight fists, she opened her mouth to make him stop, summoning her shattered resistance. But with mind-numbing ease his finger slipped inside, pushing past muscles that clenched hungrily around him.

She almost sobbed with pleasure at the gentle, insistent, seductive slide. Just that alone felt so good. Too good. It had been so long and—

'Carys? I'm waiting for you to tell me.'

From under weighted lids she saw him watch her and felt a flush cover her breasts and cheeks. This was her last chance.

'I…' The tempo of his caress changed, the angle of his touch, and all at once the world shattered around her in a storm of ecstatic energy. She felt it splinter into tiny fragments as she bucked up against his palm, tidal waves of unstoppable sensation radiating out from his touch.

Heat drenched her as the sudden climax, as complete and mind-numbing as any she'd known, blasted her apart.

Only Alessandro's jade gaze held her together. Through the

maelstrom of exquisite delight and overwhelmed senses, his eyes locked with hers. The connection between them sparked like a live wire.

An instant later he moved, surging forward in a powerful motion that thrust her back into the mattress, her legs around his already pumping hips.

Better, so much better than before. The heavy, satisfying length of him filled her completely. His breath was hot at her neck, his broad chest flattening hers, rubbing against her sensitive breasts. His arms curled beneath her and lifted her up so that each rapid thrust slid further and further till surely he touched her very centre.

Her spasming muscles had begun to ease, but now, pummelled by the unstoppable force that was Alessandro, spent nerve endings came abruptly to life again. Hearing him growl her name, feeling his teeth graze her neck at its most sensitive point only heightened the intensity of his raw, earthy loving. Tension spiralled anew as she responded to a passion so primitive she'd never experienced its like before.

The force driving him was so elemental Carys felt as if he branded her for life. She revelled in it.

One last thrust, the slide of eager hands, and she looked up into dazed green eyes as an explosion, more cataclysmic than the first, shook them both.

She heard her name, heard her own high-pitched scream, felt the satisfying hot pulse of his seed inside her as the wave took them, and then they collapsed together.

Alessandro couldn't believe he'd so lost control. One minute they were arguing and the next Carys was tipped up on the bed and he was pounding into her with all the finesse of a rampant stallion.

The sight of her coming apart at his touch, the look of bemused wonder, of yearning on her face, had tipped him over the edge. And shattered every claim he had to be a civilised man.

He had no control where this woman was concerned. Not one iota of subtlety or restraint.

For weeks he'd harnessed a desperate, growing hunger, but not for a moment had he thought the outcome would be so rough or so barbaric.

Alessandro scrubbed a hand across his face and met his hooded eyes in the bathroom mirror. Even now they glittered with unrepentant satisfaction and excitement. Because Carys, his wife, lay in the next room. In his bed.

He should be ashamed he'd taken her with such unskilled abandon. Yet even that wouldn't stop him a second time.

He reached out for a flannel and turned back towards the bathroom door.

She lay as he'd left her, limp and sated, long legs still encased in stockings and high-heeled satin shoes. The sight of those legs, the rucked up, crumpled dress, and the dark triangle of hair sent a bolt of electricity straight to his groin. His breath whistled out of his lungs as need, instant and consuming, swamped him again.

Had it always been like this with Carys?

Again that tantalising memory teased him, of Carys lying sated in another bed. This time, though, it wasn't her image that caught his attention but the emotions the scene evoked. As if he could feel what he'd felt then. Satisfaction tinged with stirring sexual anticipation. Blatant possessiveness. And…contentment.

It was the latter, the curious sense of absolute rightness, that unsettled him. The suspicion that along with his memory he'd lost something precious.

He'd never responded to another woman so. That made him wary. But he couldn't keep away. Didn't want to.

Already he hungered for her again. This time he'd put her needs first and prove he wasn't a barbaric lout who didn't know how to seduce a woman.

Alessandro avoided her eyes. Heat lashed his cheeks at the way he'd treated her.

She didn't move as he settled himself, naked, on the bed beside her. The dress he'd paid a fortune for was probably unsalvageable, but he didn't care. Didn't care about anything but the hunger thrumming again in his veins like a horde of locusts sweeping down to devour him.

She was barely dozing, worn out by his rough handling. He should let her rest. She'd been wound tight as a top at the wedding. But in conscience he couldn't let her sleep in her clothes and shoes. She was bound to be uncomfortable and wake.

He reached out and took one slim foot in his hand.

Carys stretched, half aware of something behind her, something moving down her back. But she felt deliciously replete and she clung to sleep.

It was only as hot palms slid against her bare skin that she woke fully.

She lay in bed, still in her wedding gown, and Alessandro had undone each tiny button down her spine. His hands were inside the dress, massaging and soothing so she instinctively arched against his touch.

'You're awake.' His deep voice throbbed with an expression she couldn't identify.

Cravenly she wished she'd woken alone. The memory of what they'd done scoured her brain. The hot musk smell of sex permeated the air, reminding her of how she'd climaxed so easily at his touch. Without even a move to escape!

For all her protests, her fine talk about not being a convenience, she'd succumbed without a fight. Just lay there and given herself up to the ecstasy he wrought.

Carys bowed her head into upturned hands, hunching away from him. What had she done? How could she face herself?

'Carys? Are you all right?' His roving hands stopped, gripping her shoulders beneath her dress.

'I'm fine,' she lied.

She fought the tremors of delight spreading from his touch. The secret excitement hoarded close in her heart that he'd wanted her, and no one else, in all that time. Had she no pride?

It would be too easy to fall in love with Alessandro again. Where would that get her? A one-sided relationship where she gave all and he only as much as it suited him.

But she feared it was too late. That there was no turning back. Emotion filled the bitter void she'd lived with so long.

She needed time to work out what this all meant.

Yet there was no mistaking the sizzle of anticipation in her blood as his hands wandered, evoking magic.

Was she doomed to be enraptured by him all over again?

'Let me help you out of that dress. It can't be comfortable.'

Carys slithered forward out of his reach. 'I can do it myself.' It was too soon to meet his assessing eyes. If she didn't gather her wits, he'd have no trouble reading the effect he had on her.

She made it to the edge of the bed, sitting up and holding the sagging bodice against her breasts with one palm. She stopped there, rigid, as Alessandro walked around to stand before her.

Naked.

Long-limbed, muscle-toned, a tall Adonis come to life.

An *aroused* Adonis.

Her body prickled at nape, breast and forehead as heat bloomed. She swallowed hard and tried to control her wayward pulse.

She'd just experienced the most intense climax of her life. Twice. She should not be interested in sex right now.

He shifted his weight, and she watched, fascinated as muscles flexed in broad thighs and across his taut abdomen. A dart of fire pierced her chest and spiralled lazily down into her womb.

She shut her eyes, trying to banish the heady image of Alessandro, pure potent male, before her. But there was no escape. The picture was branded on her brain.

She tried to think of Leo, of the guests beginning to leave the wedding reception. Of—

'It will be easier if I help, Carys.'

Mutely she sat as he unpinned the veil that hung haphazardly from her hair. She felt the fine lace drop away but didn't open her eyes. Not when Alessandro stood before her so close his heat invaded her space.

His hands at her elbows urged her to her feet and she complied.

She snapped her eyes open, keeping them trained on his shuttered face. What had she expected? To see a reflection of the stunned delight that had consumed her such a short time ago? Instead his hooded gaze and flattened mouth gave nothing away. Only the merest hint of a frown suggested he wasn't quite satisfied with how this had played out.

What more could he want? She'd been putty in his hands, so eager she hadn't even managed to remove her precious gown. Her cheeks burned. She was so easy where he was concerned.

It had always been like that with Alessandro.

'I can take it from there, thanks,' she said in a clipped voice. But as she sidestepped he was already dragging the bodice from her shoulders.

With a shush of silk the dress fell to wedge at her elbows. She darted a look at Alessandro, but, contrary to expectations, he wasn't scrutinising the bare flesh he'd exposed. Instead he watched her face. That look sent her stomach plunging on a rollercoaster ride.

'Let me.' As simply as that, when his hands slipped down her sleeves and tugged, she allowed him to pull the dress away. It dropped in rumpled folds around her feet and he helped her step out. Only now did she realise he'd removed her shoes. She stood before him in bra, suspender belt and stockings. Totally vulnerable.

Yet the glow in his eyes warmed her to the core and stopped her from covering herself.

She felt something swell inside. She felt almost powerful. Felt desired. Even, for a crazy moment, cherished.

'Did you mean that?' Carys found herself asking before she could think twice. 'About there not being anyone since the accident?'

It was so unlikely, especially given his cold fury when he'd accused her of betraying him. But the Alessandro she'd known had never lied. If he said it was so...

He leaned close, holding her with his gaze, and with his hands, large and warm, grasping her upper arms.

For a moment she thought he wouldn't answer. She read a play of unfathomable expressions in his shadowed eyes and felt his fingers stiffen against her bare skin.

Finally he nodded. '*Si*. There was no one.' He didn't look happy about the admission, as if it impinged somehow on his masculinity. But Carys was so elated she barely registered it. A fizzing, as if of a hundred champagne bottles, flooded her bloodstream, making her dizzy. All this time…had he been subconsciously waiting for her?

She tried to blank the preposterous notion from her head, but it lodged there, insidiously tempting.

It meant nothing. He'd been recuperating from injury, or busy with business. Yet a stubborn part of her clung to the idea his celibacy had been because he hadn't had *her*.

'Carlotta told me you hadn't been lovers,' she blurted out. 'She said you hadn't planned to marry her.'

He shrugged, still holding her, yet his face took on a more rigid cast. 'I told you I would not behave in such a way. Carlotta is a childhood friend, nothing more.'

Even now, without remembering the details himself, he was so sure of himself, so positive about his actions!

Carys wished she had half his self-belief. She'd striven a lifetime to overcome the ingrained idea she was second best, fostered by being the 'slow' member of an academically high-achieving family. And by being all but ignored by her busy parents. Even now it was so easy to let doubt take hold.

'I'm sorry I didn't trust you, Alessandro.' Tentatively she raised her hand and pressed it over his where he held her. The feel of her hand on his seemed so right.

It wasn't her fault alone their relationship had unravelled at the seams. But she realised now her readiness to believe the worst, fed by her own sense of inadequacy, as much as Livia's lies, had been a major part of it.

Her throat clogged in mixed hope and fear as she waited for his response. Tension buzzed her rigid body.

'Now you know the truth,' he said dismissively. 'The past doesn't matter.'

But it does, she wanted to cry as pent up feelings lashed her. If they'd been able to trust, to believe in each other, they might still be together. Truly together, not yoked in a marriage of convenience.

Bitterness welled on her tongue as regrets swamped her.

'I believe you didn't betray me, Alessandro. Is it so hard for you to believe I didn't betray you?'

* * *

Alessandro stared down into her earnest, flushed face and felt again the stab of unfamiliar emotion in his gut. This woman twisted him inside out. With her words as well as her delectable body.

Automatically he shied from the emotions she sought to awaken. They were too confronting, too foreign to a man who built his life on logic and self-sufficiency. Too dangerous.

'I believe, *piccolina,* that the past is the past. There is nothing to be gained in revisiting it. Instead we have our future with our son to create. Our future together.'

She blinked and he could have sworn he saw tears well in eyes that had turned from hopeful blue to dull slate-grey in a moment. Heat corkscrewed through his chest at the knowledge he was responsible. But he refused to lie, even to placate the woman he intended to live with for life.

His trust only went so far. Taking any woman's word without proof was as foreign to him as breathing underwater.

She could not seriously ask him to accept, on the word of a woman he couldn't remember, that he'd been wrong to accuse her of infidelity. He must have had excellent reasons for the accusations.

Until he knew more, he would reserve judgement. Any sane man would.

Carys shifted, trying to shrug off his hold.

'I need to hang this dress up.' Her voice was as cool and colourless as a mountain stream and she avoided his eyes.

Though she didn't berate or accuse, he felt her disappointment as a tangible force. His belly clenched with a sensation that might have been regret.

Alessandro didn't like it.

'Later.' The word emerged roughly, dragging her stunned gaze to his face.

Didn't she understand that he gave her as much as any man could in the circumstances? That he'd already gone out on a limb tying himself to a woman he didn't know simply for the sake of their son?

And for the shimmering inexplicable force that hovered between them.

No! Now he was buying into that female territory where emotions rather than sense ruled the world.

'This is more important than your dress.' His hands slid round her bare shoulders and he yanked her close, revelling in the bare heat of her torso, the delicate scratch of her lace bra and soft breasts against his thudding chest.

Without giving her time to protest he covered her mouth with his, taking advantage of her parted lips to thrust inside and claim her. She tasted of hot summer days, sun-ripened cherries and warm, luscious woman.

This was real, tangible. The attraction between them sizzled and snarled like a live current. He sank into her sweet depths with something suspiciously like relief. One hand splayed in her hair, holding her so he could ravage her mouth. The other pressed her close.

Hunger rose, raw and untrammelled, making a mockery of every resolution to remain in control. Need consumed him.

Dimly he was aware he'd unleashed an onslaught on her, not a slow seduction. But he couldn't stop, couldn't think, until gradually the rigidity left her bones and she melted into him, her hands sliding up to cup his neck. He shuddered with pleasure when she pressed into him as if she too couldn't get enough of the powerful passion driving them.

Only much later, when their chests heaved from lack of oxygen and her lax form told him she was his for the taking, did he remember his vow to seduce and not simply ravage.

Moments later he'd flicked her bra open and dragged it off. He bent and cupped one luscious breast in his hand. Its weight was perfect, made for his palm. She sighed as he closed his lips around one peak and suckled, cried out when he bit gently on her nipple. Her hands dug into his skull, keeping him close as he lavished attention on one breast then the other. And all the while his body clamoured for more.

She swayed in his hold and he nudged her back a step till she collapsed on the bed. Perfect. Before she could protest he was between her knees, shoulders spreading her thighs, his hunger an unstoppable force.

'I—' Her words died as he cupped her with his palm, gently applying pressure till he felt a response shudder through her. He nudged aside her hands that had sought to stop him. Then he took his time, stroking and teasing till her body lifted off the mattress to meet his hand.

Relief scoured him. She was as needy as he. As hungry for this passion. His body felt gripped by a vice, too tight, too hard, too impossibly aroused, just by the sight and sound of Carys responding to his ministrations.

Never had a lover's pleasure affected him so profoundly. He wanted to give her more and more, even as his whole being thrummed with the need for release.

'Alessandro!' Her protest died as he parted her folds and licked her, tasting the dewy salt tang that was pure Carys. It was addictive, as was the delicate shiver of her legs enfolding him.

It didn't take much to push her over the edge and he revelled in the sound of her gasping breath, the feel of her body curving up around him, the shudders racking her from top to toe. He smiled his satisfaction even as he forced down a desperate hunger for his own release.

He needed to show Carys that here, now, was the beginning of their life together. That it was more important than the past she clung to and that he couldn't recall.

That yawning blank disturbed him more than he'd admit, but he was determined to carve a life with his child. And, therefore, his bride. He wanted to please her, sate her, till she was completely, absolutely *his*. Till she didn't hanker for anything else. So Carys understood the magnitude of this passion between them.

And gave up badgering him with emotions and tests of trust.

What they had was enough. More than enough.

Carys surely would attest to that as he brought her to climax again. This time he leaned over her, watching her eyes shine like a starry night.

Then, only when she was spent, did he slowly join with her, careful of her exhausted body. He trembled, almost undone by the depth of pleasure at being inside her. She tugged him close and held him to her. Instantly desperate energy rose and swamped him. He gave up all pretence at control and lost himself in the ecstasy of being at one with his wife.

Impossibly, it was as good as before. Better.

He didn't understand.

But he ceased thinking as Carys wrapped her legs around his hips and told him exactly how much she wanted him.

Aeons later Alessandro's drumming heartbeat slowed and he recovered enough to roll his weight off Carys and pull her onto him. Only then did his brain engage.

Despite the incredible pleasure they'd shared, his thoughts were nothing but trouble.

Above all was the niggling, astonishing idea that sex with Carys felt too good to be just about physical release.

That it felt profoundly important.

Like coming home.

CHAPTER TWELVE

'Papa! Papa!' Leo's screams of delight resounded in the glassed-in room that housed the villa's full-length pool.

Carys looked up from her paper to see Alessandro rise out of the water like a sleek, mighty sea god, all honed muscle and heart-stopping virility. The kick of her heartbeat accelerating played havoc with her breathing.

Every night since their wedding Carys had shared a bed with him. She hadn't been able to resist. She'd learned again the feel, scent and taste of that superbly sculpted body. Learned too the passion and pleasure he could unleash in her. Yet familiarity with his magnificent body didn't lessen the intensity of her reactions. Just the sight of Alessandro, almost naked in low-slung swimming trunks, set a pulse thrumming deep in her womb.

With casual ease he threw Leo in the air then caught him again, spinning him round, toes dragging in the warm water. Leo squealed with glee, holding tight to Alessandro's sinewy forearms.

Her son. Her husband.

A flash of heat speared Carys at the sight of them together, delighting in each other's company.

Stupidly, emotion clogged her throat.

Alessandro and Leo were developing the sort of relationship she'd dreamed of for her son. At first Alessandro had been wary, almost diffident, as if dealing with a baby was tantamount to meeting an alien being. But gradually he'd become adept at handling his child and a camaraderie had begun to build between them, a relationship that was based on far more than duty.

She knew about that sort of relationship. Initially she'd feared that, though Alessandro had been adamant he wanted his son, adamant enough even to marry *her,* he'd be the sort of parent she'd suffered. The sort who provided the necessities of life, and even some of the comforts, but never quite connected with their child. The sort who saw parenting as an obligation, especially when their child was a cuckoo in the nest, unlike them or their other offspring.

'Papa!' Leo's voice grew shriller as he demanded another aerial stunt.

Carys lowered her newspaper and turned more fully towards the pool, looking over her glasses. That high-pitched tone was a sure sign that Leo was tired and over-stimulated by this exciting new game. If it continued he'd end in tears.

She opened her mouth to warn Alessandro and suggest it was time to finish, but he forestalled her. He lowered Leo into the water and gently towed him along, pointing out the richly coloured sea creatures featured at the bottom of the enormous mural covering the end wall. After a few grizzly moments Leo became intrigued, leaning forward in his dad's arms and trying to repeat some of the words.

Carys leant back. Alessandro really was developing an understanding of his son. It was there in his eyes when he looked at Leo, in the calm encouragement and occasional firm reprimands he gave. He had a natural aptitude for parenting.

He enjoyed being with Leo. Why else would he spend so much time here at the villa, ignoring the lure of the office?

Alessandro still drove himself, working long hours, but increasingly those hours became flexible. Today he'd arrived mid-afternoon, at a time when Carys and Leo were always in the pool. Instead of closeting himself in his office or taking important calls, he'd spent the last half hour in the water with Leo.

She'd done the right thing. Leo and Alessandro were building something that would last a lifetime. Respect and love. The sort of relationship she'd longed for as a kid. The sort she'd vowed her son would have. Now he'd have it with both parents.

Even if all that kept those parents together was their child. And lust.

She grimaced, ashamed to admit the all-consuming hunger Alessandro sparked in her.

The lust would fade, on Alessandro's part, at least. Carys was a novelty still, and she was here, available, all too ready to accede to his every sensual demand.

Heaven help her when he lost interest in her!

For with every day spent here in his home, every night cocooned in his arms, sated from his lovemaking, Carys felt the tendrils of her old feelings bud again. She tried to resist, to remind herself that what she felt wasn't reciprocated, that this was a marriage of convenience.

The trouble was it *felt* like more.

She squeezed her eyes shut, pinching the bridge of her nose, reminding herself she'd given up on self-delusion.

She'd made her decision: to settle for a loveless marriage. To settle for what was best for Leo.

It didn't matter that deep inside she knew 'settling' meant accepting second best, accepting the sort of inferior status she'd fought against all her life. 'Settling' felt dangerously like slicing her innermost self apart, day by day. Till one day, perhaps, there'd be nothing of the real Carys left, just the façade of a woman who was nothing more than Leo Mattani's mother and Alessandro Mattani's wife.

She couldn't allow herself to think like that!

Clearly she'd made the right choice. Seeing Leo and Alessandro together made that obvious.

It didn't matter that she still secretly yearned for—

'Carys?' Alessandro's deep voice slid over her like the caress of warm hands on bare flesh.

She looked up to discover him standing before her, legs planted wide in an assured stance that spoke of masculine power. In his arms Leo smiled down at her.

'Mumum.'

Carys thrust her newspaper and reading glasses aside and held her hands out for Leo. After a quick glance, she avoided

Alessandro's penetrating stare. Sometimes, as now, his regard was so intense it felt as if he delved right inside her.

'Here, sweetie.' She cuddled Leo close when Alessandro passed him to her, undoing her towelling robe and wrapping it around him, rubbing him dry. 'Did you have a good time?'

Leo grinned sleepily, his eyelids already drooping. 'Papa.' He turned and waved an arm at Alessandro.

'Yes, you swam with papa, didn't you?'

For the life of her Carys still couldn't meet her husband's hooded green gaze. There'd been a hint of something far too unsettling in it. She felt it flick over her, tangible as a touch.

Carys repressed a shiver of unwanted awareness and concentrated on drying Leo.

'It's time Leo had his nap,' she said eventually, sliding forward on her seat, ready to stand. Hopefully once she was in Leo's room the trembling eagerness for Alessandro's touch would abate. If she stayed any longer Alessandro would surely pick up on her edginess and guess the cause. When it came to understanding the demands of her body, he had more expertise than she!

'I just called Anna on the house phone. She'll be here in a minute to collect him and put him down for a rest.'

Carys frowned as Alessandro scooped Leo from her arms.

'I can settle him.'

Broad shoulders shrugged. 'We pay Anna to help with Leo. Let her do this while you finish reading. See? Leo's happy.'

He was right. Leo was calling out to Anna as she entered the room. There was no logical reason for Carys to insist on settling Leo herself. To do so would only arouse Alessandro's curiosity. Besides, as soon as Leo left, so would Alessandro. No doubt he'd taken enough time away from his work.

'OK,' Carys said at last, smiling to Anna and waving to Leo. Her heart swelled when Leo blew her a smacking kiss as he was carried from the room.

Her son was so happy here. She *had* done the right thing.

Carys eased back in her seat and picked up her newspaper. It was only as she rested her head on the lounge that she realised

Alessandro hadn't moved. He stood a few metres away, watching her.

Heat crawled up her throat and across her breasts. She realised her robe was wide open where she'd snuggled Leo and quickly closed it, knotting the belt tightly. There was something too unsettling about Alessandro's regard.

Instead of leaving, he took the lounge beside hers. Yet he didn't lean back to face the pool, and beyond it the manicured garden and lake. He sat sideways, facing her.

Too close! Far too close!

Those shivery little tremors inside Carys intensified, as did the hollow sensation in the region of her pelvis. He only had to look at her and desire consumed her. The realisation made a mockery of her hard-won self-control.

She searched for something to break the silence that felt too weighty for comfort.

'I haven't seen much of Livia since the wedding.' Carys could have kicked herself as soon as the words were out, for the last thing she wanted was to talk about her mother-in-law, or suggest she wanted to see more of her.

The relationship between Carys and Livia was polite and stiffly cordial, no more. Carys saw no point in confronting her about her lie that Alessandro had intended to marry Carlotta, but nor could she forget the way the older woman had deliberately misled her.

Alessandro's brows rose. 'Livia has been...busy lately.'

Carys paused, digesting the curious inflection in his tone. It sounded almost like disapproval. Alessandro and his stepmother weren't particularly close, but they had always seemed to get on.

'Really?'

'Yes.' This time there was no mistaking the spark of anger in Alessandro's eyes or the firming of his jaw. Had there been a falling out between him and Livia? Had he finally grown tired of her snobby, manipulative ways? It was too much to hope for. 'She has commitments elsewhere.'

Carys would have to be blind and deaf not to notice the warning in his tone, but she refused to back off. She knew to her cost just how much damage Livia could do. She needed to understand what was happening.

'You said she'd come to advise me on how to play the role of *contessa*.' Carys was proud of the way she kept the bitterness from her voice. Of course she needed to learn, but the implication that she was so way below standard still hurt.

His gaze narrowed and he sat straighter, shoulders seeming to broaden before her eyes. 'You're not playing a role, Carys. You *are* the Contessa Mattani. Remember that.'

'Oh, I'm hardly likely to forget.' Surrounded by luxury acquired by the Mattani family over generations, Carys felt like an intruder, an impostor. She still couldn't get used to having servants at her beck and call.

Sometimes as she walked past the family portraits in the upstairs gallery, she felt the accusing eyes of long dead Mattanis, as if they wondered how someone as ordinary as she came to be in their home.

Carys shook her head. She had to get out of this place. She was going stir crazy.

She hadn't ventured out of the grounds in the weeks since the wedding, too busy ensuring Leo settled in to his new home. And with the memory of paparazzi surrounding the church on her wedding day, too nervous to face the press on her own. Alessandro hadn't offered to take her out, but nor had she expected him to. She had no illusions about her place in his life.

'Don't worry, Livia will perform the responsibilities of the Contessa Mattani until you're ready to take over.' The steel in his eyes made her wonder if she'd have to pass some test to convince him she was ready. Obviously he doubted her ability to make the grade. 'But I think it better if someone more compatible and…reliable is your mentor in the meantime.'

Reliable? It sounded as if dear Livia had blotted her copy book. Carys was human enough to feel a surge of satisfaction at the thought of the woman's schemes coming undone just a little.

'Who did you have in mind?' For one electrifying moment she thought he was going to take on the role himself.

Then common sense returned. Even as his wife she wouldn't merit that much claim on Alessandro's time.

'I thought perhaps Carlotta.' He sat back, watching her reaction.

'Carlotta?' Carys felt relief sweep her. 'I'd like that.' After the initial stiffness they'd got on well. Carys was attracted to the other woman's honesty and dry wit. She'd enjoy spending time with the princess. 'As long as that's OK with her,' she added diffidently.

'I'm sure it will be. She's already mentioned the idea of coming to see you.'

Carys frowned. 'But I haven't heard from her.'

Alessandro leaned forward a fraction, elbows on thighs and hands between his knees. 'No doubt she was allowing the newly-wed couple time alone before making social calls.'

Carys looked dumbfounded at his words. As if the idea of a honeymoon period was a foreign concept.

Alessandro felt frustration rise again. No matter how hot and heavy their lovemaking, afterwards Carys somehow managed to put a distance between them. Just as she'd done since he'd arrived at the pool today.

Of course he didn't want her hanging on his sleeve, pretending to dote on him, but the perpetual distance between them whenever they were out of the bedroom annoyed him.

He wanted...

He didn't know quite what he wanted. But it was definitely not a wife who treated him like a polite stranger unless he was naked and inside her. *Then* she responded with all the enthusiasm he could wish for.

Fire ignited in his groin and spread, tightening thighs and buttocks, curling fingers into fists and drawing the tendons in his back and neck unbearably taut.

Just thinking about sex with Carys made him hard. While she sat there, cool as a cucumber, quizzing him about Livia!

He'd thought marriage would bring respite from the surge of hormones that made him crave Carys like a fire in his blood. Yet the more he had her, the more he wanted her. And not just in bed.

Even watching her pull her robe open to nestle their son against her breast as she dried him made Alessandro rigid with desire.

What did that say about him?

He scrubbed a hand over his jaw, trying to ease the escalating tension there.

She didn't even dress provocatively to entice him. Despite the massive injection of funds to her new bank account, she still wore the simple, cheap clothes she'd brought with her.

There were no designer gowns or expensive shoes. No new handbags or hairstyles. Not even sexy new lingerie. Each night he found himself discarding her plain cotton night shirts. She didn't even bother to acquire a skerrick of lace or silk to entice her husband.

And somehow he still found her more alluring than any silk-clad siren of his memory.

Swaddled in thick towelling, her hair drying around her shoulders, and her face washed clean of make-up, Carys made his heart thud faster and his libido claw for release.

He told himself he'd come home to spend time with Leo, and he *had* enjoyed his son's company. Young Leo had an energy and an enquiring mind as well as an open, loving disposition that made him a pleasure to be with. Yet Alessandro had been distracted time and again by the enigmatic woman at the poolside. She'd been so engrossed in her reading it was clear her husband didn't hold her interest.

He didn't understand her.

'You haven't been away from the house,' he found himself saying.

She angled her chin a fraction, in that unconscious gesture of defiance he found ridiculously appealing.

'I didn't want to brave the press. I'm not used to that sort of attention.'

Guilt punched him. Why hadn't he thought of that? He'd been so busy adjusting to his ready-made family while trying to maintain his usual constant work schedule, it hadn't occurred to him.

'I'll arrange for a quick photo opportunity in the next few days. We'll give them a chance to snap shots of the happy couple.' He paused on the thought of how inappropriate the phrase seemed. 'Then the pressure will ease. Tell the staff when you want to go out and security will be arranged. You need have no fear. You'll be well taken care of.'

'Thank you.'

Again she avoided eye contact. Frustration returned. He felt an unfamiliar desire to provoke a reaction, any reaction from her. He refused to be ignored.

'The staff can tell you the best places to shop. No doubt that's high on your agenda.' After all, she now had a substantial fortune to spend.

Cool grey eyes met his as she frowned. 'Why would I need to shop? Do you mean for an outfit to wear for this press session?' She shook her head. 'There's no need. Carlotta already had two extra outfits made for me, a suit and a dress. I'm sure one of them will do. They're both lovely.'

Alessandro waved a dismissive hand. 'No doubt whatever Carlotta provided will be suitable. But you'll want to start enjoying your money and buy a new wardrobe.' On his instructions one of his secretaries had already provided her with a card linked to her new bank account.

Carys sat back in her seat, her brow clearing. 'There's no need. I've got plenty to last me till the cooler weather comes. Then I'll have to invest in a new winter coat.'

'A new winter coat?' His voice trailed off. Winter was months away. Summer was just starting. Who did she think she was fooling? 'With all that money at your disposal you expect me to believe you have no interest in spending it?'

'I know you're providing money for expenses, but—'

'Money for expenses!' This woman was something else. She reduced her new-found wealth to the status of grocery funds. 'It's far more than that, Carys. Remember, I know exactly how much since I'm paying it.'

'There's no need to sound so accusing.' A flash of fire in her eyes sent shards of ice-hot need splintering through him. That only intensified his anger.

'And there's no need to pretend your outrageously lavish allowance is a mere pittance.' The games women played!

Carys stiffened, looking more like an ice queen than the

ordinary working girl he'd plucked from drudgery. 'I don't know what you're talking about.'

Alessandro shot to his feet, trying to work off his anger at her games by pacing the length of the pool and back. This pretence was the sort of thing he abhorred. Next she'd be complaining the funds he provided weren't enough.

'Of course you know. You read the prenup in such detail you must have checked every word twice. You have enough money in your personal account now to keep you in Gucci, Versace and Yves Saint Laurent every day of the year.'

Clouds must have passed over the sun, giving the illusion she'd paled.

Then, as he approached, Alessandro saw the way her hands gripped the arms of her chair, the stiffness in her small frame as she sat up. And in her eyes, what looked like shock.

'You're kidding.' Even her voice sounded different. Light and breathless. 'Why would you do that?'

He shrugged, refusing to put into words the suspicion that without such a financial incentive, she might one day walk out on Leo. And him.

'You need to dress as befits my wife.' Even to his own ears it sounded unconvincing. 'But you know all about it. You signed the agreement before we married. That set it all out.'

The sight of her gaze sliding guiltily from his, the way her hands tightened even more till they resembled talons clawing at the padded chair arms, brought him up short.

Instinct honed over years of business dealings told him something was wrong. Something important. The hairs at his neck rose and he stilled.

'Yes. Yes, I signed it.'

Alessandro's gaze strayed from her mouth, distorted as she bit hard into her bottom lip, to her knees, now pressed up to her chest. She looked so *vulnerable*. What on earth?

Eventually he followed the direction of her stare, to her folded newspaper and glasses. It was a prestigious English-language paper, open at the international news. He recognised the large picture of the United Nations Secretary General in one corner.

The same page she'd been reading over half an hour ago when he'd arrived.

'Carys?' He took a step closer till she turned to face him. Her expression was closed, rigid with something that looked like fear.

'What is it?' He glanced again at the newspaper. It was impossible that, even with the noise in the pool distracting her, it could take so long to read a single page.

Then he remembered the way Carys had hesitated over some passport control forms as they'd travelled.

'You *did* read the prenup,' he said to himself as much as her. 'I saw you.' He watched her swallow, almost wincing as the motion looked so difficult.

'I…started to.' Still she didn't face him. 'But in the end I decided it was just saying I'd get nothing of yours if we divorced.' She lifted her shoulders in a jerky shrug. 'So I signed. I didn't know anything about a big allowance.'

'Liar,' he whispered. 'I saw you. You were reading the last page just before you signed.'

Her head whipped around and he saw high colour flag her cheeks. Yet her face was chalky pale.

An appalling notion smote him. An unbelievable one.

'You *can* read, can't you?'

Had she been sitting there all this time, pretending to examine an article that made no sense? His stomach plunged heavily as an alien emotion kicked him hard.

'Of course I can read!' She drew herself up straighter in her chair, eyes brilliant with fury. 'How do you think I did my job if I couldn't read? Just because I…'

'Just because you…?' Alessandro stepped forward to stand before her, hands planted akimbo.

He watched her wrap her hands around her bare legs, rocking forward in the age-old motion of someone seeking comfort.

'I didn't read your precious papers.' She almost spat the words at him, they came out so fast. 'I began to but I was exhausted and stressed and…' She paused so long he thought she wouldn't continue. 'And I have dyslexia,' she said on a surge of breath. 'That's why I wear tinted glasses; they help me focus. But sometimes, especially when I'm tired or when the text is a solid mass, it's almost impossible to read, because whole lines keep disappearing and the words turn into a jumble. Legal papers are the worst.'

Silence. A silence ringing with the echo of her defiant tones.

Alessandro's heart twisted in his chest as he saw what it had cost her to share the truth. He wanted to reach out and soothe the hurt so evident in her drawn features, but guessed his touch wouldn't be welcome.

Her lips trembled into a heart-wrenching parody of a smile. 'It's not something I tell many people about.'

'But you told me, didn't you? When we were together before?' He knew it, sensed it, even though he didn't remember.

'I... Yes. You knew. Of course you did.'

Of course he did.

They'd been that close, sharing secrets as well as passion. Once again Alessandro had that sickening sense of taking a step straight into a yawning abyss. His damned memory loss had robbed him of so much. Robbed them both.

He took a deep breath, trying to make sense of what Carys had revealed.

'But you're reading the international news page.' In a paper renowned for in-depth, incisive journalism. It was no lightweight read.

Carys moved so swiftly, surging to her feet, that he stepped back a pace. Her eyes glittered blue fire as her gaze clashed with his.

'Just because I'm a slow reader doesn't mean I'm thick! You understood that before.' She paused, as if grappling for control over her hurt and disappointment.

Why couldn't he have remembered this one thing at least about her?

'I read the international news because I'm interested, even if it takes me longer than some people. Some days, like today, it's just slower than others, OK?'

'OK.' Alessandro watched the fire dim in her eyes as she wrapped her arms tight round her torso again.

Guilt carved a hole inside Alessandro's chest as he remembered how he'd all but forced her to sign the prenup on the spot. He'd already guessed she was exhausted and wrung out from stress. He'd had no compunction about seizing on her weakness and stampeding through her objections to get what he wanted, just as he would in any business deal.

But this wasn't business. It wasn't nearly so simple.

'I'm sorry,' he murmured, watching her rub her arms as if from cold. Clearly her dyslexia was an emotional issue. She was so defensive. 'I didn't mean to imply—'

'That I'm dumb?' Her lips curved up in a smile that held pain rather than humour.

'Of course not. No one would.' He didn't have any personal experience of the condition, but even he knew that.

Her laugh was hollow. 'You think not?'

'Carys?' Her distressed expression was too much. He reached out and took her by the shoulders. 'Talk to me,' he commanded as he massaged her stiff muscles, trying to ease their rigidity. Her pain made him feel uncomfortable…edgy…protective.

Again that bleak smile. 'Everyone thought I was slow-witted because I couldn't read well. *Everyone.* I was always bottom of the class. Even when I reached high school and a teacher suspected what was wrong, it was easier for people to think I was just slow.'

Alessandro frowned. 'Kids can be cruel.'

She lifted her shoulders in a weary gesture. 'Not just kids. My father is a professor; my mother ran her own business. My siblings are all academic over-achievers. They found it difficult to adjust to me. I didn't measure up.'

'Adjust to *you?*' Alessandro's jaw tightened. 'They should have been encouraging you, looking after you.'

She shook her head. 'They preferred to bury themselves in their own activities.' From the raw pain in her voice Alessandro guessed they had provided precious little support.

The idea infuriated him. Kids needed more from their parents than the bare necessities of life.

Suddenly it struck him that he and Carys had a lot in common— both had been left at too young an age to look after themselves.

'Even when I stopped working in dead-end jobs and finally found the nerve to sign up for a hotel management degree, they saw it as second best.' She paused, the dead chill in her eyes carving a chasm through his chest. 'That's all they ever expected from me...second best.'

'Carys.' He pulled her close, pushing her head down against his shoulder. His heart thumped unsteadily at the wild emotions running through him. He'd been angry and distrustful of her, yet now, seeing the hurt she tried so hard to hide, he felt compassion and a driving need to make things better.

Her pain felt like his. Sharp as a blade, it transfixed him.

He'd never experienced such empathy for anyone else. Or such a strong impulse to protect.

Automatically he rocked her against him, feeling shudder after shudder rack her taut frame.

'You're not second best, Carys. You're a wonderful mother. Anyone seeing Leo would know that. Plus you excel at your work.' He'd taken the time to find that out in Melbourne. 'And you haven't let dyslexia hold you back from tertiary study.' How she'd coped with that he had no idea. His own ability to read and quickly absorb huge amounts of information was something he'd always taken for granted.

'You're a special woman, *tesoro*. Never forget it.'

Slowly he stroked her back, feeling her tension begin to ease. But he didn't release her. He wanted to hold her. And not just because she was the woman at the centre of every erotic daydream he'd had for months.

He wanted to comfort her. The tenderness and regret that welled inside him at her story, the tide of anger on her behalf, overwhelmed him.

His mind shied from the realisation that he'd so easily misread her. Because if he dwelled on that too long, he might have to consider that he'd misjudged her in other things.

Her question on their wedding night echoed too clearly for comfort.

I believe you didn't betray me, Alessandro. Is it so hard for you to believe I didn't betray you?

CHAPTER THIRTEEN

ALESSANDRO nuzzled the silk tresses on his pillow, inhaling the scent of flowers. He wound a strand round his fingers, then brushed the end across her bare breast.

Carys shivered. Even now, exhausted from lovemaking, she responded to him. As he did to her.

It was as if she'd got into his blood, his bones.

Still it wasn't enough. 'Tell me about us,' he murmured, finally confronting the need that had gnawed at him so long. 'What did we do together...before? What was it like?'

He watched her breathing falter. Raising his gaze, he found her biting her lip. Wary eyes met his.

'You really want to know?'

He nodded. More than ever he needed to understand. Knowing the past might help him understand the present.

Huge eyes surveyed him carefully, as if seeking a hidden trap. Then she looked down to where he caressed her. Long eyelashes shielded her eyes from his gaze.

'It was like a summer storm. Like a lightning strike out of the blue.' Her lips tilted up. 'It was sudden and overwhelming. Wonderful and scary and...undeniable.'

'The sex, you mean?' She described perfectly the marrow-melting intensity of their loving.

Her moue of disappointment told him he'd got it wrong. 'No.' She tugged the sheet up, dislodging his hand. He ignored the tiny splinter of hurt that jabbed him.

'So tell me. What did we do together?'

She shrugged. 'Everything. You taught me to ski and snow-board. We went climbing and hiked some of the hills here. I cooked you Aussie style roast lamb and pavlova for dessert, and you taught me about Italian wines and the history of the area.' Her voice was so wistful he felt a pang of discomfort.

But greater still was his confusion. He'd taken her climbing and hiking? He slid a hand around her hip, lodging her concretely against him as the world started to spin.

'Alessandro? What is it? Have I sparked a memory?'

Numbly his shook his head. 'No memory.' The words were curt, but he couldn't help it. He still couldn't face with equanimity the fact he'd probably never remember.

Yet that wasn't what shocked him.

Climbing, hiking, constituted his rare, private time away from the high-pressure business world. He climbed with a friend or two. Male friends. He hiked alone. Always. Most of his acquaintances had no notion he loved the mountains even more than his fast cars. The idea of sharing that most precious private time with a woman was astonishing.

'We hiked together?' His voice sounded rusty.

Carys nodded. 'It was glorious. The countryside's so lovely. In the evening we'd sit together and discuss where we'd head the next weekend.'

'Really?' The picture she conjured was completely foreign. Yet it seemed…right. He frowned, wondering how he knew that so definitely when he remembered nothing.

'You don't believe me.' She shuffled away to prop herself against the bed head, hurt shimmering in her eyes.

He reached out to cup her face, stunned by what he'd learned. He needed to know more. But this wasn't the time.

'I believe you, Carys.' He paused. 'Tell me about Leo. What was he like as a newborn? Did you know from the first how intelligent he was?'

The sound of his son's laughter warmed Alessandro, but it was the sight of his wife, smiling as she held Leo up to look out the ferry window, that made something shift inside him. Something he hadn't ever acknowledged before.

The barrier that had kept him safely separate and self-contained from those who tried to get too close.

Alessandro drew a slow breath and exhaled, battling the turmoil inside.

This shift wasn't a sudden event. The barrier had been crumbling for weeks. Day by day the connection with Leo and Carys had strengthened, growing into something he'd never expected to feel. There was protectiveness, possessiveness, caring. Joy and acceptance.

Despite the ferry's smooth progress across the lake, Alessandro rocked back on his feet as if struck off balance.

He should have expected it, he supposed, with Leo.

His son.

Though his own parents had never indicated they felt anything for Alessandro except mild pleasure if he did well and cold dismissal if he intruded at an inopportune time, he knew what the bond between parent and child should be. When he discovered his son, he'd acted instantly to get custody, desperate to ensure Leo was in the care of a loving parent.

Even though Alessandro knew he had everything to learn about how to love.

He'd never expected it would come so easily.

He watched Leo point out the window and babble, talking to both Carys and Bruno, standing protectively beside them. Something warm inside Alessandro's chest expanded and his lips twitched as he watched his boy's animated face.

His boy.

The happiness Leo had brought into Alessandro's life, and the weighty sense of responsibility, were unprecedented.

He wouldn't change them for anything.

His gaze shifted to Carys and the way her gentle smile lit her face. She did things to him he didn't understand.

A lifetime's lessons in the ways of women had taught him he'd be a fool to give any woman his heart on a platter.

And yet, these past weeks he'd grown…comfortable with

her. Never comfortable enough to ignore the effervescent bubble of lust that was now a constant in his life. But relaxed as he'd never been with any other woman.

So relaxed he had to force himself to remember that, like the rest of her sex, she wasn't above cheating on a man.

Yet looking at her now, so thrilled that he'd given in to her request to do something 'normal' like spend the afternoon sightseeing around the lake, without a limo or a Lamborghini or any other of his 'rich man's toys', he found it hard to believe she could be selfishly calculating.

He didn't want to believe it. That was the most astonishing of all.

He found himself trusting her in so many ways. *Liking* her. Not merely desiring her.

She *was* different.

Her disinterest in cash was genuine. She really did prefer a picnic by the lake to the ostentation of Milan's top restaurants. And though she now spent money from her account, it was mainly on toys and books for Leo rather than fashion for herself.

She was completely different to his mother, who'd had barely a maternal bone in her body. Carys was a wonderful mother.

Alessandro realised his insurance policy, the prenup that provided her with a fortune if she stayed with Leo, hadn't been necessary. Nothing on this earth would drag Carys from her son. Alessandro approved of her for that alone.

And, he realised, for so many other things.

For her indomitable spirit, conquering what he realised were wounds as old and deep as his. Overcoming dyslexia and the ingrained sense of not measuring up, to get on with her life.

Her intelligence. Her quiet dignity.

Carys was the sort of wife a man could be proud of in many ways. With her warmth and generosity of spirit, he saw her taking her place beside him in the public aspects of his life. Livia had fulfilled the public responsibilities of the Contessa Mattani with panache, but with a cool intolerance for what she termed 'the ordinary people' that made him grit his teeth.

Across the cabin Carys stretched and her sundress grew

taut across her breasts. Predictably his body tightened in a spasm of hunger.

Alessandro thought of their slow, languorous lovemaking this morning, of the wonder in her eyes as he brought her to climax and pumped his life essence inside her.

His gaze dipped to her flat belly and excitement stirred. For all they knew she could even now be carrying another of his children. Raw, primal satisfaction smote him at the idea of watching her grow big with his baby. He'd missed that the first time. But now…they could build a family together and he'd participate in every moment.

'Signor Conte.'

Alessandro dragged himself from his thoughts to focus on the small, grey-haired woman before him.

Some sixth sense made Carys turn and look for Alessandro. He stood not far away, head tilted down as he listened to the rotund woman before him. The intensity of his expression, the stillness of his rangy frame, sent a skitter of prescience up her spine.

The woman looked vaguely familiar.

At her side Bruno also watched the pair, making no move to intervene. Yet something was wrong. She sensed it.

'Bruno, would you please take Leo?' She met the minder's startled gaze as she thrust Leo towards him. Barely waiting to see her son settled, she turned towards Alessandro. The woman leaned in, gripping his arm.

Begging? No, that wouldn't leach the colour from Alessandro's face. The woman tilted her head and finally Carys recognised her: Rosina, who'd been Alessandro's housekeeper when he'd lived in his home in the hills behind the lake.

Rosina had been so friendly and warm. She'd encouraged Carys in her tentative attempts to learn Italian. More, she'd provided comfort in the form of a cup of tea or a plate of fruit and admonishment not to starve herself when Carys felt her relationship with Alessandro shatter around her.

Carys squeezed through the seats, eager to greet her, but more than ever concerned by Alessandro's frozen expression. She regretted now that she'd requested they come by ferry instead of private boat or car.

After being surrounded by servants, getting used to her new life as the Contessa Mattani, and absorbing the overwhelming reality of her role as Alessandro's wife, she'd been eager for a 'normal' day with people who hadn't a clue who she was. Had it been a mistake?

By the time she reached the aisle, Rosina had gone and the ferry was coming in to dock. People rose, ready to stream ashore.

Yet Alessandro stood unmoving, as if riveted to the spot. Fear made her heart thump so hard it seemed to catapult around her chest.

She hadn't wanted to care for him, but somehow he'd deviously wormed his way back into her heart. He pleasured her to within an inch of her sanity, comforted her when she needed it, made her feel…special.

She could no longer pretend she didn't care. *Didn't love.*

Carys swallowed a welling knot of anxiety. 'Alessandro?'

He turned and for a moment it seemed as if he didn't see her. His gaze was blank, inward looking. Then he blinked, focused, and snagged her close, away from the people thronging towards the door.

'Bruno has Leo? Good.' He sounded just the same as ever, but he looked…different.

'What is it, Alessandro?' He met her eyes for a moment before looking away, towards the passengers. Somewhere in that crowd was the woman who'd talked to him so earnestly.

'Come.' He curved his arm around her back and led her to the door. 'It's all right. Leo and Bruno are on their way.'

It wasn't all right; Carys could see the pinched line of his mouth and the deep crease in his forehead.

Yet it wasn't till they were ashore and a waiting car had delivered them to the villa, that Carys got any answers. Alessandro gave a sleepy Leo into his nanny's arms, and as if too edgy to settle indoors, led the way to the private path along the lake. He seemed distracted, forgetting to shorten his long pace so she had to scurry to keep up.

'Please, Alessandro.' The look on his face, as if he'd just seen a ghost, frightened her. 'What's wrong? What did Rosina want?'

He turned then, the expression in his shadowed eyes unreadable. 'You remember her?'

'Of course. She was kind to me.' At a time when Carys had felt lost. 'Does she still work for you?' Carys realised she didn't even know if he'd kept his mountain home.

He shook his head. 'When I went to hospital, the house was shut up. She took the retirement she'd put off and moved away to be near her daughter. When I came out of hospital I settled into the family villa instead.'

Was that wistfulness in his voice? The home he'd built had been so like him, vibrantly unique and attractive. Did he miss it?

'But she said something to you.' Something significant.

Alessandro shrugged, walking ahead as her steps slowed.

'She said it was good to see me again, all recovered. Good to see us,' he added after a moment.

Carys started forward. 'She remembered me?' He nodded. 'What else did she say?' There was more. Shadows darkened Alessandro's face, each line etched as if on a lifeless mask.

'She congratulated us on our wedding. She read about it in the papers.'

'And?' Alessandro was stonewalling. After living with him she knew that much.

Suddenly he stopped and turned. 'She was there the day you left.'

The day Alessandro had told her to go. The day he'd found her, dishevelled from holding Stefano Manzoni at bay, and leapt to the conclusion she'd been fooling with her lover, not fighting off a predator. Alessandro's fury had been instantaneous and all consuming, as if the incident had thrown fuel on a long-smouldering fire.

Carys groped for the balustrade between her and the water as memories she'd tried to forget came rushing back.

'I see.'

'No. You don't.' Something in his voice made her turn. His expression baffled her. 'She said that after you left, I couldn't settle. I paced the house from end to end.'

That didn't surprise her. He'd been in a towering rage, for all that he'd kept it tightly leashed. Even his order to leave had been delivered in a lethally quiet whisper that had cut Carys to the bone and slashed through her last hopes that he could ever love her.

'Twenty minutes later I raced out to the car. Apparently I said I was going to bring you back.'

Carys gasped. Her heart stuttered then eventually took up something like its usual rhythm.

Alessandro had gone after her? He'd wanted her back?

Her eyes opened so wide they stung. Did that mean he'd realised his accusations were baseless? Now her heart pounded like a locomotive and adrenaline pulsed in her blood.

He'd chased after her…

Heat flooded Carys at the thought of him racing to stop her leaving. *Of him realising his mistake.*

'But you didn't go to the station.' She'd waited ages for a train.

'No.' Penetrating green eyes met hers. 'That was when I had the accident, speeding along the road after you.'

Dumbfounded, Carys met his shuttered gaze. Guilt replaced the buoyant surge of elation in her veins and she slumped against the balustrade as shock hit her in the knees.

'Carys!' Strong arms dragged her up against a familiar, hard torso and she shut her eyes, unwilling to face just yet the dislike which surely must be in his face now.

Did he blame her for the accident?

She did. Guilt seeped through her bones. She clutched him close, reliving the horror she'd experienced when she'd heard about his accident. But this was worse. So much worse.

Alessandro widened his stance, wrapping Carys closer to his pounding chest. Fear spiked at her sudden pallor. He told himself it was shock, expected in the circumstances, but that didn't ease his concern. He rubbed a hand down her back, willing warmth back into her trembling, chilled form.

It would be OK, he assured himself.

OK? His world had turned upside down!

You were so much in love, both of you. Of course you went to fetch her back.

The words rang in Alessandro's head, pounding in time with the heavy rush of blood surging through his temples.

No! She had that wrong. Must have.

Yet the words resonated, shocking him with their familiarity. Love? Romantic love?

He tried to reject the notion, as he'd rejected it all his life. But the emotions Carys evoked lodged deep inside and wouldn't be removed.

The fact remained that he'd gone after Carys. He'd been wild-eyed and desperate if his former housekeeper was to be believed. Though clearly she had a romantic disposition. No doubt her memory embroidered the event.

That wasn't important. What mattered was knowing if he'd changed his mind because he'd realised he'd been wrong about Carys, or whether he'd decided he didn't care what she'd done—simply had to have her back.

Either option revealed him as emotional, too strongly affected by his lover to think straight.

He didn't want to believe it.

Yet here he was, tied in knots because of this same woman. Feeling so much because of her. Even now her fresh cinnamon scent tangled in his senses, a heady distraction.

He thought through the few concrete facts he'd pieced together about her infidelity. He'd come home to find Stefano Manzoni, a man he'd never trusted, accelerating recklessly down the driveway. He'd found Carys with her blouse undone, her hair down and a fresh love bite on her neck. She'd admitted meeting Manzoni in town and letting him bring her home. Then she'd tried to deflect Alessandro's anger by accusing him instead of infidelity with Carlotta.

What else had there been that he couldn't recall? Was there any more? Had his accusation been as misguided as her belief he'd planned to marry Carlotta?

That didn't seem believable. Yet honesty made him face the possibility he'd jumped to conclusions.

Had Alessandro subconsciously waited for Carys to prove it was his money that really attracted her? That she would dump him for a man who could give her more once the going got tough? As his mother had left his father years before, hooking up with a man whose bank account made the Mattani wealth at that time look insipid by comparison.

Had Alessandro primed himself to expect Carys' betrayal?

He drew a steadying breath, tightening his hold on her, feeling her rapid heartbeat near his, the way her soft form moulded so perfectly to his.

Reluctantly he faced the truth he'd been avoiding.

Despite those few wisps of memory, the gap in his mind was as real as ever. Intimacy with Carys hadn't restored it. He could no longer kid himself that would happen.

He would never remember that part of his past. Never have his memory as absolute proof about her behaviour. He had only the comments of those, like his housekeeper and Carys, who'd been there.

He had logic.

Above all he had his own gut instinct.

What did they tell him?

Carys felt the heavy thud of Alessandro's heart, strong and steady, against her. The way he held her, as if welded to her, made her heart sing, but couldn't blot out her distress.

'I'm sorry,' she murmured at last, clutching his shirt as if to stop him retreating.

'Pardon?' He stepped back a fraction so her voice wasn't muffled against his chest. Carys only just resisted the impulse to burrow back into him, seeking comfort.

'I'm sorry.' Finally she lifted her face. 'If it weren't for me, you wouldn't have crashed. You wouldn't have…' Even now the thought of him in a coma paralysed her larynx.

'You blame yourself?' He tilted his head.

'Don't you?' She remembered the steady rain that day—that was why she'd accepted a man's offer of a lift rather than waiting for a bus. That and the fact that the evening before she'd seen

Alessandro with Carlotta. He'd spent the night in town rather than return home, and Carys had finally grown tired of waiting meekly for him to appear. No wonder she'd been distracted enough to fall into Stefano's clutches.

If only she hadn't been so gullible, so ready to believe Livia's plausible lies.

'Of course I don't. Don't be absurd.' Alessandro's eyes flashed dark fire. 'How could you be to blame? I was the one speeding, and the driver that forced me off the road was on the wrong side. It had nothing to do with you.' His gaze held hers so long Carys felt his certainty pulse through her.

'Don't take that upon your conscience, *tesoro*,' he said more gently and cupped her chin in one warm palm. Her heart squeezed tight at such tenderness. It reminded her of how he'd looked, and sounded, so long ago.

'Carys.' He bent his head and touched his lips to hers. Instantly she melted into him, her body alive with the tingle of magic only Alessandro could create. 'Sweet Carys.'

Kisses, soft yet fervent, covered her cheeks, brow, even her nose. Large hands cupped her head, holding her still. Her heart rose in her mouth. These weren't the caresses of a man desperate to bed her. They weren't about sex. They were about emotion. The sort of emotion she'd nurtured so long.

'Forgive me, Carys?'

The kisses stopped, though he didn't release her. Dazedly Carys opened her eyes. The look on her husband's face stole her breath right away. It would have claimed her heart too, if she hadn't already given that to him.

She blinked. 'What are you talking about?'

He didn't speak immediately and she had the bizarre feeling he was gathering his courage. He, the man who felt no qualms about anything, not billion-dollar deals or handling a hungry media scrum.

He breathed deep, his chest expanding so mightily it brushed hers, sparking inevitable flickers of awareness in every erogenous zone.

'These past years have been hard for you,' he murmured, his voice a suede caress that unravelled the ribbon of tension in her stomach. 'I sent you away, and because of that you were alone through your pregnancy and Leo's birth. Alone bringing up our son and making a home for him.' He paused and squeezed his eyes shut as if in pain.

Carys reached out, sliding her trembling fingers over his shoulders, feeling the tension vibrate within him.

'We survived.'

'I deprived myself of you and Leo.' Alessandro's mouth twisted up in a mirthless smile, and when he opened his eyes they were darker than she'd ever seen them. So dark it felt as if she looked right into his soul.

'I should never have let you go. Never have doubted.'

'Sorry?' His admission struck Carys dumb. She read the remorse in his face, felt the powerful energy hum through his body as if he kept a lid on a force too great to be released. But still she couldn't believe.

Long fingers slid round to cradle her face. His gentle touch set a thousand butterflies dancing inside her. A sense of something precious, something miraculous, filled her.

'I'm to blame, Carys. It's my fault. I should never have accused you of betraying me.'

She looked into his eyes and read emotion there, bare and powerful. Remorse. Guilt. Pain. And hope.

The shock of it, of having him reveal such depth of feelings rocked her on her heels. She clung to his shoulders, trying to marshal stunned thoughts.

'You weren't to know,' she found herself saying tentatively, not even questioning her need to ease his pain. 'After all, I believed Livia when she told me you were getting married.'

He shook his head abruptly. 'You weren't to know Livia had her own agenda. Whereas I…I have no one but myself to blame for leaping to conclusions.'

Carys' heart accelerated. 'Rosina told you on the boat? Told you there was nothing between me and Stefano Manzoni?'

Once more Alessandro shook his head. 'No.'

'But then…?'

'How do I know?' Again that raw, self-deprecating smile.

He reached up and took her hand, slid it from his shoulder, past the spot where his heart thundered, then pressed it down against his abdomen. 'I feel it here. Gut instinct, if you like.' He shrugged, still holding her palm against his belly. 'My sixth sense has been telling me all along that you weren't the woman I thought, but I ignored it.'

His eyes glowed emerald fire that melted the last of her defences.

'Two years ago I was wrapped up in saving the company, fixing the mess my father had left behind. I know that much, at least. Plus I'd decided all women were treacherous. I was probably waiting for you to slip up and prove me right.' He shook his head in obvious self-disgust.

Carys remembered the speed with which he'd put two and two together and made five, assuming infidelity where there was none. It *had* seemed as if he'd been all too ready to believe the worst.

She felt as if she'd whirled into an alternate universe, where nothing made sense. For a crazy instant, as he'd dragged her palm down his chest, she'd thought he was going to say it was his heart dictating this change in him. That he loved her.

Now she battled a queasy sensation of burgeoning hope and fear roiling together inside her.

'I don't understand.'

Alessandro was silent so long her nerves screamed with tension. Eventually he shrugged, a tense movement that only reinforced her awareness of his pain.

'Let's just say I've spent too many years as a target for women interested in acquiring wealth and prestige.'

Carys stared. Was it possible Alessandro thought women threw themselves at him for material things they could get from him? Didn't he understand the pull of a devastatingly sexy, macho man? She'd been a sucker for him the moment she saw him, and she'd known nothing of his wealth or position.

'And earlier...' He paused a moment before continuing. She watched his nostrils flare as if he stole a sustaining breath. 'My mother left when I was five. Dumped my father and went off to become the partner of a man whose fortune and prestige was even greater than his. I never saw her again.'

'Your father kept you apart?' Despite the rift between man and wife, to deprive a son of his mother was—

Alessandro snorted. 'My dear mama wasn't interested in me. She'd palmed me off to nannies from the first. In some ways it wasn't such a blow when she left.'

Despite his tight smile, Carys read the lie in his words. Her heart turned inside out, recognising the ancient scars he hid: the knowledge that his mother hadn't wanted him. How devastating that must have been.

Fellow feeling stirred. She felt his hurt deep in her psyche.

'After that it was a succession of nannies, most of them more interested in snaring a man with a title than looking after his son.' Alessandro didn't hide his bitterness for all that his words were clipped. 'I learned not to trust anyone.'

Carys wanted to soothe away the years of built up pain and distrust. To cradle him in her arms as if he were still that little boy distressed at losing his mother.

'But that's no excuse for my behaviour.'

Alessandro lifted her hand and pressed a kiss on her wrist. Another on her palm. Heat juddered through her and suddenly her need to comfort turned into something else. The familiar electrical current flowed from him to her and back again.

His smouldering eyes held her fast.

'Carys. I can't remember what happened between us. I probably never will. But I understand now that I jumped to conclusions and acted rashly.'

Her pulse leapt at the admission.

'Living with you these past couple of months, I realise I misjudged you. I should never have ended it the way I did.'

Her heart swelled as if it would burst as she read the warmth in his gaze.

'Sandro!' It was what she used to call him. The name she'd kept locked away in her heart for so long. Now it slipped out easily. 'Sandro, I—'

He pressed his index finger to her mouth. The male musk scent of his skin teased her. 'Let me say this first, Carys.'

He drew a deep breath and, stunned, she read hesitancy in his expression. Instinct told her this was serious. Her muscles tightened and she almost stopped breathing.

Was it possible her secret hopes were coming true?

'I never expected to feel like this about any woman. You're honest, direct, caring.' He smiled and the impact scrambled her brain. 'And we're good together. Aren't we?'

He looked so serious as he watched for her reaction, almost vulnerable, despite his innate strength.

Carys nodded carefully, trying to remain calm as a high-octane mix of excitement, love and desire ignited inside.

She tugged his hand from her mouth and squeezed it, willing him to say the words she'd waited so long to hear. The words she wanted to share with him.

I love you.

His face was sober as he pulled her close.

'I...trust you, Carys.'

CHAPTER FOURTEEN

'DID you hear me, Carys?' Carlotta tilted her head to one side, looking like an inquisitive little bird.

'Of course I heard.' Carys mustered a smile for her friend, trying to drag her mind back to the conversation.

She spent too much time fretting over what couldn't be changed. Life with Alessandro was good. More than good. He was a great father to Leo, a stupendous lover. Even now the memory of his hands and mouth on her body quickened her pulse. He was kind, attentive.

And he trusted her. Her lips twisted, remembering his words and the depths of her disappointment.

He gave her more than he'd given any other woman. All he had to give.

It wasn't Alessandro's fault he'd never learned what love was. That he couldn't offer it to her.

She would learn, one day, to be content. It didn't matter that she'd craved love all her life. Or that she bestowed it on him unstintingly. She was thankful for what she had, and soon she'd stop wishing for the moon.

The best way to do that was to keep herself busy, as she had these past couple of months.

'Yes, the tutor is terrific. I'm so glad I took your advice about hiring him.' This time her smile was more convincing. If she was going to live here, she had to master the language, which was why she and Carlotta spoke Italian when they were alone. 'I'm improving, don't you think?'

'You're a marvel,' Carlotta said with a smile. 'Your pronunciation is great, even if your vocab has a way to go. You'll be a hit when Alessandro starts entertaining on a large scale again. With that cute hint of an accent everyone will find you enchanting.'

'You think?' Carys glanced around the exclusive hotel restaurant Carlotta had chosen for lunch. Despite her new clothes and her determination to fit into Alessandro's life, she felt a ripple of unease sometimes, as if she didn't belong and everyone knew it.

The fact that Alessandro seemed to keep her apart from the demands of his social schedule didn't help either. Yes, they went out, even had friends to dine occasionally, but it was obvious he turned down a lot of invitations he would normally accept. Because he wasn't sure she'd cope?

'I *know,* Carys. According to the grapevine, the young *contessa* is charming, refreshing and beautifully dressed.' Carlotta laughed. It was she who'd steered Carys through the acquisition of a new wardrobe.

Carys smiled. 'You can take a lot of credit there.'

'Don't be so modest. Now, tell me, how are you going with your speech for the annual charity lunch? Any ideas?'

Carys nodded. 'A few.' In truth, she'd been thinking of little else since she'd heard about it. Each year the Contessa Mattani hosted a charity luncheon in the ballroom of the Mattani villa. Proceeds, along with a sizeable donation from Mattani Enterprises, went to a charity of her choosing, a different one each year. It was a tradition dating back to the time of Alessandro's grandmother.

Now it was a major event on the calendar of Italy's social elite. Anxiety skipped down her spine as she thought of hosting it and delivering a speech to a throng of the country's rich and famous.

'You *will* be there, won't you?'

'I wouldn't miss it for the world. And you'll have Alessandro by your side too.'

Alessandro hadn't spoken to her about it yet. Instead she'd learned about it from Carlotta, then had the date confirmed by the housekeeper. Tonight she'd finally remember to ask him for more details. She'd been meaning to for weeks, but somehow she often found herself…distracted around him.

Carlotta signalled for the bill. 'I'm afraid I have to rush off. Special meeting with a special client.'

'Then you go and I'll pay.'

'Sure?'

'Of course. Don't be late. I'll just sit here a little longer.' Because it was back again, that slight queasiness she'd experienced on and off lately.

'*Ciao, bella.*' Carlotta kissed her on both cheeks. 'I'll call when I'm back from Paris.'

Carys said goodbye and sat back, willing her stomach to settle. She paid the bill, sipping water, trying to stifle excitement that rose even stronger than the nausea.

She'd only felt like this once before. When she'd been pregnant with Leo. Her breasts were tender too. Or was that from Alessandro's thorough loving last night?

A ripple of pleasure tingled through her as she remembered their passion. And at the possibility she could no longer ignore. *Was she pregnant?*

A brother or sister for Leo. Another child to love and cherish. Only this time with Alessandro at her side from the start. Would he be happy? They hadn't taken precautions, so presumably he wasn't averse to the idea.

Surreptitiously she rubbed her palm over her stomach, wonder growing at the possibility.

Eventually she pushed her chair back and made for the foyer, only to falter as she saw a group of well-dressed older women in a group ahead of her.

A familiar voice spoke; a familiar elegantly tall figure blocked her path.

'Of course, I expected it. Poor Alessandro, what choice did he have? The girl was the mother of his child. But now he's stuck with the consequences.' A shrug of bony shoulders emphasised the point.

Carys put her hand to the door jamb, clinging tight as nausea hit again, stronger this time, preventing her from turning and walking away. Besides, her feet were welded to the spot by the scalding venom in Livia's voice.

'She has no breeding, no class, no idea of how to go on. How she's going to fill her responsibilities as *contessa* I can't imagine. Thank goodness I'm in the country for the day of the gala charity luncheon.' She shook her head. 'He asked me to step in and host it. Begged me. I couldn't let him down. We both know his wife would make a hash of it, and the Mattani name is too important to be made a laughing stock.'

Carys didn't hear any more vitriol. She'd finally unlocked her feet and prised her hand from the wall.

'Since the family name is so important to you, I'm surprised to hear you doing your best to taint it.'

Despite the bile rising in her throat, Carys somehow managed to sound cool and in control. Each word emerged with a crystal-clear diction that would have made her language tutor proud.

Amazing what shock and fury could produce. Especially since Carys wanted only to retreat and give in to the nausea.

Instead she stood straighter in her heels and smoke-blue suit of finest local silk. She told herself she looked elegant, even chic, like the countess she now was.

Livia spun round, hectic colour rimming her artfully made-up cheeks.

Carys looked up at the woman who'd tried to destroy what Alessandro and she had shared. For the first time she saw beyond the careful grooming and exquisite sophistication to the ugly greed and discontent beneath.

'Anyone would think you had an axe to grind,' Carys said softly and heard a collective intake of breath from the women watching so avidly. 'That you had your nose put out of joint because you'd been supplanted by Alessandro's wife.' She let a pause lengthen. 'Supplanted by a younger woman.'

The widening of Livia's eyes and a single muffled laugh from the group told Carys she was right.

She was tempted to confront Livia with her lies and machinations. But she refused to play her game and feed gossip to the curious. Instead she summoned a stiff-lipped smile. 'But we know that's nonsense, don't we?'

Livia opened her mouth then shut it, nodding abruptly.

'As for my charity lunch,' Carys continued, 'no doubt there was some misunderstanding about the arrangements. I'll ensure it's sorted and send you an invitation, Livia. I hope your friends will all attend too.'

Dimly she was aware of nods and agreement, but her focus was on the woman before her, who suddenly looked smaller and less assured. Carys didn't feel satisfaction or triumph, just a cold lump of distress in the pit of her belly.

'I must go, but I'll talk to Alessandro about having you to the villa for a meal soon. *Ciao, Livia.*' She pressed obligatory kisses to the other woman's cheeks, heard her automatic responses, then turned and concentrated on putting one foot in front of the other all the way to the entrance.

By the time she was alone in the back of the limo, her rigid control had cracked. She was shaking, her skin clammy, and her stomach heaved anew.

She tried to concentrate on the shock and defeat in Livia's eyes but instead remembered only her words.

What choice did he have? His wife would make a hash of it…he begged me…

No, Carys didn't believe it. Alessandro wouldn't do that to her. Livia had lied again. Carys wouldn't trust her as far as she could lift Alessandro's favourite Lamborghini. As soon as the shaking passed, she'd ring him and he'd confirm it.

He'd told her he trusted her.

He'd looked so sincere she'd believed him without hesitation.

But now that old doubting voice whispered again in her head. Had he said it just to woo her into compliance? To make things easier between them? Pain lanced her chest.

No! He'd meant every word.

Yet maybe trust came in different forms. He might trust her word but not think she was fit for the role of wife to a mega-wealthy industrialist.

Who could blame him?

She hadn't grown up in his world. Didn't know all the rules. And maybe—the thought sneaked up out of nowhere—he secretly believed, as others had, that her reading problems reflected on her capacity in other things.

Another surge of nausea made her hunch in her seat. She spent the next few wretched minutes riding wave after wave of pain, trying to blot out the voice of doubt.

Finally, she sat up straight, staring blind-eyed out the window. The roiling in her stomach was vanquished for now, yet she trembled in the aftermath of distress.

She lifted her chin. No matter that a craven part of her was tempted to agree with Livia, that she didn't know how to go on in these rarefied social circles. Carys was here to stay. She was Alessandro Mattani's wife and she'd prove to everyone, herself included, that she could handle whatever that entailed. She owed it to herself, and to Leo.

Her hand slid to her stomach. If she was going to bring up her family in this place, she couldn't afford to let herself sink into the shadows as she'd done when she was young. She knew what that was like, and it was a place she didn't want to visit again.

She'd worked all her adult life to make something of herself, prove to herself that she was as good as everyone else, and not live down to her family's expectations. She refused to let anyone put her in that position again.

She was tired of being made to feel second best. Even by herself.

Carys slipped her cellphone from her handbag and punched in the number for Alessandro's office. She ignored the tingle of fear running through her. Instead she reminded herself Alessandro trusted her.

Alessandro was out of his car and loping up the front steps before the echo of the Lamborghini's engine died. The front door swung silently open before he reached it.

'Where's my wife?'

Paulo moved back to let him enter. 'I believe madam is still at the pool. Master Leo has had his swim and gone up for a nap.'

'Good.' What needed saying was better done in private.

Alessandro strode towards the fitness wing, his sense of urgency growing with each step.

He'd been driving home when his efficient new assistant called, explaining that the *contessa* had rung to ask about arrangements for the charity lunch. When she'd checked, it was to find the fool of a woman who'd been his temporary PA had arranged for Livia to host the event. Despite his express instructions that his stepmother no longer be invited to represent the family or his company.

He speared a hand through his hair, frustration rising. At Livia. At incompetent temps. At himself for not double-checking.

He stalked down the corridor. All the while his assistant's voice echoed in his head. 'No, she didn't leave a message. No, she didn't say anything. She hung up after I told her about the luncheon.'

Alessandro had a bad feeling about this. He knew Carys sometimes felt unsure of herself. That was why he'd taken it slowly introducing her to society. He guessed at the scars her family's treatment of her had caused. Scars he suspected had never truly healed.

He thrust open the door to the pool, shrugging out of his jacket and tie as the warmth hit him. He dropped them on a chair, eyes fixed on the small form swimming in the pool. Usually she swam gracefully. This time there was a dogged determination about her freestyle stroke that spoke more of churning emotion than the need for exercise.

Carys let her palm slam onto the tiles at the end of the pool. She was too tired to make a proper racing turn. Her chest heaved, but still the hurt and anger bubbled inside. She'd do a few more laps, till her mind cleared.

A shadow fell on the tiles. Hands reached down.

'Let me help you out.'

Automatically she kicked out off the wall, propelling herself away. But Alessandro forestalled her by grasping her upper arms and using his extraordinary strength to haul her out to stand before him.

She didn't want to talk to him yet. Not till she was calm. Not till she'd got over the sense of betrayal. It was just a lunch, for goodness sake. Nothing to get worked up about.

Yet it felt like more. Like once again she hadn't measured up. Like last time when he'd kept her to himself rather than trust her to socialise with his friends. Like all the times her parents hadn't showed, or hadn't remembered or just weren't interested. Like she was doomed to be second best still.

'Look at me, Carys.'

She looked. He stood in a puddle as water sluiced off her body. His trousers were wet from where he'd lifted her, and his shirt clung in a way that made her want to run needy hands over his sculpted chest and torso. The knowledge fuelled her anger just as she was aiming for calm.

'You're home early.' It emerged as an accusation, belying the rapture she'd found so often when he returned in time to play with Leo, then take his wife to bed for some late afternoon loving. She bit her lip and looked over his shoulder.

A finger at her chin inexorably lifted her face towards his. There was no escaping his dark gaze or the sympathy she read there.

She didn't want his sympathy! She wanted so much more.

The futility of it hit her. She'd married Alessandro pretending not to care for him, but she'd known, deep in her heart, that she was fated to love this man no matter how unequal their circumstances or the feelings between them.

Alessandro's heart jammed against his ribs, almost stopped beating, as he saw her reddened eyes.

His indomitable Carys had been crying. The realisation gutted him. His hold on her tightened, but he resisted the need to pull her close. The set of her jaw and the flash of her ice-bright eyes were pure warning.

'I can explain—'

'I'm sure you can.' Bitterness laced her words. 'I suppose your office warned you I'd rung. That I knew you'd asked Livia to take my place.'

'It wasn't like that.' Not in the way she thought. His hands gentled on her shoulders, sliding down her slick arms in an instinctive gesture of comfort.

'Wasn't it?' Her gaze shifted. She didn't want to look at him. 'You think I'm not up to playing the role of *contessa*.'

'Don't say that!' He hated it when she talked of playing a role. As if at any moment she might decide she was tired of the act and simply leave. His fingers tightened and he planted his feet wider, instinctively ready to fight for what was his.

'So you asked Livia, *begged* her to step in.'

'That was a mistake, Carys.'

'You can say that again!' She tried to shrug out of his grip, but he refused to release her. He watched temper war with pain as her lips trembled and her eyes glowed bright with slow burning anger. He wanted to fold her close and soothe her.

'I'm you're *wife*, Alessandro. Not some employee you can put aside if you think they're not up to a job.' The words poured out in a rush. 'You *manipulated* me into this marriage. Gave me no choice in the matter. It's too late to decide now that you didn't get a good bargain when you married me.'

'Now hold on.' She'd hit on a sore spot. He knew a sneaking guilt that he'd forced her into marriage. That he'd taken unfair advantage of a woman who hadn't the resources to withstand him. He'd been utterly ruthless in getting this woman into his home and his bed.

'No, I won't hold on!' She straightened, glaring at him with something akin to hatred in her eyes. That look set his heart pounding and fear skimming through him. A fear such as he'd never known.

He couldn't lose Carys. It was impossible. Not now.

'I'm not some prop to be pulled out and shown to the public when you want a compliant wife, then shoved aside when you think I'm not up to dealing with your aristocratic friends.'

'You can't believe that's what I've been doing!' Indignation warred with sympathy. 'I've been giving you time to adjust, trying not to overwhelm you. I know this is different to what you're used to.'

She wasn't listening, just shook her head and planted her hands dead centre on his chest, pushing as if to make him move away.

He stayed planted exactly where he was. No one, not even Carys, dismissed him.

'I'm tired of this, Alessandro. Tired of being treated as second best. Tired of settling for less.'

'Settling?' His brow knotted. 'What do you mean settling?'

'This *convenient* arrangement of ours,' she said, distaste dripping from every syllable. 'It can't go on like this. I can't—'

'Convenient?' Alessandro tried to obliterate burgeoning panic, funnelling his fears instead into the wrath that surfaced when she spoke of ending their marriage. 'You accused me of that the night we got married, didn't you? You were wrong then and you're wrong now.' After all this time they were back where they'd started. Why couldn't she see how important this was? How important *they* were. 'You think this marriage is *convenient* for me?'

Azure eyes met his, unblinking. Her gaze pierced him to the soul. 'I think you got what you wanted, Alessandro. But it's not enough for me. I—'

He refused to listen to Carys request a divorce. Feelings, more tumultuous than he'd ever experienced, exploded within him, shattering the last of his iron-clad control, leaving him defenceless against the pain that ripped him apart.

'You think *this* is convenient, Carys?' He swooped down and took her mouth with his. The kiss was hard, demanding, proprietorial, almost brutal, but he could no longer hold himself in check.

She was *his*. Absolutely incontrovertibly *his*. Nothing had ever felt as right as holding Carys, kissing her. He pulled her close, enfolded her in an embrace that nothing could break.

He needed her. Wouldn't be whole without her.

The feel of her there, her heart hammering in time with his, her soft lips yielding, even giving back kiss for furious kiss, only strengthened his certainty.

'Or this?' He drew back enough to lick a line from her collarbone to her ear, feeling her judder in response, her breath catch in a gasp of pure pleasure.

'There's nothing convenient about what I feel for you, Carys.'

He drew back just enough to hold her dazed eyes with his. 'I refuse to give up the woman I love. Do you hear me? There will be no talk of divorce. I won't accept it. I won't give you up.'

This time when he kissed her, he lifted her right off the ground, securing her with one arm around her bottom, the other around her torso, pulling her to him as if he could meld her wet form into his own.

They were one, damn it. They belonged together.

'Sandro?'

'No.' The coward in him didn't want to hear her pleas to be released from their marriage. Instead he kissed her again, turning and walking the few paces till he felt the wall against his arm. He held her there, secure in his arms, her back to the wall, unable to escape, as he concentrated on ravaging her senses with all the passion welling inside him.

He could swear she responded as ardently as ever. More so. Perhaps, after all, she could be persuaded.

'Sandro.' Only lack of oxygen, the need to breathe again, allowed her to speak.

Her fingers against his lips stopped him when he would have kissed her again to stop the flow of words he didn't want to hear.

'Please, Sandro.' Such emotion in her husky voice. His heart squeezed in sheer terror as he knew he couldn't put off the moment any longer. He drew back enough to look down into her face. But he didn't relinquish his hold. He held her clamped hard against him.

'You love me?' There was wonder in her eyes, and doubt.

He was a proud man. From childhood he'd learned not to share himself, not to trust his heart to anyone else. But what he felt was too big to be hidden.

'Can you doubt it, Carys?' He lifted his hand to stroke her brow, her cheek, her swollen lips. 'I think I loved you even before I saw your picture in that brochure. Definitely from the moment I held you in my arms in my hotel suite, and almost died from the sheer ecstasy of you there, with me.' He swallowed a rising lump in his throat.

'And when I saw you holding our son…' This time his kiss

was tender, soft and fleeting. Reluctantly he pulled back, watching her eyes widen.

'I didn't know what love was till I met you, *tesoro mio*. But now I do. It's the glorious warmth I feel just thinking about you. Just remembering your smile when you're not there. It's the desire to keep you safe, to protect you and care for you every day of the rest of our lives. To share my life with you. It would kill me if you left.'

His heartbeat slowed to a sombre, waiting pulse. 'I was only half alive before I found you again. Please…' He didn't care that he laid his innermost self open and vulnerable before her. All that mattered was having Carys in his life.

'Oh, Sandro!' Her kiss was fervent but almost clumsy as she pressed her lips feverishly to his. He felt hot tears slide down his cheek and realised she was crying in earnest.

Guilt scorched him. Did he really want to trap her with sympathy?

'Sandro.' She pressed kisses to his chin, his lips, his face. 'I love you so much. I've always loved you. I thought you'd never feel the same.'

He shuddered with the shock of it. But lifting his head, he saw the truth in her eyes. She glowed incandescently as if lit from within. Even then he couldn't believe.

'But you wanted to leave me. You said so.'

Her smile, through drenched eyes and a tear-stained face, was the most beautiful thing he'd ever seen.

'No. I couldn't do that. Ever.' The words sank into his soul and settled there. A tentative sense of peace washed through him. He lowered his head to kiss her again, but she stopped him.

'I'm here for good, Sandro. I just meant I couldn't put up with accepting less than a real marriage with real responsibilities. I couldn't bear thinking you were ashamed of me, that I wasn't good enough to be your *contessa*.'

'Never say that, *piccolina*.' He hitched her higher so they were at eye level. 'You are the perfect wife for me. In every way.' He let the words echo around the tiled walls, satisfaction filling him.

'The luncheon arrangements were a mistake. I didn't invite Livia to take your place. I—'

Her lips against his stopped his words. Stopped thought. She kissed him with all the sweet pleasure and tenderness love could bestow. Alessandro felt it seep into his very bones. He cradled her close and gave back what she offered so unstintingly.

He loved this woman. Would love her till his dying day. The knowledge was glorious, terrifying and wonderful.

When eventually they pulled apart a fraction, she whispered, 'Tell me later. Much later.'

'But it's important for you to understand.'

She smiled and his heart stopped.

'And I will, Sandro.' Alessandro felt his pulse start again, rocketing into life. 'But it can wait. Nothing is more important than this.' She cupped his face in her hands and gazed into his eyes. 'I love you Alessandro Leonardo Daniele Mattani. We're going to be so happy together.'

CHAPTER FIFTEEN

'ONCE again, thank you all for your generosity.' Carys looked across the crowded ballroom, acknowledging smiles from her audience. Relief sighed through her.

Far from being an unresponsive group, those attending the lunch had embraced her and her chosen charities with disarming enthusiasm.

'And please, when you've finished your meal, feel free to come outside and enjoy the fair.'

At a nod from her, the light curtains covering the series of French doors were pushed aside and the doors flung open.

On the afternoon breeze, children's laughter mingled with the sound of music. A fairground had been set up on the lawns and those who would be the recipients of today's fundraising were enjoying themselves: children. Some from orphanages, some with disabilities and others recuperating from serious illnesses.

Carys stepped down from the small podium, acknowledging applause from all sides.

Her gaze kept straying to the tall figure at the back of the room. His nod and smile confirmed what she saw herself. That the lunch and the speech she'd sweated over so long had been successful.

She guessed he was proud of her. But it was the love in his eyes, clear even from here, that warmed her to the core.

Walking between the tables took for ever as she stopped to talk to those she knew and others eager to introduce themselves.

By the time she reached Sandro, Carys felt as if she'd shaken hundreds of hands, answered thousands of questions. And she revelled in it. The guests' support of the charities she'd chosen touched her heart.

'You're a natural,' said a warm voice as she left the final table.

She stopped, looking up into familiar hooded eyes alive with approval. Sandro took her hand and raised it to his lips. Inevitably she shivered in response and he smiled, recognising the effect he had on her.

'You made them laugh and even made them cry,' he added. 'I've never seen such unabashed enthusiasm for our fundraising before.'

Carys looked at Leo, bright-eyed and excited, on his father's hip. Her heart swelled seeing him so happy. Feeling the bond between the three of them.

She shrugged. 'A lot of them are parents. Besides, who wouldn't want to help those kids and make life a little easier for them?'

Alessandro gathered her close with his free arm and she went willingly, content to be in her husband's strong embrace. Content, at last, to be home.

'The hotel industry lost a treasure when you left,' he murmured. 'But I'm not giving you back. You make the perfect Contessa Mattani.' His voice dropped to a low purr. 'You're perfect for me, *piccolina*.' He lowered his head.

'Sandro,' she hissed. 'We can't! Not here.'

His response was to kiss her till her bones tingled and she clung to him.

Some time later she became aware of Leo leaning in for a hug, and sound swelling around them. The sound of laughter and more applause.

Alessandro looked over her head and waved to their guests, then led her out into the gardens.

'We can't just leave them,' she protested.

'Of course we can,' he assured her. 'Today is a treat for the local children.' His gaze dropped to her still-flat stomach, and he smiled, a secret, possessive smile that turned her limbs to jelly.

'Let's give ours a treat too, before we sneak away for a

weekend at our place in the mountains.' He hitched Leo higher and drew Carys further into the balmy afternoon.

She went willingly, knowing there was nowhere else on earth she'd rather be.

THE INFAMOUS ITALIAN'S SECRET BABY

CAROLE MORTIMER

PROLOGUE

'THE party is outside by the pool.'

Bella froze in the doorway, searching the shadows of the unlit room she had entered by mistake, a study or den if the book-lined walls and desk were any indication. Her hand tightened about the door-handle as she finally saw the outline of the large, imposing figure seated behind that desk.

The man was totally unmoving, and yet his very stillness was an implied danger, an echo of the challenge in his tone. By the light from the hallway behind her, Bella was just able to make out the fall of long dark hair that grew onto a pair of wide shoulders, those shoulders and a powerful chest encased in a dark top of some kind.

She swallowed hard before speaking. 'I was looking for the bathroom…'

'As you can see, this is not it,' he responded, his amused voice slightly accented. As he spoke some of the tension left his upper torso and he relaxed back in the high-backed chair, head tilted slightly sideways as the glitter of his gaze moved slowly over Bella standing silhouetted in the doorway. 'Or perhaps you cannot see…'

Bella barely had time to realise that the husky voice sounded vaguely familiar before there was the click of a switch and a light illuminated the desk in a soft warm glow. And the man seated behind it. Bella recognised him instantly.

Gabriel Danti!

Bella felt her heart plummet in her chest as she looked at the wickedly handsome man in front of her. His thick dark hair and chocolate-brown eyes were almost black in their intensity. His olive-skinned face boasted a perfectly straight aristocratic nose, high cheekbones, a mouth that was full and sensual, and a square, arrogant chin, softened only by the slight cleft in its centre.

It was the face that thousands, no, *millions* of women all over the world sighed over. Daydreamed over. Drooled over!

Italian by birth, Gabriel Danti was, at the age of twenty-eight, the defending champion of the Formula One racing car championship currently in its fifth month. This man was the darling of the rich and the famous on both sides of the Atlantic—and, as if that weren't enough, he was also the only son and heir of Cristo Danti, head of the Danti business and wine empire, with vineyards in both Italy and America.

Even while she registered all those things about him Bella was also aware of the fact that this house in the Surrey countryside was Gabriel Danti's English home, and that he was actually the host of the noisy party taking place outside by the pool. So what was he doing sitting up here alone in the dark?

She moistened suddenly dry lips. 'I'm terribly sorry for disturbing you. I really *was* looking for the bathroom.' She gave a small self-conscious grimace. How awful that the first and probably only time she had the opportunity to speak to Gabriel Danti it was because she needed to find the bathroom!

Gabriel made a lazy study of the tiny, dark-haired woman who stood in the doorway of his study. A young woman totally unlike the tall, leggy blondes that he usually escorted—and totally unlike the traitorous Janine, he acknowledged grimly to himself.

She had very long, straight hair, as black as ebony and falling soft and silky about her shoulders. A dark fringe of that same silky softness lay on her forehead, and her small, heart-shaped face was pale and smooth as alabaster—and totally dominated by a pair of the most unusual violet-coloured eyes Gabriel had ever seen. Her gently pouting lips were unknowingly sensuous and inviting.

His gaze dropped lower, to the soft woollen top she wore, which was the same violet colour of her eyes. The top two buttons were undone to reveal surprisingly full breasts—completely naked breasts beneath the thinness of her sweater, if Gabriel wasn't mistaken, which made her slender waist look even more so in comparison. Her narrow hips and legs were clearly defined in figure-hugging jeans.

That long, leisurely glance told Gabriel that he didn't know her.

But he wanted to!

Bella took an involuntary step back as Gabriel Danti stood up from behind the desk, revealing that the top he wore was in fact a black silk shirt that rippled as he stood before resettling softly against the muscled hardness of his shoulders and chest. The sleeves were turned back to just below his elbows, revealing muscled forearms lightly dusted with dark hair.

At least a foot taller than her own five feet two inches, Gabriel Danti at once dominated the space around him. And she, Bella realised in some alarm as she found herself rooted to the spot, was totally unable to move as the tall Italian sauntered across the room in long feline strides to stand mere inches in front of her. The raucous noise of the party outside instantly became muted as all Bella could see or hear was him.

She had been wrong, Bella mused as she found herself in a daze, unable to look away from the dark beauty of his face. Gabriel Danti wasn't handsome. He was stunningly gorgeous.

Bella could feel the heat radiating from his body, could smell his tangy aftershave, the male scent of him that invaded and claimed the senses, filling her with a warm lethargy, a need to move closer to all that heady maleness.

A need Bella was unable to resist as she felt herself swaying towards him. She made an effort at the last moment not to do so, lifting a hand to stop herself from curving her body along the length of his. Instead she found the palm of her hand against the black silk of his shirt, her fingers curling against the warm hardness of the chest beneath as she felt the hot, heady thrum of his heart against her fingertips.

What was happening to her?

She never reacted to men like this. At least, she never had before…

She had to—

Bella froze, every part of her immobilised as Gabriel Danti raised one of his long elegant hands that so capably handled the wheel of a racing car travelling at unimaginable speeds, and cupped her chin, the soft pad of his thumb caressing lightly across her bottom lip. The tingling warmth that ensued travelled down her throat and spine to pool hotly between her thighs.

Dark brown eyes held her own captive. 'You have the most beautiful eyes I have ever seen.' His voice was low, husky, as if he were aware that anything else would break the spell that surrounded them.

'So do you,' Bella breathed, her chest rising and falling sharply with the effort it took to breathe at all.

His throaty laugh was a soft rumble beneath her fingertips before it faded; the darkness of his gaze suddenly became intense, searching. 'Did you come here with someone?'

Bella blinked, trying to think through the slow insidiousness of his seduction. 'I—I'm here with a group of friends, Mr Danti.' She gave a self-conscious shake of her head as his eyes compelled her answer. 'Sean is the nephew of one of your mechanics.'

It didn't surprise Gabriel that this beautiful young woman knew who he was. Even if she hadn't recognised him from the photographs of him that appeared almost daily in the newspapers at the moment, the fact that this was his house and he had been sitting in the study where several framed photographs of him winning races also adorned the walls would have given him away.

'Sean is your boyfriend?' There was a slight edge to his voice that hadn't been there seconds earlier.

'Heavens, no!' she denied with a smile, her long hair falling forward across her breasts as she shook her head. 'We're just at university together. I hope you don't mind that Sean brought some friends with him, Mr Danti?' She was frowning now, her eyes almost purple. 'His uncle said—'

'I do not mind,' Gabriel cut in reassuringly. 'And please call me Gabriel.'

A slight flush darkened her cheeks. 'And I'm Bella,' she invited huskily.

'Bella?'

'Isabella.' She grimaced. 'But everyone just calls me Bella.'

Gabriel wasn't sure he wanted to be grouped with 'everyone' where this fascinating woman was concerned. He raised one dark brow. 'You are Italian?'

'No,' she laughed softly, her teeth small and white against the fullness of her lips. 'My mother allowed my father, who's a doctor, to choose my own and my younger sister's names, so he named us after two of his favourite models and actresses: Isabella and Claudia. When my brother was born six years ago my mother had the choice of names. She chose Liam. After the actor. A tall Irishman, with what my mother describes as "very sexy blue eyes"—'

'I know him,' Gabriel admitted.

'You know of him or you know him?' Bella was aware that she was talking too much. About things that could be of absolutely no interest to a man like Gabriel Danti. It was nerves, that was what it was. That and the fact that she couldn't think straight with Gabriel's fingers still curled possessively around the softness of her chin!

The Italian smiled. 'I know him. I cannot confirm the sexiness of his blue eyes, of course, but—'

'You're mocking me now,' Bella reproved self-consciously.

'Only a little,' Gabriel murmured, his gaze once more intense on hers. 'You said you are at university?'

'Was,' Bella corrected ruefully. 'I left last month.'

Telling Gabriel that Bella was probably aged twenty-one or twenty-two to his twenty-eight. 'What subject did you study?'

'Art and History,' she supplied.

'With a view to teaching, perhaps?'

'I'm really not sure yet. I'm hoping something that involves both subjects.' She shrugged slender shoulders, the movement giving Gabriel, with his superior height, a delicious glimpse of the fullness of her breasts.

Gabriel could never remember being so instantly attracted to a woman before. So attracted that he was sure her appraisal of him earlier had raised his body temperature by several degrees, at the same time making him totally aware of every muscle and sinew of his own body as well as hers. Rousing a need, a hunger, inside him that demanded the slender curves of Bella's body be placed against his much harder ones. Intimately. Preferably with no clothing between them.

Bella gave a slightly nervous laugh as she saw the way the Italian's eyes had suddenly darkened. 'If you'll excuse me, I think I'll just go and find the bathroom—'

'The bathroom is the room next to this on the right,' Gabriel interrupted, his fingers firming against her chin. 'While you are gone, I suggest I find a bottle of champagne and some glasses and then we can find somewhere more comfortable in which to continue this conversation, hmm?'

What conversation? Bella wondered, slightly bemused. She was pretty sure that Gabriel Danti didn't want to hear more about her degree in art and history or her family! 'Shouldn't you be returning to your guests?' She frowned.

His laugh was slightly wicked. 'Does it sound as if they are missing me?'

Well…no, the party outside sounded noisier and more out of control than ever. Which was some feat considering several of the guests had already thrown off their clothes and jumped into the pool naked before Bella had left to go in search of the bathroom. Which had hastened her need to go in search of the bathroom, if she was honest; the party looked in danger of disintegrating in a way Bella wasn't at all comfortable with.

It had sounded like a fun thing to do when Sean Davies had invited several of his fellow ex-students to the party being given at the Surrey home of Gabriel Danti. A chance to mix with the rich and the famous.

The fact that most of those 'rich and famous' were behaving in a way Bella would never have imagined if she hadn't seen it with her own eyes had come as something of a shock to her. It wasn't that she was a prude, it was just a little disconcerting to have a man she had last seen reading the evening news, a respected middle-aged man, jumping stark naked into Gabriel Danti's swimming pool. Admittedly it was a warm summer's evening, but even so!

'Come, Bella.' Gabriel removed his hand from her chin only to place it about her waist, his arm warm and spine-tingling as it rested against the slenderness of her back. 'Do you have any preference in champagne?'

'Preference?' she echoed. Champagne was champagne, wasn't it?

'White or pink?' he elaborated.

'Er—pink will be fine.' As a student, the only preference Bella had when it came to wines was that it not cost a lot of money! 'Are you sure you wouldn't rather just rejoin your guests?' Bella hesitated in the hallway, rather confused that this gorgeous man, a man any of his female guests would scratch another woman's eyes out in order to spend time alone with, appeared to want to spend that time with *her*...

'I am very sure, Bella.' Gabriel turned her in the curve of his arm so that she now faced him, his hands resting lightly against her waist. 'But perhaps you would rather return to your friends...?'

Bella swallowed hard as Gabriel made no effort to hide the hot sensuality burning in his eyes. 'No, I—' She stopped as she realised her voice was several octaves higher than normal. She cleared her throat before trying again. 'No, I think I would enjoy drinking champagne with you more.'

Those dark eyes gleamed with satisfaction as he raised his hands to cup either side of her face before slowly lowering his head to take possession of her mouth. Sipping, tasting, his tongue was a warm sweep against her lips as he tacitly asked her permission to enter. Then he claimed her mouth, groaning low in his throat as Bella gave in to temptation, parting her lips and inviting his tongue to surge inside.

His mouth was hot against hers now, Bella feeling

slightly dizzy from the warm rush of desire that instantly claimed her. Her breasts were firm and aching and she moved instinctively to rub that ache against the hardness of Gabriel's chest, that friction affording her some relief even as she felt more desire pooling between her thighs.

Oh, how she wanted this man. Wanted him as she had never known it was possible to want any man, the hot demand of his kiss, the hardness of his thighs against hers, telling her that he returned that need.

Gabriel had never tasted anything as sweet as the response of Bella's mouth beneath his. Never felt anything so lush, so perfect, as his hands moved down over her hips and then down to clasp her bottom as he pulled her into him, his arousal now nestled demandingly against the flatness of her stomach.

Gabriel dragged his mouth from Bella's to cast a searching look down at her. Those beautiful violet-coloured eyes were so darkly purple it was almost impossible to distinguish the black of her pupils. Her cheeks were flushed, her lips swollen from their kisses, and she looked more erotically enticing than ever. Her breasts were firm against his chest, and Gabriel was able to feel the hardness of her nipples through the soft silk of his shirt.

'Go. Before I lose all sense and make love to you out here in the hallway!' He grasped the tops of her arms tightly and turned her in the direction of the bathroom she had been seeking. 'I will return in two minutes with the champagne and glasses.'

Bella was completely dazed and disorientated as she entered the bathroom and closed the door behind her before leaning weakly back against it.

She was twenty-one years of age, had dated dozens of boys in the last five or six years, but never before had she known anyone or anything as lethal—as potent—as Gabriel's kisses!

Bella straightened to look at herself in the mirror on the door of the bathroom cabinet over the sink. Her cheeks glowed with the warmth of her arousal. Her mouth—oh, dear, her lips were swollen and slightly parted as if in invitation! Her eyes were deep pools of liquid violet, the pupils enlarged. As for her breasts...Well, if she had any sense she would leave now! If she had any will power at all, she would *make* herself leave now.

Even as she told herself these things Bella knew she wasn't going anywhere but back into Gabriel Danti's arms...

'Nice?'

'Mmm.'

'Would you like more?'

'Please.'

'Come a little closer, then. Now hold out your hand.'

Bella lifted the hand holding her glass to allow Gabriel to pour her more champagne as she sat on the sofa beside him, at the same time noting that he hadn't touched any of the bubbly wine in his own glass since placing it on the coffee table in front of them. The two of them were seated in a sitting-room at the front of the house on the first floor, well away from the noisy party downstairs.

'You aren't drinking,' she pointed out in an effort to cover up the slight shaking of her hand as she once again raised her glass to her lips and took a sip of the delicious pink champagne.

He shook his head, his arm along the back of the sofa as he sat very close beside her, that hand playing with the silken strands of her hair. 'I'm going to the track for a practice session tomorrow, and I never drink if I am going to drive the next day.'

Bella's eyes widened. 'You shouldn't have bothered opening a bottle of champagne just for me.'

'It is not just for you,' Gabriel assured her, dipping his finger into her champagne glass before running his finger lightly behind Bella's ear and along her jaw. 'I said I do not drink champagne before driving, Bella, not that I do not intend enjoying its taste,' he murmured softly, his breath warm against her ear lobe as his lips moved to follow the trail of champagne left by his finger, his tongue rasping against her already sensitised skin.

The combination of Bella and champagne was more intoxicating to Gabriel's senses than drinking a whole bottle of the expensive wine could ever have been, her skin so smooth to the touch, its sweet taste driving the heat through Gabriel's already roused body until he throbbed with the need to touch her more intimately. All of her.

He held her gaze as he deliberately dipped his finger back into the champagne before leaving a moist trail from her chin, down the delicate curve of her throat, to the exposed swell of the fullness of her breasts, his lips instantly following that heady trail.

Bella squirmed pleasurably as the warmth of his mouth lingered on her breasts. 'Gabriel—'

'Let me, Bella,' he pressed huskily. 'Let me bathe you in champagne. All of you. So that I might drink from your body.' His hand moved to cup her cheek as his thumb moved across her parted lips once more. 'Will you allow me to do that, Bella?'

Bella had accepted exactly where this was going the moment she had agreed to accompany Gabriel up the stairs to what had turned out to be the private sitting-room that adjoined his bedroom. Although thankfully the bedroom door had remained closed, otherwise she might have panicked long before now.

Not that she was panicking. Quivering with delicious anticipation more described her present state of mind! Just the thought of Gabriel dribbling champagne over her totally naked body, before slowly licking away each drop with the rasp of his arousing tongue, was enough to heat every inch of her to a tingling awareness that suddenly made the few clothes Bella was wearing feel tight and restrictive.

'As long as I can reciprocate.' She dipped her own finger into the champagne before running that finger over the firm sensuality of Gabriel's slightly parted lips. 'May I?' She paused expectantly with her mouth only centimetres away from his, violet eyes looking deeply into dark brown.

'Please do,' he encouraged.

What Bella lacked in experience she hoped she made up for in her delight at being given the freedom to explore the sculptured perfection of Gabriel's mouth in the same way he had hers. She heard his ragged intake of breath as she gently sucked his top lip into her mouth and her tongue slowly licked the heady champagne from that softness. His hand moved up to entangle his fingers into her hair as she gave the same treatment to his bottom lip, knowing as those fingers tightened in her hair that these caresses were arousing Gabriel as deeply as they were her.

Gabriel's body hardened more with each heated sweep of Bella's tongue against his lips, the throb of his thighs becoming an urgent demand. In fact, he wasn't even sure he was going to make it as far as the bedroom before stripping Bella's clothes from her deliciously responsive body and surging hotly, satisfyingly inside her!

He moved back abruptly, a nerve pulsing in his tightly clenched jaw as he stood up to hold out his hand to her. 'Come with me, Bella,' he invited as she looked up at him uncertainly.

Gabriel continued to hold that gaze as Bella placed her hand in his and rose gracefully to her feet, her breasts quickly rising and falling beneath the thin wool of her sweater.

She was like a small, wild thing, Gabriel acknowledged with growing wonder. So tiny. So delicate. So absolutely, potently desirable.

Gabriel felt his stomach muscles tighten with the force of that desire, continuing to keep a firm hold of her delicate fingers as he picked up the chilled bottle of champagne with his other hand, neither of them speaking as they went into his bedroom.

'Please don't…' Bella protested shyly as Gabriel would have turned on the bedside light.

A four-poster bed! A genuine antique if Bella wasn't mistaken, as were the drapes of deep gold brocade that could be pulled around the four sides of the bed.

What did it matter whether or not the bed and drapes were genuinely old? It was still a bed. A bed Bella had no doubts she would shortly be sharing—very shortly, if the heat of his gaze was any indication!—with Gabriel Danti.

This was madness. Sheer, utter, delicious madness!

'I want to be able to look at you as I make love to you, Bella,' Gabriel said, once again standing very close to her, but not touching her, the warmth of his body alone acting on Bella's senses like a drug. 'Will you allow me to do that?' he encouraged throatily. 'I will undress first if you would be more comfortable with that…?'

God knew Bella wanted to look at him in all his naked glory! 'Please do,' she begged breathlessly.

He reached out to turn on the bedside lamp, to bathe the room in a muted golden glow before he reached up and began to unfasten the buttons down the front of his black shirt.

Bella found her gaze fixed on the movements of those long, elegantly slender hands as they slowly slipped each button from its fastening, the silk falling back to reveal the muscled hardness of Gabriel's chest covered in another dusting of dark hair. Dark hair that thickened as it reached his navel before disappearing below the waistband of his black tailored trousers.

It was instinct, pure compulsion that caused Bella to reach out and touch his chest, to feel the tautness of his flesh beneath her fingertips as it stretched tightly across those muscles. His skin felt hot and fevered, those muscles tightening as Bella's hands moved up to slide the shirt from his shoulders before she dropped the garment to the carpeted floor.

Gabriel was as beautiful as the angel he was named

for. Achingly, temptingly gorgeous as his eyes burned hotly in the chiselled beauty of his face.

Bella wanted to see more. Wanted to see all of him!

Her hands trembled slightly as she unfastened his trousers to slide the zip down slowly, her fingers skimming lightly across Gabriel's arousal beneath black underpants, causing him to draw in a sharp breath.

His hand moved down to clasp hers against him. 'Feel how badly I want you, Bella,' he grated fiercely. 'Feel it!'

She looked up at him, their gazes fusing hotly, Bella never more sure of anything in her life as she slowly, deliberately, peeled away Gabriel's last item of clothing to release his pulsing erection.

He was long and thick, incredibly hard, that hardness moving against her hand as Bella reached out to touch him.

Gabriel felt his control slipping, groaning softly, lids closing, his jaw clenching, as his pleasure centred totally on the caress of Bella's fingers against his arousal. Selfishly he wanted those caresses to continue to their pleasurable conclusion. But more than that he wanted to see Bella, to touch her with the same intimacy as she was now touching him.

His gaze held hers as he stepped back slightly before reaching out to grasp the bottom of her thin sweater and draw it slowly up over her breasts and then her head before adding it to the pile of clothes on the carpet. Gabriel's breath caught in his throat as he gazed at the firm thrust of her breasts, the nipples a deep, dusky rose, and a waist so small and slender Gabriel felt sure he would be able to span it with his hands.

He slowly bent his head to kiss those uptilting

breasts, able to see and feel Bella's response as his tongue moved moistly across one nipple before he drew it deeply into his mouth.

Bella was lost. Totally, utterly lost as her hands moved up to clasp Gabriel's head to her, her fingers tangling in the heavy thickness of his hair as the pleasure created by his lips and tongue washed over her in dark, sensuous waves, pooling achingly between her thighs. An ache that Gabriel helped to assuage as his hand moved to cup her there, pressing lightly, Bella gasping weakly as he unerringly found the centre of her arousal.

She had no idea which one of them removed her jeans and panties, any more than she could remember how they came to be lying on the bed, bodies pressed close together, legs entwined as they kissed hotly, fiercely, feverishly.

Bella stopped breathing altogether as Gabriel's hand parted her thighs before his thumb began to touch, to stroke, the hardened nub that nestled there. Her senses became saturated with the intensity of her arousal, her hips rising off the bed to meet the thrust of Gabriel's fingers as they moved deeply, rhythmically inside her and Bella exploded with spasm after spasm of unimagined pleasure, her head moving from side to side on the pillow, her fingers curled into the sheets beneath her as that pleasure seemed never ending.

It didn't end as Gabriel moved above her, his gaze holding hers as he slowly, inch by inch, entered her still quivering body until he claimed her completely. He began to move inside her, his thrusts slow and measured, and then increasing in depth, Gabriel groaning low in his throat as he surged fiercely inside her. Bella met the fierceness of his thrusts as she—amazingly, incredibly!—felt her own release building for a second time in as many minutes.

Her eyes widened, deeply purple, as that release grew, the pleasure so achingly deep now it was almost painful in its intensity as Gabriel deliberately slowed the strokes of his erection inside her, holding her on the edge of that plateau, refusing to release her as he watched her pleasure.

'Please!' Bella gasped restlessly as her body burned and ached for that release. 'Oh, God, please!'

He continued to watch her even as he moved up onto his arms, his thrusts deepening, becoming harder, quicker, his cheeks flushed with his own pleasure, eyes glittering like onyx as Bella's second release took him over that edge with her.

Gabriel closed his eyes at the force of his release, surging, pumping, hot and fierce, his hips continuing to move against Bella's long after he had completely spilled himself as he remained hard inside her and the quivering pleasure still washed over and through him.

Finally, when he could take no more, when he felt as if he would die if the intensity of it didn't stop, Gabriel collapsed weakly onto Bella's breasts, turning only to pull the bedclothes over them both as they fell into a deep, exhausted sleep, their bodies still joined.

'It's time to wake up, Bella.'

Bella was already awake, had woken up several minutes ago in fact, and was trying to come to terms with who she was here with.

Gabriel Danti…

Just thinking of his name conjured up images of the night that had just passed. Of waking up in the early hours of the morning to find Gabriel once more hard inside her, his gaze silently questioning as he looked down at her. A question Bella had silently answered by the slow, languorous thrust of her thighs as her mouth became fused with his.

If anything, the second time they had made love had been even more intense than the first—and Bella hadn't believed that anything could possibly match their first time together!

But, having woken up alone in the four-poster bed a few minutes ago, the sound of the shower running in the adjoining bathroom telling her where Gabriel was, instead of the happy euphoria Bella should have been feeling after such a night of pure pleasure, she had instead been filled with a sense of trepidation.

Last night she had made love with Gabriel Danti. Number one driver of the Formula One racing championship. Playboy son and heir of the Danti business and wine empire.

Whereas she was the eldest daughter of an English country doctor, hopefully with a forthcoming degree in art and history.

Not only that, but Bella knew she was far from the tall, leggy blonde models or actresses that Gabriel usually escorted to the glitzy parties and film premieres he seemed to attend on a regular basis. The glossy magazines were constantly showing photographs of him with those women, most recently the model Janine Childe.

So she and Gabriel had absolutely nothing in common!

Out of the bedroom, that was…

In the cold light of dawn Bella blushed to the roots of her tangled hair as she relived each and every one of their intimate caresses of the night before.

Of course, she should have thought of all the reasons she shouldn't be here with Gabriel before she went to bed with him. She probably would have done so if she hadn't been quite so mesmerised by all that brooding Latin charm. If she hadn't been held in thrall by the hard beauty of Gabriel's face and body…

'Bella…?' Gabriel prompted again as he moved to sit on the side of the bed. 'Wake up, *cara*, so that I can say goodbye properly.'

Goodbye?

Bella's lids flew open wide as she turned her head to look at Gabriel sitting on the bed beside her. She was grateful that she had the sheet draped over her to hide her nakedness when she saw that Gabriel was fully dressed in a black polo shirt that emphasised the width of his shoulders and chest, and faded jeans that rested low down on his hips, his hair still wet from the shower he had just taken.

Gabriel's smile was quizzical as he looked down at Bella, once again fascinated by how beautiful she was. How tiny and curvaceous. How responsive…

He felt his body stir, his thighs hardening, as he recalled just how responsive Bella had been the previous evening and once again during the night. How his own response had been deepened, intensified, to match hers.

He reached out to smooth the fringe of dark hair from her brow, his gaze holding hers as he bent to kiss her, slowly, his expression regretful when he finally raised his head. 'I really do have to go now, Bella, or I am going to be late getting to Silverstone,' he murmured huskily. 'But I will call you later, okay?'

'Okay,' she whispered.

Gabriel stood up reluctantly, as aware of the minutes ticking by as he was of Bella's nakedness beneath the sheet, and knowing he had to remove himself from the temptation she represented. 'My housekeeper will call a taxi for you when you are ready to leave.' He spoke abruptly as he fought the urge he had to say to hell with the practice session and remain here in bed with Bella instead. 'As I cannot drive you home myself I have left you some money on the dressing-table to pay for the taxi,' he added lightly, remembering that Bella had only recently ceased being a student.

She frowned slightly. 'That won't be necessary.'

'Bella…?' Gabriel lowered his own brows darkly as he could read none of her thoughts in those violet-coloured eyes.

'It's fine, Gabriel.' Bella forced a lightness to her tone that was completely contradicted by the heaviness that had settled in her chest at the suddenness of Gabriel's departure.

'I will call you later, Bella,' he repeated firmly. Gabriel bent once again to kiss her on the lips before turning to leave, pausing at the door to turn and add, 'Take your time showering—there is no hurry for you to leave.'

CHAPTER ONE

Five years later…

'As PARTIES go this one is pretty amazi—I don't believe it!' Claudia gasped incredulously.

'What don't you believe?' Bella prompted indulgently, her sister having exclaimed over one wonder or another since the family's arrival in San Francisco two days ago.

Although Bella had to admit that the view of the San Francisco evening skyline from this private function room at the top of one of its most prestigious hotels was pretty spectacular. She could even see the Golden Gate Bridge lit up in all its splendour.

'Wow! I mean—wow!' Claudia wasn't looking out of the window but across the crowded room where the private party, to introduce the two families of their cousin Brian and his American fiancée Dahlia Fabrizzi, was taking place on the eve of their wedding. 'But it can't really be him, can it?' she queried as she frowned. 'Of course Aunt Gloria has been dropping huge hints the last few days about Dahlia's mother being well connected, but, still, I can't believe—'

'Claudia, will you for goodness' sake stop waffling into your champagne and just—?' Bella broke off abruptly as she turned to see who was holding her sister so enrapt, and instantly recognised the 'him' Claudia had to be referring to.

Bella hadn't seen him for five years. Five years! And yet she had no trouble whatsoever in recognising Gabriel Danti!

No! Claudia was right; it couldn't possibly be him, Bella assured herself. Not here, of all places. It had to be an illusion.

Or perhaps just a waking nightmare!

'It *is* him!' Claudia exclaimed excitedly as she clutched Bella's arm. 'It's Gabriel Danti, Bella! Can you believe it?'

No, Bella couldn't believe it. She didn't *want* to believe it!

Maybe it wasn't him, just someone who looked a lot like him?

The height was the same, but the dark hair was much shorter than Bella remembered. The eyes, although dark, were cold and aloof despite the smile that curved those chiselled lips as he was introduced to several other guests. The cleft in the chin was also the same, but this man had a scar running from beneath his left eye to his jaw to mar the harsh, sculptured beauty of his face.

Bella remembered that Gabriel Danti had been photographed sporting a long scar down the left side of his face when he was discharged from hospital three months after the horrendous crash that had put an end to his own racing career and killed two of his fellow drivers.

Months after his accident, Gabriel Danti had returned

to Italy on the family owned jet, had been photographed as he left the hospital, and then again as he entered the plane, but had rarely been seen in public since. His racing career over, he had turned his concentration on the Danti wineries and seemingly retired from the playboy lifestyle he had once so enjoyed.

'Do you remember those posters of him I had stuck all over my bedroom walls when I was younger?' Claudia laughed.

Of course Bella remembered those posters—they had given her the shivers for months following that night Bella had spent with him, her relief immense once Claudia took them down and replaced them with posters of one of the bad-boy actors of Hollywood.

'He's gorgeous, isn't he?' Claudia sighed dreamily.

'Lovely,' Bella answered insincerely, watching the man standing across the crowded room now talking to her uncle Simon.

He was several inches taller than her uncle, and had to bend slightly in order to hear the older man's conversation. He looked dark and mesmerising, his body lithe and obviously fit in the black evening suit and snowy white shirt with a black bow tie.

Could it really be Gabriel?

From the way his mere presence had ensnared the attention of all the female guests at the party Bella could well believe it was him. She just didn't want it to be!

'His hair's shorter, of course— Oh, look, he favours his left leg…' Claudia sympathised as their cousin Brian moved with the man to introduce him to several members of his own family who had made the trip over for the wedding tomorrow.

'His legs were badly crushed in the accident five years ago, remember,' Bella murmured with a frown.

'You would have thought that all the Danti millions could have fixed that,' her sister mused. 'You know, Bella,' she added slowly, 'he reminds me of someone...'

'Probably Gabriel Danti!' Bella said sharply as she finally came out of the dazed stupor that had held her firmly in its grip, linking her arm with her sister's in order to turn Claudia in the direction of the bar. 'Let's go and get some more champagne.'

'Aren't you in the least intrigued to know if it *is* him?' Claudia looked at her teasingly. She was of a similar height to Bella, but her hair was a short, wispy cap of ebony, the blue of her figure-hugging knee-length gown a perfect match in colour for her eyes.

'Not in the least,' Bella dismissed firmly, deliberately going to the farthest end of the bar away from the crowd of people where the man who looked like Gabriel Danti was now the centre of attention, several other people having drifted over to join the group, obviously as intrigued as Claudia.

Claudia gave a husky chuckle of affection as they stood at the bar waiting for their champagne glasses to be refilled. 'My big sister, the man hater!'

Bella raised dark brows. 'I don't hate all men—just those that have gone through puberty!'

'Exactly.' Claudia grinned, her face arrestingly pretty rather than classically beautiful. 'I wonder if I should go over and say hello to Brian and see if he can introduce me to— No, wait a minute...' Her attention noticeably sharpened as she looked over Bella's shoulder. 'I do believe our darling cousin is bringing him over to meet us!' Her face brightened excitedly.

No!

Bella couldn't believe this was happening!

She didn't even want to look at a man who resembled Gabriel Danti, let alone be introduced to him—

'And last, but not least, I would like you to meet the two most beautiful women I know after Dahlia,' Brian said affectionately behind her. 'Bella, Claudi, can I introduce you to Dahlia's cousin, Gabriel Danti? Gabriel, my cousins, Claudia and Isabella Scott.'

It truly *was* Gabriel Danti!

Bella couldn't breathe. Her mind had gone completely blank. Her knees had turned to jelly. In fact no part of her seemed to be functioning properly.

Luckily for her Claudia had eagerly grasped on to the introduction, and was even now enthusing to Gabriel how much she had enjoyed watching him during his career in Formula One racing, giving Bella a little time to catch her breath as she heard the familiar husky accented tones as he murmured a polite but dismissive response.

Perhaps Gabriel wouldn't remember her? Bella thought frantically.

Of course he wouldn't remember her!

Why should he remember the student of art and history called Bella who had once shared his bed for the night?

From his lack of a phone call, she could only assume he had forgotten her instantly!

'Bella...?' Brian prompted lightly as she still kept her back firmly turned towards both him and his guest.

Bella drew in a deep, steadying breath, knowing that

she had no choice but to turn and face the man she so longed to forget, as he had her.

Gabriel's expression was blandly polite as Isabella Scott turned to face him. 'Miss Scott,' he greeted evenly as he briefly took the cool slenderness of her hand in his before releasing it. 'Or may I call you Isabella?'

'I—'

'Everyone calls her Bella,' Claudia put in helpfully.

'May I?' The icy darkness of Gabriel's gaze easily held Bella captive.

Violet-coloured eyes were surrounded by thick dark lashes the same colour as that wild cascade of hair down the slender length of her spine...

Bella blinked before abruptly breaking the intensity of Gabriel's gaze to focus on something across the room. 'Bella is fine,' she answered him evenly.

Isabella Scott looked self-assured and incredibly beautiful in an off-the-shoulder gown of the exact colour of her eyes, and, if Gabriel was not mistaken, her small, pointed chin was slightly raised in challenge as her gaze returned questioningly to meet the intensity of his...

'More guests to greet,' Brian Kingston murmured apologetically as he glanced across the room. 'Excuse me, won't you, Gabriel? I'm sure Bella and Claudi will be only too pleased to keep you entertained.' He shot a teasing glance at the younger of the two cousins before turning and making his way back across the crowded room to his fiancée's side.

Gabriel's gaze was hooded as he continued to look steadily at Bella. 'Will you?'

An irritated frown appeared between her eyes. 'Will I what?' she prompted sharply.

'Be pleased to keep me entertained?' he drawled with cool mockery.

Purple lights flashed in the depths of her eyes. 'Do you need entertaining, Mr Danti?'

'In truth, I doubt I will be staying long enough for that to be necessary,' he conceded.

Gabriel hadn't intended attending this party at all this evening, but at the last moment his father had asked him to represent the Danti side of the family, as he didn't feel well enough to attend the party of his niece this evening as well as her wedding tomorrow. Gabriel had reluctantly agreed to come in his place, his intention to only stay long enough to satisfy the proprieties.

At least, it had been…

Gabriel Danti wasn't staying long, Bella triumphed with inward relief. 'I'm sure Claudia and I can manage a few minutes' polite conversation, Mr Danti.'

Gabriel Danti gave a mocking inclination of his head before turning his attention to Claudia. 'Are you enjoying your visit to San Francisco, Claudia?'

Bella allowed her breath to leave her lungs in a soft, shaky sigh as she at last felt herself released from the intensity of Gabriel's dark, compelling gaze, and she took those few moments of respite to study him more closely.

The man she had met five years ago had possessed the broodingly magnetic good looks of his heavenly namesake. Along with a lazy self-confidence and charm that was utterly captivating, and a warm sensuality in those chocolate-brown eyes that undressed a woman at a glance.

Or, in Bella's experience, made a woman want to undress for him at a glance!

The man talking oh-so-politely to Claudia still possessed those broodingly magnetic good looks—the livid scar down the left side of his face only added a dangerous edge to that attraction!—but his eyes were no longer that warm and sensual colour of melted chocolate but were instead a flat, unemotional brown, and the lazy charm and self-confidence had been replaced with a cold and arrogant aloofness.

As far as Bella was aware, Gabriel had never married—although, in all honesty, Bella hadn't particularly gone out of her way to learn anything about his life in the five years since they had parted so abruptly.

What would have been the point? The two of them had shared nothing more than a night of unimaginable and unrepeatable passion.

'Would you care for a drink?'

Bella raised startled eyes to Gabriel's, frowning slightly as she saw the glass he held out to her. Champagne. It would have to be champagne, wouldn't it?

'Thank you,' she accepted stiltedly.

Gabriel watched beneath hooded lids as Bella's cheeks warmed with colour as she took the fluted glass from him with a deftness that prevented her fingers from coming into contact with his.

His mouth twisted derisively as he asked, 'Is this your first visit to San Francisco, too, Bella?'

'Yes.'

'You like the city?'

'Very much.'

'Have you done much sightseeing since your arrival?'

'Some, yes.'

Gabriel's gaze narrowed at the economy of her replies. 'Perhaps—'

'Excuse me for interrupting, Gabriel,' his cousin Dahlia, tomorrow's bride, cut in lightly as she joined them, 'but my brother Benito is anxious to become re-acquainted with Claudia,' she added indulgently.

'Really?' The younger of the two Scott sisters glanced across the room to where Benito stood watching her intently.

Bella felt herself begin to tremble as she was over-whelmed with an impending sense of doom. If Claudia left then Bella would be completely alone with—

'You don't mind, do you, Bella?' Claudia's eyes were glowing with excitement. She had confided in Bella earlier today, after being introduced to Benito the previous evening, that she definitely wanted to get to know Dahlia's older brother better.

Obviously the attraction was reciprocated—which didn't help Bella in the least when she had no inclina-tion whatsoever to be left alone with Gabriel Danti!

'I assure you, Claudia, your sister will be perfectly safe with me,' Gabriel replied with dry mockery before Bella had a chance to say anything.

Bella shot him a glance beneath her long lashes. She still had absolutely no idea whether or not Gabriel re-membered her from their night together five years ago—and she didn't want to know, either.

She remembered *him*, and that was bad enough!

But before she could add anything to his reply Claudia gave her arm a grateful squeeze. 'Thanks, Bella,' she whispered before moving away to accompany Dahlia over to where the dark and handsome Benito stood waiting.

The sudden silence the two women left in their wake seemed deafening to Bella.

The room was full of people, at least a hundred or so of the guests invited to the wedding tomorrow, all of them chatting or laughing as they either renewed old acquaintances or met new ones. And yet as far as Bella was concerned she and Gabriel could have been alone on an island in the Arctic—the air between them was certainly frigidly cold enough for them to be on one!

'There is a more—private sitting area next to this one in which we might talk,' Gabriel bit out abruptly.

Bella raised apprehensive eyes, knowing that wariness was justified as Gabriel looked down his nose at her with a glacial brown gaze, his mouth—the mouth she had once found so sensually mesmerising!—flattened to a thin, uncompromising line above that cleft chin.

She moistened suddenly dry lips. 'I'm perfectly happy where I am, thank you, Mr Danti.'

His eyes became even more icy as he reached out and curled his fingers compellingly about the top of her arm. 'It was a statement of intent, Bella, not a question,' he assured her grimly as he began to walk towards the exit, Bella firmly anchored to his side, the stiffness of his left leg barely noticeable.

'But—'

'Do you really want to have this conversation here, in front of Dahlia and Brian's other guests?' he asked harshly as he came to a halt halfway across the crowded room to look down at her through narrowed lids.

Bella swallowed hard as she saw the unmistakeably

angry glitter in that dark gaze. 'I have absolutely no idea what conversation you're referring to—'

'Oh, I think that you do, Bella,' he retorted menacingly.

Bella thought that she did, too!

She only wished that she didn't. But Gabriel's behaviour since Claudia and Dahlia's departure all pointed to the fact that he *did* remember her from five years ago, after all…

CHAPTER TWO

'I REALLY have no idea what the two of us could possibly have to talk about, Mr Danti,' Bella told him stiltedly as he sat perfectly relaxed in the armchair across from hers in the quiet of the otherwise deserted small reception-room just down the hallway from where the family party was being held.

Gabriel's eyes narrowed on the paleness of her face as she sat stiffly upright in her own chair. 'Considering our—past acquaintance, shall we say?—I believe refraining from addressing me as "Mr Danti" in that superior tone would be a good way to begin.'

She raised her brows in what she hoped was a querying manner. 'Our past acquaintance…?'

Gabriel's mouth thinned. 'Do not play games with me, Bella!'

She shot him another glance before looking sharply away again. 'I wasn't sure you had remembered we'd met before…'

'Oh, I remember,' he growled.

She swallowed hard before speaking. 'As do I— Gabriel,' she conceded tightly.

He gave a humourless smile. 'You had absolutely no idea I would be here tonight, did you?'

Those eyes flashed deeply purple at his mocking tone. 'Why should I have done? Dahlia's name is Fabrizzi.'

'Her mother, my aunt Teresa, is my father's younger sister,' Gabriel supplied evenly.

Bella's mouth twisted. 'How sweet that you flew all the way from Italy to attend your cousin's wedding!'

Gabriel's mouth thinned at her obvious mockery. 'I no longer live in Italy, Bella.'

She looked startled. 'You don't?'

Gabriel shook his head. 'I spend most of my time at the Danti vineyards about an hour's drive away from here, but I also have a house right here in San Francisco.'

Bella could easily guess exactly where in San Francisco that house was!

She and the rest of her family had gone for a tour of the city earlier today, and part of that tour had been through an area known as Pacific Heights, where the houses were grand and gracious—and worth millions of dollars!

'Do you like living in America?' she asked curiously.

Gabriel shrugged. 'It has its—advantages.'

Bella just bet that it did! She also couldn't help wondering if Gabriel's move to America didn't have something to do with the fact that Janine Childe, the woman Gabriel had once been in love with—perhaps was still in love with?—now lived in California, too…

'Have you now finished with the polite exchange of information?' Gabriel asked.

Bella forced her gaze to remain level on his. 'What do you want from me, Gabriel?'

What did he want from her? That was an interesting question, Gabriel acknowledged grimly. Until he had arrived at the party earlier, and seen Bella across the room as she chatted with the young woman he now knew to be her sister, Gabriel would have liked to believe he had cast Bella from his mind after that single night together. But having recognised her instantly, he knew he could no longer claim that to be the case...

If anything, Isabella Scott was even more strikingly lovely than she had been five years ago, maturity having added self-assurance to a beauty that had already been breathtaking. Her violet eyes were still as stunning as ever, her hair was still long and the colour of ebony, but styled now in heavy layers so that it swung silkily against her cheeks and her throat, before cascading wildly down the length of her back. And the close fit of her violet gown revealed that her waist was still delicately slender beneath the full thrust of those perfect breasts...

What did he want from her?

He wanted not to have noticed any of those things!

His mouth set in a grim, uncompromising line. 'What do you have to give, Bella?'

Her gaze was searching as she eyed him warily, and Gabriel knew that Bella would see that he, at least, was visibly much changed from their last meeting.

The darkness of his hair was styled several inches shorter than it had once been, but the scar that ran the length of his left cheek—a constant reminder, when Gabriel looked in the mirror to shave each morning, of the guilt he carried inside—was a much more visible reminder of how much he had changed in the last five years.

Was Bella repulsed, as Gabriel was himself, by the livid ugliness of that scar?

'What do I have to give to you, in particular?' Bella repeated incredulously. 'Absolutely nothing!' she scornfully answered her own question.

Gabriel's hand moved instinctively to the jagged wound that marred his cheek. 'That, at least, has not changed,' he rasped coldly.

Bella eyed him frowningly. Why was he looking at her so contemptuously? He was the one who had seduced her only because the woman he had really wanted—the beautiful supermodel, Janine Childe— had told him their relationship was over, and that she was involved with one his fellow Formula One drivers.

That Formula One driver had been Paulo Descari. Killed in the crash that had occurred only hours after Gabriel had left Bella in his bed.

Janine Childe had tearfully claimed at the time that Gabriel had deliberately caused the accident out of jealousy, because of Paulo Descari's relationship with her.

While not convinced Gabriel would have deliberately caused that crash, five years later Bella still cringed whenever she thought that being on the rebound had been Gabriel's only reason for spending the night with her.

So how dared Gabriel now look at her with such contempt?

'I've changed, Gabriel,' she told him pointedly.

'For the better?'

Bella frowned. 'What the—'

'Did you ever marry, Bella?' Gabriel cut icily across her protest, his mouth twisting derisively as his dark gaze moved over the bareness of her left hand. 'I see not. Perhaps that is as well,' he added insultingly.

Bella took an outraged breath. 'Perhaps it's as well that you have never married either!' She came back in just as cutting a tone.

He gave a humourless smile. 'Perhaps.'

'I don't think the two of us sitting here exchanging insults is in the least harmonious to Brian and Dahlia's wedding tomorrow, do you?' she challenged.

Bella's heart sank every time she thought of attending that wedding.

She had been looking forward for weeks to this trip to San Francisco. But meeting Gabriel again, knowing he was going to be at the wedding tomorrow, too, now made it an ordeal Bella didn't even want to attempt to get through.

But she had no idea how to get out of it, either…

Gabriel watched the emotions as they flickered across Bella's beautiful and expressive face, taking a guess at the reason for her look of trepidation. 'Your parents and brother are here for the wedding also?'

'Yes,' she confirmed quietly.

He gave a ruthless smile. 'And they, like your sister just now, have no idea that the two of us have ever met before.' It was a statement, not a question.

'No,' she sighed.

Gabriel gave a mocking inclination of his head. 'And you would prefer that it remain that way?'

Bella sent him a narrow-eyed glance. 'Yes!'

'They would not understand our having spent the night together five years ago?'

'*I* don't understand it, so why should they!' Bella exclaimed. 'That night was totally out of character for me. Totally,' she added vehemently as she remembered just how eager, how *gullible* she had been.

Gabriel almost felt a hint of sympathy for Bella as he noticed that her hands were trembling slightly as she wrapped her fingers about her fluted glass sitting on the table in front of her. Almost. The fact it was champagne that bubbled inside the glass, the same wine that Gabriel had once dribbled all over this woman's body, before slowly licking it from the sensuous softness of her skin, precluded him feeling in the least sorry for Bella's obvious discomfort with this unexpected encounter.

He shrugged unsympathetically. 'I am sure that we all have things in our past that we wish had not happened.'

Bella wondered briefly if he could possibly be talking about that horrific car crash and Janine Childe's accusations, but then she saw the hard glitter in Gabriel's eyes as he looked at her, and the contemptuous curl of his top lip, and Bella realised he had been referring to her, that she was something he wished had not happened in his life, either.

She swallowed before speaking. 'Then we're both agreed that it would be better for everyone if we both just forgot our—past acquaintance?' She deliberately used his own description of that night five years ago.

The grimness of his smile lacked any genuine humour. 'If only it were that simple, Bella...'

If only.

But it wasn't. Bella, more than anyone, knew that it wasn't.

Much as she hated meeting Gabriel again like this, let alone having to sit through this insulting conversation, she also thanked God that this initial meeting had taken place this evening. It could have been so much more disastrous if it had happened at the wedding tomorrow instead...

She straightened, pushing her wine glass away from her so that she didn't risk knocking it over. 'Let's make it that simple, Gabriel,' she offered. 'We'll both just agree to stay well away from each other for the rest of my stay in San Francisco.' Which was only three more days, thank goodness; her father hadn't been able to take any longer than a week away from his medical practice.

Gabriel's gaze narrowed as he took in the smooth creaminess of Bella's skin as she flicked her hair back over her shoulders. Deliberately drawing attention to the full swell of her breasts above the fitted purple gown? Somehow, going on their previous conversation, Gabriel didn't think so.

'One dance together, Bella, and then perhaps I will consider your suggestion,' he murmured huskily.

Her eyes widened. 'One dance?'

'They have begun dancing at the party now that all of the guests have arrived,' he pointed out dryly, the earlier soft strains of background music having given way to louder dance music.

Bella looked confused. 'You want to *dance* with me?'

'Why not?' Gabriel wanted to know.

Her cheeks were very pale. 'Because—well, because—Can you dance? I mean—'

'You mean considering I am so obviously disadvantaged?' Gabriel rasped harshly, his expression grim as he acknowledged that she had obviously noticed that, as well as the scar on his face, he also favoured his left leg when he walked.

Not that the disability was anywhere near as bad as it had been five years ago. Gabriel had spent several months in a wheelchair after the accident, several more painful months after that learning to walk again. That he now had the scar and a slight limp as the only visible sign of the car crash, even if unsightly, was a miracle.

Bella gave an impatient shake of her head. 'You're about as *disadvantaged* as a stalking tiger!'

'I am pleased that you realise that,' he growled—and had the satisfaction of seeing the heated colour that instantly flooded her cheeks. 'I am definitely able to dance, Bella. As long as the music is slow,' he added challengingly.

Slow…! Bella inwardly groaned. What Gabriel really meant by that was he could dance to the sort of music where a man held the woman closely in his arms… Her mouth firmed. 'I was actually thinking of excusing myself and going to bed—'

'Was that an invitation for me to join you?' he smoothly inserted.

'No, it most certainly was not!' She flushed slightly as she almost screeched her indignation with the suggestion. Definitely an overreaction to that sort of temptation…

He shrugged. 'Then I believe I will return to the

party once you have left and ask that Brian introduce me to your parents.'

Bella glared across the table at him. 'You rat! You absolute, unmitigated—'

'I will tolerate the name calling once, Bella.' Gabriel's tone was steely. 'But only once,' he warned coldly. 'It is your choice.' Then his tone softened almost to pleasantness as he relaxed back in his chair to once again look across at her with mocking eyes. 'Consent to one dance with me or I will ask to meet your parents.'

'Why?' she groaned protestingly. 'Why do you even want to dance with me?'

'Curiosity, perhaps…?'

'Curiosity about what?' She voiced her bewilderment.

His gaze roamed over her slowly, from the darkness of her hair, across her face, and then lower, to the swell of her breasts.

Bella could barely breathe as she suffered that slow perusal, rising abruptly to her feet when she could no longer bear the deliberate insult of that gaze. 'One dance, Gabriel,' she said, abruptly giving in. 'After which, I would prefer it if you didn't so much as speak to me again!'

He smiled before rising more leisurely to his feet. 'I will let you know how I feel about that after we have danced together.'

Bella shrugged off the hold Gabriel would have taken of her arm, instead walking several feet away from him as they returned down the hallway to the function room where the party was being held.

She was nevertheless aware of everything about him,

from the mocking gleam in those dark eyes, the smile of satisfaction that curved those sculptured lips and that sexy cleft in the centre of his arrogant chin, to the lithe grace of his body as he easily compensated for the injury he had sustained in the crash five years ago.

According to the newspaper reports at the time, Gabriel's injuries had been horrific. Both legs and his pelvis crushed. Burns over much of his torso. Numerous cuts on his body, the worst of them that terrible gash to his left cheek. But as far as Bella was concerned, those scars only added to the air of danger Gabriel had already possessed in such abundance!

'Perfect,' Gabriel murmured with satisfaction when a slow ballad began to play as they entered the crowded function room. The lights had been dimmed and several couples were already dancing in the space that had been cleared in the centre of the room, including Claudia Scott and his cousin Benito. 'A pity there is not a song about a lady in purple,' Gabriel mocked, taking hold of Bella's hand as they stepped onto the dance floor.

'I would prefer it if we danced formally,' she told Gabriel stiffly as he deliberately placed his arms about her waist to draw her against him, her hands crushed against his chest.

'Did no one ever tell you that life is full of disappointments?' he murmured, a hand against her spine continuing to hold her body moulded against his as they began to move slowly in time to the music.

She pulled back slightly, her eyes glittering with anger. 'Oh, yes,' she snapped scathingly. 'Someone taught me that only too well!'

Gabriel raised dark brows. 'Then it will not surprise

you to know that I prefer that we continue to dance exactly as we are.'

Bella was past being surprised by anything that happened this evening!

In fact, she was too busy fighting her complete awareness of the hardness of Gabriel's body pressed so close to her own, his cheek resting lightly against her hair, the warmth of his hand against her spine, his other hand enveloping one of her own as he held it against his chest, to be able to concentrate on anything else.

Much as she wished it weren't so, Bella was aware of everything about Gabriel as they danced. His heat. His smell. The warmth of his breath against her temple. The sensuality of his body against hers as he moved them both to the slow beat of the music.

And Bella was also supremely aware of her own response to all of those things, her breathing soft and uneven, her skin sensitised, her breasts swelling, the nipples hardening, and a deep hot ache pooling between her thighs.

This was torture. Absolute torture.

Nor was her discomfort helped by the fact that Claudia had spotted the two of them dancing so closely together, her encouraging nods and smiles showing Bella that one member of her family, at least, was totally fooled by Gabriel's marked interest in her.

Bella pulled slightly away from him, releasing her hand from his as she deliberately put several inches between them. 'I think we've danced quite long enough, don't you?' she said stiffly, her gaze fixed on the third button of his white evening shirt.

Gabriel's mouth tightened, his gaze becoming glacial

as he inwardly acknowledged that he had definitely danced with Isabella Scott 'quite long enough'. Long enough for him to confirm that his body still responded to the voluptuousness of Bella's breasts and the warmth of her thighs pressed against his. Which was all he had wanted to know…

'Perhaps you are right,' he said and immediately stepped away from her in the middle of the dance floor.

Bella looked uncomfortable at his abrupt withdrawal, and she glanced about them self-consciously as several of the other people dancing gave them curious glances. 'You're deliberately trying to embarrass me,' she muttered irritably before she turned and walked off the dance floor, her cheeks warm with colour.

'You expressed a wish that we stop dancing.' Gabriel followed at a more leisurely pace.

'Go away, Gabriel. Just *go away*,' she repeated wearily.

Gabriel looked down at her searchingly, the glitter in those purple eyes no longer looking as if it was caused by anger. 'Are you *crying*, Bella?'

'Of course I'm not crying,' she snapped, her chin once again rising in challenge as she now met his gaze defiantly. 'It would take more than the misfortune of having met you again to make me cry!' she said scathingly. 'Now, if you will excuse me? I really would like to go to my room.'

He raised dark brows. 'You are staying here at the hotel?' It was a possibility that hadn't occurred to him.

Her eyes narrowed. 'And so what if I am?'

'I was just curious, Bella,' he pointed out.

'Are you?' She gave a mocking smile. 'I don't remember you being curious enough five years ago to be interested in anyone but yourself.'

Gabriel's mouth thinned warningly. 'Are you accusing me of having been a selfish lover?' He sounded outraged.

'No, of course not!' Bella's cheeks blazed with colour. 'This is a ridiculous conversation!' she added resentfully. 'It's time I was leaving. I won't say it's been a pleasure meeting you again, Gabriel—because we both know that isn't true!' she added before turning and walking away, her head held high.

Gabriel watched Bella as she crossed the room to make her excuses to his aunt and uncle before leaving, her hair long and gloriously silky down the length of her spine, the movements of her hips provocative beneath the purple gown, her legs appearing slender and shapely above the high heels of her purple sandals.

No, Gabriel agreed, it had certainly not been a pleasure to meet Isabella Scott again.

But it had been something…

Bella forced herself to move slowly, calmly, as she made her excuses to her hosts, Teresa and Pablo Fabrizzi, before leaving the function room to walk down the hallway to the lift, refusing to give Gabriel Danti the satisfaction of seeing her hurrying down that hallway in order to escape being the focus of his intense gaze.

She breathed easier once inside the lift, leaning weakly against one of the mirrored walls as she pressed the button to descend to the sixth floor where her room was situated.

Could anything worse than Gabriel Danti being related to her cousin's fiancée possibly have happened?

Bella couldn't think of anything.

Nor had she yet been able to think of a way to avoid being at the wedding tomorrow. But she would have to come up with something. She had to.

'You're back early,' Angela, Dahlia's younger sister, greeted warmly as Bella let herself into the sitting-room of the suite she was sharing with her siblings.

Bella put her evening bag down on the table just inside the door. 'I have a bit of a headache,' she dismissed.

'That's a pity.' Angela stood up, as tall and lithely beautiful as her older sister.

'I also thought that you've been babysitting long enough this evening and perhaps you might like to go up and join in the party for a while?' Bella added warmly, Angela having very kindly offered to take the half a dozen younger members of the English contingent of the wedding party out to a pizza restaurant for the evening, before bringing them back to the hotel and ensuring they all settled down in bed for the night.

'If you're sure you don't mind?' Angela smiled.

'Not at all,' Bella assured her. 'The dancing has only just started,' she added encouragingly.

'Take something for that headache, hmm?' Angela encouraged lightly before letting herself out of the suite.

Bella heaved a shaky sigh, taking several minutes to calm herself before going into the adjoining bedroom where her young brother lay in bed, the bedside lamp still on as he read a book. 'Everything okay, Liam?' she enquired softly as she paused beside him.

Her twelve-year-old brother grinned up at her. 'Fast asleep, as you can see.'

Bella turned, her expression softening as she looked down at the occupant of the second bed.

Her four-year-old son, Toby.

His curls were dark against the pillow, lashes of the same warm chocolate resting on his baby cheeks, his lips slightly parted as he breathed deeply, an endearing dimple in the centre of his chin.

A dimple that Bella knew would one day become a firm cleft.

Just like the one in his father's chin.

CHAPTER THREE

'YOU do not feel a woman's usual need to cry at weddings?'

Bella's back stiffened at the softly taunting sound of Gabriel's voice directly behind her as she stood with all the other wedding guests outside the church, watching the bride and groom as they posed for numerous photographs.

Hard as Bella had tried to find a reason for Toby and herself not to attend the wedding today, including a headache for herself and possible signs of a fever for Toby, ultimately she had had no choice but to concede defeat when her father had declared them both fit and well. Other than throwing herself down a flight of stairs, Bella knew she had lost that particular battle! The most she had been able to hope for was that Gabriel Danti would heed her advice from last night and just stay away from her.

The fact that he was standing behind her now showed that he hadn't!

Bella had seen him when she and the rest of her family arrived for the wedding an hour or so ago, seated in a pew further down the church. Sitting next to him was a silver-haired man whose height and facial likeness to Gabriel indicated that this was probably his father, the aristocratic Cristo Danti.

Her heart had given a jolt as she watched the two Italians unobserved before glancing down at the small boy fidgeting on the pew beside her, instantly recognising how like his father and grandfather Toby was.

As Claudia had also innocently noted the previous evening when she remarked that Gabriel reminded her of someone…!

Thank goodness Toby had disappeared with his adored uncle Liam once the service was over, and was even now playing beneath an oak tree further down the churchyard, with the group of children who had gone out for pizza the evening before.

A fact Bella took note of before she slowly turned to face Gabriel, her response to how handsome he looked in a tailored dark suit and snowy white shirt hidden behind a deliberately neutral expression as she rather wickedly responded to his comment about women usually crying at weddings. 'I'd only cry in sympathy, I'm afraid!'

Gabriel gave an appreciative smile as his hooded gaze swept admiringly over her in the knee-length dress that fitted smoothly over the curves of her slender body, a silk flower pinned behind her left ear and holding back the long length of her dark hair.

She looked cool and beautiful—and utterly self-contained.

It was an assurance that Gabriel perversely wanted to shatter. 'Perhaps that is because no man has so far asked you to become his bride?' he taunted.

Delicate colour warmed her cheeks at the intended insult. 'What on earth makes you assume that, Gabriel?' she retorted. 'Maybe I've simply chosen not to marry because I'm only too aware of how fickle a man's interest can be?' she added sweetly.

Gabriel's mouth thinned at her riposte. 'Perhaps you have been—*meeting* the wrong men…?'

'Perhaps I have.' Her gaze was openly challenging now as it met his.

Enjoyable as it was, this constant bickering with Bella would not do, Gabriel recognised ruefully. It was his cousin's wedding day, an entirely inappropriate time for open dissent between two of her guests.

Bella had obviously come to the same conclusion. 'If you'll excuse me, Gabriel? I have to rejoin my family—' She looked up at Gabriel with sharp enquiry as the fingers he had placed about her arm prevented her from leaving.

A nerve pulsed in his jaw as he looked down at her. 'We need to talk, Bella.'

'We talked yesterday evening, Gabriel—for all the good it did either of us!' she exclaimed.

'Exactly,' he agreed. 'We cannot possibly continue this estrangement between us, when our two families are now united—'

Bella's unamused laugh cut him off. 'My cousin is now married to your cousin—that hardly makes our families united!' she pointed out impatiently. 'In fact, I can't think of another occasion when the two of us will ever have to meet again!'

It was what Bella fervently hoped, at least. At the moment she would just think herself lucky if she could get through the rest of today without this whole situation blowing up in her face.

It really was unfortunate that her father happened to be a doctor, and as such perfectly able to dismiss the illnesses Bella had imagined earlier for both herself and Toby. Although, her previously mythical headache was rapidly becoming a reality during this latest conversation with Gabriel!

How could it be otherwise when she still had absolutely no idea how she was going to prevent Toby and Gabriel from coming face to face at some time during the wedding reception? If that should happen Bella had no idea what Gabriel's reaction would be... After his rejection of her, there was no way she was going to risk Toby being rejected, too, and Gabriel's menacing looks did nothing to calm her fears.

She glanced past Gabriel now as she easily recognised the sound of her young son's giggle, knowing the reason for his joyful laughter as she saw that Liam was tickling him.

Toby was a happy child, totally secure in the adoration of his mother and his indulgent grandparents, as well as his doting aunt and uncle. And Bella wished for him to remain that way.

The last three days had shown her how close the members of the Danti family were, how much they valued and loved their children. She literally quailed at the thought of what Gabriel might do if he were to ever realise that Toby was the result of their single night together five years ago, and how much of his young son's life he'd already missed out on...

'I really do have to go, Gabriel.' Her gaze avoided

meeting his now as she stepped away from him to release herself from his hold on her arm.

Gabriel watched Bella with frowning intensity as she walked away from him, that frown turning to a scowl as he heard the softness of her laughter as she was surrounded by the group of laughing children, some of them the offspring of his own cousins, the likeness to Bella of the tallest of the group making him easily recognisable as her brother Liam.

How strange it was that the people she had talked of so affectionately five years ago—her parents, her sister Claudia and her brother Liam—should now be a reality to him.

'A friend of yours…?'

Gabriel's smile stayed in place as he turned to face his father, revealing none of his inner concern as he saw the unhealthy grey pallor to the older man's face. 'I doubt Bella would think so,' he answered wryly.

'Bella?' Cristo raised silver brows before he glanced across to where Bella was now walking down the pathway chatting with her brother and another of the children.

'Isabella Scott. I met her yesterday evening at Dahlia's party,' Gabriel enlarged.

Again, he could have added. But didn't, knowing that to do so would only arouse his father's insatiable curiosity.

Cristo was the patriarch of the Danti family, and, at sixty-five and ill in health, he had begun to make definite murmurings about Gabriel marrying and producing children to continue the dynasty that Gabriel's great-grandfather had begun with the vineyards in Italy a hundred years ago, and which each succeeding generation had added to. It was Gabriel's own grandfather who had instigated the planting of the vineyards in America seventy years ago.

Gabriel had taken over the running of the California vineyards four years ago, after his father suffered a minor heart attack. But, at the age of thirty-three, unhappily for his father, Gabriel as yet felt no inclination to marry and produce the heirs necessary to continue that dynasty.

As a consequence, Cristo tended to look at every woman Gabriel so much as spoke to as a possible mother to his grandchildren.

How Bella Scott would have laughed if she had known Cristo had briefly considered her for that role!

Bella began to breathe a little easier once the wedding breakfast and speeches were over, and the guests began to wander through to the adjoining room where the evening's dancing was to begin and the socialising to continue. Giving her an ideal opportunity, she hoped, in which to excuse herself and Toby.

Her luck in keeping Toby well away from Gabriel had held during the reception, with Gabriel and his father seated at a dining-table on the furthest side of the room from where Bella sat with her own family.

Dahlia's family being Italian, there were a lot of children present, and the happy couple had chosen to seat all the children at four tables separate from their parents, both allowing the children the freedom to be themselves, and the parents to eat their meal in peace and enjoy socialising with the other adults. This arrangement had also made it impossible to know which children belonged to which parents.

Or, in Bella's case, which parent…

Taking a quick mental note of Gabriel's presence on the other side of the reception room, Bella made her excuses to her own family before slowly making her way towards the door where Dahlia and Brian stood greeting the last of their evening guests, her intention to collect Toby from where he was running riot with the other children, before making—hopefully!—an unnoticed exit.

'You are leaving so soon, Bella?'

She had counted her chickens far too early, Bella acknowledged with a sinking sensation in the pit of her stomach, looking up to see Gabriel Danti's challenging expression as he blocked her progress to the door. 'I have a headache,' she excused tightly.

He raised a mocking eyebrow. 'Weddings really do not agree with you, do they?'

'It's only the prospect of ever having to attend one of my own that I'm allergic to,' she assured him dryly.

Gabriel gave an appreciative smile. He had watched narrow-eyed as Bella made slow but determined progress down the room as she took her leave of several of the other guests, easily guessing that it was her intention to leave early.

It amused him to challenge that departure. 'I trust my own presence has not added to your—discomfort?'

'Not at all.' Those violet-coloured eyes gazed steadily into his. 'My headache is probably a delayed reaction to jet lag.'

'Of course,' Gabriel drawled. 'My father expressed a wish earlier to be introduced to you,' he added not quite truthfully.

No doubt his father would enjoy the introduction, and would draw his own—erroneous—conclusions about it, but he certainly hadn't asked for it.

'Your father?' Bella looked startled by the suggestion. 'Oh, I don't think so, Gabriel—I mean—what would be the point?' she concluded, obviously flustered.

Gabriel studied her beneath hooded lids. 'Politeness, perhaps?' he suggested blandly. 'He is, after all, now the uncle-in-law of your cousin.'

Bella didn't look convinced by that argument. 'As I told you earlier, it's doubtful that any of us will ever meet up again after today.'

He raised dark brows. 'Not even at the christening of Dahlia and Brian's first child?'

Bella hadn't thought of that! This situation really was getting extremely complicated. So much so that she wasn't sure how much longer Gabriel would remain in ignorance of the fact that she had a small son—or, more crucially, that he had one, too!

Nevertheless, she didn't feel able to make that explanation right now, so… 'That's probably years away,' she dismissed sharply. 'Who knows what any of us will be doing then?'

Personally, Bella was thinking of emigrating to Tasmania!

She tried again. 'I really do have to go, Gabriel…'

'Perhaps, as you obviously do not feel inclined to meet my father this evening, you and your family might like to visit the Danti vineyards tomorrow?'

Bella froze, a frown on her brow as she turned to look up at Gabriel with uncertain eyes. 'Why are you doing this?' she asked.

'I merely asked if you and your family would care to come to the Danti vineyards tomorrow,' he reiterated.

'You didn't "merely ask" anything, Gabriel, and you know it,' she argued. 'Just as you know that you are the very last man I wish to spend any more time with!' She was trying not to breathe hard, hoping to conceal the worst of her agitation from him.

'The very last man?' he repeated softly, eyes narrowed suspiciously. 'Why is that, Bella? What did I do to merit such a distinction? Or perhaps it is my scars that you now find so repulsive?' he added harshly.

'I'm insulted that you believe me to be so shallow,' Bella snapped to hide the fact that she had made yet another mistake where this man was concerned.

Yet when had she ever done anything else…?

Toby hadn't been a mistake!

Bella had been stunned five years ago, and not a little frightened, when she'd realised she was pregnant. But that shock and fear had quickly given way to the wonder of the new life growing inside her. Her parents' support, as well as that of Claudia and Liam, had also helped. Especially in the early months when Bella had wondered what she was going to do, how she was going to cope, and especially how she would be able to earn a living once she had a small baby to care for.

Again her parents had been wonderful, insisting that Bella remain living at home with them during her pregnancy, and for some time after Toby was born, by which time Bella had been earning enough money to be able to support them both.

Her parents' attitude to her pregnancy was doubly

admirable when Bella considered that they had done all of that without her ever telling them, or their insisting, on knowing the name of her baby's father...

But how long would they remain in ignorance of his identity if Gabriel went ahead with his intention of inviting her family to the Danti vineyards tomorrow?

She looked at Gabriel searchingly, easily noting his similarity to Toby: the darkness of his hair, the same facial structure, those dark eyes, the cleft in his chin. But was Bella only seeing those similarities because she knew of Toby's paternity? Would her parents, her siblings, see them, too?

Claudia had already seen Gabriel's likeness to 'someone', so Bella obviously couldn't risk it!

'Okay, Gabriel, I'll stay long enough for you to introduce me to your father,' she capitulated suddenly, before turning and preceding him across the room to where Cristo Danti sat in conversation with his sister.

Bella hadn't completely answered his question about being put off by his scar, Gabriel noted with a scowl as he closely followed her to make sure she didn't manage to slip away. But there had been no doubting the vehemence of her claim that he was the very last man she wished to spend any more time with.

Interestingly, Gabriel had once felt exactly the same way about Bella...

His father broke off his conversation and stood up at their approach, Gabriel frowning slightly as he noted the increased pallor in his father's face. The long flight from Italy earlier in the week, and attending Dahlia's wedding today, had obviously taken more of a toll on his father's health than was wise.

Gabriel would suggest that the two of them leave, too, once the introductions were over. 'Papa, may I present Isabella Scott? Bella, my father, Cristo Danti.'

Bella's breath caught in her throat as she looked up into that stern, aristocratic face that was so much like Gabriel's. So much like Toby's, too…

'Mr Danti,' she greeted with a coolness she was far from feeling, only her cheeks echoing her inner warmth as the older man took her hand in his before raising it gallantly to his lips.

'You are well named, Miss Scott,' Cristo Danti murmured appreciatively as he slowly released her hand.

Bella gave an awkward smile. 'Thank you.'

'You are enjoying your stay in San Francisco?'

'Very much, thank you.'

He nodded. 'I have always liked San Francisco.'

'It's certainly an interesting city,' Bella came back non-committally, very aware of Gabriel's broodingly silent presence beside her.

No doubt he was enjoying her discomfort in this stilted conversation with his father. Just as he had enjoyed being able to force this introduction on her in the first place by the veiled threat of inviting her family to the Danti vineyards when she so obviously didn't want his company at all.

'It was a beautiful wedding,' Cristo Danti continued lightly.

'Bella does not enjoy weddings.' Gabriel spoke for the first time. Dryly. Dark brows raised mockingly as Bella shot him a frowning glance.

Bella gave him another quelling glance before answering the older man. 'Dahlia is a lovely bride.'

'Yes, she is.' Cristo Danti's expression was slightly quizzical now as he glanced at his son and then back to Bella. 'Are you remaining in San Francisco long, Miss Scott?'

'Just another couple of days. And please call me Bella,' she invited.

The older man nodded. 'Perhaps before you leave you might care to—'

'Mummy, Nanny and Grandad said we're leaving now!' Toby complained irritably as he suddenly appeared at her side, the excitement of the last week, and his late night yesterday evening, obviously making him tired and slightly querulous.

Bella froze at the first sound of her son's voice, like a nocturnal animal caught in the headlights of an oncoming car.

This couldn't be happening! Not here. Not now!

Bella couldn't breathe. She couldn't move. Couldn't speak.

This was worse than anything she could ever have imagined. Worse than any of the nightmares that had plagued her dreams since she had met Gabriel again yesterday evening.

'Mummy?' Gabriel echoed beside her with soft in-credulity.

Bella forced herself to move as she slowly turned to look at him, the colour draining from her cheeks as she saw the way he was staring down so intently at Toby.

But it was Cristo Danti, the man standing at Bella's other side, who broke their frozen tableau as, his breath rasping in his throat, he slowly, but graciously, began to collapse, his eyes remaining wide and disbelieving on Toby as he did so.

As he stared at the little boy who was unmistakeably his grandson…

CHAPTER FOUR

'DO NOT speak! Not one word!' Gabriel warned harshly as he paced the hallway where he and Bella waited to hear news of his father.

Gabriel had managed to halt his father's collapse before he hit the floor. Bella had reminded Gabriel that her father was a doctor before rushing off to get him as Gabriel helped Cristo from the room with as little fuss as was possible in the circumstances.

Even so several concerned wedding guests, including the bride and groom, had followed them to hover outside the doorway of the small unoccupied room Gabriel had found to take his father to further down the hallway.

Henry Scott, Bella's father, had dealt firmly with those onlookers when he joined them a couple of minutes later, by ordering those guests back to the wedding reception and Gabriel and Bella out into the hallway while he examined his patient.

At last giving Gabriel the opportunity to deal with, to think of, the reason for his father's collapse!

That small boy—Bella's son—

His son, too…?

Bella flinched as Gabriel stopped his pacing to look down at her with dark, accusing eyes, knowing it would do no good now to deny what had been so patently obvious to Cristo Danti that he had collapsed from the shock of suddenly being confronted by his grandson.

She drew in a ragged breath. 'His name is Toby. Tobias,' she enlarged shakily. 'He's four years old.'

Gabriel's hands clenched into fists at his side. 'Four years and four months to be exact!'

Bella swallowed hard. 'Yes.'

Those dark eyes glittered menacingly. 'Where is he now?'

Bella straightened defensively. 'I took him back to sit with my mother and Liam. I— It frightened him when your father collapsed in that way.'

Gabriel looked at her coldly. 'Shock is apt to do that to a man who has already suffered three minor heart attacks in the last four years!'

Bella hadn't known that about Cristo Danti. Not that it would have made a lot of difference if she had known. Neither Gabriel nor his father were part of her own or Toby's lives.

At least, they hadn't been until now…

Gabriel, she had no doubt, wanted—no, he would demand—some answers from her concerning that. Just as the look on her own father's face, as he had looked first at Cristo Danti and then Gabriel, had told Bella he would no doubt like some answers, too, once he had finished examining his patient!

She gave a shaky sigh. 'I don't think this is the time or place to discuss this, Gabriel—'

'The time and place to discuss this would have been

almost five years ago when you first discovered you were pregnant!'

'As I recall you were no longer around to talk to almost five years ago!'

His mouth tightened. 'It was well publicised that I was in Italy at the time, at the Danti vineyards, recovering from the injuries I sustained in the car crash!'

Bella's eyes flashed deeply purple. 'And you seriously think that I was going to follow you there and tell you the news!'

'You had no right to keep my son's existence from me!' A nerve pulsed in Gabriel's tightly clenched jaw.

She shook her head. 'You gave up any right you had to know about Toby by the fact that you never phoned me as you promised and only slept with me that night out of jealousy and spite because of your ex-girlfriend's relationship with Paulo Descari!'

Gabriel's face darkened dangerously. 'I—'

'Could the two of you please save your—*discussion*—until later?' Henry Scott had opened the door of the room where Gabriel could see his father lying back on one of the sofas. 'I think your father has merely suffered a severe shock rather than another heart attack, Mr Danti, but to be on the safe side I would like to get him to a hospital for a check-up.'

'Daddy…?' Bella looked across at her father uncertainly.

He gave her a reassuring smile. 'It's okay, Bella,' he said gently. 'For the moment let's just concentrate on getting Mr Danti to hospital, hmm?'

Bella didn't need to be told any plainer that her father had guessed Toby's relationship to the two Danti men.

What must her father think of her?

More to the point, what must he think of the fact that Gabriel Danti, of all men, was unmistakeably the father of his grandson?

'I would like to see my son.'

Bella had remained behind at the hotel to put Toby to bed when Gabriel and her father had accompanied Cristo Danti to the hospital. But she hadn't made any attempt to go to bed herself. Had known—had been absolutely certain, in fact—that Gabriel would return once he had assured himself of his father's recovery.

It was almost two o'clock in the morning, but nevertheless Bella had been expecting the knock on the door of the sitting-room between the bedroom she shared with Claudia and the one Liam shared with Toby. She had changed out of the dress she had worn to the wedding, and into fitted jeans and a black T-shirt, in anticipation of this meeting.

Gabriel looked grim, to say the least, that scar down his left cheek more noticeable in his harshly set features, his eyes fierce as he looked down at her challengingly.

Bella opened the door wider so that Gabriel could step inside the suite. 'Toby is asleep,' she told him calmly as she closed the door behind him before turning to face him.

That scar on Gabriel's cheek seemed to pulse as he clenched his jaw tightly. 'Nevertheless, I wish to see him.'

'How is your father?'

'Tests have shown your father's original diagnosis to be the correct one. It was shock that caused my father's collapse and not a heart attack. He is to remain in hospital overnight for observation, but they expect to discharge him in the morning. Isabella—'

'Did my father return with you from the hospital?' Bella had already had one long, uncomfortable conversation with her mother this evening, she wasn't sure she would be up to another one with her father once Gabriel had left.

Gabriel gave a terse nod. 'He told me to tell you he will speak with you in the morning.'

Her eyes widened. 'He knew you were coming here?' Even as she asked the question Bella knew the answer; how else would Gabriel have known which suite to come to in order to see her if her father hadn't told him?

Gabriel's mouth thinned. 'He realised I would want to see my son again before I left, yes.'

Bella flinched every time he said that. No matter what his biological make-up might be, Toby was her son, not Gabriel's.

She gave a firm shake of her head. 'I don't think that's a good idea—'

Gabriel's scornful laugh cut across her refusal. 'Any concern I might have felt for your wishes died the moment I discovered you had kept my son's existence from me for over four years!' He made no effort to hide his contempt.

He had a son!

Gabriel still found it incredible that such a person existed. That there was a small, tousle-haired boy in the adjoining bedroom with his dark curls and eyes, and a small dimple in the centre of his still-babyish chin...

Having been denied all knowledge of him for over

four years, Gabriel had no intention of letting that continue a minute—even a second—longer!

'Where is he, Isabella?' he rasped furiously, her panicked glance towards the door to the right of the room enough for Gabriel to stride towards it determinedly.

'Where are you going?'

Gabriel ignored Bella's protest as he gently pushed that door open, recognising the sleeping boy in the first bed as Liam Scott before he turned his attention to the much smaller child in the second bed.

His breath caught in his throat as he looked down at the little boy he now knew to be his own son. Toby. Tobias.

He was beautiful, Gabriel acknowledged achingly. Absolutely beautiful. A perfect combination of his two parents.

Toby had Gabriel's hair colour and that dimple on his chin that would one day become a cleft exactly like those of his father and grandfather. The smoothness of Toby's brow and the long lashes that swept his cheeks were his mother's, as was that perfect bow of a mouth with its fuller top lip.

His!

This beautiful child was of his loins. Of his blood.

Bella could only stand helplessly by as Gabriel dropped to his knees beside Toby's bed, her protest strangling in her throat as Gabriel reached out a hand to touch the little boy, the stroke of his fingers against one slightly chubby cheek so gentle, so tender, that Toby didn't even stir.

Her heart felt as if it were breaking, shattering, as she watched the rush of love that softened Gabriel's harshly hewn features. As she saw that love glowing in his broodingly dark gaze as he continued to stare at his son in wonder.

And she knew without a doubt that the last four years of sharing Toby only with her family were over...

'I need a drink,' Gabriel stated flatly some time later when he had reluctantly left his son's bedside to return to the sitting-room, not waiting for Bella's reply but moving to the mini-bar to help himself to one of the small bottles of whisky before pouring it into a glass and drinking most of it in one swallow. 'So, Isabella,' he stated as he looked across at her grimly. 'What do you suggest we do about this situation?'

'What situation?' she repeated sharply, her stance wholly defensive as she stood across the room.

Gabriel looked at her through narrowed lids. He had made love with this woman a little over five years ago. That lovemaking had resulted in a child. A child whose existence she had deliberately kept from him. For that alone Isabella deserved no mercy from him.

His mouth thinned. 'The situation that Toby, despite what you may have decided to the contrary, deserves to know both of his parents rather than just one!'

Her throat moved convulsively, but otherwise she maintained her defensive stance. 'As I have already explained—'

'As far as you are concerned, I gave up the right to know my own child because *you* believe I only went to bed with you out of jealousy and spite over my ex-girl-friend's relationship with Paulo Descari,' Gabriel coldly repeated her earlier accusation. 'Neither jealousy nor spite were part of my emotions that night, Isabella,' he added curtly. 'And I certainly wasn't feeling those emotions at the time of the accident the following day either,' he bit out deliberately.

Bella moistened lips that had gone suddenly dry as she sensed the leashed violence in him. 'I didn't suggest they were, Gabriel. You did.'

He gave a scathing snort. 'It is impossible not to do so considering Janine's claims following the accident,' Gabriel snarled. 'The official enquiry proved my innocence in the matter. But perhaps you would prefer to believe that I am responsible for the accident that caused the death of two other men, rather than take my word for what happened that day?'

Bella felt the colour drain from her cheeks even as she stared at Gabriel. No, of course she didn't prefer to believe that Gabriel had deliberately caused the accident that had killed two other men. She didn't believe it!

Gabriel might be guilty of many things, but Bella certainly hadn't ever believed him to be guilty of that.

Gabriel looked at her coldly. 'I did *not* cause the accident, Isabella,' he repeated firmly. 'That was only the hysterical accusation of a woman who took advantage of the fact that I was unconscious for several days following the crash, and so was unable to deny those accusations.'

And that accusation hadn't been the reason Bella had made no effort to contact Gabriel following the car crash, either…

How could she possibly have just arrived at the hospital and asked to be allowed to see Gabriel when they had only spent a single night together?

If Gabriel wanted to see her again, Bella had reasoned, then he would contact her just as he'd said he would. Until he chose to do that—if he chose to do that!—she would just have to get on with her life as best she could.

Her pregnancy had been something Bella simply hadn't taken into account when she had made that decision.

Weeks later, after her pregnancy was confirmed, Bella had been forced to make choices, both for herself and her baby. Gabriel's failure to phone had simply reinforced Bella's suspicion that he would want nothing to do with them. Or if he did, he had the power to take her baby away from her. Something Bella would never allow to happen. It was too late now, far too late, for her to explain or undo any of those choices…

Gabriel watched the emotions that flickered across Bella's beautiful and expressive face, too fleeting for him to be able to discern any of them accurately. 'I did not cause the accident, Isabella, but that does not mean I have not carried the guilt of Paulo and Jason's deaths with me every day since.'

'But why?' She looked totally confused now.

Gabriel turned away to look out of the window at the San Francisco skyline.

How could he ever explain to her how he had felt five years ago when he'd regained consciousness and learnt of Paulo Descari and Jason Miller's deaths? Of Janine's hysterical accusations?

Added to that, Gabriel had felt utter despair, even helplessness, at the seriousness of his own injuries.

The cuts and burns to his body that were still visible, five years later, in the scar on his face and those that laced across his chest, back, and legs. The crushing of his pelvis and legs had kept him confined to bed for months, with the added possibility that he might never walk again.

Worst of all, worse even than Paulo and Jason's deaths, Janine's duplicity, had been the knowledge that their night together had meant so little to Bella that—

No!

Gabriel refused to go there. He had not thought of Bella's desertion for almost five years. He would not—could not—think of it now.

Now he would think only of Toby. Of his *son*. And Bella's second betrayal…

He turned back to face Bella, his expression utterly implacable. 'Toby is all that is important now,' Gabriel told her icily. 'I will return at ten o'clock tomorrow—or rather, today,' he corrected, 'at which time you and Toby will be ready to accompany me—'

'I'm not going anywhere with you, Gabriel, and neither is Toby,' Bella cut in immediately.

'At which time,' he repeated in, if possible, even icier tones, 'you and Toby will be ready to accompany me on a visit to my father. Toby's grandfather,' he added harshly.

Bella's second denial died unspoken on her lips.

She had talked with her mother earlier tonight. Or rather, her mother had talked with her. A conversation in which her mother had assured Bella that the relationship between herself and Gabriel was their own affair, and for the two of them alone to unravel. However, speaking as a grandmother, she had added, she had nothing but sympathy for Cristo Danti and the fact that he had only learnt this evening of his grandson's existence. That knowledge had been obviously so emotionally profound it had resulted in the older man's collapse.

An irrefutable fact against which Bella had no defence. Either earlier or now.

Her shoulders were stiff with tension. 'Firstly, let me tell you that I deeply resent your use of emotional blackmail in order to get me to do what you want—'

'Would you rather I pursued a legal claim, instead?' Gabriel challenged contemptuously.

Bella swallowed hard even as she refused to lower her gaze from his. 'That would take months, by which time I would be safely back in England.'

'I will have my lawyers apply for an immediate injunction to prevent you, or Toby, from leaving this country,' Gabriel warned scathingly. 'I am a Danti, Isabella,' he reminded her.

Her eyes flashed darkly purple at his underlying threat. 'Secondly,' she pointedly resumed her earlier conversation, 'despite the fact that I resent your methods, I am nevertheless perfectly aware of your father's claim as Toby's grandfather—'

'But not my own as his father!' Gabriel was so furiously angry now that there was a white line about the firmness of his mouth and his body was rigid with suppressed emotion.

Bella looked at him sadly, knowing this conversation was achieving nothing except to drive a distance between the two of them that was even wider than the gaping chasm that already existed.

She had known when she met Gabriel again yesterday that he wasn't the same man she had been so attracted to five years ago that she had forgotten, or simply put aside, every vestige of caution in order to spend the night in his arms.

This Gabriel was scarred on the inside as well as the outside and the coldness of his anger concerning her having kept Toby's existence a secret from him was worse than any emotional accusations might have been.

She sighed. 'Ten o'clock, I believe you said?'

Gabriel's eyes narrowed on her, searching for any sign of deception in her eyes or expression. He could see none. Only a weary acceptance of a situation she could do nothing to change.

The tension in his shoulders relaxed slightly. 'We will sit down together with Toby first and explain my own and my father's relationship to him.'

'Isn't that a little premature?' Bella protested.

'In my opinion it is almost four and a half years too late!' Gabriel snapped.

'It will only confuse Toby when you have no active role in his life—'

His scornful laugh cut off her protest. 'Do you *seriously* believe that is going to continue?'

Bella looked at him, knowing by the implacability in Gabriel's expression as he looked down the length of his arrogant nose at her—the same implacability in his tone whenever he now referred to her as *Isabella*—that it wasn't. That it was Gabriel's intention to take an extremely active role in Toby's life in future.

Precisely where that left her, Bella had no idea…

CHAPTER FIVE

'DOES Grandad live in one of these big houses?'

'He certainly does, Toby,' Gabriel answered him indulgently.

Bella would never cease to be amazed by the resilience of children and by her own child's in particular.

Having lain awake long into the night dreading, planning, how best to break the news to Toby that Gabriel Danti was his father and Cristo Danti was his grandfather, she had been totally surprised by Toby taking the whole thing in his four-year-old stride.

Even his initial shyness at suddenly being presented with a father had quickly given way to excitement as he was strapped into the back of Gabriel's open-topped sports car to make the drive over to the house where his grandfather was anxiously waiting to meet him after being discharged from the hospital earlier this morning.

Bella's own emotions were far less simplistic as she stared out of the car window, seeing none of the beauty of the Pacific Ocean in the distance, her thoughts all inwards.

Her life, and consequently Toby's, was back in

England. In the small village where she had bought a cottage for the two of them to live in, once she had been financially able to do so, after living with her parents for the first two years of Toby's life. She liked living in a village, as did Toby, and he was due to start attending the local school in September.

This situation with Gabriel, his veiled threats of the night before, made Bella wonder exactly when she could expect to return to that life.

Not that she was able to read any of Gabriel's thoughts or feelings this morning. He was wearing sunglasses now, and his mood when he had arrived at the hotel earlier had been necessarily upbeat for Toby's benefit, his attitude towards Bella one of strained politeness. Only the coldness in Gabriel's eyes earlier, whenever he had chanced to look at her, had told Bella of the anger he still felt towards her.

The anger he would probably always feel towards her for denying him knowledge of his son for the first four years of Toby's life…

'Here we are, Toby,' Gabriel turned to tell his son after steering the car into the driveway, smiling as he saw the excitement on his son's face as they waited for the electrically operated gates to open so that he could drive them down to the house.

His son…!

Even twelve hours later Gabriel still had trouble believing he had a son. A bright, happy, and unaffected little boy who had taken the news of Gabriel being his father much more pragmatically than Gabriel had responded the evening before to learning that he had a son.

Gabriel glanced at Bella now from behind his dark sunglasses, his mouth thinning as he noted the pallor to her cheeks, the lines of strain beside her eyes and mouth.

Deservedly so!

Whatever claims Janine Childe had made against him five years ago did not change the fact that Bella hadn't so much as attempted to inform him she was expecting his child, that she had actually borne him a son, or that she had then brought Toby up with no knowledge whatsoever of his father or his father's family.

'Your own family are all aware now of Toby's paternity?'

Bella was glad she was wearing sunglasses to hide the sudden tears that had welled up in her eyes at the emotional breakfast she had shared earlier with her parents and siblings.

There had been no words of rebuke or disapproval from her parents, only their gentle understanding as she explained the situation of five years ago to them—and Claudia's demand, as the two sisters had returned to their hotel suite once the meal was over, that Bella 'tell all' about the night she had spent in Gabriel's bed. A curiosity Bella had chosen not to satisfy.

She didn't even want to think about that night, let alone relive, even verbally, how completely she had been infatuated with the darkly seductive Gabriel Danti five years ago!

'Yes,' she confirmed huskily.

Gabriel nodded in satisfaction as he accelerated the black sports car down the driveway to the house that was just as grand as Bella would have expected of this prestigious area of San Francisco. It was large and gabled, slightly Victorian in style, with its redbrick structure and the white frames to the stained-glass windows.

'You're sure this…visit…isn't going to give your father a relapse?' Bella hung back reluctantly on the gravelled driveway once they were all out of the car.

Gabriel had removed his sunglasses and left them in the car, his expression mocking as he glanced down at her. 'On the contrary, I believe its possibilities will achieve the opposite.'

Bella looked up at him, a little confused by the cryptic comment. 'Sorry?'

His mouth tightened. 'Later, Isabella,' he said curtly. 'You and I are going to talk again later.'

Bella didn't much like the sound of that.

And she was really starting to dislike the way Gabriel kept calling her *Isabella* in that coldly contemptuous way!

Once Gabriel had left the previous night Bella had thought long and hard about his claim that he hadn't made love with her five years ago, or spent the night with her, in an effort to make Janine Childe jealous. After hours and hours of going over the situation in her head, Bella had finally come to the conclusion that it really didn't matter what Gabriel's reasons had been.

They had spent only that single night together. Admittedly it had been an intensely passionate, even erotic night, but nevertheless that was all it had been. On Gabriel's side, anyway. That Bella had experienced strong feelings for him after that night didn't change the fact that Gabriel hadn't felt that way about her.

As the last five years of silence on Gabriel's part showed...

He had never made any attempt to contact her again after that night although that had been his promise. Admittedly Gabriel had been involved in the car crash later that day, but he hadn't suffered memory loss. Once he had recovered enough to be able to talk, to receive visitors, that needn't have stopped him from getting in touch. Not too much to ask if Gabriel really had been interested in seeing her again. Which he obviously hadn't... That was not the kind of man she wanted as a father for her child!

She shook her head. 'I don't think we have anything left to talk about, Gabriel,' she told him firmly.

Gabriel gave a brief, humourless smile. 'We have not even begun to talk yet, Isabella!'

His father was waiting for them in the warmth of the plant-filled conservatory at the back of the house, Gabriel appreciating that the informality of such surroundings was exactly what was needed to put a four-year-old boy at his ease.

That his father found the meeting highly emotional Gabriel had no doubts, Cristo's voice husky with suppressed tears as Toby joined him and he allowed the little boy to water the orchids for him.

'I am neglecting your mother, Toby,' Cristo apologised some minutes later as he straightened. 'You may continue to water if you wish, Toby, or you may come and sit with us while your mother and I talk.'

Bella knew exactly which choice her young son would make; like most small boys, Toby had absolutely no interest in the conversation of adults!

'Bella.' Cristo Danti's voice was deep with emotion as he crossed the room to where she had sat in one of the half a dozen cane chairs watching him and Toby together. He took her hand in his to raise it to his lips as she stood up. 'Thank you for bringing Toby to see me,' he told her, his eyes slightly moist as he looked at her.

Bella felt her own tears clogging her throat as she looked at Gabriel's father, not able to discern any reproach in the directness of that brown gaze, only the slight sheen of the tears that he made no effort to hide from her.

Bella was very aware of the menacingly silent Gabriel standing beside her. 'I—' she moistened her lips nervously '—I really don't know what to say,' she stuttered, aware that statement was painfully inadequate and yet totally true.

'Gabriel has already explained all that needs to be explained.' Cristo Danti smiled at her reassuringly. 'All that really matters is that you and Toby are here now.'

Bella, besides feeling the heavy weight of guilt at Cristo Danti's complete acceptance of a situation that yesterday evening had caused his collapse, also wondered exactly what Gabriel had explained...

'You're very kind,' she told the older man as she squeezed his hand before releasing it.

'Obviously Isabella and I have much to talk about yet, Papa,' Gabriel spoke abruptly beside her. 'If you and Toby will excuse us for a few minutes...?'

Bella felt a sense of rising panic at the suggestion, not sure she was up to another confrontation with Gabriel at the moment. She hadn't slept much during what had been left of the previous night, and the morning had already been traumatic enough with the conversation with her family, followed by Gabriel's arrival at the hotel and their explanation to Toby, and now this meeting with Cristo Danti.

But a single glance at the grim determination of Gabriel's set expression was enough to tell Bella that she didn't have any choice in the matter!

'Toby…?' she prompted lightly to gain her young son's attention from watering the plants. 'Will you be okay while I just go and have a little chat with—with—your father?' That didn't get any easier with actually saying out loud!

'Of course.' Toby beamed across at her unconcernedly.

Bella wished at that moment that her young son weren't quite so gregarious; obviously she wasn't going to get any help at all from Toby in avoiding another confrontation with Gabriel.

To Toby, Bella knew, this was obviously all just a big adventure; he had absolutely no idea of the underlying tensions—or the possible repercussions!—of Gabriel Danti being his father and Cristo Danti being his grandfather.

Bella wanted to make sure it remained that way…

'I am sure Toby and I will be able to keep each other amused, Bella,' Cristo assured her.

She gave him a grateful smile, that smile fading as Gabriel stood back politely to allow her to precede him into the main house. Polite, even coldly polite, Bella could deal with—she just didn't think that politeness was going to last for very long once she and Gabriel were alone together!

'He'll probably drown your poor father's orchids for

him,' Bella murmured ruefully as Gabriel moved ahead to open a door further down the hallway.

Gabriel glanced back at her, his gaze hooded. 'I doubt my father will mind, do you?' he said pointedly as he pushed open the door to the room before standing back to allow her to enter.

It was a book-lined room, Bella noted with dismay, much like the study in the Danti's English home in Surrey where she and Gabriel had first met.

Gabriel was also aware of the irony of their surroundings as he quietly closed the door behind them before moving to sit behind the green leather-topped desk, his gaze narrowed on Bella as she chose not to sit in the chair facing that desk—and him!—but instead moved to look out of the huge picture-window, her back firmly turned towards him.

She had pulled her hair back today and secured it up in a loose knot at her crown, her exposed neck appearing fragile in its slenderness, her shoulders narrow beneath the soft material of the cream blouse she wore with black fitted trousers.

She appeared slight, even delicate, but Gabriel knew that appearance to be deceptive—Isabella Scott was more than capable of defending both herself and Toby if the need should arise. In Toby's case, as far as Gabriel was concerned, it didn't. Bella herself was a different matter, however…

His mouth firmed in exasperation. 'Ignoring me will not make me go away, Isabella!'

She turned, her smile rueful. 'If only!'

Gabriel regarded her coldly. 'You have had things completely your own way for the last five years—'

'What *things*?' she came back tartly, her body tense. 'I was twenty-one years old at the time, Gabriel. Only twenty-one!' she emphasised. 'Having a baby wasn't in my immediate plans back then, let alone one whose father wasn't even living in the same country as me when that baby was born!'

'It does no good to get angry, Isabella—'

'It does *me* good, Gabriel!' she contradicted him vehemently. 'You have made it clear you disapprove of my actions five years ago, so I'm just trying to explain to you that I did what I thought was best —'

'For whom?' Gabriel sat back in his chair to look at her intently.

'For everyone!'

Gabriel's jaw clenched. 'In what way was it *best* for Toby that he was not even aware of his father or his father's family? In what way was it *best* for him that he did not have the comforts that being a Danti could have given him—?'

'Toby hasn't gone without a single thing—'

'He has gone without a *father*!' Gabriel's voice was icy cold, his accusation indisputable.

Bella drew in a controlling breath, very aware that letting this conversation dissolve into another slanging match would settle none of the things that stood between herself and Gabriel. The main one, of course, being Toby...

She shook her head. 'I assure you that my own parents have been wonderful,' she told him huskily. 'Claudia and Liam, too. And once I was able to work I made sure that Toby wanted for nothing.'

'At what did you work?' Gabriel asked.

Bella gave a grimace. 'I was completely at a loss as to what job I could do once I discovered I was pregnant. But I had written my thesis at university on the life of Leonardo da Vinci. My tutor thought it might be good enough for publishing, so during the months of my pregnancy I approached a publishing company to see if they were interested. With a lot more hard work, and another fifty thousand words, they accepted it. I was fortunate in that its publication coincided with a fiction book on a similar theme that was very popular at the time.' She gave a rueful shrug. 'I've had two books at the top of the non-fiction bestseller list in the last three years,' she added quietly.

Gabriel realised now where Bella's self-assurance and that air of quiet self-containment came from. In spite of her unexpected pregnancy, and the difficulty involved with being a single mother, Bella had still managed to achieve success in her chosen career.

'That is—commendable.'

Bella gave a tight smile. 'But unexpected?'

Gabriel couldn't deny that Bella's obvious financial independence was something he hadn't taken into consideration when contemplating a solution to their present problem.

Although perhaps he should have done?

Her suite at the hotel would have been costly, and Bella's clothes were obviously designer-label, as were the T-shirt and shorts Toby was wearing today.

'Perhaps,' he allowed after a pause. 'But ultimately it changes nothing,' he pointed out.

Bella gave a puzzled frown. 'I'm sorry...I don't understand?'

'Toby is *my* son—'

'I believe I've already acknowledged that fact,' she snapped.

Gabriel eyed her mockingly. 'Undeniable, is it not?' he murmured with satisfaction, Toby's likeness to both himself and his father so obvious it had caused his father to collapse with the shock of it. Gabriel's mouth tightened. 'The only solution open to us is that we will be married as soon as I am able to make the arrangements—'

'No!' Bella protested forcefully, her expression one of horror. 'No, Gabriel,' she repeated determinedly, her chin once again raised in the familiar air of challenge. 'I have no intention of marrying you, either now or in the future.'

Bella was absolutely astounded that Gabriel should have suggested marriage to her. Suggested it? Gabriel hadn't *suggested* anything—he had stated it as a foregone conclusion!

Five years ago Bella had considered all of the options, despite the complication of Gabriel's feelings for Janine Childe, if she were to go to Gabriel and tell him of her pregnancy.

The offer of his financial help was obviously one of them, and Bella had rejected that on principle; no matter how hard a struggle it might be for her to manage on her own, she did not want to be beholden to Gabriel Danti in that way.

That he might want to marry her, for the sake of the baby, had been a less likely option considering they had only had a one-night stand, and one that Bella had rejected even more vehemently than she had the idea of Gabriel's financial help.

She didn't want to marry anyone just because they had made a child together.

'Do you not want to marry me because you lied when you said you are not repulsed by my scars?' Gabriel rasped harshly, his eyes narrowed to dangerous slits, a nerve pulsing in his tightly clenched jaw.

Bella shook her head. 'I'm not in the least repulsed by them,' she insisted quietly.

His gaze was glacial. 'Most women would be.'

'Well I'm not "most women",' Bella said, furiously. 'Gabriel, acknowledge Toby as your son, by all means, but please leave me out of the equation,' she pleaded.

Gabriel's mouth twisted. 'That might be a little difficult when you are Toby's mother.'

She shook her head. 'I'm sure we can work out some sort of visiting—' She broke off as Gabriel stood up abruptly.

'Is that what you want for Toby?' he asked harshly, the scar on his cheek seeming to stand out more severely. 'You want him to become nothing more than a human parcel that passes between the two of us?'

'It doesn't have to be like that,' she protested emotionally.

'If the two of us do not marry that is exactly what it will be like,' Gabriel insisted impatiently.

Bella swallowed hard, her expression pained. 'You think Toby will fare any better as the only lynchpin between two people who don't love each other but are married to each other?'

'You have said you do not find my more obvious scars— unacceptable.' Gabriel moved close enough now to see the slight flush that slowly crept into her cheeks, and the rapid rise and fall of her breasts beneath the cream blouse.

'I don't.' She frowned. 'But that doesn't mean I like the idea of marrying you!'

Bella couldn't think straight when Gabriel was standing so close to her. Couldn't concentrate on anything with the heat of his dark gaze moving slowly over her body to linger on the firm thrust of her breasts, breasts that responded in tingling awareness, the nipples suddenly hard against the soft material of her bra and blouse. A warm, aching surge between her thighs made her shift uncomfortably.

She moistened lips that had gone suddenly dry. 'Physical attraction is not a basis for marriage, either.' Even as she said the words Bella was aware that her denial lacked any force.

'Surely you will agree it is a start?' Gabriel murmured huskily, a look of deep satisfaction in his eyes.

She could barely breathe as Gabriel easily held her gaze with his, allowing her to see the warmth burning deep within those dark brown eyes. Then he stepped close enough for her to be aware of the hard press of his arousal against her and his head lowered with the obvious intention of claiming her mouth with his own...

It was like a dam bursting as their mouths fused hotly together. Bella's fingers became entangled in the dark thickness of Gabriel's hair as their bodies pressed demandingly against each other. Their kiss deepened fiercely, spiralling out of control when Gabriel's tongue moved to duel with hers as he enticed her to claim him as he was claiming her.

Bella was so hungry for this. The aching emptiness

inside her was completely filled when Gabriel pushed the soft material of her blouse aside to cup and hold her breast, the soft pad of his thumb moving urgently, arousingly, over the hardened nub.

Bella almost ripped Gabriel's shirt undone as she satisfied her own need to touch his naked flesh. The hard ripple of muscle. The dark silkiness of the hair that covered his chest. Fingers tracing the fine lines of the scars he still bore from his accident five years ago, Gabriel responding to those caresses with a low groan in his throat.

She offered no resistance as Gabriel snapped the back fastening to her bra to release her breasts to his questing hands, her throat arching, breath gasping as Gabriel's lips parted from hers to draw one hardened nipple into the hot, moist cavern of his mouth, and his tongue flickered and rasped over that sensitive nub as his hand cupped and caressed her other breast.

The ache between Bella's thighs became hot and damp, an aching void needing to be filled as she felt the hardness of Gabriel's arousal, rubbing herself against him as the hardness of his thighs pulsed with the same need. She offered no resistance when Gabriel's hands moved to cup her bottom and he lifted her so that she was sitting on the front of the desk, parting her legs so that he could move inside them, his hardness now centred on the throbbing nub that nestled there.

Bella groaned with satisfaction as Gabriel lay her back on the desktop so that he could suckle the nakedness of her breasts with the same heated rhythm as his erection thrust against the hardened nub between her thighs. Bella's breathing became shallow, a husky rasp, as her release began to burn, to explode, taking her over the edge of reason—

A soft knock on the study door sounded before Cristo Danti informed them, 'Toby and I will be outside in the garden when you have finished talking.'

Gabriel had moved sharply away from Bella the moment the knock sounded on the door, his mouth tightening now as he saw Bella's horrified expression before she pushed up from the desk and moved away from him to turn her back and rearrange her clothes. 'Isabella and I will join you shortly,' he answered his father distractedly as he pulled his shirt together.

'There is no rush,' his father assured pleasantly before he could be heard walking back down the hallway.

Gabriel frowned at Bella's back as she tried, and failed, to refasten her bra with fingers that were obviously shaking too badly to complete the task. 'Here, let me,' he rasped before moving to snap the hook back into place.

'Thank you,' she said stiffly, making no effort to turn as she quickly buttoned her blouse. 'I—I don't know what to say! That was— I'm not sure what happened…'

'Oh, I think you are well aware of what almost happened, Bella,' he drawled. 'It pleases me that you did not lie concerning my scars,' he added huskily.

Bella hadn't lied about Gabriel's physical scars; his inner ones were another matter, however…

She shook her head. 'I don't usually behave in that— in that way!'

'It is perhaps some time since you last had a man,' Gabriel pointed out dryly.

Bella turned sharply, a frown between her eyes as she

glared at him. Exactly what sort of woman did Gabriel think she was?

The sort of woman who allowed herself to almost be made love to on a desktop, apparently!

The sort of woman who had almost ripped Gabriel's shirt from his back in her need to touch his naked flesh!

Bella closed her eyes in self-disgust as she tried to reassemble her thoughts. She most certainly was *not* that sort of woman! Gabriel probably wouldn't believe her even if she were to tell him—which she had no intention of doing; it was bad enough that she knew how out of character her response to Gabriel had been without him knowing it, too!—that there hadn't been a man in her life on an intimate level since that single night she had spent with Gabriel five years ago.

How could there have been? For nine months of that time she had been pregnant with Toby. And since Toby's birth Bella had centred all of her attention on him. She certainly hadn't wanted to add any more confusion to his young life by giving him a succession of 'uncles'!

She drew in a deep controlling breath before opening her eyes to glare at Gabriel. He had pulled his shirt back onto his shoulders, but hadn't bothered to refasten it, and Bella could now see the fine pattern of scars that marred the smoothness of the olive-coloured skin. With his dark hair in disarray from her recently entangled fingers, and that unbuttoned shirt revealing his scarred chest, Gabriel looked more piratical than ever. Certainly more rakishly attractive than Bella felt comfortable with!

She raised dark, mocking brows. 'I'm sure it's been much longer for me than the last time you "had" a woman!'

Gabriel continued to look at her levelly for several tense seconds, and then a humourless smile curved those sculptured lips. 'Not all women are as—understanding, about physical imperfection, as you appear to be,' he said dryly.

Bella couldn't believe that. If Gabriel were any more perfect she would be a gibbering wreck!

'I believe that what took place just now proved that we would not lack physical gratification in our marriage,' he commented wickedly.

Bella's mouth tightened. 'We are *not* getting married,' she repeated firmly.

Gabriel looked unconcerned by her vehemence. 'Oh, I think that we are.'

'Really?' She frowned her uncertainty, not liking the assurance in Gabriel's tone at all.

Any more than she liked the smile that he now gave her. 'Really,' he drawled confidently. 'I am sure you must be aware of the benefits to you in such a marriage—'

'If you're referring to what happened between us just now, then forget it!' Bella glared at him. 'I can find that sort of "benefit" with any number of men!'

Gabriel's mouth compressed. 'There will be no other men in your life once we are married, Isabella. Now I am assured of your response, we will be married in the fullest sense of the word. As an only child myself, I am hoping it will be a marriage that will result in us having more children together. Lots of brothers and sisters for Toby.'

Bella was thrown momentarily off balance by that last claim as she easily imagined having more sons and daughters that looked exactly like Gabriel.

She gave a fierce shake of her head. 'You can't seriously want to spend the rest of your life married to a woman who doesn't love you—'

'Any more than you would wish to be married to a man who does not love you,' he acknowledged curtly. 'But the alternative is even less palatable. A long—and no doubt very public—legal battle for custody of Toby,' Gabriel said grimly.

Bella gasped as her greatest fear was made a possibility. 'You would do that to Toby?'

Gabriel gave a shrug. 'If you leave me with no other choice, yes.'

Bella looked at him searchingly, knowing by the utter implacability of Gabriel's expression that he meant every word he had just said. Marriage to him, or Gabriel would involve them all in a very messy legal battle.

She breathed in deeply. 'All right, Gabriel, I'll think about marrying you—'

'Thinking about it is not enough, Isabella,' he cut in harshly. 'Especially,' he added more softly, that dark gaze narrowed on her speculatively, 'when I suspect you are only delaying the inevitable in order that you and Toby might return to England tomorrow, as originally planned, with your family, yes?'

That was exactly the reason Bella was delaying giving Gabriel a definite answer!

She chewed on her bottom lip. 'I don't believe it's inevitable that the two of us will marry—'

'I beg to differ, Isabella.'

Her eyes flashed deeply purple. 'You've never begged in the whole of your privileged life!'

He lifted an autocratic eyebrow. 'And I am not about

to do so now, either,' he said. 'I want your answer before you leave here today.'

'You'll have my answer when I'm damned well ready to give it!' she flashed back heatedly.

Although Bella already had a feeling she knew what that answer was going to be.

What it *had* to be…

CHAPTER SIX

'WILL I see you in the morning, Daddy?'

Bella's breath caught in her throat as she waited for Gabriel to answer Toby. She was standing at the bottom of her son's bed watching the two of them as Toby lay tucked snugly beneath the duvet, Gabriel sitting at his side.

She had absolutely no doubts that Toby had enjoyed his day with his father and grandfather. The three of them had spent most of the morning out in the garden, Gabriel keeping Toby occupied with a number of ball games while Bella sat on a lounger watching them, dark sunglasses perched on the end of her nose as she allowed her thoughts to wander. The problem was, they kept coming back to the same place—Gabriel's insistence that she marry him…

As the day had progressed—a drive out to look at the Danti vineyard, and lunch eaten outside on the terrace at the magnificent villa there, and then dinner later that evening at a wonderful fish restaurant at Pier 39—it was impossible for Bella to deny that Gabriel was wonderful with Toby.

That he already loved Toby with the same fierceness that Bella did…

And that Toby loved Gabriel right back!

Looking at the two of them sitting together now on Toby's bed, so alike with their dark curling hair and chocolate-brown eyes, and that cleft in the centre of their chins, Bella couldn't help feeling that she was fighting a losing battle. That even attempting to fight this harder, more arrogant Gabriel was a waste of her time and emotions.

Gabriel glanced down at her now, the expression in his eyes unreadable. 'I think that depends on Mummy, don't you?' he murmured.

'Mummy?' Toby prompted eagerly.

Bella drew in a ragged breath before answering. 'We'll see,' she finally said non-committally.

'That usually means yes,' Toby confided as he looked up at Gabriel conspiratorially.

'It does?' The darkness of Gabriel's gaze was mocking as he glanced across at Bella.

'It means we'll see,' she insisted. 'Now it's time for you to go to sleep, young man,' she told her son firmly as she moved to tuck him more comfortably beneath the covers. 'G—Daddy and I will just be in the other room if you should need us, Toby,' she added reassuringly before bending down to kiss him.

Toby reached up to wrap his arms about her neck as he hugged her. 'It was a lovely day, wasn't it, Mummy?'

Emotion caught in Bella's throat as she looked down into her son's happily beaming face.

Could she endanger that unclouded happiness by subjecting Toby to the trauma that a legal battle with

Gabriel was sure to cause? Could she really put Toby into a position where he would almost be forced to choose between the mother he had lived with all of his young life and the father he had only just met? Could she do that to him?

Surely the answer to all of those questions was no…

'Lovely,' she answered Toby brightly before kissing him again.

'I'll see you in the morning, darling.' She ruffled his dark curls before stepping away from the bed.

'We will both see you in the morning, Toby,' Gabriel added pointedly as he moved to receive Toby's hug goodnight.

Gabriel's arms were gentle, but his emotions were not. Toby, his son, now represented everything to him, the past, the present, and most definitely the future.

'Sleep now, little one,' he said huskily as he released Toby to step back.

'You promise you'll come back in the morning?' Toby's eyes were anxious.

Gabriel doubted that Toby heard the sob in his mother's throat as she stood just behind him, but Gabriel certainly did. 'I will come back in the morning,' he assured the little boy. Whatever it took, Gabriel was determined to be in Toby's life every morning!

'What would you have done about this situation if you had already been married to someone else when you learnt of Toby's existence?' Bella challenged once the two of them had returned to the sitting-room.

Gabriel's mouth tightened. 'Fortunately, that problem does not arise.'

'But if it had?' she insisted.

He shrugged. 'I refuse to answer a "what if" question, Isabella.'

She gave a little huff of frustration. 'Doesn't it bother you that I don't want to marry you?'

It should, and it did. But Gabriel knew from Bella's response to him earlier today that on one level, at least, she did want to be with him...

Other marriages, he was sure, had begun with less.

'Not particularly,' Gabriel dismissed curtly.

Bella continued to glare at him for several more seconds before she gave a sigh of defeat. 'All right, Gabriel, I will agree to marry you—'

'I thought that you would,' Gabriel murmured as he moved to sit in one of the armchairs.

'If you will allow me to finish...?' She raised dark, expressive brows as she stood across the room from him.

'By all means.' Gabriel relaxed back in the armchair. He had won the first battle—and the most difficult, he hoped—and so could now afford to be gracious in victory.

'Thank you,' she accepted dryly. 'I will agree to marry you,' she repeated, then went on more firmly, 'but only on certain conditions.'

Gabriel's gaze narrowed as he easily guessed, from the calmness of Bella's expression, that he wasn't going to like those conditions. 'Which are?'

'Firstly, if we married I would like to continue living in England—'

'I am sure that can be arranged.' He nodded, having already considered this problem earlier today when he had decided that marriage between himself and Isabella was the only real solution to Toby's continued welfare.

It would be a simple enough process to put a

manager in charge of the vineyards here, with the occasional visit from him to make sure they were being run properly.

'The Danti business interests are international, Isabella,' he informed her. 'I will simply take over the running of our London office. Your second condition…?'

'Toby will attend schools of my choice—'

'As long as that choice eventually includes Eton and then Cambridge, I do not foresee that as being a problem,' Gabriel drawled.

'Eton and Cambridge?' Bella echoed disbelievingly.

'The Dantis have been educated at Eton and Cambridge for several generations.'

Bella shook her head. 'Toby will begin attending the local school in September. Following that he will be a day-pupil at another local school.'

Gabriel quirked one dark brow. 'Then I suggest we ensure that we have already moved into a house close enough so that he can attend Eton school as a day-pupil.'

He looked so damned smug, Bella fumed inwardly. So sure of himself.

As he had no doubt been sure of what her answer to his marriage proposal would be. Proposal? Hah! Gabriel didn't ask, he ordered; he was arrogance personified!

But, while Toby had been enjoying himself as the centre of Cristo Danti and Gabriel's attention, Bella had spent most of the day considering her options. Her limited options, she had very quickly realised, considering there was no way now of denying that Toby was Gabriel's son—even if Bella did attempt to deny it, a simple blood test would prove her a liar!

Just as there was no denying that the Dantis were a very rich and powerful family, both here and in Europe. In reality, what possible chance did she have of ensuring that she and Toby—especially Toby!—came out of a legal battle unscathed? The answer to that was only too clear. Against Gabriel Danti she had no chance.

But if she was forced to agree to this marriage, then Bella was determined to have at least some say in what she would and would not agree to!

'Thirdly,' she snapped, 'the marriage will be in name only.' She looked across at him challengingly, her eyes widening in alarm as he suddenly stood up.

Gabriel slowly shook his head. 'I am sure that you are already well aware that will not be possible.'

Because of their response to each other earlier today!

A response that still made Bella cringe whenever she thought about it—which she had tried very hard not to do all day. She never responded to men in that totally wild and wanton way. At least…she never had until Gabriel. Both five years ago and then again today…

Which was why Bella was making this the last condition to their marriage. She could imagine nothing worse than becoming a slave to the desire that Gabriel seemed to ignite in her so easily.

Even now, feeling angry and trapped, Bella was still totally aware of Gabriel in the black shirt and faded jeans. Clearly remembered pushing that shirt from his shoulders earlier so that she might touch the warm, muscled flesh beneath it. Unfortunately, she remembered even more distinctly the way that Gabriel had touched her…

She would not, could not allow her emotions, her life, to be ruled by the desire Gabriel made her feel!

She straightened her shoulders. 'Without your agreement to that last condition I couldn't even contemplate the idea of the two of us marrying each other.'

Gabriel looked at her from under hooded lids, knowing by the steadiness of Bella's gaze, the sheer determination in her expression, that she thought she meant every word she was saying, at least. Considering their response to each other in his study earlier today, Gabriel found that very hard to believe. Or accept.

Bella had come alive in his arms. Wildly. Fiercely. Demandingly. How could she possibly imagine they could live together, day after day—night after night!—and not take that lovemaking to its inevitable conclusion?

His mouth tightened. 'You wish for Toby to be an only child?'

She shrugged. 'He was going to be that, anyway.'

Gabriel studied her closely. 'You are a beautiful woman, Isabella; if we had not met again you would no doubt have married one day and had other children.'

'No,' she answered flatly. 'I decided long ago that I would never subject Toby to a stepfather who may or may not have accepted him as his own,' she explained simply as Gabriel frowned at her.

The mere thought of Toby or Bella ever belonging to another man filled Gabriel with uncontrollable fury. Toby was his. Bella was his!

His hands clenched at his sides. 'I agree to your last condition, Bella—'

'I thought that you would,' she dryly echoed his earlier comment.

'Like you, Bella, I have not finished,' Gabriel replied.

'I agree to your last condition on the basis that it can be nullified, by you, at any time.'

Bella eyed him warily. 'What exactly does that mean?'

His smile was mocking. 'It means that I reserve the right to—*persuade* you, shall we say, into changing your mind.'

Bella had no doubt that what Gabriel meant by that remark was that he reserved the right to try and *seduce* her into changing her mind any time he felt like it!

Would she be able to resist him? Living with Gabriel twenty-four hours a day, every day, would she be able to withstand a Gabriel bent on seduction?

Did she have any real choice other than to try?

'You took me by surprise earlier, Gabriel,' she stated bravely. 'In future I will be on my guard against—well, against any attempt on your part to renew such attentions!'

She sounded so serious, so firm in her resolve, Gabriel acknowledged with a grudging admiration. 'I will allow no other men in your life, Isabella,' he warned her seriously.

'And will that rule apply to you, too?' she snapped.

Gabriel eyed her mockingly. 'My own tastes do not run in that particular direction—'

'You know very well what I meant!' She glared her exasperation.

He shrugged. 'There will be no other women in my bed but you, Isabella,' he taunted.

'I'm not going to be in your bed, either, Gabriel!'

Bella did not believe she was going to be in his bed, which, as far as Gabriel was concerned, was a totally different matter. 'You have named your own conditions for our marriage, Isabella,' he rasped. 'Now I wish to tell you mine.'

Her eyes widened. 'You have conditions, too?'

'But of course.' His mouth quirked. 'You did not think that I would allow you to have everything your own way?'

'Forcing me into marrying you is hardly that!' she scorned.

Gabriel gave another shrug. 'You have a choice, Isabella.'

'Not a viable one!'

'No,' he acknowledged simply. 'But it is, nevertheless, still a choice.'

Bella sighed her frustration, just wanting this conversation over and done with now. She was tired, both emotionally and physically, and she needed time and space alone now in which to sit and lick her wounds. While she came to terms with the idea of marrying Gabriel Danti!

How different it would have been if this had happened five years ago. How different Bella would have felt if their night together had been the start of something that had eventually resulted in Gabriel asking her to marry him. She had been so infatuated with him then, so totally seduced by Gabriel's lovemaking, that Bella had absolutely no doubts she would have said yes.

Instead, what they were now proposing was nothing more than a business transaction. A marriage of convenience because both of them wished to ensure that Toby's life, at least, continued in happiness and harmony.

'What's your condition, Gabriel?' she asked.

He didn't answer her immediately, but instead walked slowly towards her, only coming to a halt when he stood mere inches away from her.

Bella eyed him warily, her nails digging into the palms of her hands as she knew herself to be totally aware of the warmth of Gabriel's body, the clean male smell of him, the golden lights that now danced in the warm darkness of his eyes as he looked down at her.

'What do you want?' she snapped apprehensively, to which he gave a slow, seductive smile. A smile Bella took exception to. 'I was referring to your condition, Gabriel,' she added hastily.

'My condition at this moment is one of—'

'Your verbal condition to our marriage!' Bella could see for herself, by the languorous desire burning in that dark gaze as it roamed slowly over the firm thrust of her breasts, and the hard stirring of his body, exactly what Gabriel's physical condition was!

'Ah. Yes. My verbal condition, Isabella,' he murmured, 'is that, in order to ensure the continued harmony of both your own family and mine, I suggest it would be better if they were all to believe that our marriage is a love match.'

Bella gasped in disbelief. 'You want me to *pretend* to be *in love* with you?'

'Only in public,' he qualified.

She glared at him. 'And in private?'

'Oh, simply in lust will do for the moment,' he said softly.

Bella's gaze narrowed. 'You arrogant son-of-a—'

'Insulting my mother will achieve nothing except to annoy me intensely, Isabella,' he warned her.

'I'm so sorry,' she came back sarcastically. 'My intention was to insult *you*, not your mother!'

Gabriel was aroused, not insulted. Marriage to Isabella promised to be a feast for the senses—all of them!

She had been beautiful five years ago, like a delicate and lovely flower that blossomed to his slightest touch. But, Gabriel now realised, he had plundered only one of her petals then. Motherhood and a successful career had ensured there was now so much more to Isabella Scott, and he found it all desirable...

He smiled slowly. 'I am not insulted, Isabella,' he assured huskily. 'Intrigued, perhaps, but not insulted.'

'Pity,' she muttered.

Gabriel's smile widened. 'You agree to my condition, then?'

She eyed him, totally frustrated with her lack of anything resembling control of this situation. 'I assure you I no more want my parents and siblings upset about the choice I'm making than you want to distress your father.'

'And so...?'

She glared her dislike of him, then grudgingly conceded. 'And so, in public at least, I will try to ensure that it appears as if our marriage is something I want.'

'Good.' Gabriel murmured his satisfaction as he lifted his hand and curved it about the delicate line of Bella's jaw, instantly feeling the way she tensed at his lightest touch before moving sharply away. 'Neither your family or my own will be convinced of our—ease with each other, if you react in that way when I touch you!' he growled disapprovingly as his hand fell back to his side.

She gave a dismissive snort. 'I promise I'll try to do better when we have an audience!'

'To merely try is not good enough,' Gabriel told her coldly.

'It's the only answer I can give you for now,' she told him wearily.

Gabriel studied her through narrowed lids, easily able to see that weariness, along with the air of defeat Bella no longer tried to hide from him.

Yes, he had won the battle by forcing Isabella's compliance in the matter of marrying him, and in claiming Toby as his son.

But Gabriel felt little triumph in that victory as he sensed that, in doing so, he might have put the success of the entire war he was waging in jeopardy…

CHAPTER SEVEN

'YOU make a stunning bride, Bella!' Claudia smiled at her tearfully as she put the finishing touches to the veil before stepping back to admire her sister's appearance.

Bella could only stare numbly at her own reflection, in a beautiful white satin wedding gown and lovely lace veil, in the full-length mirror on the door of the wardrobe in the bedroom that had been hers as a child.

Whoever would have thought, having agreed to Gabriel's marriage proposal, that only five weeks later Bella would be standing here dressed in this beautiful white wedding gown and veil, preparing to drive to the church with her father, on her way to becoming Gabriel's bride?

Gabriel's bride.

Gabriel Danti's bride.

Oh, God!

'You can't be having second thoughts about marrying a man as gorgeous as Gabriel, Bella?' Claudia teased her obvious nervousness.

'No, I can't, can I?' she agreed with forced lightness. 'Go and tell Daddy that I'm ready to leave, hmm?' she asked, waiting until Claudia had left the bedroom before turning back to look at her reflection in the mirror.

What would be the point in having doubts about marrying Gabriel when he had already legally claimed Toby as his son? The name Danti had been enough to ensure that Gabriel's claim was dealt with quickly and positively. Toby Scott was now Tobias Danti.

As Bella would very shortly become Isabella Danti.

Even that name sounded alien to her, not like her at all. Which was pretty apt when Bella hadn't felt like herself for the last five weeks. Even less so today!

The woman reflected in the mirror wearing the white satin gown and delicate lace veil over the dark cascade of her hair certainly looked like her, but Bella could feel no joy in her appearance, or at the thought of becoming Gabriel's wife.

They had shared the news of their engagement with their delighted families five weeks ago. Bella and Toby had then remained in San Francisco for two more days to give Gabriel the time to settle his affairs before he flew back to England with them.

Since arriving in England, Gabriel had been staying in the house in Surrey where Bella had first met him, but coming to the cottage every day in order to spend time with Toby.

When in the company of her family and Gabriel's they had, as agreed, given every impression that they were happy in each other's company.

Not an easy thing on Bella's part when the more time she spent in Gabriel's company, the more physically aware of him she became. Until now, on their wedding day, she felt so tense with that physical awareness it was a constant painful ache. So much for her condition that this was to be a marriage in name only...

This was her wedding day, Bella accepted heavily. And she couldn't have felt more miserable!

'Where are we going?'

'On our honeymoon, of course,' Gabriel said with satisfaction as he drove the black sports car to the private airfield where the Danti jet was fuelled and waiting to take off, the two of them having just been given a warm send-off by their wedding guests.

'What honeymoon?' Bella frowned as she turned in her seat to look at him, still wearing her wedding gown and veil. 'At no time in the last five weeks did we discuss going away on a honeymoon!'

'We did not discuss it because I knew this would be your reaction if we had,' Gabriel told her unrepentantly.

She scowled her frustration with his high-handedness. 'If you knew that then, why—?'

'It was meant to be a surprise,' Gabriel growled.

Her mouth compressed. 'Oh it's certainly that all right.'

'It is Toby's surprise, Bella,' he elaborated softly.

She looked at him sharply. 'Toby's?'

Gabriel nodded. 'Our son confided in me several weeks ago that newly married people go away on honeymoon together after the wedding.'

Bella's cheeks were flushed. 'You should have explained to him—'

'Should have explained *what* exactly to him, Isabella?' Gabriel grated harshly. 'That although his mother and father are now married, they are not in love with each other? That his mother has no desire what-soever to spend time alone with his father?'

Bella winced. When he put it like that…!

They had spent the last few weeks, individually and together, convincing Toby that they were all going to be happy as a real family. Obviously they had succeeded as far as Toby was concerned, which was why he had decided his parents going away on honeymoon together was what a 'real family' did…

'I don't have any other clothes with me—'

'Claudia was kind enough to pack a suitcase for you,' Gabriel explained. 'It is in the trunk of the car with my own.'

Well, that explained the mischievous glint Bella had seen in Claudia's eyes earlier as her sister had stood with the other wedding guests outside the hotel to wave them off!

'Toby also arranged to stay with your parents for the week we are away,' Gabriel supplied. 'With my father remaining in England and visiting him often.'

'He's certainly been busy, hasn't he?' Bella sighed as she raised her hands to take the pins out of her hair and remove the veil, her head throbbing. 'That's better.' She threw the veil onto the back seat before sitting back more comfortably.

This really had been the most difficult day of Bella's life. Starting with the conversation her father had insisted on having with her early this morning…

He had been alone in the kitchen drinking coffee when Bella had come downstairs at six-thirty, his con-versation light as she had made herself a cup of coffee.

Once Bella had sat down at the kitchen table with him it had been a different matter, however.

He had gently voiced his own and her mother's worries about the haste with which Bella and Gabriel were getting married. Was she doing the right thing? Was she really sure this was what she wanted? There was no doubting Toby's excitement but was Bella going to be happy?

Lying to her father had possibly been the hardest thing Bella had ever done.

Even now, thinking of his gentle concern for her happiness, Bella could feel the tears prick her eyes. 'So, where have you decided we're going on our honeymoon?' she asked Gabriel heavily.

Gabriel's mouth tightened at the fatigue in Bella's tone as she made no effort to hide the fact that today had been no more than a trial she'd had to get through.

She had looked stunningly beautiful as she had walked down the aisle towards him. A vision in white satin and lace.

A vision in white satin and lace who had avoided so much as meeting his gaze. Whose voice had quivered with uncertainty as she made her vows, her hand trembling slightly as she allowed Gabriel to slide the thin gold wedding band in place. Her fingers had been cold as she'd placed the matching gold band Gabriel had insisted on upon his own finger, her mouth stiff and unresponsive as Gabriel kissed her to seal their vows. Although admittedly she had made an effort to smile and acknowledge their guests as they'd walked back down the aisle together as husband and wife.

Probably because looking and smiling at their guests

was preferable to looking at him, Gabriel acknowledged grimly to himself.

'We are flying to your island in the Caribbean,' Gabriel told her.

'Don't you mean *your* island in the Caribbean?' she corrected.

'No, I mean yours,' Gabriel said. 'It is my wedding gift to you.' He hadn't meant to tell her that quite so abruptly; had intended surprising her with his gift once they arrived at their destination. He would have stuck to that plan, too, if he weren't feeling quite so frustrated with her distant behaviour.

Bella was absolutely stunned as she stared at Gabriel in complete disbelief. Gabriel was giving her a whole island in the Caribbean as a wedding present?

His mouth quirked as he obviously read some of her incredulity. 'Do not look so concerned, Isabella. It is only a small island.'

'Isn't even a *small* island a little overkill when I only gave you a pair of cufflinks?' A frown marred her brow.

Bella had only bought the cufflinks at the last moment because Claudia, as Chief Bridesmaid, said she had to; until then Bella hadn't even thought of giving Gabriel a gift to mark their marriage. What could she possibly give to the man who had everything?

Although Bella had noted, as they stood together in the church, that Gabriel was wearing the diamond and onyx links in the cuffs of the pristine white shirt he wore beneath the dark grey frock coat...

'You have given me so much more than that, Isabella,' Gabriel assured her huskily.

She looked at him warily, but she was unable to read

anything from his expression. 'I don't know what you mean,' she finally murmured uncertainly.

'I am talking of Toby, Isabella. You have given me a son,' he explained evenly.

A man who had everything—except that…

'Wow, a wedding ring and an island in the Caribbean,' she mocked. 'What would you have given me if I had only produced a daughter? A monthly allowance and visiting rights, perhaps?'

'No, I would have given you a wedding ring and an island in the Caribbean!' A nerve pulsed in Gabriel's cheek as he answered her. 'I would value a daughter no less than a son, Isabella, and I have no idea why you would ever think that I might. Or why it is you take such delight in insulting me!'

Why *did* Bella take delight in insulting him?

Because she was angry with him. Because she was angry with herself. Because she was just plain angry!

She was angry with Gabriel for forcing her into this marriage.

She was angry with herself for allowing him to do so.

She was angry because a part of her had thrilled at the sight of Gabriel as he'd stood down the aisle waiting for her, looking so devastatingly handsome in the dark frock coat and white shirt and red bow tie. She was angry because her voice had quivered with emotion as she had made her vows to him and because her hand had trembled at his slightest touch as he'd placed his wedding ring upon her finger.

Bella was angry for all of those reasons and more!

'I'm sorry,' she sighed wearily. 'It's been a long and—and difficult day.'

'For both of us,' Gabriel pointed out.

'Yes.' Bella turned her head to look at him.

Gabriel looked as strained as she felt, Bella acknowledged ruefully, lines beside his eyes and the grimness of his mouth, his skin slightly pale beneath his naturally olive complexion.

How different this could all have been if Gabriel hadn't been in love with another woman five years ago. How different today could have been if the two of them had married because they were in love with each other now.

Instead they were two strangers who had married to protect and sustain their young son's happiness.

Bella swallowed hard. 'I think, if you don't mind, that I would like to just sit here quietly for a while.' She closed her eyes.

Gabriel did mind. If Bella thought the last five weeks had been any less of a strain for him, then she was mistaken.

In company, Bella had managed, as agreed, to maintain an air of tranquil happiness, but once they were alone it had been a totally different matter. She had shown a total lack of interest whenever he had tried to discuss the wedding arrangements with her. Had been uncommunicative on the three Sunday mornings they had attended church together in order to hear the reading of their Banns.

Worst of all, once they were alone, Bella had avoided so much as touching him...

If Bella wished to punish him for forcing this marriage on her then she could not have chosen a better way to do it than with her icy silence and her obvious aversion to his lightest touch!

* * *

'You and your father certainly know how to travel in style,' Bella commented lightly as she sat across the table from Gabriel in the luxurious cabin of the Danti jet, only now beginning to appreciate the wealth and power behind the Danti name.

Well…apart from earlier when Gabriel had informed her he had given her an island in the Caribbean as a wedding gift!

Bella shied away from even thinking about what she was going to do with an island in the Caribbean and instead turned her attention back to her present surroundings.

The Danti-owned jet was the height of luxury, only six ultra-comfortable seats in the spacious and carpeted main cabin, with a bar at the cockpit end, and a door to another private compartment at the other.

Gabriel had given instructions to the captain to take off as soon as they were on board and their luggage had been stowed in the cabin at the back of the plane. A male steward had then placed two long-stemmed fluted glasses on the glass table in front of them before pouring the bubbly champagne, leaving the bottle cooling in a bucket of ice beside Gabriel and then disappearing back into the galley behind the bar and closing the door discreetly behind him.

Bella had totally avoided even looking at her own glass of champagne as it reminded her all too forcibly of that night with Gabriel five years ago. The last thing she needed to think about at the moment was that!

Gabriel nodded now. 'As you and Toby will also do now that you are Dantis.'

The sinking feeling in Bella's stomach owed nothing

to air-sickness and everything to the realisation that that was who she really was now.

Isabella Danti. Wife of Gabriel.

'No doubt Toby will be impressed,' she answered.

'But not you?'

Bella was more nervous than impressed. Nervous of being really alone with Gabriel for the first time in five weeks. A quivering wreck just at the thought of spending a week alone with him on *her* Caribbean island.

She shook her head. 'I'm not four years old, Gabriel.'

'No, you are not, are you?'

Bella shot Gabriel a swift glance, not in the least reassured by the intensity of his chocolate-brown eyes as his gaze met hers and held it captive.

She physically had to turn her head away to break that gaze before she could stand up abruptly. 'I—I think I would like to go into the other room and take off this wedding gown.'

'An excellent idea, Isabella,' Gabriel murmured huskily.

Bella frowned up at him as he rose slowly to his feet, his height and the width of his shoulders at once dominating the cabin. 'I think I'm quite capable of changing my clothes on my own, thank you,' she told him sharply.

Gabriel gave a mocking inclination of his head. 'I thought you might need some help with the zip at the back of your gown.'

Good point, Bella realised. The wedding gown was medieval in style, with long, close-fitting lace sleeves that tapered to a point at her wrist, their snug fit making it impossible for Bella to reach the zip that ran the whole length of her spine without risking ripping the sleeves at the seams. It hadn't been a problem earlier today, because Claudia had helped her to dress, but Bella couldn't say she was exactly comfortable now with the thought of Gabriel helping her to *un*dress…

Comfortable? The thought of Gabriel touching her at all was enough to send her already fractured nerves into a complete tailspin!

She was never going to wear this gown again anyway, so what did it matter if she *did* rip the sleeves?

'I'm sure I can manage, thank you,' she replied distantly as she turned away.

'I need to change into less formal clothing, too,' Gabriel insisted quietly as he reached the door to the back compartment before Bella and held it open for her to enter.

Bella looked up at him uncertainly, knowing by the hard challenge she could see in his eyes that Gabriel expected to continue—and that he was actually enjoying!—arguing with her. On the basis that some sort of response from her was better than none, perhaps? Probably, Bella acknowledged wryly, even as she experienced a perverse desire not to give him that satisfaction.

'Fine,' she accepted airily before striding past him into the cabin at the back of the plane.

Only to come to an abrupt halt as she found herself, not in another sitting-room as she had supposed, but in a room totally dominated by the king-size bed in its centre!

Gabriel's eyes darkened with amusement when he saw Bella's stunned expression as she took in the luxuriously appointed bedroom with its fitted wardrobes, gold thick-piled carpet, and the deep gold and cream silk linen that covered the bed, several throw cushions of the same rich material against the sumptuous pillows.

Unfortunately Bella didn't stay stunned for very long as she turned to look up at him accusingly. 'I hope you don't have any ideas about adding my name to the list of women you've no doubt seduced in here!' she snapped.

Gabriel's humour faded at the deliberate insult. 'You have the tongue of a viper!'

She raised mocking brows. 'It's a little late for second thoughts, don't you think, Gabriel? We were married earlier today, remember?'

'Oh, I remember, Isabella,' he rasped harshly. 'Perhaps it is time that I reminded you of that fact also!' He closed the door gently behind him.

Bella took a step back as she obviously read the intent in his eyes. 'I meant what I said, Gabriel—I am not about to become another notch on your mile-high bedpost!'

Gabriel's jaw clenched as he took that same step forward. 'I meant what I said five weeks ago, too, concerning the right to change your mind about our marriage being in name only!'

Her eyes widened in alarm. 'Not here!'

'Wherever and whenever,' he promised.

She backed away from him. 'I told you I will not become another notch—'

'If you look at the bed again, Isabella, you will see that there is no bedpost.' Gabriel's voice was dangerously soft. 'And we are at least three miles high.'

'Your three-mile-high club, then,' she persisted as she faced him bravely, only the uncertainty Gabriel could read in her eyes telling him of the nervousness Bella was trying so desperately to hide.

Gabriel took another step forward, standing only inches away from Bella now, and able to see the nerve pulsing at the base of her throat and the slight trembling of her lips.

Full pouting lips that were slightly parted, that perfect bow of a top lip a temptation, the bottom one becoming a lure as the tip of Bella's tongue moved moistly between them.

An invitation, whether Bella meant it to be so, that Gabriel had no intention of resisting!

'Turn around, Isabella, so that I can unzip your gown,' he suggested gruffly.

She swallowed hard. 'I don't—' She broke off with a gasp as Gabriel ignored her protest and stepped behind her. She felt the touch of his fingers as he slowly began to slide the zip down.

Bella's second protest went unspoken, her back arching involuntarily as she felt the delicious ripples of awareness through her whole body as that zip slowly— so very slowly—moved down the length of her spine, her breath catching in her throat as Gabriel parted the satin material and she felt the warm caress of his lips against the bareness of her shoulder.

Desire. She instantly felt a hot, burning desire that ripped through her body at the first touch of Gabriel's mouth against her heated flesh, the moist rasp of his tongue as he licked and tasted her only intensifying that burning heat.

Much as she denied it, much as she fought against it, Bella knew she wanted him.

Wanted Gabriel passionately.

Knew that she had been fighting that want, that need, for the last five weeks, afraid to even touch him in case she revealed that ever-escalating desire. With the result that each minute she spent in his company had been torture, and full of an aching desire that had always seemed only seconds away from release.

It was a passion that Bella had only been able to keep in check by presenting Gabriel with a veneer of icy coldness. An icy veneer that had melted with the force of an avalanche the moment his mouth touched her naked flesh!

Her neck arched, her head resting back against Gabriel's shoulder as his hands slid inside the unzipped gown to move about her waist and then higher as he cupped the nakedness of her breasts beneath the satin gown, her own hands moving up to rest on top of his as she pressed him into her, wanting his caresses.

She cried out, desire surging between her thighs as Gabriel's thumbs moved across her turgid nipples, her body taut with expectation, not able to breathe as she waited for the second caress, gasping, almost sobbing as Gabriel's lips moved heatedly, moistly against her throat as he took those throbbing peaks between his thumbs and fingers and squeezed rhythmically.

'Gabriel?' Bella groaned as her bottom moved against the hardness of his arousal. 'Gabriel, please…!'

'Not yet, Bella,' Gabriel refused huskily even though his own body throbbed with that same need for release.

They had a long flight ahead of them, hours and hours before they reached their destination, and before that happened Gabriel intended to discover and fulfil every one of Bella's fantasies, as he hoped that she would fulfil every one of his.

Stripping the white satin wedding gown from Bella's body was only the first of the fantasies that had kept him awake night after night for the last five weeks!

Gabriel heard her moan of protest as he slowly moved his hands from inside her gown, her breath catching in her throat seconds later as she realised he had only done so in order to slide the gown from her shoulders and down her arms before he bared her to the waist and then slowly allowed the gown to pool on the floor at her feet.

Bella's eyes were closed and Gabriel stared down at how beautiful she looked in only a pair of brief white lace panties and white stockings.

Her throat was exposed, her lips slightly parted and moist, her lids half closing over eyes of deep purple as Gabriel's arms moved about her and his hands once again cupped her breasts before his thumbs moved to caress the deep rose nipples.

'Yes!' she exclaimed. 'Oh, God, yes, Gabriel…!'

Gabriel pulled her back against him so his lips could roam freely, erotically up the length of her throat to the sensitivity of her ear lobe, his teeth nibbling on that lobe even as one hand continued to caress the firmness of a perfect nipple and his other hand moved lower still.

Bella's skin felt like velvet as his fingers splayed across the bare expanse of her waist and down over the jut of her hip. Gabriel opened his eyes to look down to where his hand cupped and teased her breast, his own skin so much darker than the creamy magnolia of hers.

His teeth bit the softness of her ear lobe even as his gaze moved lower to where his fingers quested beneath the silk of her panties to the dark curls he could see clearly through the sheerness of the material, parting the dampness of those curls and seeking the sensitive nub nestled amongst their darkness. Seeking and finding as his fingers began to stroke her there.

She was so hot and slick, her sensitive folds swollen with need, a need Gabriel intended building until Bella cried out, begged for him to give her the climax her body craved.

Bella moaned low in her throat as she felt the brush of Gabriel's fingers against her, her legs parting to allow him greater access, an invitation he accepted as he plunged one long, satisfying finger deep inside her, followed by another as his thumb continued to stroke against her swollen nub and his other hand squeezed and caressed her breast in the same mind-blowing rhythm.

Again and again.

Those caresses becoming fiercer. Deeper. Faster.

The heat rose unbearably, building, growing ever stronger as Bella's hips moved to meet the deep thrust of Gabriel's fingers inside her.

'Don't stop, Gabriel!' she gasped breathlessly. 'Please don't stop!'

'Let go, Bella!' he groaned hoarsely against her throat. 'Give yourself, *cara*!'

'Yes…' she breathed raggedly. 'Oh, yes! Oh, God, yes…!' Bella gasped and writhed against Gabriel's hand as her climax surged out of control and wave after wave of burning, shattering pleasure rippled through her.

Gabriel held her captive as his fingers continued to

pleasure her, Bella climaxing again and again, her body quivering and shaking at Gabriel's slightest touch.

'No more, Gabriel!' she finally sobbed as she collapsed weakly in his arms.

CHAPTER EIGHT

BELLA woke slowly, slightly disorientated as she looked around the unfamiliar room.

And then she remembered.

Not just where she was, but everything that had happened since she had entered this bedroom.

Bella turned her face into the pillows, the aching protest of her body as she curled into a foetal position reminding her all too forcefully of the way Gabriel had touched and caressed her.

So much for her claim, her determination, that her marriage to Gabriel would be in name only —they hadn't even left British airspace before she'd succumbed to his caresses!

It was—

She looked sharply towards the door as she heard the handle turning softly before it was opened, her expression becoming defensive as she saw Gabriel standing in the doorway.

The cream polo shirt and jeans he wore showed that he had remained in the bedroom long enough to change his clothes after Bella—after she— After she what? Collapsed from the sheer ecstasy Gabriel had given her time and time again until she simply couldn't take any more?

Oh, God…!

Her mouth tightened. 'If you've come to gloat—'

'I came to see if you were awake yet,' he corrected coldly. 'We will be landing shortly, and you need time to dress before we do.'

Which reminded Bella all too forcibly that she was completely naked—apart from her panties and hold-up stockings—beneath the bedclothes.

It also reminded her that although she had been almost naked Gabriel had remained completely dressed throughout their earlier— Their earlier what? Sexual encounter? Lovemaking? It could hardly be called the latter when there was no love for each other, on either side.

Sexual encounter, then.

How awful did that sound?

'Thank you,' she accepted with polite dismissal.

Gabriel scowled across the cabin at Bella for several long seconds. Knowing her as he did, he hadn't been expecting her to fall lovingly into his arms when she awoke, but her coldness, her accusation that he had come here to gloat over her earlier capitulation, was unforgivable.

His expression was grim as he crossed the cabin in three long strides to stand beside the bed and look down at her. 'It is not me you are angry with, Isabella—'

'Don't presume to tell me what I'm feeling,' she said resentfully, her eyes glittering with suppressed emotion as she glowered up at him.

Gabriel sat down on the side of the bed, trapping her beneath the bedclothes as he put a hand either side of her to lean over her. 'We are husband and wife, Isabella; there is absolutely no reason for you to feel embarrassed because of what happened between us earlier—'

'I'm not *embarrassed*, Gabriel—I'm *disgusted*. With myself as much as with you!' she added, her expression defiant as she met his gaze squarely.

Gabriel wanted to reach out and shake her out of this mood of self-recrimination. But if he were to touch her again now, even in anger, he knew that he wouldn't be able to stop himself from making love with her again.

Just looking at Bella, her hair a cloud of darkness against the gold colour of the pillows, her mouth a sensual pout, and knowing her body was almost completely naked beneath the bedclothes was enough to make Gabriel shift uncomfortably as his thighs became engorged with arousal. His own lack of release earlier had become an aching throb he'd remained totally aware of while Bella slept.

He stood up abruptly, needing to put some distance between himself and Bella before speaking again, but before he could do so she got in first. 'Just don't count on a repeat performance, Gabriel,' she snapped.

Where Bella was concerned Gabriel didn't take anything for granted. Not one single thing. 'We will be landing in ten minutes, Isabella, so I suggest that before we do you get some clothes on,' he bit out tersely.

She kept the covers pulled up against her as she sat up, her hair falling silkily about her shoulders. 'I thought you said it was a small Caribbean island?'

'It is,' Gabriel confirmed. 'We will complete the rest of our journey by helicopter.'

Bella had never been in a helicopter before, and wasn't sure how she was going to respond to being in such a small aircraft.

She was even less comfortable when she realised that Gabriel intended piloting the small black wasp-looking craft himself!

She looked at him uncertainly as he climbed into the seat beside her after stowing their cases in the back. 'Are you sure you know how to fly one of these things?'

'Very sure,' he drawled. 'I assure you, Isabella, you will be completely safe in my hands,' he added mockingly as she still didn't look convinced.

Bella shot him a narrow-eyed glare before turning away to look out of the window beside her at the bright sunshine reflecting on the beautiful blue-green ocean beyond a beach of white-gold sand.

A relaxed pose that didn't last any longer than it took for Gabriel to start the engine and move the controls to lift the helicopter from the ground!

Bella reached out to clutch at Gabriel's arm as the helicopter bucked and swayed as it rose into the air. 'I think I'm going to be sick!' she cried frantically.

'You will not be sick if you look out at the sea and not down at the ground,' he instructed.

Easy enough for him to say, Bella groaned inwardly as her stomach continued to heave in protest for several long minutes, only settling down to a slight queasiness as the helicopter levelled out and she could finally appreciate the beauty of the scenery.

The sun was bright and very hot, the sea so blue and clear that Bella could see the sandy bottom in several places, even more so as they began to approach a small island edged by unspoilt beautiful beaches and covered in lush green foliage and trees.

Gabriel flew the helicopter over the beach, almost but not quite touching the tops of the trees, Bella's eyes widening as she saw he was heading towards a white-painted villa on top of a hill, only slightly inland and surrounded by more trees and huge brightly coloured flowers.

'Home.' Gabriel nodded in answer to Bella's questioning look as he began to lower the helicopter onto the patch of flat green grass next to the villa. 'What did you expect, Bella?' He turned to her once they were down on the ground. 'That I was bringing you to a shack in the middle of nowhere?'

Bella hadn't really given a lot of thought as to where they would stay once they reached the island. The fact that Gabriel had given her an island as a wedding gift had seemed fantastic enough!

'It is slightly primitive in that there are no servants here to wait on us,' Gabriel warned.

Bella smiled wryly. 'I won't miss what I've never had, Gabriel.'

'A Frenchman owned the island previously, and he had the villa built several years ago,' Gabriel told her as he climbed out of the helicopter. 'Obviously, if you want to change the décor then you must do so.'

'It's beautiful as it is,' Bella murmured as she took her sunglasses off to follow him inside the villa.

The floors were cool cream-and-terracotta-coloured marble, the cream furniture in the sitting-room kept to a minimum, with several glass-topped tables placed conveniently beside the armchairs and sofa. The kitchen was even more surprising, everything white, including the cooker and huge refrigerator and freezer.

'We have our own generator and fresh water supply,' Gabriel told her as she moved slowly about the room. 'Or rather, you have your own generator and fresh water supply,' he corrected ruefully.

Bella blinked, totally overwhelmed now that she was actually here. 'This really is all *mine*?'

Gabriel nodded. 'Do you like it?' His expression was guarded.

Almost as if he expected her to throw his gift back in his face. Not literally, of course, but verbally at least. Not surprising considering her remarks when Gabriel had first told her about the island!

'I love it!' Bella assured him emotionally. 'I—thank you, Gabriel,' she added slightly breathlessly.

Gabriel stood across the kitchen, his own sunglasses pushed up into the darkness of his hair. Hair that he hadn't bothered to have cut the last five weeks, its longer length making him look more like the man Bella had met and briefly fallen for five years ago.

She turned away abruptly. 'How on earth did everything get here? The materials to build the villa? The furniture?' she quickly asked to cover her sudden and complete awareness of Gabriel as he stood there so still and yet so lethally attractive.

Gabriel shrugged. 'The same way that the food in the freezer and refrigerator got here.' He opened the fridge door to show her all the food stored on the shelves. 'By boat,' he supplied ruefully as Bella still looked puzzled.

Bella eyes narrowed. 'Are you telling me that I didn't

have to suffer that helicopter flight at all? That we could have come here by *boat*, instead?'

Gabriel held back a smile at her slightly indignant expression. 'I thought it would be more…dramatic… to arrive by helicopter,' he admitted.

'Oh, you did, did you…?' Bella said quietly as she placed her bag down on one of the work-surfaces.

'I did, yes,' Gabriel muttered warily, not able to read Bella's mood at all as she strolled over and opened the freezer door, taking out a tray of ice cubes before moving over to the sink. 'Of course, you must be thirsty,' he acknowledged. 'There is a selection of drinks in the— What are you doing?' He frowned as Bella approached him brandishing a handful of ice cubes before reaching out to grasp the collar of his polo shirt and dropping them inside. 'Bella!' Gabriel gasped in protest at the first uncomfortable touch of the icy-cold cubes against the heat of his flesh.

'I thought you were looking a little hot, Gabriel,' she drawled as he stepped back to shake the frozen cubes out of his clothing, several of them shattering on the marble floor.

'Damn it, Bella —' Gabriel broke off as Bella began to laugh at his discomfort.

It was the first time, Gabriel realised, that he had heard her laugh without cynicism or sarcasm since they'd met again five weeks ago.

His breath caught in his throat as he stared at her, those gorgeous violet eyes shining with good humour, her teeth tiny and white against her pale pink lip gloss, a healthy colour in her cheeks.

Bella was the most beautiful woman Gabriel had ever seen!

'Perhaps I deserved that,' he allowed gruffly.

'Perhaps you did,' she confirmed unrepentantly. 'Next time we come by boat, yes?' she said as she moved to pick up the shattered ice cubes.

Gabriel remained silent as he hunkered down on his haunches to help her, unwilling to break the sudden truce by making any comment that Bella might take exception to, satisfied for the moment that there would be a next time…

'What are you doing, Gabriel?'

He threw his cheroot to the ground, grinding it beneath the sole of his shoe before turning slowly to look at Bella as she stood behind him in the moonlight.

Their uneasy truce had continued while they walked along the beach earlier, and through the dinner they had prepared together and then eaten outside on the terrace that overlooked the moon-dappled ocean. The two of them had returned outside after they had cleared the dishes away, the silence between them companionable rather than awkward as they finished drinking the bottle of red wine Gabriel had opened to accompany their meal.

Bella had excused herself half an hour or so ago in order to go to the master bedroom to prepare for bed, Gabriel opting to stay outside a little longer, still reluctant to say or do anything that might shatter even the illusion of the companionship they had found together since the ice-cube incident.

They were due to stay here for a week, and Gabriel

would prefer that they not spend all of that time at loggerheads!

Looking at Bella now, in a pale-lilac-coloured night-gown, the silk material clinging to her breasts and moulding to the gentle curve of her hips, Gabriel knew that he wanted to strip even that flimsy garment from her before making love with her.

Something, after her comments earlier on the plane, that was sure to shatter even the illusion of companionship that they'd shared so far!

He thrust his hands into the pockets of the black trousers he had changed into before dinner. 'I thought you would prefer your privacy after such a long and tiring day.'

Bella looked at him searchingly, but was totally unable to read Gabriel's mood beneath the remoteness of his expression. 'Aren't you coming to bed?' she finally prompted hesitantly.

'Later, perhaps,' he rasped dismissively. 'I am not tired yet.'

Bella hadn't exactly had sleep in mind when she'd asked that question!

The island was beautiful, and totally unspoilt, she had discovered as she and Gabriel had strolled bare-footed, if slightly apart, along the shoreline before dinner. The water had lapped gently against their feet, the smell of the exotic blossoms wafting in the warm softness of the breeze, and all adding to the seduction of the evening.

To the air of awareness that lay hidden just below the surface of even the slightest glance that Bella and Gabriel exchanged.

At least, she had thought it had.

Gabriel's reluctance to come to bed now seemed to imply that only she had felt that aching awareness.

Because Gabriel's lovemaking earlier had only been a way of showing her that he really could make love to her wherever and whenever *he* felt like it, as he had put it so bluntly?

That, having already proved his point once today, Gabriel now felt no urgency to repeat the experience?

How utterly ridiculous of her to have imagined that, because the two of them hadn't argued for the last few hours, they could have actually reached some sort of understanding in their relationship. Gabriel had never made any secret of his reason for marrying her—his only reason for marrying her!—and that reason was Toby.

Bella felt the humiliated colour burn her cheeks. 'You're right, Gabriel, I would prefer my privacy,' she said. 'As such, it would be better if you used one of the other bedrooms, and kept out of mine, for the duration of our stay here.'

Gabriel's gaze narrowed on the pale oval of her face in the moonlight, her chin raised in challenge, that same challenge reflected in the deep purple of her eyes.

'Don't come any closer, Gabriel!' she warned as he took a step towards her.

A warning Gabriel chose to ignore as he came to stand only inches away from her, his eyes glittering darkly as he looked down the length of his arrogant nose at her, and his hands clenched at his sides as he obviously fought the urge to reach out and shake her until her teeth rattled.

Bella felt her own anger starting to fade as she instead found herself fascinated by the nerve that pulsed beside that livid scar on Gabriel's tautly clenched left cheek.

He looked so gloriously handsome with his long hair slightly tousled onto his shoulders, the black silk shirt and tailored trousers only adding to that darkness, his eyes also appearing a glittering black in the moonlight.

Bella had never known another man with the grace and beauty of Gabriel. Had never been as physically aware of another man in the way she was Gabriel. Had never wanted another man in the way she constantly seemed to want Gabriel.

As, God help her, she wanted him even now…!

She swallowed hard. 'You're right, Gabriel, it's been a long and tiring day. Far too long and tiring for this conversation,' she said huskily. 'I—I'll wish you a goodnight.'

His mouth twisted self-derisively. 'I very much doubt that it will be that!'

Bella looked at him searchingly for several seconds before shaking her head ruefully. 'We really must try to find a way to stop insulting each other, Gabriel.'

He winced. 'The only time we manage to do that is when we are making love together, but…' He shrugged. 'Goodnight, Isabella. I will try not to wake you when I come to bed.'

Bella was frowning as she turned and walked slowly back inside the villa, too utterly weary to fight him any more concerning their sleeping arrangements. Especially as Gabriel had already made it plain she would lose!

She very much doubted that she would be able to fall

asleep when she knew that at any moment Gabriel would be coming to share what was now *their* bed.

Very much doubted that she would be able to sleep at all with Gabriel in bed beside her…

CHAPTER NINE

'Do you know how to scuba-dive, Isabella?'

'No.' Bella looked up from eating her piece of toast as she and Gabriel sat outside on the veranda eating their breakfast. 'Do you?'

As Bella had already guessed, it had not been a restful night's sleep, and she had still been awake but pretending not to be when Gabriel had joined her in the bedroom half an hour or so after she had gone to bed. That Gabriel had fallen asleep within minutes of his head resting on the pillow had made absolutely no difference to her own feelings of tension, and Bella had lain awake for hours after the even tenor of Gabriel's breathing told her he remained fast asleep beside her.

Bella's only consolation was that Gabriel was already up and making breakfast when she finally woke up shortly after nine o'clock. But her eyes still felt gritty from lack of sleep, and all she really felt like doing was going back to bed!

'I would hardly have asked otherwise,' Gabriel pointed out before taking a sip of his coffee. 'Would you like to learn?'

He looked disgustingly well rested this morning in a white short-sleeved shirt and white trousers, Bella noted, disgruntled. Much more relaxed than he had a right to be, as far as she was concerned.

'I suppose I could try,' she agreed irritably. 'As long as you aren't one of those awful teachers who gets cross with their student.'

'I have no doubts you will be a very attentive pupil, Isabella,' Gabriel teased, knowing by the heavy look to her eyes and the weary droop of her mouth that she hadn't slept well.

Gabriel had known she was still awake when he joined her in the bed the night before, her back firmly turned towards him as she had tried to give every appearance of being asleep. A deception Gabriel had allowed her to keep; it was enough for the moment that she accepted that they would be sharing a bed in future.

She gave him a sharp glance. 'I sincerely hope you were referring to scuba-diving!'

'What else?' he taunted.

Bella continued to eye him suspiciously for several long seconds, and then she gave a dismissive shrug. 'Why not? I obviously have nothing else to do today.' She stood up suddenly.

Gabriel looked up at her searchingly. 'Perhaps you would have preferred to go somewhere a little more…entertaining…for our honeymoon?'

Bella raked him with a scathing glance. 'Oh, I think this is entertaining enough, don't you?'

He laughed softly. 'Let us hope so.'

Bella refused to meet the challenge in his gaze. 'I'll go and get changed.'

Although she wasn't too sure about that once she saw the skimpiness of the bikinis that Claudia, obviously in on the secret of their honeymoon destination, had packed for her!

There were two of them. A black one that consisted of two very small scraps of material that barely covered anything, top or bottom. And a pink one, which admittedly had a little more material in the bottom half, but unfortunately the top plunged deeply at the front, meaning that when she put it on her breasts spilled over it revealingly.

Quite what Claudia had been thinking of when she chose them, Bella had no idea—but she could take a good guess.

Bella forgot her own self-consciousness in the pink bikini the instant she came out onto the terrace and saw that Gabriel was wearing the briefest—and sexiest— pair of black swimming trunks she had ever seen!

Fitting low down on his hips, the material barely covered that revealing bulge in the front of the trunks. A bulge Bella found it difficult to look away from…

Gabriel looked up from checking the scuba gear, his expression hardening as he saw the way Bella was staring at him. 'Do my scars bother you, after all?' he ground out harshly.

'Scars?' she repeated vaguely, trying to concentrate on something other than those skimpy bathing trunks. 'Oh. Those scars.' She nodded as she took in the revealing criss-cross of scars that marked his chest and back, several deeper marks that looked like surgical incisions on his left leg, both below and above the knee. 'I've already told you they don't bother me, Gabriel,' she said with a frown.

'That was before you had seen the full extent of them,' he said stiltedly. 'Some women would be bothered by their unsightliness.'

Some women *would*? Or they already *had*? Perhaps Janine Childe, for instance…?

Bella stepped outside. 'We all have scars, Gabriel. It's just that some of us have them on the inside rather than the outside. Besides,' she continued as he would have spoken, 'what does it matter to you how I feel about them?'

Gabriel's eyes were narrowed to dark slits. 'You are the woman who will have to look at them for the rest of your life.'

The rest of her life?

She took a deep breath as she realised she hadn't actually thought about her marriage to Gabriel with exactly that time-frame in mind before…

She suddenly realised she hadn't said anything and Gabriel was still waiting… 'I wouldn't worry about it, Gabriel. All men look the same in the dark—' She broke off as Gabriel's hands suddenly closed firmly about her upper arms. 'Let go of me!' she gasped.

His grasp didn't relax in the slightest. 'I am not interested in what you think of other men, Isabella. In the dark or otherwise!' He shook her slightly, his expression now distinctly dangerous.

Bella stared up at him, unable to see anything but the darkness of his anger as he glared down at her. 'Your scars don't bother me, Gabriel, and that's the truth,' she finally said evenly.

His gaze remained dark and stormy on her face for several more seconds before he released her so suddenly that Bella stumbled slightly. 'I will be several more minutes checking the scuba equipment, so perhaps you would like to go for a swim while you are waiting,' he suggested abruptly.

Bella gave one last, lingering glance at the stiffness of his scarred back before turning away to walk in the direction of the beach.

Another day in paradise…

'That was the most wonderful experience of my life!' Bella gasped excitedly once she had waded out of the sea and removed her breathing mask.

'The *most* wonderful?' Gabriel arched mocking brows as he removed his own scuba gear before sitting down on the blanket spread on the white-gold sand, the long darkness of his hair pushed back from his face, rivulets of sea-water dripping enticingly down his shoulders and back.

'Well…one of them,' Bella corrected hastily. 'Holding Toby in my arms seconds after he was born was probably the most wonderful,' she added huskily.

A frown darkened Gabriel's brow. 'I would have liked to have shared that experience with you.'

'It's been a lovely day, Gabriel, let's not spoil it with another argument.' Bella sighed as she dropped down onto the blanket beside him before slipping her arms out of the straps of the scuba gear and dropping it back on the sand behind them. She pushed the dampness of her hair back over her shoulders and sat forward to clasp her arms about her knees and rest her chin on her bent knees. 'Besides, I very much doubt even you would have been allowed into the delivery-room.'

Gabriel arched one dark brow. 'Even me…?'

She nodded. 'Not even the Danti name would have got you in there,' she teased. 'There was a bit of a scare at the last moment,' she explained as Gabriel continued to look at her enquiringly. 'My blood pressure went off the scale, Toby became distressed, and they had to rush me off to Theatre to deliver Toby by Caesarean section.'

Gabriel tensed. 'Your life was in danger?'

'I think both our lives were in danger for a while,' Bella admitted. 'But luckily it all turned out okay in the end.'

The frown between Gabriel's eyes didn't lessen. 'Is that likely to happen with a second pregnancy?'

Bella gave him a surprised glance. 'I don't know. It never occurred to me to ask. Gabriel?' She stared at him as he stood up abruptly to walk the short distance to the water's edge. 'Gabriel, what's wrong?'

Gabriel's hands clenched at his sides. Bella could ask him that, when she might have lost her life giving birth to Toby? When they might both have lost their lives and he, Gabriel, Bella's lover and Toby's father, would not have even known!

'The way I see it, both you and I have almost died and have the scars to prove it—' Bella broke off abruptly as Gabriel turned, his expression fierce. 'I was only trying to make light of the situation, Gabriel,' she reasoned.

His eyes narrowed to steely slits. 'You think the risk to your life is a subject for humour?'

She grimaced. 'I think it's something that happened four and a half years ago. It's nothing but history now. We're all still here, after all.'

Gabriel knew that Bella was right, but having just learnt that she might have died giving birth to Toby made him wonder—fear?—that a second pregnancy might be as dangerous...

'May I see your scar?'

Bella looked up at Gabriel warily as he loomed over her and blocked out the sun, his face darkly intense.

He wanted to see her scar from the Caesarean section? Her below-the-bikini-line scar?

She swallowed hard. 'Can't you just take my word for it that it's there?'

There was a slight easing of the tension in his expression. 'No.'

'Oh.' Bella chewed on her bottom lip. 'I would really rather not.' Her arms tightened protectively about her knees.

'Why not?'

Because it was far too intimate, that was why! Because she already felt totally exposed, vulnerable, in the brief bikini, without baring any more flesh!

'Maybe later,' she said, turning away.

'Now.'

Bella frowned her irritation as she looked back at him. 'Gabriel, we don't have to literally bare all of ourselves to each other in the first few days of marriage!'

He gave a hard smile. 'You have seen *my* scars, now I would like to see yours.'

'I would rather not,' she came back crossly.

'Men and women all look alike in the daylight, too, Isabella,' Gabriel murmured throatily.

No, they didn't!

There was simply no other man like Gabriel. No

other man with his broodingly dark good looks. No other man with the power to make Bella's knees tremble with just a glance from the warmth of those chocolate-brown eyes. No other man who made her feel so desirable. No other man who could make her totally lose control at the merest touch of his hand...

There just was no other man as far as Bella was concerned.

Oh, God!

Bella felt her cheeks pale even as she stared up at Gabriel with a feeling of helplessness. She loved him. Loved Gabriel.

Had she *ever* really stopped loving him?

Probably not, Bella acknowledged with a feeling akin to panic. She had fallen in love with Gabriel that night five years ago, and even though she had never seen him again she had continued to love him.

That was the reason she had never been interested in even going out with another man for all these years.

That was the reason she had never felt even remotely attracted to another man in that time.

Because she was already in love with Gabriel Danti, and always would be!

And now she was married to him. Married to the man she loved, would always love, and yet could never tell him of that love because it wasn't what Gabriel wanted from her. It had never been what Gabriel wanted from her, and even less so now. All Gabriel wanted was his son; Bella just happened to come along with the package.

She stood up abruptly. 'I think not, thank you, Gabriel,' she told him stiffly. 'I'm tired. I'll go back to the villa and take a nap before dinner.'

Gabriel remained on the beach, his gaze narrowed in thought as he watched Bella walk into the trees and up towards the villa, her hair a black silky cloud down the slenderness of her back, the gentle sway of her hips wholly enticing.

What had happened just now?

One minute Bella had been challenging him as she always did, just as he had been enjoying that challenge as he always did, and the next it seemed she had completely shut down all her emotions.

Perhaps that was as well when Gabriel knew he daren't risk another pregnancy for Bella until he was sure she would be in no danger…

'Tell me what happened five years ago, Gabriel.'

'As in…?' Gabriel's expression was guarded as he looked across the dinner table at Bella.

'As in the accident, of course,' she said impatiently.

'Ah.' Gabriel sat back to take a sip of the white wine that he had opened to accompany the lobster and salad they had prepared together and just eaten.

Bella frowned. 'What did you think I meant?'

Gabriel looked at Bella beneath lowered lids as he admired her and thought how lovely she looked in her simple black knee-length gown. Its thin shoulder straps and the bareness of her arms revealed the light tan she had attained at the beach earlier, the heavy cloud of her dark hair cascaded loosely over that golden hue, and her face was bare of make-up except a pale peach lip gloss.

Bella had never looked more beautiful. Or more desirable.

'What did I think that you meant?' Gabriel repeated slowly. 'The night we spent together, perhaps?'

'I think we're both already well aware of what happened that night!' Bella pointed out tartly. 'Impressionable student meets sexy racing-car driver,' she enlarged as Gabriel raised questioning brows. 'And the rest is history, as they say!'

'What do *you* say, Bella?'

What should Bella say?

She could say that she had behaved like a complete idiot five years ago. She could say that she should have had more sense than to fall for all that rakish charm and spent that one glorious night in his arms. She could say that she should never have committed the complete folly of falling in love with a man like Gabriel Danti!

'Oh, no, you don't, Gabriel.' Her smile was tight. 'You're not going to distract me from my original question by annoying me.'

'I'm not?'

'No, you're not!'

He quirked dark brows. 'I am curious as to why our talking about the night we spent together five years ago should cause annoyance.'

'Gabriel!' she protested.

'Bella…?'

Maybe if he had continued to call her Isabella in that cold and distant way then Bella would have refused to answer him. Maybe. But when he said her name in that sexy, husky way she had no chance!

She sighed. 'I really don't want to argue with you again tonight, Gabriel.'

He nodded. 'Fine, then we will not argue.'

'We can't seem to do anything else!'

He shrugged his shoulders beneath the cream silk shirt he wore.

'We are here together for a week, Bella, with no other distractions. We have to talk about something.'

'I've already told you what happened that night. I'm more interested in what happened afterwards,' she said firmly.

Gabriel's mouth tightened. 'You are once again referring to the car crash in which two men died.'

The sudden coolness in his gaze, the slight withdrawal Bella sensed in his manner, told her how reluctant Gabriel was to talk about the accident.

At least as reluctant as Bella was to talk about that night they had spent together!

She gave him a direct look. 'I assure you I'm not going to be hurt by anything you have to say concerning your feelings for Janine Childe.'

'No?' Gabriel's eyes glittered in the moonlight that shone in the ever-encroaching darkness.

'No,' Bella said. 'You aren't the first man to go to bed with one woman when you're actually in love with another one. I very much doubt that you'll be the last, either!' she added with a rueful smile.

Gabriel's jaw tensed. 'You believe me so utterly dishonourable?'

'I believe you were a man surrounded by Formula One groupies who were only too happy to go to bed with defending champion Gabriel Danti, whether he was in love with someone else or not,' Bella explained practically.

'Formula One *groupies*?' Gabriel exclaimed.

'Oh, stop being obtuse, Gabriel,' Bella teased gently. 'Women of all ages find that macho image as sexy as hell, you know that.'

'Did you?' He sounded amused now.

'We weren't talking about *me*—'

'Why did you go to bed with me that night, Bella?'

He had called her Bella again! Her defences were already in tatters after the momentous recognition earlier of her love for this man, without that!

'Because you were sexy as hell, of course,' she said brightly. 'Now could you just—'

'Past tense, Bella?' Gabriel cut in softly, an edge to those husky tones. 'You no longer find me sexy?'

If Bella found Gabriel any sexier she would literally be drooling down her chin at how gorgeous he looked this evening with the dark thickness of his hair flowing onto his shoulders and the way that cream silk shirt emphasised every muscled inch of his chest.

If Bella found him any sexier she would be ripping that shirt from his back just so that she could touch bare flesh.

If she found Gabriel any sexier she would be on her knees begging him to make love to her again!

And again.

And again…

Just thinking about it made Bella's breasts firm and swell, the nipples hardening against the soft material of her dress, and an aching warmth begin to start between her thighs.

She shot him an irritated glance. 'You should have a public health warning stamped on your forehead!' She scowled as he began to smile. 'I'm glad *you* think it's funny,' she muttered.

Gabriel continued to smile as he regarded Bella across the width of the table. Without Bella realising it—or particularly wanting it?—they were becoming easier together in each other's company.

He sat forward slightly. 'Your public health warning should be on your breasts.'

Colour suffused Bella's cheeks. 'My *breasts*…?' she choked.

Gabriel nodded. 'They are beautiful, Bella. Firm. Round. A perfect fit in my hands. And your nipples are—'

'I'm not sure this is altogether polite after-dinner conversation, Gabriel!' she gasped when she could once more catch her breath.

Gabriel allowed his gaze to lower to the part of her anatomy under discussion as they pressed firm and pouting against the material of her gown. A clear indication that their conversation had roused Bella as much as it had him.

Yet he could not—no, he dared not—make love to her. The fear of further loss and trauma in his life made Gabriel determined not to put Bella's life at risk with a possible second pregnancy.

His mouth tightened as he realised the disastrous predicament he'd landed them both in. 'You are right, Isabella, it is not.' He stood up suddenly.

'I— Where are you going?' Bella frowned as Gabriel strode off towards the beach.

He turned on the pathway, the moonlight turning his hair to ebony and reflecting in his eyes. 'I require some time to myself,' he said distantly.

Gabriel needed some time to himself…

He couldn't have told Bella any more clearly that after only two days alone together he was already bored in her company!

'Fine.' She nodded abruptly. 'I'll see you in morning, then,' she added lamely, still slightly stunned by the way Gabriel's mood had changed so swiftly from seduction to a need to go off by himself. After spending so many weeks resisting him, Bella was also shocked by the fierce desire that she *wanted* to be seduced.

'No doubt,' he answered curtly.

And, Bella realised painfully, he looked far from pleased at the prospect…

The two days it had taken Gabriel to find himself bored with her company was the same two days it had taken Bella to realise she was more in love with him than ever!

CHAPTER TEN

'BREAKFAST, Bella.'

Bella felt as if she were fighting through layers of fog as she roused herself from a deep and troubled sleep, inwardly wincing as she remembered exactly where she was. And who she was with…

Once again Bella had pretended to be asleep the previous night when Gabriel had finally come to bed about two hours after her, and had known by the restlessness of Gabriel's movements as he lay beside her that he was no more asleep than she was.

Still they hadn't spoken. Hadn't touched. Had just lain there, side by side, awake but totally uncommunicative.

'Your coffee is becoming cold, Bella,' Gabriel told her sharply.

Bella could smell that coffee, and warm buttery croissants, finally opening her eyes to frown up at Gabriel as he stood beside the bed holding a breakfast tray. He was already fully dressed, his hair still damp from the shower, evidence that he had been up for some time.

'Why the breakfast in bed, Gabriel?' Bella sat up against the sumptuous pillows, having decided attack was her best form of defence after the way the two of them had parted the previous evening.

He shrugged. 'It seemed like something a new husband should do for his bride.' He placed the tray across her knees and stepped back.

'No one has ever brought me breakfast in bed before,' Bella muttered uncomfortably, keeping her gaze averted from him to instead look down at the pot of coffee and the freshly warmed croissants with a deliciously tempting pot of butter.

'As we are leaving later this morning I thought it best if I ensure you have something to eat—'

'Leaving?' Bella cut in incredulously, the breakfast tray forgotten as she stared up at Gabriel. 'As in going back to England leaving?'

He gave a haughty inclination of his head. 'As in going back to England leaving,' he confirmed evenly.

Bella was completely stunned as she watched Gabriel begin to take his clothes from the wardrobe obviously in preparation for packing them.

Gabriel had decided they were leaving. After only two days of their planned week-long honeymoon!

She gave a confused frown. 'This is all rather sudden, isn't it?'

What on earth were her family going to make of them cutting their honeymoon short like this? Especially Toby!

Gabriel saw the doubts flickering across Bella's face. A face that showed the strain of the last few days and nights in the heavy tiredness of her eyes and the unhappy slant to her mouth.

The same strain that Gabriel was feeling. Although he doubted that Bella's strain was for the same reason as his own!

He shook his head. 'You are unhappy here, Isabella.'

'So are you!' she shot back.

His mouth tightened. 'We were not talking about me.'

'No, we weren't, were we?' Bella said. 'Why is that, Gabriel? Why is it that you can never give me a straightforward answer to a straightforward question?'

Those dark eyes narrowed warningly. 'Perhaps because the questions you ask have no straightforward answer.'

She sighed in disgust. 'You're doing it again!'

Gabriel was well aware of what he was doing. But he could not tell Bella of his fears, of his need to leave here, before he once again put her life at risk if she conceived a second time. 'If you think that your family will be concerned at our early return from our honeymoon, then I suggest you go straight to your cottage. That way no one even has to know we are back.'

Bella frowned. 'What's the difference between us staying here for another five days or hiding out in my cottage?'

Gabriel gave a humourless smile. 'I said that *you* could go straight to your cottage, Isabella, not that I would be joining you there.'

Her face blanked of all expression. 'I see...'

'Do you?' Gabriel said grimly.

'Oh, yes,' Bella snapped as she placed the breakfast tray on the bedside table before swinging her legs to the floor and sitting up. 'I can be ready to leave in half an hour or so, if that's okay with you?'

Gabriel had thought Bella would be pleased at the idea

of leaving the island today. That she would be even happier at the idea of being relieved of his company once they were back in England. But instead she merely looked angry.

'There is no rush,' he told her. 'I have radioed ahead and instructed that the plane be fuelled and ready to leave as soon as we arrive.'

'Now I know where Toby gets his organisational skills from!' Bella huffed as she stood up. 'I would like some privacy to get showered and dressed, if you wouldn't mind, Gabriel?' She looked at him challengingly.

'Would it matter if I did?' he growled.

Her eyes flashed violet fire at him. 'Not in the least!'

His mouth thinned to a severe line. 'As I thought. Eat some of the breakfast, Isabella,' he instructed. 'You will feel less sick on the helicopter if you have eaten.'

'No—I'll just have something to be sick with!' she contradicted him mutinously.

'That is true, also,' Gabriel murmured dryly.

Bella glared. 'Please don't attempt to try and sugar-coat it for me!'

She looked so beautiful as she faced him across the room, her face flushed with anger and the darkness of her hair a wild tangle about her shoulders, the long, pale cream nightgown clinging to the lushness of her curvaceous figure.

It was all Gabriel could do to stop himself from taking the few steps that separated them before gathering Bella into his arms and making love to her until she screamed for mercy!

Instead he stepped towards the bedroom door. 'I will be outside if you should need me.'

'I won't,' she assured him firmly.

No, she probably wouldn't, Gabriel acknowledged ruefully as he strode outside into the sunshine to take deep, calming breaths of the fragrant air.

Much as he had done the previous evening as he walked along the moonlit shoreline and reminded himself all the reasons he dared not make love to Bella again...

'I thought you said you had to leave?' Bella reminded Gabriel many hours later as, having driven her to her cottage, he now lingered in the sitting-room.

The helicopter flight to the mainland had been less traumatic than the one going to the island, Bella having been prepared for the uneven flight this time.

The long flight on the Danti jet back to England had been free of incident, too—probably because neither of them had suggested going anywhere near the temptation of the bedroom at the back of the plane!

Once they'd landed in England Bella had protested the need for Gabriel to drive her back to the cottage. She could find her own way, she'd said. But it had been a battle she had lost. As she lost all of her battles against Gabriel...

But having been delivered here safely, Bella now expected him to leave. In fact, she was counting on it. Mainly because if Gabriel didn't soon go and leave her to her privacy, Bella knew she was going to give in to the hot tears that had been threatening to fall all day!

'Are you not going to at least offer me a cup of coffee?' Gabriel asked.

Her eyes widened. 'It's late, Gabriel, and I thought you had somewhere else to go.'

He frowned. 'I did not say that.'

'You implied it.'

Gabriel was well aware of what he had implied. As he was aware, now the time had come to part from Bella, that he was reluctant to do so.

'I am not sure it is the right thing to do, to just leave you here on your own.'

She laughed humourlessly. 'I've lived on my own for two years, Gabriel—'

'You have lived here with Toby,' he cut in firmly. 'That is not the same thing.'

No, it wasn't, Bella accepted ruefully, already aware of how quiet, how empty, the cottage seemed without her small son's presence.

'I'm a big girl now, Gabriel; I'm sure I'll manage,' she said dryly.

His eyes darkened in intensity, that familiar nerve pulsing in his clenched jaw. 'I am well aware of the fact that you are a big girl, Isabella.'

'Then I suggest you stop treating me like I'm six years old rather than twenty-six!'

His mouth flattened into a disapproving line. 'Showing concern for your welfare is treating you like a child?'

Bella shook her head impatiently. 'No, actually treating me like a child is doing that!'

'How would you have me treat you, Isabella?' Gabriel glowered his frustration with this conversation.

Bella became very still, very aware of the sudden tension in the room. She could almost feel the crackle of electricity that arced between herself and Gabriel…

She swallowed hard. 'I think you should just go.'

Gabriel thought so, too. In fact, he knew so! Before

he did something he would later regret. Something they might both have reason to regret.

Except…

Bella looked tired after their long journey, her eyes purple smudges in a face that was pale with exhaustion, and the fullness of her lips bare of lip gloss. But nevertheless there was a beguiling determination to the stubborn lift of her chin, that challenge reflected in the brilliance of her eyes and the proud stance of her tiny body.

Gabriel felt the throb of his arousal just looking at her.

Telling him it was definitely time that he left!

'I should go, yes,' he acknowledged huskily.

'Yes.'

'Now.'

'Yes.'

'Bella—'

'Gabriel…?'

He drew in a ragged breath. 'I need to go!'

'You do.'

Except Gabriel moved *towards* Bella rather than away from her as he crossed the room in two long strides to pull her hard against him even as his head lowered and his mouth claimed hers in a need as primitive and as old as time.

As wild and primitive as his fierce, uncontrollable desire to possess Bella again…

Gabriel's hands moved to become entangled in her hair as he kissed her hungrily, fiercely, his lips parting hers and allowing his tongue to plunge deeply into the heat beyond. Bella's mouth tasted of honey, and was hot, so very hot, as she drew him deeper inside her.

Gabriel curved her body into the hardness of his as he continued to kiss and claim her. His hands spread over her bottom as he pulled her against him and pressed her to the ache in his thighs, his arousal hard and pulsing, demanding, the need to possess her so strong that Gabriel could think of nothing else, feel nothing else but Bella.

He wrenched his mouth from hers to bury his face against the satin smoothness of her throat, licking, tasting, biting. 'We should stop this now, Bella!'

'Yes,' she breathed shakily.

'I cannot be gentle with you!' Gabriel groaned, knowing it was true. He had waited too long. Wanted her for far too long!

Bella already knew that, had felt his urgency the moment he took her in his arms. An urgency that she echoed, that had ignited the moment he'd touched her. No, even before he'd touched her! This physical awareness had been there between them all day, Bella realised now, burning just below the surface of even the most mundane of conversations.

'I won't break, Gabriel,' she encouraged, her throat arched to the erotic heat of his questing mouth, her fingers entangled in the silky softness of his hair. 'Just don't stop. Please don't stop...' She quivered with longing, several buttons ripping off her blouse as Gabriel parted it to bare her breasts to his lips and tongue, drawing one swollen tip into the heat of his mouth hungrily as one of his hands cupped and squeezed its twin.

Bella sobbed low in her throat as the pleasure ripped through her, to become centred as a hot ache between her thighs. She was so swollen there, so needy as she pressed against Gabriel's arousal, she could barely think straight.

He moved against her, his hardness, his length and thickness, a promise of even greater pleasure. A pleasure Bella had no intention of letting Gabriel deny either of them. She wanted him inside her. Wanted to look up at Gabriel, to watch his face as he stroked long and hard inside her. Wanted to hear his groans of pleasure as they matched her own. To hear his cries as they reached that pinnacle together.

'Not this time, Gabriel.' She moved away as his hand went to open the fastening of her jeans. 'I want to touch you first. Kiss you. All of you,' she added huskily, her gaze deliberately holding his as she unbuttoned his shirt before slowly slipping it down his arms and dropping it onto the carpeted floor. Her fingers looked much paler than the darkness of Gabriel's skin as she touched the hard wall of his chest. 'You're so beautiful, Gabriel…!' she whispered before she began to kiss each and every one of his scars, her tongue a delicate rasp against the heat of his skin as she tasted him.

Gabriel knew that his scarred body was far from beautiful, but he ceased to care about anything else as Bella's lips roamed across him freely, her tongue flickering against him even as her hand flattened against the hardness of his arousal, his erection responding immediately as that hand moved against him slowly, rhythmically. Gabriel felt his blood pulsing, pounding, increasing in urgency.

They had spent five weeks together before their wedding and two days alone on a romantic Caribbean island. And yet it was here, and now, in Bella's tiny cottage, when he knew they would be apart for several hours, that Gabriel completely lost control!

'I need—Bella, I need—' He broke off with a groan as Bella unfastened his jeans and pushed them out of the way so that she might fulfil that need.

Her mouth was so hot as she took him inside her, her tongue moist and her fingers curling about him as she caressed the length of him.

Gabriel became lost in the pleasure of this dual assault upon his senses, his neck arched, his muscles tensing, locking, as he fought to maintain control.

Just a little longer. He wanted—needed to enjoy being with Bella just a little longer, and then he would leave, Gabriel promised himself silently as Bella manoeuvred him gently backwards so that he sat down in an armchair, her hair a wild tumble about his thighs as she knelt in front of him.

Just a few minutes more of being inside the heat of Bella's mouth. Of her wicked little tongue moistly caressing the length of his shaft. Of her fingers about him as he instinctively began to move to that same mind-blowing rhythm.

Bella raised her lids to look at Gabriel, deliberately holding his gaze with hers as her tongue swirled provocatively about the head of his pulsing erection. Licking. Teasing. Tasting.

Gabriel's face was flushed with arousal, his eyes fevered, his jaw clenched, and the muscles standing out in his throat as he fought not to lose that control.

'No more!' he growled even as he reached down and pulled Bella away from him, grasping her arms to lift her up so that his mouth could capture hers. Bella straddled him as they kissed wildly, feverishly, Gabriel's hands hot against her back as his mouth made love to hers.

Gabriel stood up, their mouths still fused wildly together. His hands cupped about Bella's bottom to lift her up with him before he lay her down on the carpeted floor, lifting his head to part her already ruined blouse and then feast on her naked breasts.

He kissed first one nipple and then the other, Bella whimpering softly when he finally raised his head to look down at the swollen fullness of her breasts. His gaze deliberately held hers as he moved to his knees beside her to brush the pads of his thumbs over those achingly sensitive nipples, watching the way Bella's eyes darkened and she groaned low in her throat even as she arched up into that caress.

Gabriel continued to hold that gaze as he unfastened her jeans and peeled them down her thighs to remove them completely, parting her legs so that he could move in between them. His hands were big and dark against her abdomen as he caressed her in slow swirling movements in a deliberate path to the soft, dark curls that were visible to him through the cream lace of her panties.

Bella was breathing hard as she watched Gabriel touching her, his fingers warm and gentle. A low moan escaped her as he swept one of those fingers against the lacy material that covered the cleft between her legs, her hips moving up to meet that tantalising caress.

That finger moved against her again.

Again Bella moved up to meet that caress.

And again.

Teasing her. Pleasuring her. Torturing her.

'Yes, Gabriel…!' Bella finally pleaded as she moved against him in frustration.

He peeled her panties down her thighs and legs to discard them completely, his eyes intense as he looked down at her before slowly lowering his head. First his hands touched her, then his lips, softly, tenderly as he kissed the scar that hadn't been there five years ago.

But Bella had no time to dwell on that as his fingers parted the dark curls beneath and his mouth moved lower…

Dear God!

Pleasure unlike anything she had ever known before radiated out to every part of her body as the sweep of Gabriel's tongue against that pulsing nub brought her to the edge of release and then took her crashing over it in wave after wave of such intensity it was almost pain.

Bella was mindless with pleasure, her breath releasing in a sob as she felt Gabriel part her sensitive folds and enter her, first with one finger, and then with two. As his tongue continued to caress that aching nub her head moved wildly from side to side and her hands clenched as Gabriel took her to a climax that was even more intense than the first.

It wasn't enough.

It would never be enough!

Bella surged up to push Gabriel down onto the carpet and pull off his remaining clothes before moving up and over him, her hands resting against his shoulders as the heat between her thighs became a hot caress against the hardness of his shaft, her breasts a temptation just beyond his reach as she bent slightly towards him.

'No, Bella—' Gabriel broke off with a groan as she opened herself to him and took him into her, inch by slow inch, until he was completely inside her. Her heat, her tightness wrapped around him. 'We must not do this—'

'*I* must,' she insisted.

Gabriel ceased breathing altogether as Bella began to move with an agonising slowness that sent the pleasure rocketing into his brain and down to his toes.

Gabriel felt himself grow even harder, bigger, no longer able to bear the torment of her breasts above him as he moved his head up and captured one of those rose-tipped breasts into his mouth.

Bella plunged down to take him deeper, before moving up so that only the very tip of him remained inside her. Before plunging down again and again. Gabriel was so big now, so long that it felt as if he touched the very centre of her.

His hands moved to grasp her hips and guide her movements as he felt his imminent release, hearing Bella's cry as she reached a climax at the same time as he did.

CHAPTER ELEVEN

'WE SHOULD not have done that!'

Bella had collapsed weakly against the dampness of Gabriel's chest as the last of the pleasure rippled through her body, but she raised her head now to look down at him incredulously. '*What* did you just say?'

Gabriel's expression was grim as he returned her gaze. 'I should not have done this, Bella—'

She gasped in shock, moving abruptly back and then away from him, clasping her ruined blouse about her nakedness as she disengaged their bodies before standing up. 'Get out, Gabriel,' she choked.

'Bella—'

'Just *get out*!' she repeated shakily, turning away to find her panties, her legs trembling slightly as she tried to balance before pulling them on over her nakedness.

How could Gabriel do this to her? How could he?

What she had thought of as being something beautiful, utterly unique, had now become nothing more than something she wished to forget.

To wish had never happened!

'Would you just put some clothes on and leave, Gabriel?'

He rose slowly to his feet, magnificent in his naked-ness, his hair tousled about his shoulders, his chest broad and muscled, thighs powerful still, his legs long and elegant.

Bella turned away from looking at all that raw, male beauty. 'I don't want you to say anything, Gabriel. I don't want you to do anything. I just want you to get dressed and leave. Now,' she insisted.

'Bella—'

'Now!'

'You misunderstood my reasoning just now, Bella—'

'Don't touch me!' She moved sharply away from the hands he placed on her shoulders, shying away from even that physical contact.

Gabriel frowned fiercely as he saw her expression. 'You did not seem to find my touch so distasteful a few minutes ago,' he rasped.

'Any more than you did mine,' she retaliated. 'I guess we both just got so carried away with the moment we forgot to look at the broader picture!'

Gabriel's eyes narrowed. 'And what might that be?' he asked softly.

'Will you just get some clothes on?' she repeated im-patiently. 'I find it a little disconcerting talking to a man when he's completely naked.'

'I'm not just any man, Isabella, I am your husband,' he pointed out harshly as he swiftly pulled his jeans back on and fastened them.

'I know exactly who and what you are, Gabriel,' she said. 'What I meant, Gabriel, is that the only reason you married me was because of Toby—'

'Isabella—'

'Would you have even thought of offering me marriage if not for Toby?' she challenged.

'Neither of us will ever know now what would have happened after we met again in San Francisco—'

'*I* know,' Bella said scornfully. 'I very much doubt we would ever have seen each other again after San Francisco if you hadn't learnt of Toby's existence!'

Gabriel drew in a deep, controlling breath. 'This is perhaps not the time to talk about this. You are distraught—'

'I'm *angry*, Gabriel, not distraught. With myself,' she added. 'For falling—yet again!—for your seduction routine!'

'My seduction routine?' he echoed incredulously.

Bella nodded. 'No doubt honed over years spent on the Formula One racing circuit! And don't bother trying to deny it,' she warned. 'I still remember the practised way you seduced me five years ago!'

He scowled. 'That was five years ago, Isabella—'

'Then you must be pleased to know that you haven't lost any of your seductive skills!' she snapped.

Gabriel studied her closely, wanting to take her in his arms, to explain his fears for her—

'Insulting me is only making this situation worse, Bella,' he told her softly instead.

'Worse? Could it be any worse?' she cried. 'We've just ripped each other's clothes off in a sexual frenzy—in my case, literally.' She looked down at her gaping blouse, the buttons scattered on the carpet at their feet. 'I don't want to talk about this any more, Gabriel,' she told him flatly, her expression bleak. 'All I want is for you to leave.'

Gabriel's mouth firmed. 'I will return tomorrow—'

'Don't hurry back on my account!' she exclaimed.

'We need to talk.'

'I very much doubt that there's anything you have to say that I will want to hear,' she told him wearily.

A nerve pulsed in Gabriel's clenched jaw. Bella looked so beautiful with the darkness of her hair tangled about her shoulders, and her lips still swollen from the heat of their kisses, so utterly desirable, that all Gabriel wanted was to take her in his arms and make love with her again. And again.

'Nevertheless, I will return later tomorrow,' he bit out with grim determination.

She raised mocking brows as he made no effort to leave. 'I hope you aren't waiting for me to tell you I'll be looking forward to it!'

'No, I am not expecting you to say that.' Gabriel gave a humourless smile. 'Your honesty is one of the things I like most about you, Bella.'

'One of the few things, I'm sure,' she said knowingly. 'If you'll excuse me, now?' She turned away. 'I would like to take a shower and then go to bed.'

Alone, Bella could have added, but didn't. What was the point in stating the obvious?

She raised her chin defensively. 'Goodbye, Gabriel.'

'It will never be goodbye between the two of us, Isabella,' he stated calmly.

No, it never would be, Bella accepted heavily once Gabriel had finally gone. They would continue with this sham of a marriage for as long as it took. For as long as Toby needed them to do so.

For Toby...

Her small, happily contented son had absolutely no

idea that his very existence had condemned his parents to a marriage that was completely devoid of love.

Except Bella's love for Gabriel.

A love she would never—could never, reveal to him...

'Where have you been?'

'Where does it look as if I've been?' Bella answered Gabriel sarcastically as she carried on taking the bags of shopping from the boot of her car. 'I wasn't expecting you back just yet,' she added as Gabriel took some of those bags out of her hands.

She had seen the powerful black sports car parked outside the cottage as soon as she turned her own car down the lane, a heaviness settling in her chest as she easily recognised Gabriel sitting behind the wheel.

Despite her exhaustion Bella had lain awake in bed for hours the previous night, unable to stop thinking about Gabriel. About the wild ecstasy of their lovemaking. And then of his declaration that they shouldn't have made love at all...!

Consequently it had been almost dawn before she had finally fallen asleep. Almost midday before she'd woke up again, feeling as if she hadn't slept at all. Several hours, and half a dozen cups of black coffee later, before she'd summoned up the energy to dress and go out to shop for food.

Which was where she had obviously been when Gabriel had arrived at the cottage. Much earlier than she had expected—it was only a little after five o'clock—and looking much too rakishly handsome for Bella's comfort in a black polo shirt and faded jeans.

'Thanks,' Bella accepted coolly as he carried half a

dozen of the bags through to the kitchen for her. 'Can I get you a coffee or anything?' she said offhandedly, her face averted as she began to unpack the bags.

But—as usual!—she was still very much aware of Gabriel as he stood only a couple of feet away from her as she put the groceries away in the cupboards. Silently. Watchfully.

'Better yet,' she added brightly, 'why don't you make yourself useful and prepare the coffee while I finish putting these things away? Gabriel…?' she said uncertainly when he didn't answer her. In fact, Bella realised with a frown, he hadn't said a word since asking where she had been…

Gabriel looked at her quizzically, easily noting the dark shadows beneath her eyes, and the hollows of her cheeks, the pallor of her face thrown into stark relief by the fact that her hair was drawn back and secured at her crown with a toothed clasp.

Dressed in a deep pink T-shirt that clung to the fullness of her breasts, and jeans that emphasised the slenderness of her hips and legs, and with her face completely bare of make-up, Bella looked ten years younger than the twenty-six years she had only yesterday evening assured him she actually was.

Gabriel's mouth tightened as he thought of yesterday evening. 'I will make the coffee. Then I wish for the two of us to talk.'

She stiffened. 'Not about last night, I hope?'

He gave a stiff inclination of his head. 'Amongst other things.'

Bella made a movement of denial. 'There's nothing left for us to say about last night—'

'There is *everything* for us to say about last night!' Gabriel contradicted her furiously before visibly controlling himself. 'I will not let you put even more barriers between us, Bella. If you prefer, I will talk, and you need only listen…?'

Bella eyed him warily, having no idea what he could have to say that she would want to listen to. He had said far too much last night!

'And if I don't like what you have to say?' she challenged.

'Then I will have to respect that,' he said curtly.

Bella continued to look at him wordlessly for several long seconds before giving an abrupt nod of her head. 'Fine,' she said. 'Just make the coffee first, hmm?'

What should have been a relaxed domestic scene, with Bella putting the groceries away and Gabriel making the pot of coffee, was anything but! Bella was far too aware of Gabriel—on every level—to feel in the least relaxed.

How could she possibly relax when Gabriel was just too vibrantly male? Too ruggedly handsome. Too physically overpowering. Too—too everything!

But, having finally put all the shopping away, two mugs of hot coffee poured and Gabriel already seated at the kitchen table, there was nothing else Bella could do to delay sitting down and listening while Gabriel talked.

'Well?' she prompted sharply after several seconds, the silence between them so absolute that Bella could hear every tick of the clock hanging on the wall above the dresser.

Gabriel's expression was pained. 'I realise you are still angry with me, Bella, but I do not believe I have done anything to deserve your contempt.'

Not recently, Bella acknowledged self-derisively, having accepted during her deliberations last night that she was just as responsible for what had happened between them the previous evening as Gabriel was. That she had wanted him as much as he had appeared to want her.

She sighed heavily. 'I'm not angry, Gabriel,' she admitted ruefully. 'At least, not with you.'

He gave her a searching glance. 'You are angry with yourself because we made love last night?'

'We had *sex* last night, Gabriel—'

'We *made love*—'

'You can call it what you like, but we both know what it really was!' Her eyes glittered angrily.

Gabriel drew in another controlling breath. 'I thought I was going to talk and you were going to listen?'

'Not if you're going to say things I don't agree with!' she snapped.

Gabriel didn't know whether to shake Bella or kiss her! Although he very much doubted that Bella would welcome either action in her present mood.

'I will endeavour not to do so,' he teased.

'You just can't guarantee it,' Bella acknowledged dryly.

Gabriel shrugged. 'It is not always possible to know what is or is not going to anger you.'

'Well, as long as you steer clear of last night or anything that happened five years ago, you should be on pretty safe ground!'

Gabriel grimaced. 'Ah.'

Her eyes widened. 'You *are* going to tell me about five years ago…?'

'It was my intention to do so, yes.'

'But—you've never wanted to talk about it!'

'The situation has changed— Bella…?' he questioned as she stood up abruptly and moved to stand with her back to the room as she stared out of the kitchen window.

Bella's neck was so delicately vulnerable, her back slender, her shoulders narrow—far too narrow, Gabriel acknowledged heavily, for her to have carried alone the burden of her pregnancy and then the bringing up of their son for the last four and a half years.

'Please, Bella…?' he asked again softly.

It felt as if Bella's heart were actually being squeezed in her chest as she heard the gentleness in Gabriel's tone.

When they were on the island she had asked Gabriel to tell her what really happened five years ago. At the time she had genuinely wanted to know the answer. But now—now when Bella already felt so vulnerable and exposed by her realised love for him, by the wildness of their lovemaking the previous evening— she really wasn't sure she could bear to hear Gabriel talk about his feelings for another woman.

Especially if he were to tell her he still had those feelings for Janine Childe…!

Coward, a little voice inside her head taunted mockingly. Bella had always known that Gabriel hadn't, didn't, and never would love her, so what difference did it make if he was now willing to talk about five years ago?

It shouldn't matter at all!

But it did…

Bella stiffened her shoulders, her expression deliberately unreadable as she turned back to face Gabriel. A defensive stance that almost crumbled as the gentleness she had heard in Gabriel's tone was echoed in the darkness of his eyes as he looked across the kitchen at her.

Damn it, she didn't want his pity!

She wanted his love. She had wanted that five years ago, and she wanted it even more now. But if she couldn't have that then she certainly didn't want his pity!

Her shoulders straightened and her chin raised in challenge. 'Go ahead,' she finally invited tightly.

Gabriel continued to look at her silently for several seconds, and then he gave a decisive inclination of his head. 'First I need to tell you where I have been since we parted yesterday evening—'

'You said we were going to talk about what happened five years ago!' Bella cut in impatiently. Having built herself up, having placed a shield about her shaky emotions, Bella now needed to get this conversation over with before that barrier crumbled into dust!

Gabriel sighed at the interruption. 'My actions since we parted yesterday are relevant to that past. Sit with me, Bella?' Gabriel encouraged huskily as he saw that her face was paler than ever, those dark shadows beneath her eyes emphasised further by that pallor.

The fact that Bella actually did as he asked told Gabriel how much his presence, this conversation, had unsettled her. The last thing he wanted to do was hurt Bella any more than he already had, and yet it seemed his mere presence had managed do that.

He rubbed his eyes wearily. 'I will leave any time you ask me to do so, Bella.'

She gave a humourless smile. 'Is that a promise?'

'If you wish it, yes,' Gabriel assured her wryly.

Her eyed widened at his compliance. 'Are you sure you haven't received a blow to the head while you've been away?'

'Very funny, Bella,' he drawled.

'One tries,' she teased lightly.

Gabriel wasn't fooled for a moment by Bella's attempt at levity, knew by the wariness in her eyes and the tension beside her mouth that it was only a façade.

As his own calm was only a façade.

A nerve pulsed beside the livid scar on Gabriel's cheek. 'Bella, when we were on the island you asked me what really happened five years ago, when three Formula One cars crashed and two other men were killed as a consequence. Do you still want to know the answer to that question?'

'Yes, of course!'

'And you will believe me if I tell you the truth?'

'Of course I'll believe you, Gabriel.' She looked irritated that he should doubt it.

He smiled briefly. 'As was stated at the time, the findings of the official enquiry were that it was a complete accident, but I knew—I have always known—that it was Paulo Descari, and not I, who was responsible for our three cars colliding.'

'But—' Bella gasped. 'It was deliberate?'

Gabriel's jaw clenched. 'I believe so, yes.'

Bella stared at him, her expression once again blank. Why on earth would Paulo Descari have done such a thing? Unless...

'Because Janine Childe had decided she had made a

mistake? That she returned your love, after all?' Bella realised heavily. 'Had she told Paulo Descari she was ending their relationship in order to come back to you?'

Gabriel's expression was grim as he stood up abruptly. 'Neither of those things was possible, I am afraid, Bella,' he rasped. 'The first for the simple reason that there was no love on my side for Janine Childe to return. The second because it was I who had ended our brief relationship, and not the other way around as Janine so publicly claimed only hours after the accident. But I do believe Janine may have taunted Paulo with our relationship,' he continued. 'He tried to provoke an argument with me that morning, was so blind with jealousy that he would not believe me when I told him I had no feelings for Janine.' He sighed heavily. 'I was not physically responsible for the accident, Bella, but I have nevertheless always felt a certain guilt, not only because of my complete indifference to Janine, but because I survived and two other men did not.'

'But that's— You have no reason to feel guilty, Gabriel.' Bella gasped. 'You could so easily have died, too!'

'And instead I am here. With you,' Gabriel murmured huskily.

How long would it take for Bella to realise, to question, after the things he had just told her, the night the two of them had spent together five years ago?

Gabriel watched as the blankness left Bella's face to be replaced with a frown, that frown disappearing, too, seconds later as she looked across at him questioningly.

Gabriel drew in a controlling breath. 'I was unconscious for several days after the accident, and so was unable at the time to deny or confirm Janine's claim that I had caused the accident because I was still in love with her.' His top lip turned back contemptuously. 'By the time I was well enough to deny her accusations I simply did not care to do so,' he added flatly.

'Why didn't you?' Bella demanded incredulously. 'Surely you must have realised that Janine Childe's claims gave people reason to continue to have doubts despite the findings of the official enquiry?'

His eyes narrowed. 'Did you have reason to continue to doubt them, too, Bella?'

She shook her head vehemently. 'Not over your innocence, no.'

Gabriel had thought, had hoped this would be easier than it was. But it wasn't. Baring his soul in this way, with no idea of the outcome, was excruciating.

'I don't understand why you didn't speak out, Gabriel,' Bella said. 'From what you've said, you were supposed to be the one who died that day!'

He turned away. 'Jason was dead. As was Paulo. When people die, Bella, all that is left is the memories people who loved them have of them. What good did it do anyone, but especially Paulo and Jason's families, for me to claim that one man had possibly been deliberately responsible for the death of the other?'

Bella could see the logic behind Gabriel's words—she just couldn't make any sense of it!

'That was…very self-sacrificing, of you,' she murmured gently.

'More so than even I realised,' he acknowledged harshly.

She looked up sharply as a realisation hit her. 'You

really didn't make love to me that night because you were upset at losing Janine Childe to another man, did you?'

His smile was rueful. 'No, I did not.'

'Then—that morning you—' She moistened dry lips. 'You said you would call me. Did you really mean it?'

'Yes.'

'You did?' The beat of Bella's heart sounded very loud in her ears as her thoughts—her hopes, rose wildly.

'I did,' Gabriel confirmed heavily. 'Our night together had been—surprising.'

'Really?'

'Yes.' Gabriel took a deep breath. 'Unfortunately that altercation with Paulo meant I did not have chance to ring you before the practice session, and obviously I was unable to do so afterwards. Then, once I recovered and there had been no word from you, I believed you did not want to know.'

Bella's hands were clenched so tightly that she could feel her nails piercing the skin of her palms. Gabriel hadn't been in love with Janine Childe, not then and certainly not now. Gabriel had meant it that morning five years ago when he had said he would call her.

Tears blurred Bella's vision, Gabriel just a hazy outline as he stood so still and silent across the kitchen. 'I thought—I didn't believe I would ever see you again after that night.'

'A belief that became fact,' Gabriel rasped.

'But not because you wanted it that way!' Bella protested achingly.

'No.'

'Gabriel, I—I don't know what to say!' She stood up

restlessly. 'I was sitting at home that night when the announcement of the crash came on the evening news. Saw the two bodies lying on the ground. You being carried away on a stretcher before they placed you in the ambulance and rushed you off to hospital. It was the worst moment of my life.' She gave a disbelieving shake of her head. 'Or, at least, I thought it was, until Janine Childe appeared on the television immediately afterwards claiming that you were still in love with her.'

'It never occurred to me—I never realised that her lies would have convinced anyone, but I suppose I knew the real Janine, and you didn't." Gabriel frowned.

'It was the one about your being in love with her that I thought to be true,' Bella admitted. 'I didn't know you well, Gabriel, but I certainly never believed you capable of deliberately harming another man.'

'Bella, what would you have done that day if you had not believed I was in love with Janine?'

'I would have come to you, of course!' she exclaimed. 'I wouldn't have cared who had tried to stop me. I would have made them let me see you!'

'Why?'

Bella raised wary eyes to his. 'Why…?'

'Why, Bella?' Gabriel repeated gruffly.

Because she had fallen in love with him that night, that was why! Because she was still in love with him!

Gabriel's eyes narrowed as he saw the uncertainty flicker across Bella's face. The wariness. The desire not to be hurt again.

Gabriel felt that same desire, both five years ago and again now.

He drew in a deep breath, accepting that one of them

had to break the deadlock between them. 'Perhaps if I were to tell you why it was that I had no interest in what people believed happened that day…?'

Bella blinked, her throat moving convulsively as she swallowed hard before speaking. 'Why didn't you, Gabriel?'

His mouth twisted. 'For the same reason that nothing mattered to me when I regained consciousness two days after the accident.' He shrugged. 'Because you were not there, Bella,' he admitted bluntly. 'You were not there. Had never been there. And no matter how much I wished for it during those three months I spent in hospital, you still did not come.'

Bella looked totally stunned now. 'I don't understand…'

'No, I do not suppose that you do,' he accepted ruefully as he was the one to take the two steps that separated them before raising one of his hands to curve it about the coolness of her cheek. 'My beautiful Bella. My brave beautiful Bella.' He smiled emotionally. 'After all this time, all you have suffered, you deserve to know the truth.'

'The truth…?'

'That I fell in love with you that night five years ago—'

'No…!' Her cry was agonised and Gabriel only just managed to prevent her from falling as her knees gave way beneath her.

'Yes, Bella.' Gabriel's arms moved about her, his cheek resting against the darkness of her hair as he gathered her close against his chest. 'Impossible as it must seem, I fell in love with you that night. I have loved you always, Bella. You and only you. So much so that there has been no other woman in my life, or my bed, these last five years,' he added gruffly.

Bella clung to him as his words washed over and then into her. She had been stunned by what he had told her about the accident and by Janine Childe's duplicity, but this was even more shocking.

Gabriel loved her. He had always loved her.

The tears fell hotly down Bella's cheeks as she clung to him.

As she cried for all the pain and disillusionment they had unwittingly caused each other through misunderstandings. For all the time they had wasted…

She pulled away from him slightly before looking up into his face, her heart aching as she still saw the uncertainty in his face. 'Gabriel, impossible as it must seem, I fell in love with you that night five years ago, too.' Bella held his gaze with hers as she deliberately repeated his words. 'I have loved you always, Gabriel. You and only you. So much so that there has been no other man in my life, or my bed, these last five years.'

His expression didn't change. He didn't blink. He didn't speak. He didn't even seem to be breathing as he continued to stare down at her.

'Gabriel?' Bella's gaze searched his face worriedly. 'Gabriel, I love you. I love you!' she repeated desperately as she reached up to clasp his arms and shake him slightly. 'I never meant to let you down after the accident, I just thought I had been a one-night stand to you. Gabriel, please—'

'You did not let me down, Bella,' he cut in harshly. 'You have never let me down. *I* was the one who let *you* down when it did not even occur to me that you might believe I was in love with Janine. *I* was the one who let *you* down by not even thinking you might become pregnant from our night together. How can you love me after what you have suffered because my pride would not let me be the one to seek you out again? How can you love me when my arrogance, my intolerance, meant you had to go through your pregnancy, Toby's birth, the first four and a half years of his life, completely alone?'

'Gabriel, I'd really rather you didn't continue to insult the man I love,' Bella interrupted shakily. 'And I wasn't alone,' she reassured him, 'I had my parents. My sister and brother.'

'I should have been there for you, too,' Gabriel growled in self-disgust. 'Instead of which, when we did finally meet up again, I only made matters worse by forcing you into marrying me.' He shook his head. 'I should not have done that, Bella.'

'You're Toby's father—'

'He was not the reason I forced our marriage upon you, Bella. It was —' He stopped and then sighed. 'Having met you again, having realised that I still love you, I could not bear the thought of having to let you go again!'

Gabriel hadn't married her just for Toby, after all?

Bella looked puzzled. 'But if you felt that way—if you do still love me—'

'I love you now more than ever, Bella,' he assured her fiercely.

'Then why did we leave the island so abruptly?'

'We left the island so suddenly for the same reason I should not have allowed our lovemaking last night to go as far as it did,' Gabriel cut in grimly. 'You almost died giving birth to Toby, Bella. I would not—I did not want to put your life at risk by another unplanned pregnancy, and so I decided we had to leave the island before I gave in to the temptation being alone there with you represented. That we needed to consult an obstetrician before we made love again. Instead of which, as soon as we were back here, I allowed—!' He shook his head. 'I had an appointment to see a specialist in Harley Street today, needed to know that a second pregnancy would not endanger your life. He was most unhelpful,' Gabriel said, patently annoyed, 'and said he could not pass comment before first examining you.'

'You spoke to an obstetrician about me...?' Bella echoed dazedly.

Gabriel frowned darkly. 'What if you are pregnant right now, Bella?' His face had gone pale at the mere thought of it. 'What if our time together last night results in another child?'

A slow, beatific smile curved Bella's lips as she realised their sudden flight from the island, Gabriel's grimness after they made love last night, had all been for one reason and one reason only.

'Then I, for one, would be absolutely thrilled,' she assured him breathlessly. 'I thought you wanted lots of brothers and sisters for Toby?' she cajoled as Gabriel still looked haunted.

'Not at the risk of losing you,' he stated definitely.

'We don't know for sure that there is any risk,' Bella teased him, no longer daunted by the fierceness of Gabriel's moods. He loved her. They loved each other. Together they could overcome any obstacles that might come their way.

'Until you have seen this obstetrician we do not know for sure that there is not, either,' Gabriel persisted.

'Have a little faith, Gabriel. Remember you're a Danti!'

Some of the tension started to leave Gabriel's body as Bella's eyes laughed up into his. 'Are you mocking me, Bella?'

'Just a little.' Her throaty chuckle gave lie to the claim. 'I'm all for taking risks, Gabriel. In fact, I think a little more risk-taking right now might be good for both of us...' she added huskily, taking his hand in hers to begin walking towards the stairs, shooting him a provocative smile over her shoulder as she did so.

Gabriel followed Bella like a man in a daze, totally unable to deny her anything. Knowing that he never would be able to deny her anything. That, having found her again, knowing she loved him as much as he loved her, that she always had, he intended spending the rest of his life loving as well as protecting Bella.

Their daughter, Clara Louisa, was born safely and without complications exactly a year later, followed two years later by the equally safe birth of their twin sons, Simon Henry and Peter Cristo...

MISTRESS, MOTHER... WIFE?

MAGGIE COX

To my singing teacher, Jeanette Barnes,
who has become a good friend and makes the
most comforting cup of tea in the world!

CHAPTER ONE

IT WAS a pastime she liked to employ when things got a little slower towards the end of the evening. She'd scan the remaining customers who were lingering over their drinks at tables or at the bar and conjure up a tale about them. Making up stories was meat and drink to Anna… it was the thing that had kept her sane and protected when she was a child. Her little made-up worlds had all been so much safer and fulfilling than reality, and there were many, many times she'd sought refuge there.

Now, as though tugged by a powerful magnet, yet again she considered the handsome, square-jawed individual staring into space in the furthermost corner of the room. He'd occupied the stylish burgundy armchair for at least two hours now, had neither removed his coat nor glanced interestedly at the other well-heeled patrons even once. It was as though they were completely off his radar. All he seemed to be focused on was the inner screen of his own troubled mind.

There was definitely an intense, preoccupied air about him that intrigued Anna. After all, what dreamer with a yen for making up stories *wouldn't* be intrigued or provoked by such fascinating material? Making sure she was discreet, she studied him hard. She hadn't personally looked into his eyes yet, but already she guessed they would have the power to hynotise whoever was caught in their gaze. A small shiver ran down her spine.

Having checked the room to see if she was needed anywhere, she let her gaze return to the mystery man. He had straight mid-blond hair, with hints of silver in it, and appeared to be growing out a cut that had probably been both stylish and expensive. Everything about him exuded wealth and good taste, a well as the sense of power and entitlement that often accompanied those attributes. Although his eye-catching broad shoulders appeared weighed down by his concerns, he also wore a fierce need for privacy that was like an invisible electronic gate, warning all comers that they encroached upon his space at their peril. Had an important deal gone sour? Had someone deceived him or seriously let him down in some way? *He didn't look like a man who suffered fools gladly.*

Anna sighed, then studied him again. No...she'd got it all wrong. The black coat he was wearing suddenly sang out to her. He'd lost someone close. Yes, that was it. He was grieving. That was why his expression was so haunted and morose. As she studied his formidable chiselled profile, with the deep shadow of a cleft centred in that square-cut chin, it seemed almost impertinent to speculate about him further if she'd guessed the truth. *Poor man...* He must be feeling totally wretched.

The third Scotch on the rocks he'd ordered was drained right down to the bottom of the glass, Anna noticed. Would he be ordering another one? Bitter personal experience had taught her that alcohol never solved anything. *All it had done for her father was make his black moods even blacker.*

The hotel bar closed at eleven-thirty and it was already a quarter past, she saw. Collecting a tray, she circumnavigated the tables with her usual light step, her heart thudding like a brick dropped into a millpond as she overrode her natural inclination to stay well clear. In front of the man, she schooled her lips into a pleasant smile.

'I'm sorry to disturb you, sir, but will you be requiring another drink? Only, the bar will be closing soon.'

Glittering blue-grey eyes that contained all the warmth of a perilous icy sea swivelled to survey her. For a startled second Anna told herself it served her right if she received a frosty reception, when his body language clearly signalled that he wanted to be left alone. But just then a corner of the austere masculine mouth lifted in the mocking semblance of a smile.

'What do you think? Do I look like I'm in need of another drink, beautiful?'

There was the faintest Mediterranean edge to his otherwise British accent. But in any case he was wrong. *She wasn't beautiful.* If it weren't for the rippling waist-length auburn hair that she freed from her workday style every night when her shift ended, Anna would consider herself quite ordinary. Yet the unexpected compliment— mocking or otherwise—was as though he'd lit a brightly burning candle inside her.

'I wouldn't presume to think I knew what you needed, sir.'

'Call me Dan,' he said, giving her the commonly abbreviated form of his name which he went by in London, not wanting to hear Dante, the name his mother had gifted him with, tonight of all nights.

The invitation almost caused her to stumble. She dipped her head beneath the glare of his riveting gaze because it was almost too powerful to look into for long.

'We're not supposed to address the customers personally,' she answered.

'And do you always follow the rules to the letter?'

'I do if I want to keep my job.'

'This establishment would be extremely foolish if they were to get rid of a girl like you.'

'You don't even know me.'

'Maybe I'd like to.' His smile was slow and deliberate. 'Get to know you better, I mean.'

That roguish grin was like a guided missile that hit all her sensitive spots at once. Inside, the implosion almost rocked Anna off her feet.

'I don't think you do,' she remarked, serious-voiced.

'You're probably just looking for a handy diversion, if the truth be known.'

'Really? A diversion from what, exactly?' A dark blond eyebrow with tiny glints of copper in it lifted in amusement.

'From whatever unhappy thoughts that have been bothering you.'

The smile vanished. His expression became as guarded as though a wall made of three-foot-deep granite had thundered down in front of it.

'How do you know I'm disturbed by unhappy thoughts? What are you…a mind-reader?'

'No.' Anna's teeth nibbled anxiously at her lip. 'I just observe people and—and sense things about them.'

'What a dangerous occupation. And you're compelled to do this why? You don't have any of your own material to contemplate? You must be a rare human being indeed if that's the case…to have managed to negotiate your way through life without any problems at all.'

'I haven't…gone through life without any problems, I mean. How would I have learned anything or be able to empathise with other people if I'd been problem-free? I'd also be quite superficial…which I'm not.'

'And here I was, thinking you were just a simple, uncomplicated barmaid, when in fact you're clearly quite the little philosopher.'

Anna didn't take the comment as an insult. How could she? As well as the pain glittering in his winter-coloured eyes, locked inside his scathing tone was the suggestion of the blackest kind of despair.

A heartfelt desire to help ease it in some way swept passionately through her.

'I'm not looking for trouble... You just seemed so alone and sad, sitting there, that I thought that if you wanted to talk...well, I'd be a good listener. Sometimes it's easier to tell your troubles to a stranger than someone you know. But anyway, if you think that's impertinent of me, and another drink would help more, then I'll gladly get you one.'

The man who'd told her to call him Dan raised a shoulder, then dropped it again dismissively.

'I'm not the unburdening kind, and if you were hoping I might be then I have to tell you that you're wasting your time. What's your name?'

'Anna.'

'That's it...just Anna?'

'Anna Bailey.'

A cold sweat broke out across her skin, where previously his disturbing glance had kindled the kind of heat that made dry tinder burst into flames. Was he going to report her or something? She hadn't meant to insult him. Her only desire had been to help if she could. Was he an important enough customer for a complaint from him to help her lose her job? *She prayed not.*

The comfortable family-run hotel in a quiet corner of Covent Garden had become her home for the past three years, and she loved everything about it—including her work. She didn't even mind if she sometimes had to work long hours. Her employers were so kind—generous to a fault, in fact—and her recent pay-rise had helped make life a whole lot more comfortable than when she'd worked at jobs she'd hated and for too little money. Lord knew she didn't want to go back to struggling again.

'Look, Mr, er...'

'I told you to call me Dan.'

'I can't do that.'

'Why?' he snapped, his expression irritated.

'Because it wouldn't be professional. I'm an employee here and you're a guest.'

'Yet you offered me a shoulder to cry on. Is that on offer to all your guests, Anna?'

She flushed. 'Of course not. I just wanted to—'

'So the only thing that prevents you calling me by my first name is that you're a stickler for the rules and you work here, while I'm a paying customer?'

'I'd better go.'

'No—stay. Is there any other reason you can't be more informal? Like the fact that you've got a husband or boyfriend waiting for you at home, perhaps?'

Anna stared helplessly.

'No.' She cleared her throat, then glanced round to see if anyone was observing them.

Brian—her young, dark-haired colleague—was wiping down the half-moon-shaped bar and chatting to a customer at the same time, whilst a smartly dressed middle-aged couple sat tenderly holding hands as they lingered over their after-theatre drinks. They'd regaled Anna earlier with tales of the play they'd been to, and their infectious enjoyment was contagious. Twenty-five years married and they were still like young lovers around each other.

Sighing, she turned back to find him broodingly examining her. The sudden jolt of her heartbeat mimicked another heavy brick splashing into a pond as his glance interestedly and deliberately appraised her figure. His gaze lingered boldly on the curve of her hips and the swell of her breasts, trailing sensuous fire in its wake. There was nothing provocative about the purple silk blouse with its pretty Chinese collar and the straight grey skirt that denoted her uniform, but when he studied her like that—as if he were imagining her naked and willing in his bed—Anna felt as if there was nowhere to hide.

A trembling excitement soared through her blood at his near-insolent examination. An excitement that was like a gargantuan powerful wave dangerously poised to sweep her into uncharted waters she'd never dared visit before.

'In that case...I've had a change of heart,' Dante drawled, smiling. 'Maybe sharing my troubles with a sweet girl like you is just what I need tonight, Anna. What time do you finish?'

'Around midnight, by the time Brian and I have cashed up.' How was it possible for her voice to sound so level when inside a roaring furnace was all but consuming her?

'And how do you normally get home? Do you get a cab?'

'I live in, actually.'

Just like a popped balloon, her last defence deflated and it was no longer possible for her to pretend that the handsome, hard-jawed stranger hadn't affected her deeply. The truth was that he held a dangerous fascination for her. She was hypnotised by the simmering aura of sensuality implicit in his rough velvet voice and in the twin lakes of his troubled haunting eyes. As a result, her bones seemed to be held together by running water instead of strong connective tissue. Unable to think straight, Anna knew her returning glance was nervous as she gathered the round wooden tray up close to her chest as though it were a shield.

'Have you made up your mind about the drink? Only I've got to get back to the bar to work.'

'Another drink can wait.'

Unbuttoning his coat for the first time that evening, Dante handed her his empty glass with another long, slow, meaningful glance. His lean fingers brushed hers. *Did she imagine that they lingered there against her skin much longer than necessary?* His touch was like being grazed by lightning—deliberate or not.

'I'm staying here too tonight, Anna. And I think that we should have a drink together when your shift ends… don't you?'

A definite refusal was on the tip of her tongue, but inside the dogged belief clung that perhaps she really *could* help him by being a good listener. Her lips pursed tight to prevent it. But when she turned away it was as if some kind of aftershock from their encounter had seized her, because her limbs were shaking almost violently as she crossed the room to rejoin Brian...

There was no understanding such alternating and violent sweeps of emotion, thought Dante. He had just flown into London from his mother's funeral—the funeral of the one person in the world he had truly loved, who had always been there for him no matter what, who had been like a beacon of light he turned to when he ached to remember that beauty, grace and selfless kindness existed in the world.

Now that she was gone he was heartbroken...truly heartbroken. But another woman also occupied his thoughts right now. His body had somehow acquired a compelling desire to know the touch of a red-haired young witch with sherry-brown eyes that glinted beguilingly like firelight—a girl he had only just met whom he had all but mocked disparagingly when she'd shyly offered him a listening ear. Was it so rare that he met up with a genuinely nice girl that he had to punish her when he did?

His mother would turn in her newly dug grave! Bitterness and despair rising in his gorge, Dante ripped off his wristwatch to discard it onto the nearby polished side-table. His coat followed suit, but he let it fall carelessly onto the bed instead. Several hundred dollars' worth of the finest cashmere—but what did it signify? His wealth had neither made him a better man nor a more generous one.

His personal assessment was brutally frank. All the businesses and property he had accumulated through mergers and acquisitions had demonstrated to him was how driven and ruthless he'd become. Yes, driven and ruthless—because of an underlying fear of losing it all. An impoverished childhood and a father who had deserted him had seen to that. He'd been so poor in the small mountain village in Italy where he'd grown up that his mother had been forced to earn their bread by dancing and singing for men in seedy bars in the nearby town, and Dante had long ago set his hungry intention for any career he might settle upon to make him wildly and disgustingly rich so that he might rescue them both.

His wealth would act as an insulating buffer between him and the rest of the world, he'd told himself. Then no one would have the chance to hurt him or his mother again, and neither would she have to humiliate herself by parading her beauty in front of men for money. Dante had carried that insulation with him into his marriage and into any other romantic relationship he'd briefly flirted with, forever seeking to protect his emotions. He'd become cold…not to mention a little heartless.

'No wonder they call you the ice man of the business world,' his American ex-wife, Marisa, had taunted him.

'You're so dedicated to the title that you even bring it home with you!'

At first his mother had been fiercely proud of his rocketing success. He'd bought her the house of her dreams in Lake Como, and made sure she always had plenty of money to buy whatever she wanted. But lately whenever he'd visited her she'd started to profess concern. With one failed marriage and a string of unhappy relationships behind him, it had only seemed to Renata that her son had lost all sense of priority.

It should be the people in his life who were important, she'd told him—not his business or the grand houses he bought—and if he continued in this soulless way then she would sell the richly decorated house on its exclusive plot by the lake and purchase a hut in the hills instead! After all, she'd been raised as a shepherd's daughter, and she wasn't ashamed to go back to where she'd begun even if *he* was. *Someone* had to show him what values were.

Dante grimaced at the hurtful memory of her distressed face and quavering voice when she'd said this to him in the hospital...

To diffuse his despair he deliberately brought his mind back to the titian-haired Anna Bailey. His reaction was purely male and instinctive, and his body tightened instantly. It was as though someone had stoked a fire beneath his blood and set it ceaselessly simmering. Reaching for his discarded watch, he impatiently scanned the time, all but boring a hole in the door with his naked, hungry glance as he waited for her to arrive—not once allowing himself to think that she *wouldn't*...

As if needing to enquire about something, her brooding new friend had leaned across the bar on his way out and whispered softly to Anna, *'Let's have that drink together in my room. I'm staying in the suite on the top floor. It would mean a lot to me...especially tonight. Please don't disappoint me.'*

His lips had been a hair's breadth away from her ear and his warm breath had all but set her alight. The seductive sensation had been the mesmerising equivalent of an intoxicating cocktail she was powerless to refuse. She knew it would make her dizzy and light-headed, but it still held a potent allure she couldn't ignore.

Anna had watched Dan's tall broad-shouldered physique as he left the bar with her heart thumping. Now, in the privacy of her room, she blew out a trembling breath, dropping down onto the padded stool in front of the dressing table because she hardly trusted her legs to keep her upright.

The enigmatic stranger was staying in the only suite in the building. It was the most luxurious and gorgeous accommodation she had ever seen. With its beautiful Turkish kelims hanging on the walls, artisan-created bespoke furniture and under-floor heating, no expense had been spared in its creation and it cost a small fortune to stay there for even *one* night.

Biting her lip, Anna peered into the dressing table mirror to gauge if her expression was as terrified as she felt. Was she really contemplating visiting a male guest in his room? Talking to that lovely couple who'd been to the theatre earlier, she had felt such a pang of envy at their closeness. It wasn't very often she succumbed to feelings of loneliness, but somehow tonight she *had*. What had he meant when he'd whispered, *It would mean a lot to me...especially tonight?* Was he feeling lonely too? Had the funeral she guessed he'd attended been for someone really close to him? His *wife* perhaps?

A heavy sigh, part compassion, part longing, left her. If anyone saw her go to his room then she really *could* lose her job. Was the loneliness that had infiltrated her blood tonight making her a little desperate? Not to mention reckless? Sighing again, Anna went into the bathroom to splash her face with cold water.

Back in the main room, she glanced unseeingly at the television that sat there. Somehow a late-night movie or talk show didn't hold any draw for her. Neither did curling up in bed alone with her thoughts appeal. She'd sensed an inexplicable overwhelming connection to the man who had whispered in her ear downstairs and it was somehow impossible to ignore it. Tomorrow he might be gone, she reasoned feverishly.

She would be wondering what might have been—and the feeling would gnaw away at her if she didn't act.

With fingers that shook, she freed her hair from the neatly coiled bun she'd got so adept at fashioning for work, then pulled a careless brush through the river of auburn silk that flowed down her back. Pinching her cheeks to make them pinker, she quickly changed into a dark green top and light blue jeans. He only wants to *talk*, she reassured herself as she walked out into the corridor. But her pulse beat with fright because he might have been looking for something more…something that in her heart of hearts she secretly longed for.

Flicking an anxious glance towards the small elevator that would soundlessly deliver her to the topmost floor, Anna sucked in a breath as she walked towards it.

The memory of Dan and his haunting mist-coloured eyes came back to her, cutting a swathe through her sudden doubt. Just because he was rich it didn't mean that he didn't suffer like everyone else…didn't mean that he didn't need help sometimes. And from her very first glimpse of him Anna had known he was tortured by something…

The polite welcome he'd intended got locked inside his throat when Dante opened the door to the vision that confronted him. She wore her bright auburn hair loose, and it resembled a burnished autumn sunset cascading down over her shoulders. His stomach muscles clamped tight and the saliva in his mouth dried to a sun-baked desert.

Finding his voice, he murmured, 'Come in.'

Stepping inside, Anna smiled. It was shy and brief, but it still gave him a jolt that had his heart thrumming with undeniable excitement.

'What can I get you to drink?' Moving across the gold and red Chinese rug that covered the main area of the polished wooden floor, Dante paused in front of the dark mahogany glass-fronted cabinet that contained several bottles of spirits behind it and rested his gaze on Anna.

'Nothing, thanks. Alcohol and me don't mix, I'm afraid. Just one sip is enough to make me dizzy.'

'A soft drink, then?'

'Please...just see to yourself. I'm fine, really.'

Dropping his hands restlessly to his hips, he let a rueful grin hijack his lips.

'I think I've probably had quite enough for one night.'

'You've decided not to drown your sorrows after all?'

'Not now that you've consented to visit me, Anna.'

She crossed her arms over her dark green top, and Dante couldn't think of a colour that would complement her pale satin skin more. Without warning, the fresh, searing pain of his recent loss swept over him. It returned with renewed force and he wanted to reach out, anchor himself to life again, remind himself that even though his mother had gone beauty and grace were still his to appreciate if only he'd take the trouble to see it. If he brushed up close to such admirable qualities in Anna would it relieve him of the bitter, despairing thoughts that pounded on him so disturbingly? Thoughts that confirmed his growing belief that he must be no good?

Yes, his nature was clearly unlovable and unworthy of regard—hadn't his own father abandoned him?—so perhaps he deserved abandonment by the people close to him? Especially when he'd been so ruthlessly focused on making himself rich that he scarcely saw the needs of anyone else.

'It upsets me when you look like that,' Anna confessed softly.

'Like what?'

'As if you don't like yourself very much.'

'Is there no hiding from that all-seeing gaze of yours?' Dante retorted uncomfortably.

'I just want to help you if I can.'

'Do you? Do you really?'

'Of course I do. Why do you think I came? Would you like to talk about it?'

'No, sweetheart. Talking is *not* what I need right now,' he answered, gravel-voiced.

And for a man who had prided himself on achieving anything he put his mind to in life it was ironically too difficult a task to keep the raw need that surged through his body like a tidal wave completely out of his tone.

CHAPTER TWO

IN SLOW motion he reached for Anna's hand. His eyes—those intense, burning, ethereal eyes—held her willing prisoner, right then becoming her whole world.

'What do you want?' she whispered, hardly able to hear over the pounding of her heart. 'What do you need?'

'You, Anna…right now I want and need *you*.'

After that, words became unnecessary. His fingers were slipping through her hair, anchoring her head so that she was placed perfectly for his kiss when he delivered it…when the touch of his lips ignited a heartfelt need that had slumbered achingly inside her for years and promised to more than satisfy it.

She'd always thought that maybe her impassioned secret desires were doomed to remain unrequited. On the rare occasion when she'd allowed herself to overcome her mistrust and be caressed by a man, the experience had never remotely lived up to her hopes. All it had done was leave her feeling vulnerable, scared that she would end up alone and unloved until the end of her days. But now, as his warm velvet tongue so hungrily and devastatingly swept her mouth's interior, the flavours she tasted rocked her.

Along with passion, fervour and consuming need, Anna was alive to the anger, despair and pain that she tasted too. But she didn't let such stark emotions scare her…not when they mirrored feelings of her own that she'd often been too afraid to bring into the light. Because of that she innately understood the tumult that flowed heatedly through his blood—good *and* bad—even if she didn't know the details.

Crushed to his warm hard chest in its dark rollnecked sweater, she felt musky male heat and sexy woody cologne captivate her senses as he ravished her in the starved, insatiable way she'd always dreamt of being loved by a man. Holding on to his hard-muscled biceps to keep from falling, Anna feverishly and willingly paid him back in kind… And in her head echoed the advice from her mother that she'd never forgotten: *Only give yourself to someone you love…*

On the bed in a room where in their haste to be together they hadn't even paused to turn on a light they raided each other's clothes with trembling hands—desperate for skin on skin contact and more drugging openmouthed kisses that promised to last all night long. And if he'd temporarily lost his mind in taking this young red-haired beauty to bed then Dante heartily welcomed the state. She was the first really good thing that had happened to him in ages, and he wasn't about to question his good fortune.

The intoxicating feminine scent of her body had already taken up residence in his blood, and it thrummed with wanting her. The arresting sight of that rippling blanket of fiery hair on the silk cream pillow behind her head made a stirring, ravishing picture that he would not soon forget. Now, as his hands eagerly caressed the smooth, slender contours of Anna's body, the breathless gasps she emitted made him blind to any other sensation but their wild and heady mutual desire. He was all but desperate to plunge inside her, to forget everything except the unrestrained thundering joy of the chemistry that had exploded between them from almost the first glance, to relegate the darkness that had recently threatened to suffocate him, to the shadows.

Sensing her stiffen a little as he explored her heat with his fingers, Dante rose up to cup and stroke her face. A duty that should have been at the forefront of his dazzled mind suddenly stabbed at his conscience.

'I'm sorry, Anna...I should protect you. Is that what you are concerned about?'

'It's okay,' she sighed, dark eyes shy. 'I'm protected already. I'm on the pill.'

For an indeterminate amount of time Dante got lost in her wide fire-lit stare, and then he came to and kissed her. The caress seemed to gentle her. Then, his blood flowing with increasing desire and demand, slowly, carefully, he drove himself deep inside her. The heat that exploded around him was incredible.

Anna's sherry-brown eyes smouldered and brightened at the same time, but Dante had not missed the momentary flash of apprehension in her beautiful glance either. Too aroused and aching to wonder about it for long, he felt his body naturally assume the age-old rhythm that would take him to the destination and release he longed for...a destination that could and *would* free him for a while from the merciless torment that had deluged him when his mother had breathed her last laboured breath in his arms. Instead of grief and misery, ecstasy and bliss would be his. And for a blessed short time, at least, all the hurt would be swept away...

His strength of purpose all but overwhelmed Anna as she watched him move over her, his arrow-straight hips slamming into hers as his loving became ever more intense, ever more voracious. By instinct and by desire she wound her long legs round his back, until he was so deep inside her that she felt as if her body no longer existed just as one. Instead, she and he had become a single entity, with two hearts beating wildly in tandem and mind, body and spirit in stunning accord. She had given herself to him without doubt that it was the right thing...*destined*, even.

Would it scare him to know that she thought that? A girl he had just met, to whom he probably wouldn't even give the time of day normally?

In the soft darkness that seemed to be growing ever

lighter as Anna's eyes grew more accustomed to it his smooth muscles rippled like warm steel beneath her trembling, caressing fingers. His breath was harshly ragged as he alternately devoured her lips and then, with that same hot, tormenting mouth, moved lower to caress her breasts. He suckled the rigid aching tips in turn, and Anna couldn't withhold the heated moan that broke free. It was as though her very womb rejoiced when he touched and caressed her.

When he rose up again to capture her lips in another hotly exploring and intimate kiss, something inside her started irrevocably to unravel, to spiral dizzyingly out of control. At first, because she was nervous of being so vulnerable and exposed in front of him, Anna tensed, trying to stem the sensation. But at that same moment she stared up at him, to find the corners of his oh-so-sensuous lips lifting in what might have well been a quietly knowing smile, and she completely gave up trying to control what was happening.

Instead, she allowed the fierce, elemental power of the tide that swept through her to take her where it willed. She was scarcely able to steal a breath as the heart-racing journey commandingly held sway. *It was like freefalling over a hundred-foot waterfall.* Feeling stunned, she didn't know if her mind or her heart raced more. Tears surged helplessly and she bit her lip to quiet the sounds that inevitably arose inside her throat.

Anna knew then that she was changed for ever by what had just occurred. Even her mother, with all her

tenderly given advice, could not have prepared her for
the powerful emotions that flooded her at surrendering
herself to this man. Her gaze met his in genuine wonder.
Moving even deeper inside her, his hard glistening body
pinned her to the bed, keeping her there for long pulsat-
ing seconds. The blue-grey eyes that were so reminiscent
of a restless stormy sea now scorched her as he silently
surveyed her. The raw feeling and emotion he unwittingly revealed ripped achingly through Anna's heart.

Even though they were engaged in the most intimate
act of all, he still seemed so isolated and alone. Like
a lighthouse, with nothing but the sea surrounding it.
She longed to be able to swim to him and reach him.
But then, with an echoing shout that sounded as though
it had been dragged up from the depths of his soul, a
shudder went through him, and he stilled. Scalding heat
invaded her.

'Anna…' he rasped, clasping her face between his
hands and shaking his head as though she was an
enigma he'd never resolve.

When he laid his head between her breasts, Anna
rubbed away her tears and then enfolded him in her
arms, stroking the impossibly soft fair hair almost as
though he were a hurt child in need of love and care.

'It will be all right,' she soothed softly. 'Whatever's
happened to make you so sad, it will pass given time.
I truly believe that. One day soon you'll start to enjoy
life again.'

'If you know that, then you have access to the kind

of faith that's a million light years away from where I am right now. And if my life runs true to form, it'll probably *stay* a million light years away.'

His warm breath skimmed her tender exposed skin like a lover blowing a kiss, while at the same time the shadow of beard covering his hard jaw lightly abraded her. But it was the utter desolation she heard in his gruffly velvet voice that disturbed Anna.

'You mustn't give up,' she urged, sliding her hands either side of his sculpted high cheekbones to make him look up at her.

Although he was surprised by her words, he couldn't disguise his anguish. 'Don't waste your reassurances on me, Anna. I'm okay. I'll survive... I always do.'

'You don't think life can be better than just surviving?'

'For you, angel, I hope it can be. You deserve it—you really do.'

'Sad things, bad things have happened to me too,' she offered shyly. 'Apart from childhood stuff. After a couple of years of doing jobs I hated I found one I really liked and excelled at. But I lost that post when some ruthless hotel magnate bought out my previous employers and installed his own staff. I didn't let myself be sad about it for long, though. I had no choice but to pick myself up and face the unknown. Luckily fate brought me here, to the Mirabelle. Sometimes help arrives when you most need it, you know?'

'Perhaps it does if your conduct has warranted it.'

'I wish you could tell me what's happened to make you feel so low. I thought—I thought perhaps because you were wearing black you might have just lost someone?'

Breathing silently for a while Dante didn't speak. Then he sighed. 'I already told you I'm not the unburdening kind. But I don't feel low right now, *cara*... How could I, lying here in your arms, hearing your heart beat beneath my cheek, having just enjoyed the pleasures and consolation of your beautiful body?'

Hot colour poured into Anna's cheeks. 'If I've brought you some comfort then I'm happy. But I think it's time I went. I really should get back to my room and get some sleep...I've got to make an early start in the morning.'

'So working in the bar isn't your only job?'

'No. I do a bit of everything. I'm learning the trade, so it's great. It's a small family-run hotel and we all muck in. In the mornings I'm a chambermaid.' She dimpled shyly.

'Stay.' Winding his fingers possessively round a spiralling length of her vivid burnished hair, Dante raised it tenderly to his lips. 'I want you to stay until morning. Would you do that for me, Anna? I can't promise you more than this one night, but I promise that I'll hold you close until the dawn comes up... If that's enough...if you're willing to accept just that...will you stay?'

Five years later

Anna flew into the large hotel kitchen, hurriedly unbuttoning her raincoat as she scanned the busy room for

Luigi, the head chef. Defying the stereotype that proclaimed all good chefs should be on the large side, he was tall and thin, with a pointy chin and an abundance of curly black hair with threads of silver tied back in a ponytail. She found him straight away, the back of his chef's whites towards her as he weighed ingredients at one of the scrubbed steel counters, whistling an aria from a well-known opera.

'Did the produce arrive?' she asked breathlessly. 'I spoke to the manager at the deli and he told me it had already left in the van. Is it here?'

Turning round to acknowledge her, the first thing Luigi did was to look her up and down, then wag his finger. 'Have you eaten breakfast this morning? My guess is that you haven't, and yet you run around at a hundred miles an hour as if you can exist on fresh air alone!'

'As it happens I had a croissant at the deli while I was waiting to talk to the manager.'

Crossing her arms over her damp rain-spattered coat, Anna challenged him to disbelieve her. It was sweet that he took such an interest in her welfare and what she ate, but she was no longer the naive twenty-four-year-old she'd been when she first came to the hotel. She was thirty-two, in charge of her own destiny, and the assistant manager to boot!

'A croissant, eh? And how do you expect to survive on such a poor substitute for food as that until lunchtime? A croissant is nothing but air too!'

'It wasn't just air. It had apricot and custard in it, and it was extremely filling and very nice.' Sighing patiently, Anna let her rose-tinted lips naturally form a smile. 'Now, will you please answer my question about the produce delivery? Anita's expecting an important delegation for lunch today, and everything has to be just perfect.'

Luigi threw up his hands dramatically. 'And you believe it *won't* be? You should know by now that Luigi delivers nothing *but* perfection!'

'You're right. I do know that.'

'And, yes, the delivery has arrived—and the black olives are excellent as usual.'

'What a relief. So everything is fine, then? I mean, there aren't any problems?'

With her gaze swinging round towards Cheryl, who was the sous chef, and the three young kitchen assistants scurrying busily about the kitchen, Anna included them all in her question. She hadn't been made assistant manager without developing an ability to notice everything— from the mundane to the much more important—and she was very keen for all to be well.

Anita and Grant, the hotel's owners, had always prided themselves on running a tight ship, but an extremely friendly one too. They cared about their staff. That was why Anna had stayed on. And when she'd fallen pregnant they hadn't said she had to leave. Instead, the couple had been unstinting in their support of her, seeing her potential and insisting she occupy the

charming two-bedroom apartment in the basement of
the hotel as part of her remuneration for working there.
They had also helped her find a reliable and decent
local nursery for her baby, and encouraged her to take
an online management course with a view to promoting
her and helping her to earn a better salary. Consequently,
Anna was fiercely loyal as well as immensely grateful
to the couple.

'Everything's fine in the kitchen, Anna.' Cheryl
nodded, but then the slim, pretty blonde bit down anxiously on her lip and continued, 'Except we couldn't help
wondering why Anita and Grant had a delegation from
one of the most well-known hotel chains in the country
coming here for lunch. Can you tell us anything about
it?'

Anna's insides cartwheeled at the question. This afternoon the couple who owned the hotel had scheduled
a meeting with her to discuss something important, and
all last night and early this morning, as she'd got her
daughter Tia ready for kindergarten, she'd been fretting about what the subject might be. The charming
little hotel in its smart Georgian building was situated
in a very desirable corner of Covent Garden, but Anna
wasn't oblivious to the fact that the country was plunged
deep into a recession and reservations and consequently
takings were definitely down.

Were they going to be bought out by a more commercial hotel giant, and as a consequence would she lose

a job she loved again? And not just her job this time, but her home too? *It hardly bore thinking about.*

But now, seeing the obvious anxiety on not just Cheryl's but on the other staff members' faces too, she knew she had a duty to reassure them.

'To be absolutely honest with you I know nothing about it. My advice to you all would be to just concentrate on your work and not waste time on speculation. It won't help. If there's anything concerning us that we need to know, you can be sure we'll all get to hear about it soon. Now, I must get on. I've got to relieve Jason on Reception. He's standing in for Amy, who's phoned in sick.'

Time dragged interminably slowly as the hotel chain's delegation of three enjoyed the superb three-course lunch Luigi and his staff had prepared. Afterwards the two men and their female colleague were closeted in a meeting with Anita, Grant and their son Jason, the manager, for two and a half hours. Anna had never been a clock-watcher, but that afternoon she was.

It was a quarter to five by the time the phone rang on Reception to invite her into Jason's office for the promised meeting with him and his parents. In the meantime, Linda, the girl who did the late shift on the desk, had turned up, and now sat beside Anna powdering her nose.

Standing outside the manager's office, Anna smoothed her hands nervously down over her smart navy skirt, captured a stray auburn tendril that had come adrift from her ponytail, tucked it back into her *faux* ivory clip and then rapped briefly on the door. Greeted by three identically reassuring smiles, she nonetheless sensed immediately that all was not well.

'Dear Anna. Come and sit down, my love.'

The tiny brunette with the stylish elfin haircut, and the smooth, unlined face that belied the fact she was only a year away from the big sixty, welcomed her warmly, as usual.

'Firstly, you'll be pleased to know that the lunch Luigi prepared for our visitors today went extremely well. They were very impressed.'

'The man can certainly cook,' chipped in Grant, Anita's handsome silver-haired husband. 'You could almost forgive him for having an ego the size of an elephant!'

Anna immediately deduced he was nervous, and she perched on the edge of her seat, wishing her mouth wasn't suddenly so sickeningly dry, and that her stomach hadn't sunk as heavily as a giant boulder thrown into the sea. Searching for reassurance, her dark eyes met Jason's. The tall, slim young man whose features were a male version of his elfin mother's tried for a smile, but instead it came off as a resigned grimace. That was the moment when the alarm bells clanged deafeningly loud for Anna.

'So...' Her hands linking together nervously in her lap, she leaned forward even farther in her chair. 'What was the delegation from that commercial hotel chain doing here? Are we in trouble, or something?'

Anita started to speak, but Grant quickly took over.

'Yes, love.' He sighed, pulling a handkerchief out of his suit trousers to lightly mop his brow. 'Serious financial trouble, I'm afraid. Like many other small businesses, the recession's dealt us a heavy blow, and I'm sure you're aware that we've been losing money hand over fist. You've noticed how the reservations have fallen? It's really only the regulars that have stayed loyal to us. If we're to hold our own against some of the more popular hotels we need to reinvest and refurbish, but with the coffers practically empty, and banks refusing loans left right and centre, it's not likely to happen. Consequently, we've had no choice but to try and get some other form of help.'

'Does that mean that you're going to sell the hotel?' There was such a rush of blood to her head that Anna scarcely registered her boss's answer. All she could think of right then was Tia... How was she going feed and clothe her child if she lost her job? More urgently, where were they going to *live*?

'We were offered a buyout, but we haven't accepted the offer yet. We told the delegation that the hotel had been in the family for three generations and we needed some time to think things over.' Anita's usually sunny smile was painfully subdued. 'We have to get back to them by the end of the week. If we do agree to the buyout then unfortunately it means that none of us stay.

They'll want to refurbish and give the place their own look, run it with their own staff. I'm desperately sorry, Anna, but that's our position.'

She was struck silent by the news she'd just heard, but her mind was racing at a hundred miles an hour. Then, because she was also devoted to and protective of the interests of the family that had been so good to her and Tia, Anna forced a reassuring smile to her numbed lips.

'It's a difficult situation you're in,' she quietly acknowledged, 'and it's hardly your fault that there's a recession. The staff—including myself—will all eventually find other jobs, but what will you guys do? The hotel's been in your family for so long, and you love it...I know you do.'

'It's kind of you to be so concerned, love.' The big shoulders that strained Grant's suit jacket lifted in a shrug. 'I'm not saying it'll be easy, but we'll be fine. We've got each other, and that's what matters most in the end, isn't it...? The people you love, I mean.'

Not usually given to expressing his feelings in public, he squeezed Anita's hand. 'And we'll do whatever we can to help you find another flat, Anna. We certainly won't be walking out this door until we know you and Tia are safely settled somewhere. As for jobs... Well, with all the experience and qualifications you've gained these past few years, some grateful hotel will eagerly snap you up. You're a lovely girl and a complete asset... they'll quickly learn that.'

'So you'll let us all know by the end of the week what you've decided?'

'Perhaps sooner… Anita, Jason and I plan to spend the evening mulling things over. As soon as we've decided we'll let you and the rest of the staff know the decision we've reached.'

Getting to his feet, Grant sent Anna a friendly broad smile. 'It's five o'clock, and it's time you were running along to get that little angel of yours from aftercare at kindergarten, isn't it?'

Glancing down at the slim silver-linked watch on her wrist, Anna shot up from her seat. She hated to be late collecting Tia, and as always ached to see her child and learn about her day. Tonight, when she was in effect in limbo about their future, she would make an extra fuss of her, and hold her even tighter before putting her to bed.

CHAPTER THREE

STUDYING the sunlit view of the Thames from his Westminster apartment window, Dante suddenly moved impatiently away, jettisoning his mobile onto the bed. He'd just flown back from a business trip to New York, was feeling fuzzy-headed and tired, and yet the conversation he'd just had with a business friend of his had definitely acted like a triple dose of strong black coffee injected straight into his bloodstream.

The Mirabelle Hotel… It was a name he'd never forgotten. Even after five years. The family who owned it were apparently in dire straits financially, and had been forced to consider a buyout from the commercial hotel chain that his friend Eddie was on the board of. The place was situated in a prime location in central London, and as far as Eddie was concerned it should have been a done deal. But he'd just heard that the owners had quite unbelievably rejected the offer. They had some old-fashioned notion that the business had to stay in the family, come what may.

Eddie had verbalised his astonishment at the number

of people who let their hearts rule their head in business. 'Will they ever learn? How about it, Dante?' he'd asked. 'Fancy giving it a shot? I don't doubt the place is a potential goldmine.'

He had ended the call after agreeing to meet with his friend for a drink later, but Eddie's parting remark had set Dante's mind racing. *That incredible night he'd stayed at that particular hotel had changed his life.* A veritable angel had motivated him to want to do some good in the world instead of just simply taking what he believed his hard work entitled him to. Not only had his aims become less ruthless and driven, but he had discovered a much more exciting avenue, and a way of doing business that far exceeded what he had achieved before in terms of personal satisfaction. It would definitely have had his mother cheering him from the sidelines if she'd lived to see the changes he'd made.

Although he was on the board of several blue chip companies, and still in mergers and acquisitions, Dante had sold off most of his businesses and now specialised in helping family-run concerns make their businesses more viable. He'd also reverted to his mother's surname, instead of the British one he'd adopted when he'd first started out in business here. Once again he was *Dante Romano*, and he had to admit it felt good to be much more authentic. Friends like Eddie still called him Dan, but that was okay. It was a fair enough shortening of Dante.

The Mirabelle Hotel…

Dante flopped down onto the king-sized bed with its opulent aubergine counterpane and picked up his phone. What had happened to the titian-haired beauty he'd spent the night with? Anna Bailey. The memory of her slid into his mind like the diaphanous caress of sensuous silk. *Closing his eyes, he could almost taste her.* He could even recall her perfume...something musky, with hints of orange and patchouli in it. It had been in her long flowing hair, and there had been traces on her milk-and-honey skin too.

His reflection deepening, Dante arrestingly recalled the sumptuously erotic, quivering pink mouth that he'd ached to plunder from almost the first moment he'd encountered it. The experience had been an utter revelation...as though it couldn't have been more right or perfect. For an endless-seeming moment he'd been dizzy with longing for her—his lovely lady of the night, who'd reached out to rescue him when all he could see ahead was blinding darkness.

His eyelids snapped open. Of all the businesses he could hear about that were in trouble...why the Mirabelle? One thing was certain—he couldn't let such an uncanny opportunity pass him by without at least checking it out...

She'd had another sleepless night. Duvet and pillow flung in frustration on the floor during the night. Her bed had become a taunting enemy instead of the safe, comforting haven she craved. And when she'd finally got up, Anna had uncharacteristically snapped at Tia as well.

As soon as she'd seen the child's luminous blue-grey eyes sparkle with tears across from her at the breakfast table, she'd immediately wanted to kick herself. Drawing the little girl urgently onto her lap, she'd kissed and hugged her and told her about a hundred times how sorry she was. Mummy didn't mean to shout. She was just a little bit stressed, she'd explained.

'What does *distressed* mean?' Tia had questioned, absently, playing with a long curling tendril of Anna's unbound auburn hair.

Perhaps her daughter had unwittingly stumbled upon the truth of what she was feeling? She *was* distressed.

'I'll explain when you come home from school, darling,' she'd hedged, praying the child would forget to ask. It wasn't something a four-year-old should be remotely acquainted with, to Anna's mind. Childhood should be joyful and carefree...*even if her own had been a million miles away from such an idyll.*

The Cathcarts had told Anna that they'd turned down the offer of a buyout from the big hotel chain. So when she'd entered the office the following morning to discover that her employers were considering a fresh offer—this one from an independent source who had been told about them by one of the delegation from the hotel chain—her insides had mimicked the nail-biting ascent and descent of a frantic rollercoaster ride for the second time. Once more the possibility of losing her job and home loomed worryingly large.

'Your parents said that an interested investor wants to help them improve profitability and modernise. Can you explain exactly what this means?' Anna had asked concernedly as she left the owners' office to walk with Jason to his.

'Don't look so worried, Anna. It's good news. Major investment is just what the Mirabelle needs. What we're hoping is that this guy will be interested enough to invest a large chunk of his own money in the business to help turn it around. He'll be the majority shareholder, but he won't own it outright. I've been checking out his record and it's quite impressive, to put it mildly. His interests are truly international, but his main concern is helping family-run businesses become more profitable. If we accept an offer from him to invest, it means that we stay running the hotel under his guidance and expertise. We'll have the chance to really take things to another level…even in the recession.'

Jason opened the door for Anna to precede him as they took their coffee into his cramped, cluttered office. Pushing some papers aside on a desk that scarcely had a corner free of paper debris, he left his mug of coffee on a stained cork coaster. An air of bubbling excitement underlaid his usually level tone.

'When he goes into a business with a view to helping it perform better,' he continued, 'he takes a good hard look at how it's being run and then advises on the changes that will make it more efficient and profitable. He particularly specialises in helping to resolve any conflicts that might be preventing people from working successfully together.'

Anna's brow creased. 'There aren't any conflicts amongst us, though, are there? Unless you mean Luigi's tendency to lord it over the others in the kitchen... They do get a bit fed up with him from time to time, but aren't all head chefs a bit like that? Egotistic and dramatic, I mean.'

'Generally I think that we all get on great. But that doesn't mean there isn't room for improvement.' As he paced the floor, it appeared as if Jason's enthusiasm was hard to contain. 'Unaired resentments can fester... we all know that. And this guy is a real people person. We thoroughly checked him out before inviting him over for a meeting. Apparently one of the first things he does is to interview everyone to discover how they feel about their job. He passionately believes that their attitude contributes to how well they work, and he has a unique reputation for getting staff and management to work more successfully together. The best thing of all is that the family get to stay doing what they love. We don't have to just sell up and go. Who knows? If the hotel starts to make a real profit, we might eventually be able to buy it back completely. The staff will remain too of course. It means you won't have to search for another job, Anna, isn't that great? Having someone like this Dante Romano guy invest his money in the hotel and take a look at how we can improve things could be the best opportunity we've had in ages!'

'And what's the pay-off for this man? I mean…what's in it for him besides making a profit? I doubt that he's going to do all this out of the goodness of his heart.'

She couldn't help it, but Anna wasn't entirely convinced. It all sounded too good to be true. Perhaps her nature wasn't as trusting as it could be, but then bruising experience had taught her to be alert to the glossily wrapped Christmas present that contained nothing but an empty shoebox.

The earnest dark-haired young man before her in the charcoal-grey suit that was showing signs of fraying at the edges of its cuffs abruptly stopped pacing.

'Of course there's a pay-off for him, Anna. He's a businessman! But his interest in helping us sounds perfectly genuine. I know you're only being protective of Mum and Dad but they're experienced hoteliers, don't forget. They won't agree to anything that remotely smacks of a scam or a rip-off. Yes, this guy might become the main shareholder—but he won't be running the business…*we* will. Plus, his policy is to take a longer-term view of situations, so he won't be in a hurry to just look at what he can get out of the business and then head for the hills.'

'You sound as though you believe this is the answer to all your family's prayers, Jason.'

It did indeed seem the ideal solution in terms of enabling them all to stay put, but Anna would rather hunt for another job and flat elsewhere if it meant that Grant and Anita wouldn't be out of pocket and the couple would have the means to start a good life again somewhere else. What if it really *was* in their best interests for them to sell the Mirabelle to a big commercial hotel giant?

'Nothing's been decided yet, Anna.' Compounding her guilt at being sceptical, Jason sounded subdued. 'But Romano is coming for lunch, and after he's eaten we'll have a proper meeting to thrash things out. Hopefully we'll be able to report back on what's been decided later on that afternoon. Would you mind going to talk to Luigi, to make sure he's got everything he needs to impress our visitor with his menu?'

'Of course.'

Carrying what remained of her half-drunk coffee to the door, Anna flashed him a smile to make up for her less than enthusiastic response earlier, but her stomach still churned at the prospect of the unknown changes that lay ahead for them all. She paused to glance back at the Cathcarts' preoccupied son, guessing that he probably saw the chance of working with this Romano chap as something that would enhance his reputation and ability—assets that were sometimes overshadowed by his much more confident and experienced father.

'I just want you to know that I'll do everything I can to help you and your parents, Jason. I love this hotel too, and I know it's been a very worrying time for all of you.'

'Thanks, Anna...I've always known I can count on you.'

The memories crashed in on Dante the instant he walked through the glass-panelled entrance into the cosily old-fashioned lobby, with its chintz armchairs and worn brown chesterfields.

After that incredible night with Anna he'd left the hotel in the early hours of the morning to jump in a cab and catch a flight to New York. His mother's death had plunged him into a tunnel of despair for a frighteningly long time. It had taken a good year or more for him to be able to function anywhere near normal again because, disturbingly, his work and everything he'd achieved had become utterly meaningless. Life had only started to improve when the warm memory of Anna's tenderness and his mother's unfailing belief that he was a much better man than the world suspected broke through the walls of his grief and his self-imposed isolation and helped him start to entertain the possibility of a very different, much more fulfilling future.

That was when Dante had decided to change his driven, selfish approach to something far more wholesome...

The Cathcarts were a delightful couple, with admirably solid values when it came to business and family. But Dante, although charmed by their unstinting hospitality and the superlative lunch, sensed that some of those solid values were a bit too entrenched in the past and needed to be brought up to date.

At lunch, his cool gaze assessed as much as it could as they talked, including the worn velvet hangings at the stately Georgian dining room windows, the tarnished silver cutlery and the slightly old-fashioned uniforms of the waiting staff. Afterwards he was invited to the Cathcarts' office to discuss the nuts and bolts of an investment.

As the fragrant, elegant Anita Cathcart poured him some coffee—at Dante's nod adding cream and sugar— he sat back in the comfortable leather chair, loosened his silk tie a little and relaxed. The hotel *was* in an absolutely prime location and could—as Eddie had foreseen—potentially be a goldmine. Because of lack of funds and the large debt they had accrued with the bank, it was clear the Cathcarts weren't able to make the best of their incredible asset, and that was where Dante came in.

'We'll get started soon, Mr Romano. We're just waiting for our assistant manager to join us. She's more like family than an employee, and we'd like her to be in on what we decide. She'll be along any minute now.'

Jason, the Cathcarts' slightly built son and manager, smiled diffidently at Dante as he sat down opposite him at the meeting table. He was clutching a pen and a spiral notebook and his hand shook a little. *What was the story with him?* Dante wondered. Was the manager's role too big an ask for him, or was it just that he struggled to assert himself under his parents' guardianship of the hotel?

'Was she informed about the meeting?'

'Yes…of course. It's just that she—'

'Then she should be here on time, like everyone else.'

His chastising glance encompassed them all, but Dante nonetheless tempered it with a trace of a smile. He heard the door behind him open and turned expectantly. A woman with hair the same hue as a bright russet apple stepped inside, bringing with her the faint but stirring scent of oranges and patchouli…

His thoughts careened to an abrupt halt…like a driver applying the emergency brake before hitting a wall. He stared in shock. *Anna…dear God, she still worked here?*

'I'm so sorry I'm late,' she breathed, porcelain skin flushing. 'I was—'

The startled leap in her sherry-brown eyes told Dante she recognised him. His heart—which had all but stalled—pumped a little harder as he realised he'd been genuinely afraid she might have forgotten him. *What a blow that would have been to his pride, when out of all the women he'd seen over the years she was the one that haunted him…*

'Mr Romano,' Grant Cathcart was saying, 'I'd like to introduce you to our stalwart assistant manager…Anna Bailey.'

Rising automatically to his feet, Dante extended his hand, praying hard that his voice wouldn't desert him. Anna's palm was fragile and slightly chilled as it slid into his. Their gazes locked as though magnetized, and though he sensed her tremble, inside he believed that he trembled *more*.

'Miss Bailey…I'm very pleased to meet you,' he heard himself announce.

'The feeling is mutual, Mr—Mr Romano,' she replied politely.

Her warm velvet voice bathed his senses in liquid honey. Arresting memories of their unforgettable night together came pouring back in a disturbing heated rush. Realising that his hand still covered hers, Dante reluctantly withdrew it.

'Why don't you come and sit down, Anna love?' Anita invited. 'There's plenty of coffee in the pot if you'd like some.'

'I'm fine, thanks,' Anna murmured distractedly.

As Dante watched her, she moved like a sleepwalker to a seat at the opposite side of the table, next to Jason, and he didn't miss the spark of warmth in the other man's dark eyes as he silently acknowledged her. *Was something going on there?* A hot flash of jealousy hit Dante a glancing blow as he resumed his seat.

'Well, if everybody's ready, we'll make a start, shall we?' With a respectful glance in their visitor's direction, Grant Cathcart organised his notes and prepared to address the meeting.

* * *

Dante Romano. No wonder she'd never been able to find him! What had instigated the name-change? she wondered. Underneath, was he still as ruthless and cutthroat as it had said in the newspaper reports she'd read when she'd been searching for him? But what did it matter when it had already been decided by the Cathcarts that he was going to be their saviour?

As well as investing a substantial amount of money in the Mirabelle, Dante Romano was taking the hotel, its owners and its staff firmly under his wing. Being satisfied that Anita and Grant were completely happy with the arrangement was one thing. *Only time would tell if Anna would be equally happy.* There was a very big—in fact a *huge* hurdle she had to cross before then.

Shaking her head, she emitted a small groan as she added chopped up red and green peppers to the stir-fry she was busy cooking for herself and Tia.

She'd half believed she was hallucinating when she'd walked into the office to find Dan, or *Dante* as he called himself now, sitting there. And she'd had such a jolt when his incredible winter-coloured eyes had bored into hers. In those electrifying few seconds the world could have ended, and she hadn't been able to drag her hypnotised gaze away.

Five years ago she'd never even asked him his full name. When he'd asked her to stay with him for the night but not to expect anything more she'd agreed— and she'd promised herself she wouldn't speculate on where he would go or what he would do when he left her, even if it ultimately meant he was going from her arms to someone else's.

Consoling herself that she'd helped comfort him in his hour of need, and that no matter how emotionally painful it was it would have to be enough, Anna had never intended to try and track him down afterwards. But when she'd found herself pregnant with his child she'd reasoned that she owed it to him to let him know. However, discovering that the suite's occupant Dan Masterson was a veritable 'shark' in the world of international business, who didn't care who he brought down in his empire-building quest, had definitely given her pause. He might have been tender with Anna that night they'd spent together, and he might have been troubled, but could she knowingly risk inflicting such a driven ruthless man on her child?

She'd decided *no*, she couldn't. Besides, she'd definitely received the impression from her one-night lover that he wasn't interested in a relationship, so why would he be interested in the fact that he'd left his one-time-only lover pregnant? she'd reasoned.

Leading up to that night five years ago she'd been working so hard, what with all the different jobs she did at the hotel—sometimes even working double shifts back to back—and because she'd been extremely tired, she'd absent-mindedly forgotten to take one of her daily contraceptive pills. It had only dawned on Anna to check when early-morning nausea had become a worrying recurrence.

Some months after Tia had been born she'd revised her decision not to get in touch with Dan and decided to try once more to locate him. *It had been as though he had vanished.* The only information about him she'd been able to glean was stuff from the past. There had been nothing to indicate what he was doing nearly eighteen months after they'd met.

From the living room came the delighted chuckle of her small daughter as she knocked down the building blocks she'd had as a toddler that she'd been happily shaping into a wobbling tower for the past ten minutes or so. A wave of sadness and terror deluged her mother all at once. What would Dan—or Dante, as she should call him now—think when he found out that their passionate night together all those years ago had made him a father? How poignant that he hadn't had the privilege of knowing his own delightful daughter. Anna had no doubt that it would have enhanced his life in a myriad different ways. But what could she have done when it had seemed as though he didn't exist any more?

With genuine regret she squeezed her eyes shut, then quickly opened them again. Her terror came from the fact that she knew he was a very rich and influential man indeed—rich enough to invest in a major share of the hotel that was the means of her employment and her place to live. How would it reflect on Anna if Dante's was the controlling share? What if he decided she wasn't up to her job—or, worse still, that he wanted to try and take Tia away from her? A man as wealthy as him must have access to all kinds of power…particularly *legal* power.

Abruptly switching off the burner beneath the wooden-handled wok, Anna wrapped her arms protectively round her middle as she crossed the tiled kitchen floor to examine the collage of baby and toddler photographs of Tia that were framed on the wall there. Behind her, the suddenly ringing telephone made her jump.

'Hello?'

'Anna? It's me—Dante. I'm still in the hotel. You rushed off rather quickly after the meeting and I think we need to talk. I believe you have a flat downstairs—can I come down and see you?'

CHAPTER FOUR

ANNA was struck dumb by Dante's request. What should she do? If she agreed for him to come down to the flat, how to prepare him for her news when Tia was there, large as life, playing happily in the living room? There was no time to prepare for anything!

'I'd love to talk to you—I really would—but—'

'But?'

She could imagine him sardonically curling his lip. He knew she was hedging. God, why couldn't she be a better actress?

'I'm making dinner at the moment. Why don't we arrange to meet up tomorrow? You're coming in to start working with Grant and Anita, aren't you?'

'I think I'd rather come and talk to you right now, Anna. I'll be with you in about five minutes.'

He put down the phone. Anna was left staring at the receiver in her hand as if it was a grenade she'd just pulled the pin from.

'Tia, we're going to have a visitor in a minute. We'll have dinner after he's gone, okay?'

She sped round the compact living room, sweeping up strewn toys into her arms like a whirlwind, then throwing them onto the end of the faded gold couch as if she was aiming to knock down coconuts at a carnival stall. When Dante arrived she would hide her emotions as best she could, she promised herself, yanking her oversized emerald sweater further down over her hips. Yes, she would hide behind her assistant manager's mask—be unflustered and professional, as if she could totally handle whatever he cared to throw at her. No matter that she hadn't been able to so much as *look* at another man since he'd left, because her heart had been irrevocably stolen by him.

She didn't have a hope of concealing her feelings behind a managerial mask under the circumstances. How could she?

'Who's coming to see us, Mummy?' Feeling a tug on her trouser-leg, Anna's gaze fell distractedly into her daughter's. The child's big blue-grey eyes—eyes, she realised with another frisson of shock, that were *identical* to her father's—were avid with curiosity. 'Is it Auntie Anita?'

'No, darling. It's not Auntie Anita.' Chewing anxiously down on her lip, Anna forced herself to smile. 'It's a man called Dante Romano and—and he's an old friend of mine.'

'If he's your friend, why haven't I seen him before?' Tia's husky little voice was plaintive.

'Because—'

The knock on the hallway door just outside completely silenced whatever it was that Anna had been about to say. Rolling up her sweater sleeves, she reached for Tia's hand and led her as calmly as she was able over to the couch, where she sat her down. Crouching in front of her, she tenderly stroked back some golden corkscrew curls from her forehead.

'Don't be nervous, will you? He's—he's a very nice man, and I'm sure he'll be very pleased to meet you.'

As she hurried out into the hallway a surge of irrepressibly strong emotion made tears flood into her eyes. Not now! she moaned silently, wiping them away with the back of her hand. *Why don't you wait to hear what he has to say before you start crying?*

'Hi.' His handsome smile was devastatingly confident, and Anna could scarcely contain the anger that suddenly rose up inside her, let alone analyse it.

'Hello,' she murmured in reply, praying he wouldn't see the evidence of her tears. 'Come in.'

Had he called at a bad time? Dante speculated. Her beautiful brown eyes appeared slightly moist. He guessed she would rather have put off his visit until tomorrow, but the fact of the matter was he couldn't wait until then to see her and talk to her again. Ever since Anna had walked into that office he'd ached to get her alone, find out what she'd been doing all these years... maybe even ask if she'd ever thought about him since that extraordinary night they'd spent together.

Folding her arms, she stood squarely in front of him,

leaving him with the distinct notion he wasn't going to be invited in any farther. Fighting down the sense of rejection that bubbled up inside him, he swept his glance hungrily over her pale oval face. The dazzling fire-lit brown eyes were wary, he noticed, and the softly shaped mouth that was barely glazed with some raspberry-coloured lipgloss was serious and unsmiling.

'You said you wanted to talk...what about?'

It wasn't a very promising start. Apprehension flooded into the pit of Dante's stomach.

'What a greeting. You make it sound like you're expecting an interrogation.' He shrugged, momentarily thrown off balance by her cool reception.

'It's just that I'm busy.'

'Cooking, you said?' He quirked a slightly mocking eyebrow and sniffed the air.

'Look...how do you expect me to greet you after all this time? The truth is you're the last person I ever expected to see again! For you to show up now, because you're the new investor in the Mirabelle, is obviously a shock...a shock that I was totally unprepared for.' Pursing her lips, she was clearly distressed. 'I don't know how to put this any other way, Mr Romano, and please don't think me presumptuous, but I think that whatever else happens round here our relationship should remain strictly professional for as long as we have to work together.'

'Why? Afraid you might be tempted to instigate a repeat performance of the last time we got together?'

Stung by her aloof air, and the distance she seemed so eager to put between them, Dante said the first thing that entered his head. Trouble was, he'd be *lying* if he said the thought of them being intimate *hadn't* crossed his mind. It was practically all he'd been dwelling on since setting eyes on her.

Blushing hard, Anna gazed down at the floor. When she glanced up at him again her dark eyes were spilling over with fury.

'What a hateful, arrogant thing to say! Bad enough that you only thought me good enough for a one-night stand, but to come here now and assume that I—that I would even—' She gulped in a deep breath to calm herself. 'Some of us have moved on.'

Dante nodded, sensing a muscle flex hard in the side of his cheek. 'And you *have* moved on, haven't you, Anna? Assistant Manager, no less.'

'If you're suggesting I got the position by any other means than by damned hard work then you can just turn around and leave right now. I certainly don't intend to meekly stand here while you mock and insult me!'

His lips twitched into a smile. He couldn't help it. Did she have any idea how sexy she was when she was angry? With that fiery-red hair spilling over her shoulders and those dark eyes flashing...it would test the libidinous mettle of any red-blooded heterosexual male. To Dante it felt as if a lighted match had been dropped into his blood, and it had ignited as though it were petrol.

'I didn't come here to insult you, Anna. I merely wanted to see you again in private…that's all.'

'I heard you shouting, Mummy.'

A little girl with the prettiest corkscrew blond curls Dante had ever seen suddenly emerged from a room along the hall. Deep shock scissored through him. She'd addressed Anna as 'Mummy'.

Definitely flustered, Anna ran her fingers over the child's softly wayward hair, captured a small hand in hers and squeezed it.

'Tia…this is the man I told you about. Mr Romano.'

'Why are you calling him Mr Romano when you told me his name was Dante?'

The girl was engagingly forthright. Dante smiled, and the child dimpled shyly up at him.

'Hello, Tia.' Staring into her riveting misty-coloured eyes, he frowned, not knowing why she suddenly seemed so familiar. Quickly he returned his attention to Anna. 'You got married and had a child?' he said numbly. 'Was that the "moving on" you referred to?'

'I'm not married.'

'But you're still with her father?'

Her cheeks pinking with embarrassment, she sighed. 'No…I'm not.'

'Obviously things didn't work out between you?' Dante's racing heartbeat started to stabilise. So she was alone again? It must have been tough, raising her child on her own. He wondered if the father kept in touch and assumed the proper responsibility for his daughter's welfare. Having had a father who had shamelessly deserted him and his mother when it didn't suit him to be responsible, Dante deplored the mere idea that the man might have turned his back on Anna and the child.

'Perhaps—perhaps you'd better come in after all.' Saying no more, Anna turned back towards the room along the hallway, Tia's hand gripped firmly in hers.

Barely knowing what to make of this, Dante followed. The living room was charming. The walls were painted in an off-white cream-coloured tone, helping to create a very attractive sense of spaciousness and light. It was the perfect solution in a basement apartment where the long rectangular windows were built too high up to let in much daylight.

'Please,' she said nervously, gesturing towards a plump gold-coloured couch with toys strewn at one end, 'sit down. Can I get you something to drink?'

She'd gone from hostile to the perfect hostess in a couple of seconds flat. It immediately made Dante suspicious. He dropped down onto the couch.

'No, thanks.' Freeing his tie a little from his shirt collar, he gave Tia a smile then leant forward, his hands linked loosely across his thighs. 'What's going on, Anna? And don't tell me nothing... I'm too good a reader of people to buy that.'

She was alternately twisting her hands together and fiddling with the ends of her bright auburn hair. The tension already building in Dante's iron-hard stomach muscles increased an uncomfortable notch.

'Tia? Would you go into your bedroom for a minute and look for that colouring book we were searching for earlier? You know the one—with the farm animals on the front? Have a really good look and bring some crayons too.'

'Is Dante going to help me colour in my book, Mummy?' The little girl's voice was hopeful.

'Sure.' He grinned at her. 'Why not?'

When Tia had left them to run along the hallway to her bedroom, Anna's dark eyes immediately cleaved apprehensively to Dante's. 'That night—the night we were together…' She cleared her throat a little and his avid gaze didn't waver from hers for a second. 'I got pregnant. I didn't lie when I told you I was on the pill, but because I'd been working so hard I missed taking one… Anyway…Tia's yours. What I'm saying—what I'm trying to tell you—is that you're her father.'

He'd heard of white-outs, but not being enamoured of snow or freezing weather had never experienced one. He imagined the blinding sensation of disorientation that currently gripped him was a little like that condition. Time ticked on in its own relentless way, but for a long moment he couldn't distinguish anything much. Feelings, thoughts—they just didn't exist. He quite simply felt numb. Then, when emotions started to pour through him like a riptide, he pushed to his feet, staring hard at the slender redhead who stood stock-still, her brown eyes a myriad palette of shifting colours Dante couldn't decipher right then.

'What are you up to?' he demanded. 'Has someone put you up to this to try and swindle money from me? Answer me, damn it!' He drove his shaking fingers through his hair in a bid to still them. 'Tell me what you just said again, Anna—so I can be sure I didn't misunderstand you.'

'Nobody put me up to anything, and nor do I want your money. I'm telling you the truth, Dante. That night we spent together resulted in me becoming pregnant.'

'And the baby you were carrying is Tia?'

'Yes.'

'Then if that's the truth, why in God's name didn't you find me to let me know?'

'We agreed.' She swallowed hard. Her flawless smooth skin was alabaster-pale, Dante registered without sympathy. 'We agreed that we wouldn't hold each other to anything...that it was just for the one night and in the morning we'd both move on. You were—you were so troubled that night. I knew you were hurting. I didn't know what had happened, because you didn't tell me, but I guessed you might have just lost someone close. You weren't looking for anything deep...like a relationship. I knew that. You didn't even tell me your last name. You simply wanted—*needed* to be close to someone and for some reason—' She momentarily dipped her head. 'For some reason you chose me.'

Barely trusting himself to speak, because his chest

felt so tight and he was afraid he might just explode, Dante grimly shook his head.

'You could have easily found out my last name by checking in the reservations book. From there you could have found a contact address. Why didn't you?'

She hesitated, as if she was about to say something, but changed her mind. 'I—I told you. I didn't because we'd made an agreement. I was respecting your wishes… that's all.'

'Respecting my wishes? Are you crazy? This wasn't just some simple mistake you could brush aside, woman! Can't you see what you've done? You've denied me my own child. For over four years my daughter has lived without her father. Did she never ask about me?'

'Yes…she—she did.'

'Then what did you tell her?'

Her expression anguished, Anna was clearly struggling to give him a reply.

'When Tia asked me why her daddy wasn't around I—I just told her that you'd been ill and had to go away to get better. What else could I tell her when I had no idea where you were or even if you'd care?'

Lifting a shaky hand to his forehead Dante grimaced painfully. 'And whose fault is that, when you couldn't even be bothered to find me?'

Her skin turned even paler. 'I understand why you'd want to blame me, but at the time the decision not to see each other again was ostensibly *yours*, if you remember?'

'And while I've been relegated to the back of your mind as some past inconvenient mistake...has there been anyone else on the scene?' Dante demanded, his temper flashing like an electrical storm out of a previously calm summer sky. 'Another man who's played father to Tia?'

'No, there hasn't. I've been raising her on my own, and at the same time trying to build a career so that I can support us both. I don't have time for relationships with other men!'

This last statement had clearly made her angry. The tightness in Dante's chest eased a little, but not much. He was still furious with her. Frankly, the idea that his child might have witnessed a parade of different men filing through her mother's life filled him with horror and distress. Children needed stability, support, *love*... The thought brought him up short. He had accepted without dispute the fact that Tia was his daughter—accepted the word of a woman he had only known for one too short and incredible night. Yet the moment he had gazed into Tia's eyes—eyes that were the same unusual light shade as his—Dante had somehow known that she belonged to him.

'Well, now you *will* make time for a relationship, Anna. Your comfortable little idyll of having things just the way you want them is about to change dramatically. You've dropped the bombshell that I am father to a daughter, and now you will have to accept the consequences.'

'What consequences?' The colour seemed to drain out of her face.

'What do you think?' Dante snarled, his hands curling into fists down by his sides. 'What do you think will happen now that I know I fathered a child that night? Did you think I would calmly walk away, saying, *"Oh, well"*? From this moment on I fully intend to be a father to our daughter, and that means I want a legalised relationship with you—her mother. Purely for the child's sake, you understand, and not because it fills me with joy to be with you again, Anna! Not after the terrible deceit you have played on me. So, no… I won't be calmly walking away so that you can happily continue the way you were. It's not just the hotel that will undergo a great change now that I am here.'

'I won't prevent you from playing an important part in Tia's life now that you know the truth…if that's what you want,' Anna replied quietly, though her expression mirrored a silent plea, 'but we don't need to be in a relationship for that. Five years ago you made it very clear that you weren't interested in taking things any further. I accepted that. I've made a good life for myself working at the hotel. The owners have been more than kind to me and Tia, and I'm extremely grateful to them for all they've done. As far as I can see there's no need for that arrangement to change.'

Rubbing his fingers into his temples, Dante breathed out an impatient sigh. He didn't like referring to the past, but in this case he would have to.

'Five years ago I was bordering on burn-out from working too hard and too long...then my mother died. She was Italian. The name I use now is my proper full name—the name my mother gave me. I only mention it because the night we met I'd just flown back from her funeral in Italy. I was living in New York at the time, but I couldn't get a direct flight back there so made a stopover in London for the night. Having just been bereaved, I was hardly in a fit state to contemplate a relationship with anyone. But, like you with Tia, my mother raised me on my own as a single parent, and I saw first-hand how hard life was for her. It made her old before her time, and I worried about her constantly. I'll be damned if I'll visit that hurtful existence on my own child. That being the way things stand, you have no choice but to enter into a relationship with me—a relationship that can have only one destination... Our marriage.'

Sympathetically examining the compellingly hand-some face with those searing stormy eyes—the face that she had fantasised over and dreamed longingly about for five long, lonely years—Anna willed her emotions not to get the better of her. She was gratified to hear at last an explanation as to why Dante had appeared so haunted and troubled that night, and for the second time in their association her heart went out to him. But while she understood the fears that their own situation must be raising inside him, because he too had been brought up without a father, she balked at the idea of tying herself to him merely for convenience. Dante Romano might be the father of her beloved daughter, but he was still an unknown quantity to Anna. It would be nothing less than reckless to marry him—even though privately she still held a torch for him and always would.

'I'm really sorry that you lost your mother, Dante. I could see at the time how devastated you were. But I won't be told I'm going to have to marry you just because you're Tia's father. That would be crazy. We don't even know each other. And for your information I don't want to marry anyone. I'm happy just as I am, doing my job and taking care of Tia. I won't stop you from being in her life—I'd be glad of it, if that's what you honestly want. But, like I said before, you and I don't have to be in a relationship for that.'

'Like hell we don't!' He scowled at her.

'And there's one more thing.' Feeling nervous, and knowing she was on shaky ground already, Anna rubbed a chilled palm down over her sweater. 'I'd be grateful if you didn't say anything to Grant and Anita about us knowing each other…at least not yet. It's such an awkward situation, and I *will* tell them, but I need some time to think about how best to broach the subject. Please do this one favour for me, and I promise I'll tell them soon.'

'I'll let you off the hook for a couple of days,' Dante agreed reluctantly. 'But then you *will* be telling them, Anna—about us *and* Tia. You can be absolutely sure about that.'

'I found my colouring book and my crayons!' Rushing back into the room like a tiny blond cyclone, Tia blew out a happy breath and headed straight for Dante.

For a moment he stood stock-still, his lean, smartly suited figure apparently all at sea. Anna realised that, like her, he was desperately trying to get his emotions under control. *Put yourself in his shoes*, she told herself. How would you feel if you were suddenly confronted with the astonishing fact that you'd fathered a child? A child you hadn't even known existed up until now?

'Will you help me colour in my book, please?'

The tall broad-shouldered man whose dark blond hair was slightly mussed from his agitated fingers had let Tia pierce his heart with her big soulful eyes, Anna saw. Her teeth clamped down on her lip, but it didn't stop them from trembling.

'I promised I would, didn't I?' she heard Dante agree huskily, and then he slipped his hand into his daughter's and allowed her to lead him back to the couch. Before he sat down, he shucked off the dark blue exquisitely lined jacket of his business suit, throwing it carelessly onto the cushions.

His arresting light eyes met Anna's. 'I'd like that drink you offered earlier after all,' he commented. 'Coffee would be good. I take it with milk and two sugars, thanks.'

CHAPTER FIVE

BY THE time Dante was ready to leave that evening—
having accepted Anna's invitation to join them for dinner—Tia was completely besotted with the man.

Although Anna's senses had been minutely attuned to
the fact that the man she had so recklessly given herself
to that magical night five years ago was now sitting opposite her at her dining table there had been no struggle
to make awkward conversation. Not when her daughter
had chatted enough for them both. So engaged had she
been with Dante's company that for the first time ever
she'd protested loudly about going to bed. She had only
agreed to go if Dante would read her a bedtime story—
which he duly had.

When he'd emerged from her bedroom half an hour
later his air had been subdued and preoccupied. It had
been obvious that he was trying hard to come to terms
with a situation he probably couldn't have envisaged
in a thousand years. After all, Anna had told him she
was on the pill, so what need had there been for him to
worry?

Assuming he would want to discuss things further, she'd risked giving him a smile, but he had shown no inclination to linger…the opposite, in fact. How was she supposed to confess that she wasn't as heartless as he'd assumed, and that she *had* planned to let him know about her pregnancy, but when she'd discovered his ruthless reputation in the business world she'd been scared that when the baby was born he might try and take him or her away from her? Then, when she'd tried again later, it had been as though 'Dan Masterson' had simply vanished off the radar.

'We've got a long day of discussion and planning about the hotel tomorrow,' he said to her now. 'There'll be plenty of time after work in the evening for us to discuss our personal situation in more depth.' There was a fierce glint in his eyes that said *do not doubt that*. 'For now I'll say goodnight, *innamorata*, and I will see you in the morning. Sleep well. You're going to need to be doubly alert for all we have to face tomorrow,' he added, a dark blond eyebrow lifting a little mockingly even though his voice and manner was still distant and aloof.

Innamorata—didn't that mean *sweetheart* in Italian? Anna shivered hard. Having asserted that she wasn't interested in a relationship, she wondered if Dante would still adhere to his insistence that they marry? A tug of uncertainty mingled with the faintest of faint hopes in the pit of her stomach. *What if he concluded that his association with Tia was the only one that really counted?*

A lonely feeling crept over her. And when she was still lying awake in the early hours of the morning because she couldn't get Dante out of her mind, Anna seriously worried how on earth she was going to get through her working day without at some point falling asleep on the job.

Reflecting on the new partner's all-business tone when he'd left, as well as his warning that she needed to be 'doubly alert', she imagined that would go down like the proverbial ton of bricks. It certainly wouldn't reveal her at her best. And as for the news he had just so shockingly learned…would Dante be so angry with her for not revealing his daughter's existence to him that he would try to punish her in some way? For instance, would her job and her home be under threat now that he was in the driving seat?

Thumping her pillow in pure frustration, Anna released a pained groan. Then, with her eyes determinedly shut, she sent up a swift plea to the universe for the incessant worry going through her mind to grind to a halt so that she might at least get a couple of hours' rest before having to rise for work…

'You're late, Miss Bailey.'

The clipped pronouncement came not from the owners of the hotel, nor Jason their son, but from Dante. He was seated at the head of the meeting table in Grant and Anita's office, wearing another mouthwateringly tailored dark suit that he'd teamed with an elegant black shirt—the only splash of colour came from his vivid cobalt silk tie and his disturbing light eyes...eyes that now pierced Anna like the dazzling beams of sunlight reflecting on water as she stood in the doorway, wrestling with her embarrassment at being reprimanded.

So the gloves were off, were they? Clearly he'd reflected on her news of yesterday and he *did* mean to punish her. Making it clear he was the one in charge, he'd probably make her rue the day she'd kept Tia a secret from him and then had the temerity to say she wouldn't marry him.

'I'm sorry. I'm afraid I had a bit of a sleepless night. When I did manage to drop off I ended up sleeping through the alarm.'

'Tia's not coming down with something, is she?' Anita's perfectly arched brows lifted concernedly.

Straight away, Anna saw Dante's smooth lightly-tanned forehead tighten too.

'No, she's fine. I just couldn't sleep, that's all.'

Frown disappearing, he scanned a document in front of him on the table, then lifted his gaze to examine her coolly. 'That kind of lame excuse for being late is unacceptable, Miss Bailey. I'd advise you to get a louder alarm clock if you want to keep your position here.'

Even her employers' mouths dropped opened at that. As the avuncular Grant shifted uncomfortably in his seat, Anita directed a sympathetic smile at Anna and mouthed *don't worry.*

'Dante?'

The older woman moved her attention immediately back to the outrageously handsome man at the head of the table. Although her voice was soft it didn't lack authority.

'Sleeping through the alarm happens to the best of us from time to time—and we've always called our staff by their first names...especially Anna. As we indicated to you before, she's not just an employee. She's a friend too.'

'And that's precisely what goes wrong in family businesses,' Dante returned, sharp as a blade. 'Whilst I'm all for informality, to a degree, it's still important to monitor it so it doesn't get out of control, or your staff will start taking advantage of your goodwill.'

'How dare you?' With her heart beating a tattoo that wouldn't shame a military marching band, Anna glared at the owners' new partner and took affront at the superior tone in his voice. 'I would never dream of taking advantage of my employers' goodwill. I owe them everything...they've given me a job, a home—'

Pulling out a chair next to Jason and dropping down into it, she firmly closed her lips to stop any further angry words from recklessly pouring out. What was between Dante and her was personal, she thought furiously. She wouldn't drag her personal resentments into work meetings and neither should he!

So she hadn't been able to sleep last night? Dante reflected with satisfaction, ignoring her outburst. His glance swept helplessly over her delicate, now flushed features. Well, neither had he. Learning only a few short hours ago that he was the father of the most engaging and beautiful child he'd ever seen had never been going to help him get the best night's rest known to man. Neither was the fact that Anna had seemed far from keen on the idea of marrying him. *As in the past, rejection was like a scythe, slicing open his heart.* But Dante had already decided she could refuse him all she liked—because in the end he was determined to have his way. As far as his daughter was concerned he would use any means possible to ensure she had the upbringing and the future she deserved. But right now he needed to deal with what was in front of him—his promise and commitment to the Mirabelle, to turn the business around and have it flourishing again. Already his mind was buzzing with ideas for changes and improvements. And he would begin as he usually began when he went into a business to update it and improve its profitability—he would interview the staff…

'Can I pour you some coffee?' Reaching for the newly filled cafetière, Dante glanced expectantly at Anna as she sat down on the other side of his desk.

'No, thank you.' Her sherry-brown gaze briefly acknowledged him then quickly moved away again.

Irritation and disappointment threatened his effort to

be as good-humoured and fair as possible. Was she still brooding about him ticking her off earlier? As much as his pride wanted to cajole her into viewing him more favourably, right now this interview needed to get underway as well as remain professional, and Dante knew a battle of wills wouldn't help. Their personal issues would have to wait until later tonight.

'Fine… Good. We'll make a start, then, shall we?'

'As you wish.'

'For goodness' sake, you don't have to sit there like you're about to climb the steps up to the guillotine! All I'm doing is interviewing you about your job.' Tunnelling his fingers through his hair, Dante knew his breath was slightly ragged as he fought to regain control of his temper. What was it about this woman that always inflamed him? Whether it was lustful desire or a burst of bad temper she always seemed to inspire some kind of volatile reaction.

'Am I going to keep my job, or are you planning to replace me with someone else in your clean sweep?'

'What?' His dark blond brows drew together in puzzlement. Anna was slumped back in her chair, and the fear in her eyes was suddenly clear as daylight to Dante.

'I mean, in your drive to improve things, is my job under threat?'

A flash of memory of that night they'd met came back to Dante, and he recalled her telling him that she'd lost her previous job to a 'ruthless takeover'.

'I'm only interviewing you to find out what your responsibilities and duties are, and if you enjoy your work. I have no plans to replace or fire anyone right now, so your job is quite safe.'

'Oh...' Her sigh was relieved. Her restless hand lifted to play with the tiny heart-shaped crystal on the end of a slim gold chain she wore round her neck. *Had an admirer bought her that?*

His equilibrium coming under disagreeable fire yet again, Dante leaned forward to level his gaze. 'Now that we've got that out of the way, perhaps you could give me a rundown of your duties?'

'I will... Only...'

'What?'

'I'm worried that because you're clearly angry with me about Tia you might deliberately find something wrong about the way I do my job so—so that you can get back at me in some way.'

'What?' Stunned, Dante widened his blue-grey eyes. 'Do you really think I'd resort to the kind of tactics that would jeopardise my daughter's well-being? Think about it. If I tried to punish you in some way, would it not have repercussions for her too? I'd hardly allow that.'

'You see? That's where our sticking point is. I don't know you well enough to know *what* you might be capable of.' Her slender shoulders lifted in a shrug. 'All I know is that it's been a confusing and worrying time, what with the threat of Anita and Grant possibly having to sell up and leave, and then—and then out of the blue you show up, and I learn that you're the man who's looking to invest in the hotel and will become the new senior partner. More importantly, I then have to break the news to you that Tia is your daughter. I had no idea how you'd react. We only spent a night together. You might feel utterly compromised and furious. Or you might…' Her voice faltered a little. 'You might want to try and take her away from me. Can you wonder why I couldn't sleep last night?'

Dante pushed to his feet, because the restlessness and annoyance that deluged him wouldn't allow him to remain sitting.

'Why would I want to try and take her away from you? Don't you think—to use an English expression—that would be rather like shooting myself in the foot? I can see that she adores you, and you her. From what I've seen you've done an admirable job of raising her by yourself. But I'm sticking by my original conviction that she needs her father in her life too. She needs two parents…which is why I said we should marry.'

'Why would you want to tie yourself to a woman you knew for just one night?' Anna's voice was slightly husky as she asked this, and a tiny perplexed crease puckered her brow.

'Because that one night resulted in a child…a child I didn't even know about until yesterday!' He drove his hands into his trouser pockets as he moved away from the desk, briefly presenting her with his back.

Was the impression he'd left her with so poor that she hadn't considered even for a moment trying to contact him? It didn't make Dante feel very good *or* wanted. It just made him mad. Briefly thinking of his father and his ex, he wondered what *rare* quality he had that made it so easy for people to walk away from him. And to make them think he wouldn't be concerned about his own flesh and blood.

'Dante?'

Garnering his composure, he turned back to face the striking redhead on the other side of the desk.

'What is it?'

'I didn't tell you before because I didn't quite know how to put it, but I *did* initially try to contact you when I found out I was pregnant. I did find out your name, and I even looked you up on the internet.'

'And?' Dante interjected impatiently, his heart thudding.

'Your reputation was quite—quite intimidating. To be perfectly honest, it worried me. I didn't even know if you'd remember me, let alone believe me when I told you I was pregnant. Anyway...' Glancing away, Anna heaved a sigh. 'I decided perhaps it was best after all if I didn't contact you. But some months after Tia was born the conviction that you had a right to know about her took hold of me again. For days I followed every lead I could to try and track you down, but it was as though you'd disappeared. Of course now I realise that it was because you'd changed your name. I went back to believing that maybe it had never been on the cards that we should meet again. In any case, for all I knew you could have married and had children with someone else. And besides…that night we were together you did tell me it was a one-time-only thing and that I had to accept that…remember?'

Dante remembered. He sombrely reflected on how he'd regretted that over the years. There had been many lonely nights when he would have been thrilled to have Anna in his arms again. But, to be brutal, at the time all he could have offered her was sex. Not even companionship had been an option. Not after his mother's death. He'd been in too dark a place to take anyone there with him. But it still hit him hard that because of his ruthless reputation Anna had been frightened of trying to make contact. And later, when she'd wanted to try and find him again, he had changed his name back to Dante Romano. He could no longer blame her for anything. Everything that had happened was *his* fault.

'We cannot turn back the clock. That is beyond even *my* power, ruthless reputation or no.' His lips twisted ruefully. 'What has happened in the past has happened, and all we can do now is face what's in front of us today. Besides…our personal issues probably shouldn't be discussed in work time. We'll talk tonight, as previously agreed. Right now I have an interview to conduct.'

He sat down again, automatically switching his brain to work mode. He'd turned that ability into a fine art over the years whenever emotions had threatened to swamp him. The woman sitting opposite him was silent.

'Anna?'

For a moment she seemed troubled. But then the corners of her pretty mouth curved into a smile.

'You mean you're not going to call me Miss Bailey any more?' she teased.

The look on her face was somewhere between angel and imp, and Dante all but groaned—because it was as though someone had shot a flame-tipped arrow straight into his loins. A charged memory of her whispering softly into his ear and moving over his body, erotically sliding her mouth over his as her long hair, carrying its scent of oranges and patchouli, drifted against him surfaced powerfully.

'When we're working together, and in the company of our colleagues, I may from time to time call you Miss Bailey. When we're alone...' his voice lowered meaningfully '...I'll call you Anna.'

'Right.' Beneath her flawlessly satin skin, a soft pink bloomed like a summer rose.

Gratified that he still had the power to discomfit her, Dante couldn't help the smile that escaped him.

'We'll carry on then...yes?'

'Yes, all right.' She straightened her back, but her expression seemed transfixed and he had to prompt her again.

'Anna?'

She patted down her hair.

'Sorry. To answer your question—my first responsibility is to the manager…to help support him in fulfilling the hotel's promise of delivering an impeccable service to the customer.'

'And how do you and Mr Cathcart get on? Do you communicate well? Are there any problems there, for instance?'

'There aren't any problems. Jason—Mr Cathcart and I have always got on. He's kind and fair…just like his parents.'

'So you like him?'

'Yes, I like him. We work very well together.'

'Good…that's good to hear.'

Twirling his pen absently between his fingers, now it was Dante's turn to fall into a trance. Studying the arresting face before him, the face that had haunted his sleep many nights in the past, he had a hungry need to just look and appreciate. To his mind, Anna Bailey's features were perfect. The finely shaped brows above those dancing long-lashed brown eyes, the slim and elegant nose and the pensive pretty mouth—there was a serenity about her that was more than a little appealing to a man who had lived his life mostly in the fast lane.

Did Jason Cathcart enjoy that aspect of her company too? He had certainly been voluble in his praise of Anna's talents and abilities during his interview with Dante earlier. A fierce little knot of jealousy throbbed painfully under his ribs. Did the man wish they were more than colleagues? he wondered. A disturbing image of him getting cosy with Anna and Tia almost stole his breath.

'And is Mr Cathcart good at leading and inspiring his staff, would you say?' he asked, gravel-voiced.

'Definitely.' A flicker of apprehension crossed Anna's face. 'You interviewed him earlier. Surely you formed an impression of him?'

'I did,' Dante answered abruptly. 'And that, of course, will remain confidential. Now, what other responsibilities does your role entail?'

Even though he would have preferred to quiz Anna further about *her* impression of her colleague, he knew it shouldn't be in the arena of a professional conversation concerning her job. Corralling the urge to ask her outright if she had more personal feelings towards Jason, he listened intently as she described other aspects of her role as assistant manager, determinedly making himself focus on the interview at hand and not get sidetracked by emotion.

CHAPTER SIX

THE ring on the doorbell just after she'd checked to see if Tia was asleep made Anna's heart skip a beat. She knew it was Dante. He had vowed he'd return later, after going back to his apartment. They'd agreed he would drop by after she'd put Tia to bed so that they could talk in private.

Glancing at the two slim-stemmed wine glasses she'd left on the coffee table, she nervously smoothed down the multicoloured jersey tunic dress that she'd hastily donned over black leggings and cinched with a vivid green belt, praying she didn't look as flustered as she felt.

'Hi.'

She hadn't known how starved she was for the sight of his sculpted, strikingly good-looking face until she was confronted by it at the door. Her pulse went wild. In turn, Dante's disturbing gaze ran up and down her figure with equally hard-to-hide intensity, and every flicker of his glance was like lighted touchpaper to already simmering embers.

'Come in,' she invited, her voice hoarse, practically pressing herself into the wall to let him pass.

'Nice perfume,' he remarked, low-voiced, as he entered, his eyes reflecting electric blue sparks tonight, rather than the dramatic hue of stormy seas. 'Sexy.'

'Thanks,' Anna murmured, her mind going unhelpfully blank at the compliment.

'I've brought some very good Italian wine.' He placed a dark slim bottle into her hands. 'It's a Barolo. It comes from a region known as Piedmont, where they're famed for making the best wines.'

'That's kind. I've got some dry white chilling in the fridge, but if you prefer red then that's fine with me. We can have either.' Shrugging self-consciously, she shut the door behind them, adding, 'I don't mind.'

Wishing she didn't feel as if she'd been shaken hard, then stood on her head, Anna led the way into the living room.

'When we first met, I didn't know you were Italian,' she remarked lightly.

'Only on my mother's side.'

'What about your father?'

'He was British.'

'That explains why you used the surname Masterson, then. You don't have much of an Italian accent, either.'

'I stopped residing in Italy a long time ago.'

'Why? Did your parents move to the UK?'

His fascinating eyes darkened almost warningly. 'No.

They didn't. They parted company when I was very young…younger than Tia, in fact.'

'And you didn't want to stay in Italy?'

'Enough questions for now, I think.'

There was a definite tightening to Dante's perfectly symmetrical jaw, and Anna clamped her teeth down on her lip, embarrassed at the flow of curiosity that had unstoppably rushed out. But frustration niggled her—because how were she and her daughter supposed to get to know him if he was so reluctant to reveal himself?

'Why don't you sit down?' she suggested, awkward now.

Dropping down onto the couch, his expression relieved, Dante undid the single button on his tailored black jacket to reveal a midnight-blue cashmere sweater. The golden lights in his hair glinted fiercely beneath the soft glow of one of the nearby lamps, the odd silver strand here or there making him look mouthwateringly distinguished. As if she wasn't already provocatively aware of his charismatic presence, the exotically eastern tones of his aftershave sensuously made a beeline into Anna's solar plexus and caused a near meltdown.

'Open the Barolo,' he said casually, gesturing towards the bottle in her hands. 'It's a cold, rainy night outside and it will warm us up.'

His barely perceptible smile pierced her heart. Why did it seem so hard for him to relax? What was it about his past that still racked him with shadows? she mused.

'Okay...I will.'

Briefly disappearing into the kitchen to locate the corkscrew, Anna was grateful for a few moments to herself. It was clear that the inflammatory attraction that had flared out of control that night five years ago had not dimmed one *iota*. At least not for *her*. To be frank, the realisation filled her with trepidation. How could she be clear-headed and wise and do the right thing for her and Tia if all Dante had to do was walk into a room to have her temperature shooting off the scale?

In the living room once more, she gladly gave the task of pouring the wine to him. Right then her hands weren't anywhere near steady enough to do it without the possibility of spilling some. As she crossed the room to the single plump armchair, Anna felt Dante's glance track her progress.

Before raising his glass to his lips, he asked, 'Is the baby asleep?'

Charmed and taken aback that he should refer to Tia as 'the baby' with such affection in his voice, she knew her smile was unreserved. 'Yes, she is.'

'I'd like to look in on her before I go tonight.'

'Of course.'

'There's so much about her I want to know... What food she likes, her favourite colour, the book she likes the most.'

His gaze seemed to take him away to distant shores for a moment, and Anna caught her breath as a merciless stab of guilt assailed her.

But before she could comment he continued, 'We should have a toast. To Tia and her happy future.'

'Tia and her happy future,' she concurred a little huskily, her mouth drying, because she knew that the future was one of the most pertinent things they had to discuss tonight. What would it entail? Not just for her precious child, but for Anna herself now that Dante had reappeared?

Sipping at her wine, she allowed the alcohol to swim warmly into her blood for a moment, hoping it might relax her. 'This is nice…it reminds me of violets somehow.'

'You have a good nose. Barolo *does* have a bouquet of violets. You could have a new career in wine-tasting.'

'Will I need a new career?'

'Your interview wasn't *that* bad.'

'How comforting,' she quipped, unable to hide the surge of annoyance that surfaced. 'I've had no complaints about how I carry out my job so far.'

'There's no need to be defensive. You've nothing to fear from me, Anna. I certainly don't have any plans to fire you from your job.'

To her alarm, Dante set his wine glass down on the coffee table and got to his feet. Then he was standing in front of her, his nearness making her feel quite light-headed.

'Put your wine down for a minute,' he commanded quietly, voice low.

Captured by his hypnotic glance, Anna obeyed. He held out his hand and helped her to her feet.

'That dress you're wearing hurts my eyes.'

Embarrassment made her want the floor to open up and swallow her.

'I know it's a bit dazzling, but I grabbed the first thing out of my wardrobe, to tell you the truth.' She was fumbling for a foothold but couldn't find one. Had his shoulders always been this wide…his chest this broad and strong? The male heat he emanated so—so *drugging*?

'It's dazzling not because of the riot of colour but because it's on *you*. Dazzling like this glorious hair of yours.' Capturing a handful of burnished copper silk between his fingers, Dante raised the fiery strands to his lips and kissed them.

Anna couldn't move. It took every ounce of iron will she possessed not to give in to the overwhelming impulse to lay her head against his chest and wrap her arms round his waist. The intoxication of his presence almost made her forget why he was there…*almost*.

'I am so glad you haven't had it cut short since I saw you last.'

'I—I wouldn't do that… But, Dante—we—we need to talk,' she murmured, her own voice sounding like a dazed stranger's.

'We can talk like we talked when we first met. Like this… Do you remember, Anna?'

The heat of his lips touched the side of her neck,

searing the delicate skin there with an indelible brand.
'I remember,' she husked, her limbs turning to liquid
silver. 'But we should— We need to…' A helpless little
moan escaped her as Dante moved his lips up to her ear,
his mouth planting a hot, devastatingly erotic kiss on
her highly sensitive lobe. The molten heat that pooled in
Anna's centre threatened to make her lose her capacity
to think at all.

'What do we need to do?'

With a smile in his voice that was a seductive cocktail
of fine malt whisky and luxurious honey, Dante settled
his hands on her hips and firmly pulled her against
him. The hard male contours encased in his fluidly
elegant tailored suit and the suggestion of barely contained impressive masculine strength made Anna shiver.
Mesmerised by the haze of longing in his burning gaze,
she nervously swallowed. She yearned to succumb to
the desire that was flowing with equal ardour through
her veins, but an anguished moment of clarity returned,
making her stiffen in his arms.

'What did you mean when you said you weren't going
to fire me from my job? I don't like the sound of that…
It makes me feel like you potentially *could* fire me if
you wanted to. I can't say that fills me with confidence…
not when I have a child to support, and depend on my
job for a roof over our heads.'

There was a flash of impatience in his eyes.

'The point is that you don't need to depend on your
job to sustain you, *or* for a roof over your heads! I meant

it when I said we should marry. And when we're married I'll take care of you both.'

'You make it sound so straightforward and easy. I'm not an investment you're interested in, Dante. I'm a fully functioning independent human being with my own ideas and thoughts on lots of subjects—including marriage. It's completely wrong of you to assume that I'd instantly give up everything I've worked so hard for to throw in my lot with a man I barely know. A man who only wants marriage because he's discovered that the one-night stand that we had resulted in a child!'

He set Anna free with a muttered oath and stalked across the room, scraping his fingers through the dark blond strands of his previously groomed hair. His glare was blistering in its intensity. 'What better reason to marry someone than because you made a child together? Tia deserves to have her father in her life. I want that for her and I want that for me—and as a "fully functioning independent human being" you have no right to deny us!'

'I'm not saying I'd deny you. But marriage isn't for me. I...' She lowered her gaze to stare down at the floor, 'I like my independence... I like the fact that my hard work has finally got me somewhere and now I have opportunities... I'm captain of my own ship and it's a good feeling.'

'So you like being captain of your own ship—but do you honestly like being alone? Raising a child on your own is far from easy, no matter how many opportunities for advancing your career come your way. When the baby is ill do you welcome being her sole carer, with no one but yourself to rely upon to make the best decisions for her welfare? And when she's ill what do you do if you can't take time off work for fear of losing your job and your income?'

Moving back across the room towards her, Dante had that faraway look Anna had seen before in his eyes.

'Once when I was five I had the measles…had it quite severely. My mother had no choice but to go out to her job in the evening—it was literally a matter of whether we ate or starved. She asked a close neighbour if I could stay with her for the evening, but the woman refused because she had five children of her own and didn't want to risk them getting infected. My mother left me in bed. The neighbour promised to regularly check up on me while she was gone. I had a raging fever, and by the time my mother came home I was convulsing. We didn't have a telephone. She ran with me through the night to a man she knew who owned a restaurant, and he called a doctor. If it weren't for that I probably wouldn't have made it.'

His tone bitterly rueful, he shook his head. 'My mother went to hell and back that night. If she had had someone to help her, someone who cared equally for my welfare, she wouldn't have suffered the torment and guilt that she did. And I have no intention of ever letting my daughter be in the precarious position I was…no matter what your assurances.'

Barely knowing how to answer him, Anna wept inside for the agony Dante and his mother must have endured that terrible night. It was the kind of nightmare scenario every mother dreaded.

Before she realised it her impulse to touch him, to comfort him in some way, overtook her, and she laid her hand against the side of his face. His skin was velvety warm, pulsing with the vibrant strength she'd detected earlier. 'I love that you care for Tia so deeply already. But I'm lucky, Dante... I may be a single mum, but I have friends—people who really care for Tia—people who would help us at the drop of a hat.'

'That may be so, but I have no intention of leaving my child's well-being to the precarious fair-weather attention of mere friends! No matter how much you might trust them, Anna. So...' He winced a little when she withdrew her hand, almost as if she'd struck him. 'There's only one solution to our dilemma, and I've already told you what that is. Now it's just a matter of arranging things. The sooner the better, I think.'

Stroking her hands up and down her arms, Anna sensed their tremble.

'I'm not getting married...I told you.'

'Then regrettably, you're pushing me into taking action I'd much rather not take,' Dante retorted. 'But I will take it if it means I can be with my daughter. I'll go to court to get full custody of Tia.'

Was it only to her own hypersensitive hearing that her heartbeat sounded so deafeningly loud? Anna thought.

She'd been musing on a mother's worst nightmare but surely this was one of the most horrendous threats a woman could face? That her child's estranged parent might sue for custody and take her away—maybe to live in another country entirely? Searching for compassion in Dante's flint-like stare, worryingly, she found none.

'No!' she protested loudly, tears stinging the backs of her lids.

He lifted an eyebrow, but looked no less resolved on his course. 'If you don't want me to take such an action, then I suggest you stop putting obstacles in the way and agree to our marriage.'

'That's so disrespectful. You'd resort to something as low as blackmail to get your own way?'

'I told you.' His broad-shouldered shrug was unapologetic. 'I'll do anything I can to be with my daughter… the daughter you have so callously denied me knowledge of for four years because my so-called reputation made you believe I didn't deserve to know about her. And you have the audacity to stand there and lecture *me* on respect!'

'I didn't keep her from you deliberately.' Wanting to cry in frustration as well as pain, Anna stared pleadingly into the heartbreakingly handsome features of the well-dressed man in front of her. 'Don't you think I would have preferred to be in a good relationship with my baby's father than be asked not to try and get in touch after we parted that night? I know it was a difficult time for you, but it didn't exactly make me feel wanted to know that you could just walk away from me and never look back. And how do you think I felt when I discovered I was pregnant? Especially when it was the first time I—' She bit her lip on what she'd been going to say and continued, 'I was shocked, lonely, scared... I experienced every one of those states—but even taken together they don't come near to describing how I felt.'

She noticed that Dante's glance was quizzical.

'It was the first time you...what, Anna?'

Backing up nervously, she reached for the glass of wine she'd left on the side-table near the armchair and drank some. She let the alcohol hit before raising her chin with a defiant air born of Dutch courage. Her dark eyes focused firmly on Dante.

'It was the first time I'd slept with a man.'

The oath he swore was in Italian, and because she was shaky after revealing her news Anna returned her glass to the table, waiting for the tirade of disbelief that she was certain would explode towards her.

But when next he spoke Dante's voice was surprisingly quiet, his words measured. 'You were untouched when I took you into my bed...that's what you're telling me?'

'I was. Couldn't you tell I was no experienced seductress who made a habit of going to bed with male guests? I'd barely even been kissed before!'

'Yet you were molten heat in my arms. Everywhere I touched you, you made me burn.'

Praying for some way to steady the deluge of emotion that tumbled forcefully through her, Anna despaired of ever feeling calm again when she saw the renewed flame of Dante's desire sinfully reflected back at her…just as if it had never gone away. With a disparaging toss of her head, she answered, 'I think I lost my mind a little that night. I would never usually behave in that way with a strange man…with *any* man for that matter.'

'We lost our minds together, Anna.' He sounded seductively accepting and non-judgmental. 'And the result was little Tia. Can you regret such an outcome?'

'Never.'

'Then we have to deal with this situation like adults, instead of feuding children, and that means our daughter's welfare takes priority.'

'You mean…' Anna surveyed him with a frown. 'You mean you still believe marriage is the only answer?'

'I do.'

'If that's the way you want to go, how about trying a trial period of living together first?'

'Too uncertain—and it hardly represents the security I want for Tia.'

'Surely that depends on how we deal with it? If we're committed to making it work, then living together could be just as secure as marriage.'

'No. That's not what I want.'

'And if I refuse? You'd really take me to court for custody?'

'I would.' His piercing glance was as unyielding as ice.

CHAPTER SEVEN

IT DIDN'T exactly enhance his self-esteem or his pride, having to potentially resort to blackmail to persuade Anna to marry him, but since he had made the earth-shattering discovery that he was a father, Dante's determination to help bring up his daughter was cast-iron. There was nothing the redheaded beauty could say that would deter him.

But in truth he was taken aback that she could so easily refuse him. He'd met plenty of women on his travels who considered him quite the catch.

Once upon a time his ex-wife Marisa had said those very words to him. *'You're quite a catch, Dante... It's a wonder that you've been allowed to say free and single for this long...'*

But that assertion by her had soon turned to ashes when she'd discovered that for her husband raw ambition came first and his most intimate relationship a very poor second. Even when his marriage had been in its dying stages he hadn't sought to rescue it, or been able to express his emotions. Marisa had walked into the arms of another man and Dante had simply let her—if he was honest, feeling nothing but relief.

Now the greatest shock that he had ever received...the news that he was a *father*...reverberated doubly on learning that Anna had been a sexual innocent when he'd slept with her. It also made him remember the flicker of apprehension in her eyes when, for a few moments as she lay beneath him, he'd sensed definite tension in her slender frame. What must she have thought when he'd asked her to spend the night and then warned her not to expect anything else? Not a phone call, not even his real name—nothing! What an introduction to the world of adult relationships she'd had.

Fast forward five years on, and Dante knew that if he'd met Anna today he would never have let her go... not for all the million-dollar real estate in the world. With her gorgeous flame hair flowing unhindered over her shoulders and her brown eyes sparkling like fire-warmed brandy she was vivacious, pretty and completely unpretentious. Her eye-catching dress with its patent green belt highlighted how tiny her waist was, and the black leggings she wore cleaved lovingly to her long, model-slim legs.

Studying her now, he acknowledged that she made the blood pound through his veins like no other woman he'd ever met. So, even if she despised him for putting her in such a compromising position, he would endeavour not to disappoint her as he had disappointed his ex. He certainly wouldn't give her cause to accuse him of ignoring her. He would also show her that he intended to be the best father to Tia that a child could have. She would not want for anything materially, and for as long as he lived Dante would dote on her. There would be no need for Anna to be lonely either, because he fully intended to keep her warm at nights and reintroduce her to the delight and pleasure of passionate lovemaking...

Having returned to the old-fashioned floral armchair, she now sat nursing her wine glass, her glance wary and resentful when it locked with his.

'I'll have to tell the Cathcarts about us,' she murmured.

'Yes, you will.' Shrugging off his jacket, Dante dropped it onto the arm of the couch. Turning back to Anna, he smiled enigmatically. 'But don't worry... they'll have plenty of time to absorb the news.'

'Why's that?'

'Because after discussing the changes that need to be implemented I'm going to suggest we close the hotel for a month while it's being refurbished and modernised. In that time we will travel to Lake Como with Tia, where you and I will marry.'

'You're intending to close the Mirabelle for a whole month?' Slamming her wine glass precariously on the side-table, Anna widened her brown eyes in disbelief. 'What about the staff? What about their jobs? They can't possibly afford to take a whole month off.'

'It will be paid leave.' An irritated muscle flinched hard in the side of Dante's cheekbone. He'd just told her he was taking her to Lake Como to marry him and all she could think about was what was going to happen to the staff! It seriously irked him that Anna's soft heart did not include fretting about *him* in such a concerned manner.

'Can you afford to do that?' she asked in wonder.

He could have replied that he could buy and refurbish the hotel and fund the staff's leave several hundred times over and still have change, but Dante didn't. The stunning house he owned in Lake Como would be a surprise and hopefully a delight to her when she saw it, and perhaps would bring home to her just how wealthy her soon-to-be husband actually was. But there was a hollow feeling in the pit of his stomach that he should take refuge in something so superficial when in truth he wanted Anna to regard him totally for himself, to see the man behind the thousand dollar suits and impressive portfolio, *not* what his money could buy.

'I have interests in several very successful businesses worldwide, Anna, so trust me...' His hand cut expressively through the air. 'Worrying about whether I can afford it is not something that even has to enter your head.'

She was puzzled that he seemed so annoyed. Had she dented his ego by querying whether he could afford to do as he'd said? But, more perturbing than that, Anna was under siege from far more unsettling concerns. Events were moving at a pace she hadn't remotely expected, and one major issue was disturbing her above all else.

Dante's insistence that they marry was making her feel as though he wanted to control and possess her, and was disturbingly reminiscent of her father's behaviour as she was growing up.

Frank Bailey had had two major passions in his life... his love affair with booze and his diminutive, too passive wife—Anna's mother, Denise. He'd been so possessive and jealous that he'd completely banned her from even having friends, because he couldn't bear her attention to be on anyone else but him. That jealousy had even transferred itself to Anna if he thought she was too demanding—which even as a small child she rarely was. But her father had been able to misread the most innocent situations, and had made his judgements with an authority that chilled the blood.

Consequently, Anna had lost count of the times she'd witnessed his rage—and that included being frequently belittled by him verbally. An occurrence that had become even more frightening and threatening to her peace of mind when he was drunk. She knew intimately that mental torment was just as destructive as physical violence. There were too many times when, upon hearing her father's key in the door, she'd sat on her bed quaking with terror, praying to disappear, praying for a greater power to make her so small that he wouldn't even notice she was there.

In agitation, she rose to her feet. 'Dante...about us going to Lake Como to—to get married...'

'What about it?'

She obviously *had* upset him, because his handsome face was fierce for a moment. But, however unapproachable he seemed, Anna refused to be intimidated by him.

'I'll go with you on one condition.'

'I have already told you that—'

'Hear me out.' Although shaking inside, her tone was unerringly firm, and there was a definite flash of surprise in Dante's light-coloured eyes. 'I don't want a wedding arranged until I see how we get on together. And I won't have you issuing me with threats of going to court for custody of Tia either. I've seen the damage it can do to a woman's spirit to have a man try to control her, and I won't accept it from anyone...not even and *especially* the man who fathered my child!'

'You're speaking from personal experience?' Although Dante's voice had turned quiet, it was underscored with shock and a sense of impatience too—as if he wanted to hear the full extent of what Anna had endured.

'Yes, I am.' She crossed her arms in front of her, knowing there was no point in keeping her past a secret. It wouldn't serve her in the long run, however painful it was to talk about it. Ghosts could only haunt a person if they colluded with them to keep them hidden. 'My father was a cruel and jealous drunk, and he made my mother's life a living hell.'

'Where is he now?'

'No longer in this world…thank goodness.' An icy shudder ran down Anna's spine.

'And your mother…where is she?'

'She's gone too.' She briefly pursed her lips, fighting hard to win the struggle over her tears. 'They said at the hospital that she died of heart disease, but I know that's not what killed her. She was simply tired and worn out… beaten down by living with my brute of a father.'

His glance glinting with anger as well as sympathy, Dante stepped towards her. 'Was he a brute to you too, Anna?' he demanded huskily.

'A man with a propensity for intimidation doesn't care who he tries to intimidate. He just gets off on the power. His children are the easiest targets of all—especially when they're too scared to answer back in case they get another verbal lashing. And the situation becomes even more horrendous when the impulse to dominate and show what a big strong man he is is fuelled by alcohol.'

Shame and despair cramped her throat for a second. 'Have you any idea what it's like to have foul beer or whisky-smelling breath right in your face, and a mocking voice yelling at you how useless you are? How worthless? Anyway, I don't want to talk any more about this right now.' She made as if to move towards the kitchen. 'I don't think I can drink any more wine, lovely as it is. I think I'll make some coffee. Would you like some?'

'No.' Dante laid his hand on her arm to prevent her from turning away, but he didn't curl his fingers to grip it. Right now he needed to tread very carefully. He could see the fear and terror in her eyes from her disturbing memories and it shook him deeply. 'We'll do as you suggest. We'll go to Lake Como and live together for a while before embarking on marriage. Does that make you happier, Anna?'

Perversely, the look of relief crossing her face was like a hammer blow to Dante. He didn't want to possess Anna—he knew that would be wrong. In the light of what she'd experienced with her bullying father it would be *doubly* wrong. Just the thought of such a man hurting her in any way brought out the most base of animal instincts in him to deal with *anyone* who threatened her or Tia. Ultimately all he wanted to do was take care of them both—to show Anna that beneath the facade of wealth and success his genuine heartfelt desire was for family and connection. He wanted the chance to prove that underneath the outward material trappings and his drive for achievement existed the good, responsible, caring man that his mother had always insisted was the *real* Dante Romano.

'Thank you,' she answered softly.

Reluctantly he let go of her arm, even though touching her through the material of her dress made him long for so much more.

'Perhaps while you make your coffee I could look in on Tia? I just want to sit beside her bed and watch her sleep for a while,' he said.

'Go ahead. Take as long as you like.'

* * *

Half an hour later, Anna opened Tia's bedroom door to find Dante comfortably ensconced in the cosy slipper chair beside their daughter's bed, his elbows resting against his long-boned thighs in his exquisitely tailored suit trousers and his body quite still. His avid gaze was transfixed by the angelic blond child who lay sleeping peacefully beneath the Walt Disney character–decorated pink duvet, one arm flung out by her side and the other clutching her favourite chewed teddy bear.

Anna needed a moment. It was as though one of her favourite made-up stories had come to startling, vivid life, and she hardly dared breathe for fear of disturbing it and making it disappear.

But Dante had heard her come in and, turning in his chair, treated her to the most disarming, knee-trembling smile she'd ever seen.

'She's so beautiful,' he breathed quietly. 'I don't want to leave her…not for a minute or even a second. I've missed so much of her growing up.'

Anna didn't mistake the catch in his voice. Advancing into the room, which was illuminated only by the soft night light glowing in the corner, she dropped her hand on his hard-muscled shoulder, silently thrilling to feel the sensuous warmth that emanated through the luxurious cashmere of his sweater.

'She's still got a lot of growing up to do, Dante…she's only four. And children quickly adapt to new situations and people. One day she'll forget there was even a time when you didn't mean the world to her.'

Covering her hand and holding it against him, Dante held Anna's gaze with a passionate heated look. 'I want her to know I'm her father. I want her to know as soon as possible. Can you understand that?'

Gripped by the pain in his voice, Anna breathed out slowly. 'I do. Of course I do. But we just—we just have to pick the right moment.'

'Tomorrow when you pick her up from school we'll take her somewhere for tea. It will give her and me the chance to get to know each other a little. But I don't want her to be kept in the dark about who I am for long, Anna.' He let go of her hand. 'I don't think I could bear that.'

'We'll tell her soon,' she said reassuringly, seeing by his expression how in earnest he was about Tia knowing he was her father.

Clenching his jaw for a moment, Dante exhaled a heavy sigh. His eyes flashed like distant lightning in a velvet midnight sky.

'Good…that's good. Now, I think it's probably time I left. We have much to do tomorrow. I'll see you in the morning, Anna.' His lips brushed briefly against her cheek as he stood up. 'Try to get some proper sleep tonight, eh?'

The sensuous trail of his cologne and the seductive warmth that was the legacy of his lips lingered on Anna's skin long after he had gone…

She asked if Anita could spare a few minutes to talk during their afternoon tea break. Expressing her usual

amicable concern, the older woman kindly welcomed
Anna into the office she shared with her husband—an
entirely organised and *smart* office in comparison with
her son Jason's. Grant had gone out to visit a new sup-
plier and wouldn't be back until later, she confided.

She appeared much happier, Anna noticed—as if
a world of worry had been lifted from her shoulders.
Dante's rescue package for the Mirabelle was already
making a difference, she realised. There was no doubt in
her mind that he would turn the hotel's fortunes around.
He was an accomplished, experienced investor, and even
their sous chef Cheryl, and Amy and Linda the recep-
tionists, were already referring to him as their 'knight
in shining armour'. She didn't know why their praise
and ingratiating admiration should put her back up, but
it did.

'What's troubling you, sweetheart?' Stirring her tea,
Anita sat back in one of the three easy chairs arranged
round a coffee table, surveying Anna with concern.

'Am I that easy to read?' the younger woman
quipped.

'Not always… But for some reason today I definitely
sense that you're anxious about something.'

'It's about Dante,' Anna began, her fingers knotting
together in her lap.

Her cheeks flamed red when Anita raised a curious
eyebrow. The casual form of address had slipped out,
because he'd been on her mind almost constantly since
last night. Especially when she remembered that look

on his face and the tremor in his voice when he'd passionately declared that he wanted Tia to know he was her father.

'I mean Mr Romano,' she corrected herself quickly.

'What's wrong? I know he's been a little…shall we say *abrasive* with you, dear—but he can be extraordinarily thoughtful of people too. He's already won friends here. And when he's talked to me and Grant about plans for updating the hotel he's consulted our opinion at every turn. There are exciting plans afoot!' Her lips splitting in a grin reminiscent of an excited schoolgirl, Anita all but hugged herself. 'We're going to call a staff meeting later, to give everyone an update, but as you're our assistant manager I may as well tell you confidentially that Dante has deemed it a good idea to close the Mirabelle for a month while the modernisation gets underway. All the staff will get paid leave.'

'How do you feel about that?'

'We're perfectly happy. Not only is it necessary, but it's a great idea too. Grant and I haven't had a break in so long. We plan to devote some time to our much neglected garden, and spend some genuine quality time together. You should think about having a little holiday, Anna…you work so hard and you and Tia deserve it.'

'Maybe I will.' Shrugging lightly, Anna wished she could hear herself think over the clamouring of her heart. 'Look, Anita…there's no way of couching this or making it sound less surprising…I've got something important to tell you.'

'You're not handing in your notice?'

'No.' Anna took a nervous swallow. 'It's something much more personal. You know I've never told you before who Tia's father is?'

Anita stared, her gaze intrigued. The ticking wall clock suddenly seemed noisily loud.

'Well, it's—'

'Yes?'

'It's Dante Romano.'

Beneath her carefully applied make-up, her boss paled a little in shock. 'Dante Romano? But how can that be? As far as I'm aware he's never been here before, so how could you two have met?'

'He *has* been here before.' Clearing her throat, Anna smiled awkwardly. 'It was about five years ago. I was working the late shift in the bar, and he—he was there having a drink. He'd just returned from Italy, where he'd been to his mother's funeral, and had stopped en route to New York, where he was living at the time.'

'And you and he…?'

Lifting her chin, because she wouldn't be ashamed of that incredible life-changing night, Anna met her boss's brown-eyed glance without flinching.

'There was an immediate attraction and we slept together that was how I fell pregnant with Tia.'

CHAPTER EIGHT

'ANNA, can I have a word?'

She was walking by Jason's office when he opened the door and beckoned to her. Having had their staff meeting, everyone was now perfectly aware of the imminent plan to close the hotel for a month while it was being modernised, but she hadn't had an opportunity to discuss it with the manager—especially the news that he'd been made project manager to oversee the refurbishments while everyone else was away. No doubt that was why he wanted to see her. It was a big step up for him, and a huge responsibility. But Anna had no doubts that Jason could do it.

Regarding her relationship with Dante, Anita Cathcart had suggested that they keep it to themselves for a while—at least until the changes were underway and the staff had returned from leave. It was cowardly, but Anna's relief that she wouldn't be the focus of curious speculation just yet was boundless.

Shutting the door behind them Jason invited Anna

to sit down. 'You look very nice,' he commented, his glance running lightly over her outfit.

'I'm collecting Tia, then we're going out to have tea.'

'Going anywhere special?'

'I'm not sure yet, but we'll find somewhere nice, I'm sure. We're spoiled for choice in Covent Garden, aren't we?'

Her heart was thudding a little at the idea of telling her little girl some time soon that Dante was her father, and her smile was uncertain. But Jason seemed preoccupied with own problems as he started to restlessly pace the floor.

When he stopped pacing to nervously return his attention to Anna his dark eyes were shining. 'I've met someone,' he said in a rush.

'You have?' He'd been single for a long time, and didn't have much confidence in blind dates or being hooked up by some well-meaning friend as a means of finding 'the one', so Anna was genuinely pleased for him.

'I won't say any more just yet, in case I jinx things, but we're seeing each other this weekend.'

'Oh, Jason, that's wonderful—and of course you won't jinx things!'

Getting to her feet, she threw her arms round him in an affectionate hug.

Someone rapped on the door and stepped into the room before Jason could invite them. *It was Dante.* Anna had no reason in the world to feel guilty, but when his frosted gaze alighted on them, radiating obvious disapproval, she felt awkward and embarrassed—like a child caught red-handed, raiding the fridge after bedtime.

'I've been looking for Anna,' he said to Jason without preamble. 'A staff member suggested I see if she was with you. Looks like I hit the jackpot.'

'We were—we were just talking.' Flashing him an uncomfortable smile, Jason stepped quickly away from the girl at his side.

'Well, if you've finished *talking*, Anna and I have to go. We have some important business to attend to.'

'Isn't she taking her daughter out to tea?' The younger man's brow was furrowing.

'I see that you like to keep completely up to date with Miss Bailey's diary, Mr Cathcart. It would be nice if you could be as diligent in looking over that list of new equipment for the hotel that I left you, and let me have your thoughts first thing in the morning. This is an absolutely vital responsibility you've accepted, becoming project manager, and the work begins right here, right now. Don't let me down.' Holding the door open for Anna, Dante was impatient. 'We really have to go,' he said firmly.

'You didn't have to be so snooty or condescending to Jason. We've done nothing wrong.'

She had to practically run to keep up with Dante's annoyed stride as she followed him out into the hotel car park. Reaching a gleaming silver Jaguar, she heard an electronic key open the doors. He stopped dead, and she could see he was struggling with his temper.

'So you fling your arms round every male you work with, do you?'

'That's ridiculous. Of course I don't! He'd just told me some good news and I was pleased for him…that's all.'

The resentment in Dante's mercurial eyes receded only slightly.

'He likes you,' he said flatly.

Was he jealous? Anna let the thought swirl around for a bit, then mentally filed it to look at later. But she couldn't help her lips curving into a smile.

'And I like *him*. But not in the way you're insinuating.'

He would have liked to have quizzed her more, she saw, but instead he glanced down at the linked gold watch glinting on his wrist beneath his cuff and opened the passenger door for her.

'We'd better get going if we're not going to be late collecting Tia.'

'Where are we going for tea?' she asked lightly, before climbing into her seat.

'The Ritz Hotel.'

Dismay washed over her.

'You might have told me that earlier… I would have worn something smarter than this dress.'

It was a plain white linen dress that she'd teamed with

a businesslike black jacket, and the ensemble had had many outings in the past. It was perfect for a mild spring day like today, when there was just a gentle breeze blowing, but, knowing where they were heading, she was suddenly seized by the idea that it was nowhere near presentable enough for such a notoriously swish hotel.

His appreciative glance on the slender length of leg she unwittingly flashed as she sat down in her seat in a huff, Dante grinned and disarmed her completely.

'There is nothing wrong with what you are wearing, so there's no need to fret...*le guarda piu di bene a caro prezzo*.'

'And that means?'

'It means that you look more than fine.'

Dipping his head to survey Anna before closing her door, he let his light-filled gaze linger teasingly on her lips for a moment. Then it intensified. Suddenly there didn't seem to be enough air for her to breathe.

'Let's go and collect our little one, shall we?' Closing the passenger door, he moved with his usual fluid graceful stride round the Jaguar's bonnet to the driver's seat.

Tia wanted another scone and jam, and with Anna's agreement Dante leaned forward to spread the strawberry jam for her. *He'd never felt so proud.* Not one of his achievements had elicited the euphoria that poured through him now, when he surveyed this beautiful golden-haired child and knew he'd played an important part in her being.

Moving his glance across to Anna, he discovered her sherry-brown eyes were furtively studying him. With her river of auburn hair spilling unfettered down her back, and her quiet understated beauty, it was inevitable that she drew many admiring glances from the other guests taking afternoon tea. Mentally, Dante puffed out his chest. She was the mother of his child, and one day soon…*very soon* if he had his way…she would be his wife too. Yet, because of what she'd revealed about her cruel and controlling father, he needed to curb any inclination to manipulate her—even if waiting for her to say yes to marriage frustrated the hell out of him.

Her distressing childhood with such a despicable bully genuinely pained him. If Anna had been anything like their daughter, then she must have been the most exquisite, engaging little girl, and had surely deserved a man far more worthy to take care of her than the poor excuse for a father she'd had?

'This is a *golden* room,' Tia announced, licking strawberry jam off her lips as she chewed her second mouthwatering scone. 'There's a golden arch and golden tables and golden—what did you say those sparkly lamps on the ceiling were?'

'Chandeliers.'

'Yes—and golden chairs too! A king or a queen could live here. The people that own this place should call it the golden room—don't you think, Mummy?'

Reaching out to clean away some of the jam stains on her cherubic face with a linen napkin, Anna smiled. 'This is a very famous room, Tia, and it already has a name. It's called the Palm Court.'

'But,' Dante said softly, his voice lowering conspiratorially, 'from now on the three of us will always call it the golden room...deal?'

He held out his hand and Tia shook it enthusiastically, clearly delighted that the man who had brought them to such a magical place thought it was a good idea too.

'You have to shake Mummy's hand as well, Dante.'

'Of course...how silly of me to forget to do such an important thing.'

As soon as he took Anna's slim cool palm into his, the rest of the room faded away. The only thing Dante knew for sure was that his heart beat faster and heavier than it had before he'd touched her, and that if they had been alone he would have shown her in no uncertain terms that he desired her...*desired her beyond belief*. Immediately recognising the flare of heat suddenly laid bare in the liquid brown depths of her beautiful eyes, he inwardly rejoiced.

'You're meant to just shake her hand, not hold it for ages and ages!' his daughter protested huffily, pulling his hand away from her mother's with a distinctly old-fashioned look.

'Mind your manners, Tia, that was very rude.' Anna admonished her, looking embarrassed.

'I'm sorry.' The tips of the dark blond lashes that

were so like Dante's own briefly swept her cheeks in contrition, but a scant moment later her eyes shone with unrepentant mischief again. '*You're* not cross with me, are you?' She dimpled up at him.

That knock-out smile could melt his heart at a hundred paces, her father silently acknowledged. Tenderly he grazed his knuckles over her velvet cheekbone. 'No, *mia bambina*…I don't think I could be cross with you if I tried…you are far too charming and lovely for that.'

'She certainly has her moments.' Taking a sip of her Earl Grey tea in its exquisite porcelain cup, Anna replaced the delicate vessel back in its saucer before grimacing at Dante.

'Meaning?'

'Meaning that occasionally she can be a bit wild.'

'I wonder where she gets that from?' His tone was silky smooth and playful.

Surprising him with a grin, Anna tipped her head to the side.

'I can't imagine you ever doing anything that wasn't measured and considered, Dante. You just seem so organised and in charge to me—as if nothing life can throw at you could ever give you a moment's doubt about your place in the scheme of things.'

'You are wrong about that.' Feeling the need to put her right about her assumption, Dante was suddenly serious. 'Being part-Italian, passion is in my blood. Neither can I admit to never having a moment's doubt. Do you know a human being who can?'

'No,' she answered thoughtfully, 'I don't think I do.'

'What are you talking about, Mummy? It doesn't sound very interesting.'

Tia was clearly miffed at not being privy to the grown-ups' conversation. Turning her gaze to her daughter, Anna appeared to be thinking hard.

'Tia? There's something important I want to tell you.' Glancing over at Dante, she lowered her gaze meaningfully with his.

His heart pounded hard. He hadn't expected her to raise the subject on this outing, but now, realising that she was going to, he mentally began to arrange his armour—so that if Tia should protest the idea in any way the blow wouldn't wound him irreparably. Logically he knew it would take time for his daughter to learn to love him, but Dante craved her love and acceptance of him more than he could say.

'Mummy? I know you want to tell me something important, but I want to ask Dante something.' The child put her elbows on top of the white tablecloth and then, with her chin resting in her hand, studied him intently.

'What is it, sweetheart?'

'Are you married?'

Resisting the urge to laugh out loud at the uncanny aptness of the question, he endeavoured to keep his face expressionless so that Tia wouldn't think he wasn't giving her question the proper consideration.

'No, my sweet little girl...I'm not married.'

'My mummy's not married either. I wish she was. I wish she was so that I could have a daddy, like my friend Madison at school. Not all the children in my class have daddies, but she does, and I think she's very lucky—don't you?'

Powerful emotion struck Dante silent. As if in slow motion—as if time had ground to a dreamlike halt—he saw Anna's pale slim hand reach out to pull Tia's hand away from her chin and tenderly hold it.

'Darling, I want you to listen very carefully to what I need to tell you. Will you do that?'

Her blue-grey eyes widening like twin compact disks, Tia nodded gravely.

'Dante and I knew each other a long time ago—remember I told you that? Anyway, we liked each other very much. But unfortunately…because something very sad happened in Italy, where he came from…he had to go away.' Sighing softly, Anna gave him a brief heartfelt glance. 'When he left… When he left, I found out that I was expecting a baby.'

'A baby? That must have been me!'

'Yes, darling…it *was* you.'

Her innocent brow puckering, Tia swung her gaze round to alight firmly on Dante.

'Does that mean that you're my daddy, then?'

'Yes, my angel.' His throat feeling as if it had been branded with an iron, Dante attempted a smile. 'It does.'

'You mean my *real* daddy? Real like Madison's daddy is her *real* daddy?'

'Yes.'

'Then we must be a real *family*.'

Never had anyone looked clear down to his soul as his daughter did at that breathtaking moment, and he knew...*knew* beyond any shadow of doubt...that she saw him for who he really was. It was the most unsettling yet exhilarating feeling Dante had ever experienced.

'And if we're a real family then you have to come and live with us—because that's what real families do, you know. Mummy, can I have a chocolate éclair now?' Tia turned pleadingly towards her mother. 'If you don't want me to eat a whole one, in case I'm sick, can I share it with you and have just half?'

'Okay, but I think after that you should call it a day on the cake front, don't you?'

As Anna glanced at Dante with a tremulous smile, he silently formed the words *thank you*. Then, reaching towards the multi-tiered cake stand, he plucked a chocolate éclair from it and with the small silver knife by his plate proceeded to cut it in half...

It had been a day of truth-telling. Along with the relief that had followed it, an incredible fatigue rolled over Anna, dragging at her limbs and making her eyelids so heavy that she could hardly stay awake.

Having left Dante in the bedroom, watching Tia as

she drifted off to sleep after the story he'd read her, she kicked off her shoes and stretched out on the couch.

She'd told him that children quickly adapted to new situations and she'd been right. Already Tia was calling him Daddy—as if by voicing her acknowledgement of who he was gave her even more right to claim him as her own. It touched Anna almost unbearably to see father and child together, bonding as naturally as if there had never at any time been a separation. It was wonderful…a dream come true. *But where did that leave her?*

She'd been a single parent for so long. It wouldn't be easy to let go of that role, even when she knew it was probably best for Tia that her father was in her life at last. Was it wrong of her to feel so afraid? To live in fear that her autonomy over their lives would be taken away? And would it be wise to contemplate letting her loneliness be soothed by this rugged and virile urbane man to whom she'd relinquished her innocence one night five years ago, knowing that because of the wall she'd glimpsed behind his eyes more than once he'd probably never be able to love her the wholehearted way that he loved his daughter?

'How are you doing?'

Anna's eyes had been drifting closed, and suddenly Dante was there in front of her, staring down at her with his soulful light eyes in a way that would have made her knees knock together if she'd been standing.

'I'm fine, thanks. Just a bit tired, to tell you the truth.' She started to sit up, but he gestured that she stay just as she was and then dropped down to sit on the edge of the couch beside her.

The strong, long-fingered hands that she'd noticed when they first met and had privately thought poetic and artistic were linked loosely in front of him, and a lock of dark blond hair flopped sexily down in front of his forehead. His sculpted lean profile and long luxuriant lashes made him look like a movie star, and for a distressing moment Anna wondered what an outstanding male specimen like him could possibly see in someone as ordinary as her.

'It's been quite an incredible day, huh?'

And as Dante smiled at her with surprising warmth her suddenly wobbly self-esteem was completely banished beneath the breathtaking gaze that was directed straight at her...

CHAPTER NINE

'Tia loved the Ritz. She'll probably look round the Mirabelle now and think it quite shabby after being there.'

'That will be the last thing this hotel will be when we get through with all the improvements I have in mind. Did I tell you I've hired a team of designers from Milan to oversee the refurbishment?'

'Milan? Gosh.'

'This place is already in a league of its own as a Georgian building with a fascinating history. With modernisation and refurbishment it's going to be one of the most stylish and sophisticated establishments in London.'

'Anita and Grant deserve it to be. They've unstint-ingly lavished their love on it ever since Grant inherited it from his parents. Can I ask you something?'

He nodded.

'Talking about Milan…I was wondering…'

'Yes?'

'Does that mean you've made your peace with Italy?

It's just that you seemed reluctant to discuss it. You told me you left a long time ago, and I sensed that you had deliberately distanced yourself from it.'

'I had... But when I went back for my mother's funeral I remembered things about the place that I loved and missed. Gradually over the years I've grown to love it again. That's why I bought a house there...the house we will stay in when you and Tia return with me. Does that reply satisfy your question?'

Touching the tips of his fingers to her cheek, Dante studied her intently. Anna fell silent, hardly knowing what to say. He'd admitted that he'd distanced himself from his homeland but he hadn't said *why*. Would he ever trust her enough to disclose some of the secrets from his past? she wondered. But Lake Como was the other subject she needed to address.

'It's a big step for me to go with you to Italy. To tell you the truth, I feel a little vulnerable going there with you, Dante. I don't know the language, and I know you won't like this but I'm also wary of being pushed into something I'm not really ready for. Do you understand that?'

'It is not my intention to push you into anything or to make you feel vulnerable,' he replied thoughtfully. 'I simply want us to have a holiday together, for us to get to know one another and for Tia to get to know me. When you are ready, and *only* when you are ready, will we talk about marriage.'

'Do you mean it?'

He studied her gravely. 'My word is my bond.'

'I suppose I could do with a holiday. And, like you say…it will give you and Tia a chance to get to know each other a bit more.'

'And as for not speaking the language…I will make it my personal mission to teach you,' Dante promised. 'I will have you speaking like a native Italian before you know it! Tia too.'

'It's getting dark.' Nervously Anna glanced up at the swiftly fading evening light, evident through the room's high windows. At the same time she heard the lilting song of a lone blackbird. For some reason it made her feel a little melancholy. 'I ought to turn on the lamps.'

'Don't.' The command in Dante's tone gave her a jolt.

'It's gloomy…I'd like some light in here.'

'You're uncomfortable with the dark? There's no need when I am right here beside you, Anna. I would never let anything or anyone hurt you.'

His heated glance was in earnest, she saw. Instantly a swarm of butterflies fluttered wildly inside her.

'Yes, but I still want to… I still need some…some light.'

As she made to move, Dante slid his hand round to the back of her head, to bring her face slowly but inexorably towards his. The last thing she registered was his hot, languorous gaze before his mouth fell on hers to ravish it without restraint, his warm velvet tongue gliding and coiling sensually with hers, his breathing a grated rasp as the shadow of his beard scraped her chin.

A sea of honey lapped inside Anna. It was as though she'd been left languishing in a cold dark cave for five long years and now at last she was wildly, deliriously free again—free to breathe in pure heady oxygen and be deluged in light. The pleasure and joy that soared inside her was untrammelled as her hands pushed through the silky strands of Dante's fair hair to anchor his head as he anchored hers, all the better for their lips to meld and sup as though their hunger would never be assuaged. *Not in this lifetime…*

'No… Not—not here.' She gulped down a shaky breath as his hands tugged at the zip fastener on her dress. 'My bedroom.'

They didn't let each other go as they entered the dim, cool enclave of Anna's room. It seemed essential to keep touching, to keep holding on in case some nightmare schism should cut through their longing and keep them apart for ever.

With the heel of his Italian loafer Dante shut the door behind them. He shucked off his footwear just before falling onto the bed with her, somehow manoeuvring her on top of him as he kissed her senseless. The zipper on her linen dress was skilfully undone, the sleeves tugged urgently down over her shoulders. With dreamlike effort Anna helped Dante remove it completely, then she was astride his hard lean hips again, bending her head to give and receive drugging, passionate kisses that made her head spin and her heart gallop. Her long waving hair was a protective shield that kept the world from intruding as it drifted sensually over them both.

Cupping his face as she leant forward, Anna marvelled at the strong, chiselled contours, at the sublime slopes and plains that denoted his fascinating masculine features. But it was the vulnerable, naked look of utter longing in his eyes that undid her. Stilling in shock, she hardly registered breathing.

'I thought perhaps I'd dreamt wanting you this much...but now I see that I didn't... Or if I did the dream was just a tantalising glimpse of the incredible reality that is you, Anna.'

Finding no words that could adequately describe the force of what she was feeling, Anna began to slide the buttons through the buttonholes of his fine cotton shirt with trembling fingers. When the smooth, tanned musculature underneath, with its dusting of hair, was exposed to her, she pushed the material aside, sliding her hands over the flat male nipples and taut ribcage to explore him, to feel the throb of his heartbeat beneath her palm. She was thrilled to realise that it beat with desire for *her*. Lowering her head, she pressed her lips to Dante's deliciously warm skin.

She was following the trail of silky dark blond hair towards his belly button when he made a low, husky sound, slid his hands beneath her hair and urged her eagerly upwards again. The next thing she knew he was helping remove the scrap of plain white silk that denoted her panties and sliding down his zipper.

When he placed himself at the soft moist centre of Anna's core, easing his way inside her and then plunging upwards, she threw back her head with a whimper. The very notion of pleasure broke all its bounds. It hardly seemed an adequate description for the utterly consuming sensations that effervesced through her body. Not since she'd surrendered her innocence to Dante five years ago had such violent waves of ecstatic bliss been hers. *This* was the completeness she'd longed for—the deep connection her soul had ached to experience again. The one primal force that could drive away all melancholy and doubt.

The feeling brought it unerringly home to her why she had never wanted another man since that first time with him...why she had resigned herself to being alone for ever—because no man could possibly come close to making her feel what Dante made her feel.

Utterly losing himself in their wild, urgent coupling, Dante buried himself so deep inside her dizzying heat that he swore he would melt. Expertly opening the catch on her bra, he quickly discarded the garment to fill his palms with her perfect satin-tipped breasts, stroking his thumbs across the tender nipples. Gazing up into Anna's lovely face he saw the stunning crown of burnished hair that rippled river-like down over her pale smooth skin and knew there wasn't another woman in the world to match her for beauty and grace. *Or who could crack the frozen ice round his heart.*

He should have searched for her long before this… *why hadn't he?* Unbelievable that he'd let his fear of rejection keep him from the one woman who'd selflessly given herself to him all that time ago when he was most in need.

With urgency and passion Dante's fingers bit into the soft flesh of Anna's svelte hips, holding her to him as if he could never let her go. A long soft moan followed by her ragged breathing feathered over him as she climaxed, and suddenly he couldn't hold back the tide that lapped forcefully at the shores of his own longing, and had no choice but to let it completely sweep him away…

'Come here.' He helped her lie across his chest, then wrapped his arms around her. It was a new experience for him to hold a woman like this after making love. Not just to appease her, but simply for the sheer joy of being close—to sense the beat of her heart slowly but surely aligning with his. When they finally came to live together he would enjoy that pleasure every single day he realised. Weaving his fingers through her long flowing hair Dante kissed the top of Anna's head.

She stirred, raising her face to his. 'That was rather wonderful. But now I feel absolutely incapable of doing anything else.' She smiled.

'And exactly what did you have planned for the rest

of the evening that our enjoyment of each other has interrupted, *innamorata*?'

Her smile didn't fade. Instead it grew impish, just like their daughter's. 'Well...for starters I've got a pile of ironing to do.'

'And this is essential?'

'It might not be.' Her voice lowered seductively, and renewed desire—swift and hot as a lava-flow—made Dante bite back a groan. 'It depends what distractions are on offer as an alternative.'

'You've become a shameless temptress in my absence, I see.' In one swiftly deft move Dante took hold of Anna's arms, moved her to the side of him, then captured her beneath him. The laughter in her pretty eyes instantly died. 'As long as you haven't been practising your seductive arts on some other poor defenceless male, I won't complain.'

She looked stricken for a moment. 'I swear to you I haven't.'

The tension that had suddenly gripped him at the idea of Anna being with someone else eased.

'Then is *this* the kind of distraction you were looking for, hmm?' he enquired huskily as he firmly parted her thighs and once again hungrily joined his body to hers...

'Is that an aria by Puccini you're whistling, Anna?' Pausing in his food preparation for lunch, Luigi narrowed his gaze in surprise as he studied the hotel's slim assistant manager, who had come into the kitchen to collect the menu.

'Yes, from *Madame Butterfly*. I hope you don't think I was murdering it, or being sacrilegious or something?'

'Not at all… I am only curious as to what has made you seem happy lately?'

She could have answered *a week of nights making passionate love with the Mirabelle's handsome new major shareholder*, but of course she didn't. Only Anita and her husband Grant knew the truth about her relationship with Dante. And they had agreed that the information would stay private until they returned from the month's break they were all taking while the hotel was being modernised.

The idea of her and Tia travelling to Lake Como the following day with Dante was exciting, but Anna would be lying if she didn't admit it terrified her too. Having late-night trysts with her lover was one thing, but *living together*? That was a whole other scenario entirely. And she would be totally on his turf, so to speak—dependent on his kindness and goodwill to see her through, when she was feeling unsure about the prospect of trusting a man long-term and fearing he might want to control her.

But then he *had* given her his promise that he wouldn't try and push her into anything she wasn't ready for, she remembered.

'I suppose I'm just happy at being able to take a whole

month off to spend with Tia,' she answered Luigi, poignantly realising it was an event that had not occurred since her daughter was a newborn baby. *And if it wasn't for Dante, it wouldn't be happening at all.*

Taking a couple of steps towards the chef, she clutched the paper with the menu written on it to her chest. 'A little bird told me that you're going to Provence for a French cookery course...is that true, Luigi?'

With a dismissive flourish of his hand, he sheepishly lowered his gaze. 'Signor Romano suggested it, and is paying for me to go. If we want to get a Michelin star for the Mirabelle then of course I will do it...even if French cooking is not my subject of choice. But I am surprised that a fellow Italian can be so enthusiastic about the cooking of another nation!'

'Mr Romano is well travelled and wise, Luigi. And being able to diversify the menu will help our lunchtime trade and maximise sales, so it's great that you're going to Provence.' Anna patted his arm encouragingly. 'You'll love it, I'm sure.'

'We will see.'

After a car journey to Heathrow, then a four-hour plane journey, followed by another car ride on which they took a detour for an hour to eat at a charming restaurant Dante knew, they finally arrived at his five-storey villa in Lake Como.

It was situated in prime viewing position at the lake, on a high-banked sward where the last rays of the sun played upon the surface of the water, giving it the appearance of glinting diamonds. The scent of bougainvillaea, azalea and other heady blossoms floated on the balmy Mediterranean air, rustling through Anna's unbound hair and lightly teasing Tia's wild corkscrew curls. Both females studied the house in its fairy-tale surroundings in silent awe. Having retrieved their luggage from the boot of the Mercedes that had been waiting for them at the airport, Dante stepped up beside Anna and slid his arm around her waist. As was becoming a habit, his touch electrified her.

'It's a stunningly beautiful house, Dante,' she remarked, shyly meeting his searching blue-grey glance.

'And it will be made even more beautiful by the presence of my two beautiful girls,' he asserted warmly.

It totally made her melt when he said things like that. Her heart was already his, but when he let his guard down and spoke what seemed to be his true feelings out loud Anna honestly felt as if she would follow him to the ends of the earth and back, and not care what discomfort or challenges confronted her so long as she could confront them with him.

'Is this our new house, Daddy?' Tia piped up beside them.

For answer, Dante scooped the little girl up into his arms and planted a loud, affectionate kiss at the side of her cheek. 'This is our house in Italy, *mia bambina.*' He grinned. 'But we have other homes around the world too.'

Mentally, Anna gulped. Having called her cosy basement flat in Covent Garden home for the past eight years, it was quite some dizzying leap to realise that if she and Tia were to live permanently with Dante they would be moving around quite a lot. And if the other properties he owned had anything like the stunning architecture and formidable size of this one then Anna could possibly be feeling overwhelmed for a very long time indeed!

'Let's go inside, shall we?'

'What do you think of the place now that you've had a couple of hours to acclimatise yourself?'

Dante walked up behind her as Anna stood on the balcony off the drawing room, gazing out at the stunning lake view. With a breathtaking vista of the Alps in the distance, it was guaranteed to capture all her attention. Even breathing in the warm Mediterranean air acted like a soothing salve. It made her realise how much in need of a holiday she'd been for ages.

After kissing Tia a loving goodnight, and tucking her into bed in her new bedroom, she'd been standing here ever since Dante had gone upstairs to read her a bedtime story. Now her heart leapt as he walked onto the balcony to join her. Gesturing in disbelief at the lake, with its perfectly serene surface and the twinkling lights reflected on the water from some of the surrounding buildings now that night was falling, she slowly shook her head.

'Sometimes words are inadequate, and this is one of those times. I don't think I've ever seen a more stirring or sublime scene.'

'Well, it's yours to enjoy for however long you want… you know that.'

She fell silent.

'Come inside and sit down,' he invited—but not before Anna registered what might have been uncertainty in his eyes.

Re-entering the elegant lamplit room, which was full of stunning antiques and sublime paintings, with a huge fireplace inlaid with white marble at its head, Anna smiled.

'I feel like I'm on the movie set of a film about some sophisticated Italian noble. There's so much beauty here that I can hardly take it in.'

'You are right. There *is* so much beauty.'

His low-voiced comment was loaded with meaning—meaning that Anna couldn't fail to comprehend. She couldn't glance at him without wanting him, and knew that no matter how much she tried to contain her desire he must see it in her eyes every time their gazes met.

Gesturing, she sat on the sumptuous sofa. Dante joined her. Gathering her slender palm into his, for a while he just simply turned it over and examined it—just as if it were some priceless jewel he was contemplating purchasing.

'I don't know how you can ever bear leaving this place,' she remarked, her heart quietly thudding. 'It's like paradise on earth.'

'For a long time I couldn't see it that way. But lately I've begun to see how lucky I am being able to have a home here.'

'Is this where you're from? Como, I mean?'

He let go of her hand.

'No. I bought this house because my mother loved Como and had a home here. When I was young she always fantasised about living here one day...but the truth is that she was a very simple and contented soul, and would have been happy anywhere as long as she knew I was happy.'

'She sounds wonderful.'

Dante smiled. 'She was.'

'So where were you raised, if not here?' Anna prompted him gently.

CHAPTER TEN

'I was raised in a small village inland, far away from the mountains and lakes. It wasn't anything like here.' He pushed to his feet as though the memory made him restless and uneasy. 'It didn't have the cultural delights or beautiful vistas of Como, and the people who lived there were neither rich nor privileged. But there was a strong sense of community, so I've been told. However, we didn't stay. When my father walked out on her, my mother had no choice but to move to the nearest town to try and make a living.'

'Your father walked out on you and your mother?'

'He did.' Only briefly did Dante meet Anna's gaze and hold it. 'It was a long time ago. I don't even remember him.'

'So...you don't know much about him, then?'

He grimaced. 'Only that he was British and an archaeologist. He'd been working on a dig nearby, looking for Roman ruins, when he met my mother. As far as I'm aware archaeologists aren't exactly high earners. At least I've far exceeded anything my father could have made, and my mother didn't die impoverished—as *he* left her!'

The strained silence that fell after his reluctantly voiced confession made Anna's heart sore. Dante had become a man without the love or guidance of a father, or even close male relatives, and bereft of that important bond had had to forge his own way in life. He'd had to bury what must have been a deep-seated need for love and connection from his male parent, papering it over with material pursuits and the seemingly glamorous but ultimately not permanently fulfilling rewards of success.

All Anna had yearned for as a child was the unconditional love and support of her parents. No amount of money would have made her dire situation any better. It probably would have made things *worse*, because more money would have meant her father had had more income to spend on drink. But right now it was clear to her that no matter how wealthy or successful Dante had become a big part of him still yearned for the father's love he'd never had...

Moving over to where he stood, she touched her palm to the strong heart beating beneath his fine linen shirt.

'I think you've done an amazing job of turning your life around after such a challenging start, Dante,' she told him. 'But more than what you've achieved materially, you're a good man...a man any father would be proud to call his son.'

'Am I?' For a disturbing few moments his glance was tortured. 'You only say that because you don't know what I've done to get where I am today.'

Anna's dark-eyed gaze didn't waver. 'If you've done anything wrong, in my opinion it's only that you've become too hard on yourself.'

'You're just naive—that's why you say that.'

'I had to grow up too fast—just like you, Dante—and I've learned that we don't help ourselves when we constantly criticise what we've done in the past. We did the best we knew how to do at the time. How can anyone— even *you*—do more than that?'

'You learned when you started to look for me that I had a "ruthless reputation". The papers did not lie, Anna. I did whatever I could to make my fortune. I had no scruples as long as I won the deal—as long as it meant more money and power. I was so driven I didn't even care that I helped people to lose their jobs. I certainly didn't have sleepless nights worrying about how they would support themselves or their families afterwards! Even my mother started to despair of me. She warned me against alienating good people. One day I would need trustworthy friends, she said—not phoney ones who were driven by fear and greed like I was.

'Well…it took my mother's death and then meeting you, Anna, to make me wake up to the truth of my life. To make me want to work and live with more integrity… to make me want to help people instead of exploit them for what I could get. It took me a while to change things, but when I realised that the changes I had to make had to be quite radical one of the first things I did was to revert back to my Italian name. I only used my father's name because, coming from a poor background, with only the most basic education, I wanted to distance myself from Italy and all that it meant to me. Ironic, really, when I didn't even know the man and he didn't stay around for long—'

'Oh, Dante... What an incredible journey you've had to come back to yourself.' Anna's heart was so full it was hard to keep her tears at bay.

He shook his head, as if he was uncomfortable with the tenderness in her voice, as if his painful story couldn't possibly warrant it. 'There are shadows beneath your eyes, *innamorata*.'

His hand glanced softly against her cheekbone, his blue-grey eyes as hypnotically mesmerising as the moon-lit lake outside the window, and Anna wanted to lose herself in those fascinating depths for a long time.

His next words robbed her of the chance.

'We've had a long day's travelling. You really should take the opportunity of having an early night. In the morning the housekeeper I hire to look after the villa when I'm here will arrive with her daughter, who also helps out. They'll prepare breakfast for us, and also find out if there's anything we need.'

'What are their names?'

'The housekeeper and her daughter?' Dante shrugged, as though surprised by the question. 'Giovanna is the mother and Ester the daughter. No doubt they'll immediately fall in love with Tia when they meet her—both of them adore children, and Ester has a little son of her own. Anyway…like I said, you look tired. You should have a leisurely bath, then an early night. I'll join you later.' He turned away from her.

'I hope you don't regret sharing what you just shared with me?' Concerned, as well as disappointed that he seemed intent on spending the rest of the evening without her, Anna restlessly coiled a long strand of her bright hair round her finger. 'Do you?' she pressed.

'Go to bed, Anna. We'll talk again in the morning.'

'Why don't you answer me? I don't want to go to bed and leave you brooding here on your own.'

A faint smile appeared on his fine-cut lips as he turned to survey her.

'So you want to be my rescuer again? Just as you tried to rescue me from my morose mood all those years ago?'

Fielding the comment, Anna lifted her chin. 'Is it so wrong of me to want to reach out to you? To show you that I care about how you're feeling?'

Remaining silent, Dante looked away again.

With frustrated tears making her eyes smart, Anna swung round on her heel and marched out of the room…

After watching the coloured house lights reflect off the dark lake for a long time, Dante stepped back into the drawing room at around one in the morning. The Campari on the rocks he'd made himself was barely touched. Leaving the crystal tumbler on a rosewood table, he stretched his arms high above his head, grimacing at the locked tension in his protesting muscles.

With everything he had in him he wanted to join Anna in the stately canopied double bed. But how could he when he knew she must secretly despise him for the way he had conducted himself in the past? It had even prevented her from getting in touch with him to tell him about Tia. No, it was Anna who was good and deserving of help...not him. Fear of failure and loss had been the dark, soul-destroying forces he'd been guided by. And because his associations with Italy had been tainted with hurt from his childhood he had fled to England to make his fortune, consciously choosing to lose his accent and forget his roots to reinvent himself as the untouchable businessman, the ice man.

All in all, it didn't make a pretty picture. Bringing Anna and Tia here had raised painful spectres from his past when he'd started to believe he had let them go. What he wanted most of all was a new start for himself and his family—not to focus on his past mistakes and feel unworthy again. But could he blame Anna if ultimately she couldn't forgive him for his deplorable history?

Intensely disliking the feeling of not having his emotions under control the way he wanted, Dante scrubbed an agitated hand round his shadowed jaw. He'd be better in the morning, he told himself. A few hours' solid sleep and he'd be more like himself again. Reaching for the button on a discreet wall panel that controlled the lighting, he pressed it, lingering for a solitary moment as the room was plunged into darkness.

Tonight he *wouldn't* seek comfort in Anna's tender arms, as he ached with every fibre of his being to do. Somehow, after practically dismissing her on her first night in Como, he didn't believe he deserved it. Instead, he would retreat to one of the other palatial bedrooms and spend the night alone...

She'd left the curtains open, and in the morning, sun streamed into the room, straight at her. Anna had to shield her eyes. Her spirits plunged in dismay when she realised that Dante hadn't joined her as he'd promised he would. He'd been absolutely right about her being tired, but she was shocked at the speed with which she'd fallen asleep. She had remained in that condition up until now too. She was in a strange country, and a strange house, as well as beginning a month's trial period of living with him. You'd think any one of those things would have kept her awake...but, no.

A deep sigh of regret escaped her. She should have stayed with him last night—should have found a way to reach him, to let him know how much she cared. If she'd stayed then he would have seen that she didn't agree with his unspoken belief that he didn't deserve love and care. He would have seen that Anna was fiercely loyal to the people she cared about. Yet she was still wary of disclosing her feelings when there was the ever-present fear that he might want to take away her autonomy...

But right now she needed to see her little girl and see how she was faring. She too had slept in a strange room, in a strange bed. Glancing at the clock by the bedside, she gasped when she saw the time. What kind of a mother was she that she could blithely oversleep and leave her child to fend for herself?

Guiltily grabbing her pastel blue cotton robe from the end of the bed, she yawned—and then couldn't resist peering out at the wrought-iron balcony and the sublime view of the sun-dappled lake. A canopied boat full of early-morning tourists floated leisurely by. She caught her breath. There was a real holiday atmosphere in the air that to Anna was just like a dream. Even more so when she thought about spending her time here with the two people she cared most about in the world...

Tia had apparently long vacated her bed. Seeing clothes scattered round the pretty room, with its lovely antique furniture and tall open windows, Anna realised she had even dressed herself. Had Dante taken her downstairs for breakfast?

Laughter and the suggestion of jovial conversation drew her to the high-ceilinged oak-beamed kitchen. As she hovered in the doorway, conscious of the flimsy robe she had hastily flung on over her white cotton nightdress, she dragged the edges together and stared. Two women—one younger, and one perhaps just past middle-age, both dark-haired, with strong-boned Italian faces and bright eyes—were bustling round the kitchen, carrying plates of food to the table and beaming at Tia, who sat there with Dante just as though she was in her absolute element.

As if he intuitively knew she was there, Dante turned in his high-backed oak chair and smiled. *Any words Anna might have been going to say utterly dried up.* Bathed in the sensual sea of his storm-coloured gaze, she felt her limbs turn as weak as cooked strands of tagliatelli.

'*Buongiorno,*' he greeted her, his low-pitched 'bedroom' voice sounding slightly husky.

Flustered, all she could manage right then was an awkward nervous smile. Rising from his chair, Dante crossed the room to kiss her cheek, his lips lingering warmly at the side of her face so that her senses were crowded by his fresh clean scent and disturbingly arousing body heat. His fit lean body was encased in fitted black jeans and a loose white linen shirt, and frankly he was more sinfully tempting than any honey or sugar-laden breakfast she could think of.

Unquestioningly aware of the devastating effect he had on her, he smiled for a second time into Anna's mesmerised dark gaze and curved his arm round her waist. 'Come and meet Giovanna and Ester,' he urged, leading her across the stone-flagged floor to the long oak table where the two women had paused in their serving of food to furnish Anna with twin welcoming smiles.

They greeted her in their native Italian, but then the younger woman said in faltering English, 'It is—is so nice to see you—I mean to meet you, *signorina*.'

'Please,' Anna said warmly, taking her hand, 'call me Anna.'

'Mummy? Why aren't you dressed yet?' Tia demanded, her mouth crammed with ciabatta bread and jam. 'Do you even know what the time is?'

'Yes, I know what the time is, Tia Bailey, and I know I've slept in—but I was more tired than I realised. And by the way, Miss Bossy Boots…did you forget to say good morning?'

'Sorry, Mummy, but me and Daddy have been up for ages and ages!'

'Really?'

'The early bird catches the worm…isn't that what they say?'

Seeing the teasing glint in Dante's eyes, Anna felt a rush of dizzying warmth flood into her chest. Stooping to kiss the top of Tia's curly blond head, she felt her heart warm doubly when she detected no tension whatsoever in her child about this new unfamiliar situation. Very quickly, it seemed, she had made herself quite at home.

Glancing round at the rest of the company, she became uncomfortably conscious that she was still in her nightwear. 'I'm so sorry I got up so late. I'd like to return to my room to dress, and then I'll be back down as soon as I can—if that's okay?'

'Of course it's okay.' Dante's tone was slightly irked. 'There aren't any rules about what you can and can't do here, Anna. This is your home. Giovanna will keep some food hot for you in the oven until you return.'

By the time Anna returned to the kitchen Giovanna had disappeared upstairs to make the beds, and at Dante's request Ester had taken Tia into the gardens for a while so that she could play. The woman had beamed at him, clearly jumping at the chance to spend time with his engaging little daughter.

Staring down into a mug of strong sugared black coffee—*his troubled mind hadn't allowed him to sleep at all well last night*—he glanced expectantly towards the door as Anna appeared. She was wearing a lemon tunic dress, with sleeves that ended just past her elbows and a hemline that finished just above her knees. Her long shapely legs were bare. With her stunning auburn hair left free to tumble down over her breasts unhindered she was a vision of loveliness that put Dante's already charged senses on hyper-alertness. The mere sight of her acted as an incendiary flame on his frustrated libido, making it virtual *agony* to stay sitting and not go to her and haul her urgently into his arms.

'Tia's in the garden with Ester,' he said instead, knowing that would be the first thing that would concern her. 'Is that okay?'

'Of course.' Moving to the table, Anna briefly

squeezed her eyes shut as she leaned her arms over a chair. 'I can't tell you how good that coffee smells.'

'I'll get you some.'

'It's all right. I'm quite capable of helping myself. I don't want to disturb you when you look so relaxed, just sitting there.'

She brought a mug of the steaming beverage she'd poured from the percolator back to the table, and sat down opposite him. She looked so pretty, fresh and artless that his heart pounded with longing. Replaying their conversation of last night for the umpteenth time in his mind, he wondered if she would ever truly be able to accept him for himself and not hold his past against him.

'Tia indicated you were up early. Couldn't you sleep?'

Tumbling headlong into the liquid depths of her big brown eyes for a moment, he edged the corner of his mouth into an almost painful rueful grin. 'No, Anna... I could not sleep. Did you think I could without you in my bed?'

Blushing, she stared down into her coffee cup for long seconds. 'I would have stayed with you last night... talking downstairs, I mean.' She lifted her gaze to his. 'But you clearly didn't want me to. Whenever I try to get close to you, Dante, it seems you push me away. Do you intend on doing that for ever?'

His grin vanished. What could he tell her when his whole system was in such an agony of need? *Mental, physical, spiritual*… He could go mad with it all. He pushed his mug of coffee from him with such force that the dark liquid slopped messily over the sides. He heard Anna's shocked intake of breath even as he rose, but he was suddenly beyond worrying about anything but the powerful need to hold her, to breathe her in as though she was life-giving air in the increasing sense of claustrophobia that seized him, the prison of his past that had kept him in the dark for so long.

Hauling her out of her chair against him, Dante buried his face in her hair while his feverish hands desperately sought the warmth of her body through her thin cotton dress.

'Anna… Oh, Anna…'

Sensing her tremble, he tipped up her face and plundered her mouth until his lips ached and his heart thundered as though it would burst inside him.

'Do you want me, Dante?' As she dragged her mouth away from his, her voice sounded broken and tearful.

'Yes… Yes, I want you. I always want you! Are you going to punish me for that?'

'No, my angel.' She pushed back some of the dark blond hair that had flopped onto his brow, and her touch was so soft, so infinitely tender that Dante couldn't speak. His muscles all but screamed with the tension that built inside him, and he prayed for it to ease soon.

'You punish yourself enough without me doing the same,' she finished sadly.

Uttering a dramatic oath, he slid his arm beneath her

and lifted her high against his chest. Bereft of words, because devastating emotion had right then robbed him of
the ability to speak, he carried her out through the door
and up the winding staircase with its ornate wrought-
iron stair-rail to their bedroom...

'What are you looking at?'

In front of the stunning cheval mirror, brushing
out her long bed-tangled hair, with the balcony doors
slightly ajar to allow in a delicious thermal of sultry
Mediterranean air, Anna glanced over her shoulder at
Dante with a smile. Bare-chested and tousle-haired, he
lay back against the bank of white silk pillows with the
kind of lascivious, knowing look that made her insides
clench and her toes flex hard.

An impossible ache arose inside her that all but
begged her to join him in bed for another greedy helping of wild reckless loving. She could hardly credit her
own body's hungry libidinous needs. Already tingling
and aching from the voracious homage her lover had
paid to her in bed, Anna was seriously torn between
rejoining Dante and going down to the garden to give
some attention to Tia, and to thank her generous-hearted
young minder for looking after her.

'I'm looking at *you*. Where else do you expect me to
focus my gaze when you stand there in that thin robe
that hugs every delicious curve and reminds me that I
should never have let you get out of bed?'

'Well, you've got to stop looking at me like that—or

I'll be a wreck for the rest of the day because I won't be able to concentrate on anything else but you! And I want to see some of the sights of this beautiful place, Dante... For instance that medieval monastery you mentioned.'

He got out of bed, stepped into black silk boxers, then moved barefoot across the polished parquet floor to join her. Such a simple human manoeuvre shouldn't look so mouthwateringly arresting, but when a man had a body as fit and compelling as Dante Romano's, it did.

'So...a ruined medieval monastery is preferable to looking at me, is it?' he teased, his hands settling over her hips while his mouth planted a hot, sexy little kiss at the juncture of her neck and shoulder.

Anna's loosely tied cotton robe slid off one satiny shoulder as the languorous heaviness between her thighs returned.

'I—I didn't say that,' she moaned, readjusting her robe over her shoulder, then trying to disentangle herself from her lover's arms. 'What are Giovanna and Ester going to think? I already got up late, and then you per-suaded me back to bed. They'll think I've got no morals or sense of decency at all!'

He laughed. It was such a spontaneous, joyous sound that Anna could hardly credit him as being the same man who had been so gripped by inner turmoil and pain earlier.

She'd cradled him in her arms for a long time after that first stormy coupling they'd fallen into when they'd come to bed, because she'd sensed he needed it. It had been all the more poignant because even a strong, powerful man like him needed the reassurance that he was cared for, she realised—even when his whole demeanour practically screamed to deny it.

'You don't have to worry about them. They are both women of the world. Besides...Giovanna put her head round the door about ten minutes after we came up here and saw that we were...busy.'

'What?' Covering her face with her hands, Anna groaned. 'Why didn't you tell me? Oh, my God...how am I ever going to look the woman in the eye again?'

'Beautiful Anna...you are making far too much of this when there really is no need. We already have a daughter. Don't you think that Giovanna and Ester have already guessed that we've been intimate?'

His teasing gaze brimmed with laughter again, and Anna lightly hit him on his toned tanned bicep. 'That's not funny!' Whirling away from him, she grabbed up her clothes from the arm of the chair, where she'd carelessly thrown them earlier, and headed for the sumptuous marble bathroom. 'You are utterly impossible—you know that?'

Dante was still grinning from ear to ear as she dramatically slammed the door shut.

CHAPTER ELEVEN

AMBLING through the quaint cobblestoned streets and alleyways of the bewitching lakeside town, Dante glanced at the titian-haired beauty beside him and wondered what he'd done to deserve the sense of satisfaction and contentment that kept washing over him.

Wearing a shift dress printed with pink poppies, her bright hair streaming loose down her back like Millais's *Ophelia*, she was the most eye-catching woman in the vicinity. More than that, the buzz he got from just holding her hand, strolling along like any other entranced tourist, couldn't be measured. All the money and success in the world couldn't match the pleasure of it. And as he walked Dante saw his home and the stunning Renaissance architecture that abounded with fresh eyes.

Another first was that for once he was simply being himself. It didn't matter who he was or where he came from. He'd shed the 'billionaire businessman' persona with alacrity, and there was such a euphoric sense of liberation about that that he almost wanted to announce it to the world. Instead, his hand lightly squeezed Anna's. In return, he received a traffic-stopping smile.

Tia was the only thing that was missing to make the day absolutely perfect. She had begged to be allowed to go with Ester and collect her son Paolo from kindergarten, after which she'd been invited to stay for lunch and to play with him for the afternoon. With Anna's consent first of all, Dante had agreed that she could go. He wouldn't have if he hadn't trusted Ester and her mother, Giovanna, completely. Giovanna had been his mother's closest and dearest friend, and that was how she and her daughter had come to take care of Dante's house for him—both when he was there and when he was away.

But although he was missing Tia already, they would all eat dinner together this evening, and he was appreciative of having some free time with Anna. This morning when they'd returned to bed she had surrendered *everything* to him. It had been as though she'd let all her carefully erected barriers down at once—even perhaps her fear of being controlled. She had simply accepted his sometimes too passionate loving with equal ardour and longing, her breathless sighs and eager exploring hands on his body letting Dante know that she was right where she wanted to be...no question.

Honestly, he had never known a woman so generous and giving—*in* bed and *out* of it. If he thought about losing her or letting her go his heart missed a beat. Frankly, it frightened him to realise how much she had come to mean to him. *Would she ever agree to marry him?* He almost felt sick at the idea she might not.

Stopping suddenly beside him, Anna pushed her huge sunglasses back onto her head to study him. 'I can hear a lot of wheels grinding and turning.' She grinned.

'What do you mean?' he asked, perplexed.

'I mean the wheels in your busy mind, Dante. What have you been thinking about?' Her brown eyes crinkled at the corners against the bright sunlight.

Pushing aside the sudden fear that arose inside him like a malevolent cloud blocking out the sun, Dante made himself smile. 'Nothing very interesting, I'm afraid. I was merely enjoying holding your hand and us being able to have this time together.'

'You weren't worrying about work? About what's going on at the Mirabelle or what million-dollar deals you're going to be making next?' Her tone was gently teasing.

'You believe all I think about is work when I'm with you?' He frowned, but then, when he might have descended into feeling guilty or frustrated that she could have such perception, he stroked his fingers across her soft cheek and followed it up with a playful pinch. 'Let me assure you, *innamorata*…my thoughts are *definitely* not about work when I'm with you. Could you doubt that after what happened this morning? There are still places on my body that throb and burn from making such uninhibited love with you. It's a wonder I can walk at all!'

Hot colour seared her cheeks and Anna lowered her gaze.

Dante chuckled softly. It was such a delight and also the biggest aphrodisiac to see her blush.

'You said there was a park that was a century old not too far away,' she commented, determinedly meeting his glance again, even though her cheeks still carried the heated evidence of her embarrassment. 'Can we go there?'

'We'll need to jump on the ferry, but why not?' he agreed, secretly delighted that he could give her such a simple pleasure.

'A ferry?' Anna beamed. 'Oh, I'd love that!'

And she did love it.

Her excitement was charmingly contagious. Dante received vicarious pleasure from travelling over the glinting blue lake on the passenger ferry with her, viewing the stunning homes that hugged the shoreline and the glimpses of medieval walls and towers in the background, even though the trip was hardly new to him and he had seen the sights many times before.

Seated on a slatted wooden bench half an hour later, in a park on the waterway that was full of Linden trees as well as a plethora of pink and red rhododendrons and white camellias, Anna swivelled round to observe Dante more closely. 'Tell me something about you that I don't know,' she urged smilingly.

Knowing there was no way of ducking out of the

question, Dante sighed, then answered quietly, 'I've been married before.'

Her beautiful smile vanished. 'Married? Not when we first met?'

'No.' His throat felt a little tight, and his voice sounded rusty. 'It was a long time before we met, Anna. I'd been divorced for about three years before I stayed at the Mirabelle that night.'

'Oh...' The relief in that breathless exhalation was tangible. 'What was her name?'

'Her name?' It never failed to astonish Dante how women always wanted to know the most inconsequential details. Another time it might amuse him. But not right now. Not when it had suddenly occurred to him that Anna might have strong reservations over marrying a man who had been divorced...especially when he told her the reason *why*. 'Her name was Marisa.'

'Was she Italian?'

'No. She came from California. I met her when I was living in New York. She worked at one of the financial establishments I dealt with there.'

'How long were you married?'

Reaching round a hand to rub the back of his neck, Dante sighed. 'Three years. She left me for someone else, if you want to know. But our marriage had hit the rocks long before that.'

'Why?'

Anna was twisting her hands together in her lap, and he sensed her definite unease. He cursed himself for bringing up the subject in the first place. To her question, 'Tell me something about you that I don't know,' he could just as easily have replied, *I'm a big fan of the opera, fine art and Italian football.* Telling her anything along the lines of the personal interests or hobbies he had would have been fine. Not that he'd ever had time for anything as normal or mundane as a hobby.

'She resented my extreme devotion to work. Whilst she loved what the rewards of that work could buy, she craved my attention too—and to be fair I wasn't as attentive of her as I could have been.'

'But it must have hurt when she left you for somebody else. Were you in love with her?'

Dante could hardly believe that he was seeing sympathy reflected in Anna's lovely dark gaze. He couldn't attest to understanding it, and was momentarily confused.

'No,' he answered honestly, 'I wasn't in love with her. Although when we first met I probably fooled myself that I was. She was vivacious, attractive and clever, and I had a couple of friends at the time who were also interested in her.' Ruefully, he shook his head. 'I suppose it was the thrill of the chase. That was the kind of thing that obsessed me then. Who could win the best deal, buy the best property, woo and win the most unattainable woman? Anyway, Marisa decided I didn't need to do much chasing after all. The wealthy lifestyle I could give her was a great incentive, you understand?'

His laugh was short and harsh. 'For a time we shared

similar aims. I was driven to succeed more and more, and so was she. She definitely wasn't the kind of woman who hankered after having a family. I suppose I kidded myself that the superficial interests we shared were enough to make our partnership work. That was until she met the young designer who came to remodel our New York apartment and had an affair with him.'

'And where is she now?'

'As far as I know she's remarried and living happily in Greenwich Village in New York, but it doesn't really concern me.' Standing up, he reached down a hand to help his silent companion to her feet. 'Let's walk on, shall we?'

Had he cared enough for his ex that he really *had* been hurt when she'd had an affair and then left him? Anna sucked in a breath, suddenly believing she knew why he seemed to have this need to take charge and control situations. Both his father and his wife had left him—it didn't matter that their marriage hadn't been a union made in heaven—and that had to have left some deep emotional scarring. It also must have pained him to learn he was married to a woman who'd seen his wealth as his greatest asset. To not be loved for yourself but instead to be wanted because of the lifestyle you could provide must be shattering.

Refusing to be downhearted because Dante had revealed he'd been married before—with his confession about his past the other night, at least now he was opening up to her a little bit—Anna smiled, sincere and relaxed. 'Yes, let's walk,' she agreed.

Walking along beside this broad-shouldered hand-some man, in his sexy designer shades, with every passing female no matter what her age glancing help-lessly at him, she returned her attention to the beautiful sights and scents of the park, with its plethora of flowers, ornate water fountains and sculptures. No matter what transpired between them she would never forget her month's sojourn in this magical place, nor its match-less, timeless beauty, she vowed. Even now, on only the second day into her visit, she hated the thought of leaving...

'And Paolo says I can visit him again any time I want. He speaks Italian, but his mummy told me what he said. He's so nice, Daddy. I really, really like him!'

His little daughter had scarcely paused for breath since Ester had brought her home. She'd been talking so excitedly about her visit with Ester's son that she had hardly touched the wonderful food that Giovanna had prepared for them. She'd made spaghetti Bolognaise especially because Tia had requested it.

Seated at the rectangular oak table in the wooden-beamed dining room with its huge marble fireplace, Dante had never enjoyed a meal more. Never in his life had anything felt more right than being here in Italy with Anna and his daughter.

'Well, sweetheart,' he said, beaming down into Tia's

bright eyes, 'I'm sure you will see little Paolo again very soon. But now you should try and eat something, eh?'

She took a mouthful of food, chewed it thoughtfully, then gazed back at him. 'Paolo said his daddy was dead.'

Opposite him, Anna put her fork carefully down on her plate. Dante sensed her concern. 'I know, *piccolina*,' he replied gently, laying his hand over Tia's. 'He was a friend of mine, and it was very sad when he died.'

'Does that mean that you're going to die soon, Daddy?'

Swallowing hard, Dante felt the question hit him like an iron fist in the belly. Just the thought of being separated from his child and her mother any time soon made him want to hold them in the circle of his protection with all his might—and woe betide anyone who tried to rip him away!

'Nobody knows when they are going to die, my angel... But I'm sure that heaven is not ready for me yet—especially not when I need to be here to take care of my girls!'

His throat was cramped and sore as he lifted his glance to Anna's. Just when he wanted to say more, his mobile phone rang. Glancing down at the caller ID as he took it from his shirt pocket, he saw it was from the Mirabelle.

'I'm sorry, but I really should get this. It's from Jason at the hotel,' he explained, swiftly moving away from the table and out into the corridor.

'Is everything all right?'

It wasn't the Mirabelle that was her topic of choice, Anna reflected as Dante came back into the room. What he'd said about needing to be here for her and Tia had touched her heart as nothing had ever done before, and now, setting eyes on his incredible sculpted features and winter-coloured gaze, she had an almost painfully irresistible desire to touch him and hold him. But he was holding out his phone to her, looking slightly perturbed.

'Everything at the hotel is fine… He just wanted to update me on the latest developments. Jason would like to speak with you.'

'Oh…'

Getting to her feet, and uncomfortably sensing Dante's disapproving gaze as he handed her the mobile, Anna followed his example and went out into the imposing corridor with its wall-mounted chandeliers and softly glowing lamps to take the call.

'Hi, Jason…what's up?'

'A couple of things.' His voice was friendly, but concerned. 'I heard that you were in Como with Dante. How's it going?'

'You know about me and Dante?'

'Mum and Dad told me yesterday. It was a shock, but I've had a funny feeling something's going on between the two of you ever since he showed up. Is it true that he's Tia's father?'

'Yes, it's true.'

Jason was a great colleague, and a friend, but she braced herself for his possible condemnation and hoped that if and when it came she could stay calm.

She heard him sigh. 'It must have been so hard for you, raising Tia all alone and not feeling able to contact Dante to let him know that you were pregnant. If I loved someone that much I could no more keep it to myself than fly to the moon!'

Mentally, Anna did a double-take, but her gaze was caught by the shining disc of the full moon reflecting off the dark lake outside the open casement window where the scent of heady Mediterranean blossoms floated in. Her heart squeezed with the magic of it all.

'What do you mean "if I loved someone"?'

'I can see now that you're crazy about him, that's all. You wouldn't be in Como with him if you weren't. I'm glad for you—so glad. There's nobody I know who deserves to have a happy ending more than you!'

'I *do* love him, Jason…you're right.' Acceptance and acknowledgement of her deepest feelings lapped through her like a warm velvet wave, and she crossed her arm over her waist as if to hug herself.

'So…when will the happy day be?'

'What?'

'If the man hasn't asked you to marry him then he needs his head tested.'

Chewing anxiously down on her lip, Anna glanced towards the not quite closed heavy oak door of the dining room and moved a little bit farther away from it. 'He did ask me to marry him, but I suggested we have a trial period of living together first.'

'What on earth for?'

'It makes sense, doesn't it?'

'When did loving someone ever make sense?'

To Anna's amusement, Jason sounded almost exasperated with her.

'If you love him and he loves you, and you already have the most adorable little girl together, then what's the point in having a trial period? You should be beating a path over the sun-baked cobblestones to the nearest church and sending us all invitations to the wedding quicker than I can say *la dolce vita*!'

'Should I?' she smiled. This new enthusiasm she was hearing in his voice was infectious. 'You said there were a couple of things... What else did you want to say?'

'I just wanted to let you know that included in the hotel modernisation your flat is to be converted too. I hope I haven't put my foot in it by telling you that— maybe Dante's told you about it already?'

Anna frowned. 'No, he hasn't. This is the first I've heard about it. What about all my stuff? I don't want all my belongings just thrown somewhere!'

'Don't be daft. I'll make sure everything is stored away safely—you know I will. There was just one other thing before I go.'

'Not another bombshell, I hope?'

'It's a surprise more than a bombshell. You know we were talking about romance just now...?'

The joy in his voice was hard to mistake, and Anna's curiosity grew.

'Don't keep me in suspense, Jason—tell me!'

'I think I've found my soul-mate.'

'You have? Oh, my God!' She squealed into the phone in sheer delight.

CHAPTER TWELVE

DANTE waited until Tia was in bed before confronting his fears about Anna's phone conversation with Jason Cathcart. She was sitting in front of the ornate dressing table mirror in her robe, brushing out her long fiery hair, when he walked up behind her and placed his hands on her slender shoulders. The material of the robe was thin enough for him to feel the shape of her bones, and beneath his touch he sensed her stiffen.

He wanted to say something like, *You sounded happy when you spoke to Jason,* but instead the words that came out of his mouth were sharp, bordering on accusing. 'What did Jason want? He had no business wanting to talk to you about work while you're on leave.'

Watching her expression in the dressing table mirror, he saw the satin-smooth skin between her brows pucker. 'Not even to tell me that my flat is being converted while I'm away and all my stuff is being put into storage?'

His hands reluctantly fell away as she turned to accusingly look up at him. 'I'm sorry I didn't get round to talking to you about that. With so much going on I—'

'Slipped your mind, did it? I can't pretend I'm not cross about this, Dante, because I am. That's my home that's being dismantled while I'm away.'

The subject really *had* slipped his mind since they'd arrived, and now Dante could have kicked himself. He knew how important her own place was to Anna, but there was something else he'd planned without telling her too.

It seemed now was the time to confess all.

Shaking his head slightly, he moved away across the floor. 'I owe you an apology…a big one, I know. But with the extensive refurbishment and modernisation going on at the hotel you couldn't expect your flat not to be included. However, I also want to tell you that I plan to buy a house for you and Tia—independent of whether you agree to move in with me permanently or not. A real place of your own that will come with no conditional strings attached and will be yours to do exactly what you like with.'

Without a doubt Anna was taken aback. Coiling her hair behind her ear, she didn't reply straight away, but seemed to be collecting her thoughts. When she did finally speak her expression was as touched and surprised as a small child upon whom a gift she'd never dreamt would be hers had been bestowed. 'You don't have to do that. It's an extremely generous gesture—*too* generous, really—but—'

'I want to do it for you, Anna.' Returning to stand in front of her again, Dante knew he meant it in earnest.

'I never want you to feel that your home is dependent on anyone ever again—either your employers or even *me*.'

'I don't—I don't know what to say.'

He grinned. 'Just say thank you and we'll forget about it.'

'Thank you.'

'Was the flat being converted all that Jason wanted to talk to you about?'

For some reason the question made Anna smile. 'It wasn't, actually.'

'No?' Dante sensed his irritation return. 'Then what else did he want to talk about?'

'It was a personal matter.'

'And you're his only confidante?' He was tunnelling his fingers through his hair and pacing the floor in a bid to contain his temper.

'We're good friends as well as colleagues.' Her slightly husky tone was the epitome of reason and calmness, but Dante felt his insides twist with jealousy and frustration.

'Good friends?' he said mockingly, throwing his arms wide as he came to a stop in front of her again. 'Isn't the man capable of having a male friend for a confidant?'

'Your tone suggests you think he might fancy me. Is that what's bothering you, Dante?'

'Can you blame me if it is?'

'That sounds a little possessive to me, and I don't like

it. I want to be free to talk to who I like without you being suspicious of me. I do have integrity, you know, and if I give my word that something is true then you'd better believe it.'

'If I'm concerned when you share confidences with a young, good-looking male it doesn't mean I'm trying to control or possess you. It simply means that I'm the man who has your best interests at heart, and naturally I care about who you associate with. You're the mother of my child, after all. That gives me certain rights whether you like it or not.'

Sighing, Anna fell silent for a moment, then got to her feet. 'Rights to discuss what's best for her as her father, yes,' she said. 'But those rights don't include trying to control *me*.'

'*Il mio Dio!*' He stared at her in disbelief. 'Did you not hear what I just said? I'm not trying to control you. Just because your father treated your mother like some—some possession he could do as he liked with, it doesn't mean that I'm cut from the same poor-quality cloth! I understand how the possibility of me being like that might scare you, Anna...' Moving closer to her, Dante slipped his hand onto her shoulder again, his heart pounding as though the starting pistol at a race had just cracked against his ear. 'I know you have great integrity, and I do believe you when you tell me that Jason is just a friend.' His lips stretched ruefully. 'But I can't help feeling a little jealous when I hear you being so animated on the phone with him.'

'Well, there's no need to be jealous.'

Her lustrous brown eyes had grown even darker, and her tone was soft, almost caressing. Now Dante's heart pounded hard for another reason. Dared he trust what he thought he saw in those silky warm depths?

Anna sighed. 'Jason told me that he's found his soul-mate at last and he's in love.'

'Really?' Relief was like a dam bursting inside him.

'I was so happy for him, because he'd started to lose faith in finding the love of his life. I told him the perfect person was just waiting somewhere, and that when the time was right, they would appear. So all's well that ends well, as they say.'

'And do you believe that the perfect person is waiting for every one?'

'I do.'

'I didn't realise you were such a romantic.'

'There's a lot of things you don't realise about me, Dante!'

Now she had a maddeningly secret smile playing about her lips, and he was plunged into confusion again. If he lived to be a hundred he would never understand women...never! All she seemed to want to do was torment him.

'Is there something else you have to tell me? If there is, for pity's sake just come out and say it.' He scowled at her.

'First of all, Jason would never fancy me because

I'm the wrong sex, and secondly...I've found my own perfect person. Yes, and he's standing right here in front of me. So, Signor Romano...there wasn't the remotest need for you to be jealous.'

Looping her arms around him, she planted an achingly moist and provocative kiss against his lips. Desire was like a thunderbolt flashing through him. Catching her by the waist, Dante impelled Anna urgently against his already hardening body. Beneath the ridiculously thin robe she wore an equally insubstantial nightgown with shoestring straps. He was already visualising tearing off both garments and having her firmly beneath him.

'Marry me.' His lips, tongue and teeth clashed voraciously with hers as heat, want and devastating need broke all their bounds. Breaking off the kiss with a harsh affected breath, he cupped her face to stare deeply into her eyes. 'You *have* to marry me, Anna.'

'Of course I do... That's what I want too.'

Words failed him. All he could do right then was stare at her in wonder. Then, when he trusted he could speak, he raised his eyebrow and asked, 'When did you decide that?'

'The first time we were together, of course—when I saw you sitting in the lounge bar looking so handsome, indomitable and fierce. I knew the intimidating facade you projected wasn't the truth. Underneath I sensed you were hurting so bad you didn't know where to go or what to do. I suppose I grew up having a finely tuned antenna for people's pain. My mum's marriage was so hurtful and destroying, how could I help it?' Her eyes turned moist for a moment. 'But she believed in true love. I don't know how she held on to such a belief when she was married to a man like my father, yet she did. And she wanted the very best for me. She always told me that when I gave myself to a man it should be to the man I love. I want you to know that I do love you, Dante... I always have and always will.'

'And you forgive me?'

'For what?'

'For not trying to contact you and then changing my name, not knowing or *believing* that you might want to contact *me*, or that you would even *want* to see me again after my telling you we could only have one night together?'

'We've both made mistakes. If we can't forgive each other and move on then it's hopeless. That's not a message I want to give our daughter—that if she makes a mistake there'll be no forgiveness.'

'*Ti amo.*' Dante smiled, his lips visiting a series of heartfelt passionate little kisses on her eyelids, nose, cheeks and mouth. 'I love you, Anna, with all my heart and soul. Sometimes I think love is not a strong enough word to express how I feel. That evening in the hotel bar I thought I was incapable of feeling anything remotely warm towards another human being again, but you proved me wrong. Yes...' His voice grew tender. 'You reached out to me so unselfishly, even accepting

my little speech about not being able to offer you anything else but that one night. And then, like an idiot, I
let you go. I've had to come to terms with some hard
losses in my life, but if I lost you again... If I lost Tia
now that I've discovered her...I don't think I would ever
recover.'

'Well, you're not going to lose either of us, my
love.'

'Is that a promise?'

With her heart in her eyes, Anna nodded. 'I swear
it.'

Leaving her for just a moment, Dante crossed the
room to the panel beside the door and turned down the
lights. A warm scented breeze blew in off the lake.

'You can turn them off completely. There's a ravishing full moon shining just outside the window. Didn't
you see it?'

Going to the balcony doors, Anna pushed them
opened a little wider. For a few seconds she stepped
outside to stare up at the moonlit sky. A sliver of white
cloud was drifting lazily across the fiercely bright orb
in the inky darkness, just as if some divine artist had
painted it right there, right at that moment, for her to
see. The illuminating and magical scene made her shiver
with delicious anticipation.

Joining her, Dante urged her back against his warm
hard chest. As Anna relaxed against him he undid the
belt of her robe and slipped the garment from her shoulders. The robe was immediately cast aside onto a nearby

wrought-iron chair. Then, through the paper-thin cotton of her nightdress, he cupped her breasts.

The heat from his hands, the perfect weight and shape of them against her most tender flesh, made Anna arch into his palms, her nipples puckering and hardening. Catching the rigid velvet tips between thumb and fore-finger, he squeezed and tugged a little, arousing a vol-canic need that poured into her centre like liquid honey heated over the hottest flame. Pressing himself against her bottom, Dante left her in no doubt he was as turned on by their arousing foreplay as she was.

Turning into his arms, Anna urgently tore at the but-tons on his shirt, making him smile as in her haste her fingers fumbled and missed the openings, causing her to curse softly beneath her breath.

'What are you trying to do to me, my angel?' he mocked gently, his hollowed out cheekbones emphasised even more by that devastatingly handsome smile.

'I'm trying to get you naked! What do you think I'm trying to do?'

With one fluidly mesmerising movement, Dante ripped his hand down the centre of the fine linen mate-rial and made the buttons fly off into the unknown.

Face to face with his magnificent tanned chest, the ripple of smooth sculpted muscle over a strong de-fined ribcage, Anna pressed a slow, loving kiss onto the warm hard flesh matted softly with dark blond hair. Then his hands were entwined in her hair, and he lifted her head up so that he could once again claim her lips with a demanding, almost savagely passionate kiss of his own.

'When you get me naked,' he said, the timbre of his voice sounding as though it had rolled over sun-baked gravel, 'what do you intend to do with me, *innamorata*?'

Looking straight into his moonlit blue-grey eyes, Anna smiled. 'I'm going to keep you awake until the early hours of the morning…and I should tell you that I've got an extremely vivid imagination. How do you like the sound of that?'

Dante nodded. 'I like it very much, you little witch. As long as you don't fall asleep on me when I take you on the little outing I have planned for us tomorrow.'

'Oh? Where would that be?'

'I'm taking you to see my mother's house.'

'You are?'

'I want to show you what I've done with it…the new use I've put it to.'

'I'm intrigued. I would love to see where your mother lived, Dante…to get a sense of the person she was. I know she meant the world to you.'

'Well, tomorrow you will. But right now…' He fixed her with the most meltingly wicked gleam she'd ever seen. Then he scooped one strong arm under her bottom, another round her waist, and lifted her high into his arms, so that she was suddenly on even more intimate terms with his eye-catching masculine chest and his drugging male heat. 'Right now I am taking you to bed...any objections?'

Anna gulped, her heart drumming hard. 'No...I can honestly say I've no objections at all, Signor Romano.'

Brimming with anticipation, along with a genuine sense of excitement, Dante hoped that Anna and Tia would enjoy the visit he had planned to the villa on the other side of the lake.

The house he had brought them to, across the water in a luxurious motorboat, sat almost majestically back from the lakeshore, its frontage a long verdant garden that ran down to its own landing stage. He was about to reveal something about himself that he had revealed to less than a handful of friends and acquaintances, and he wanted Anna to love it. Apart from fathering his lovely daughter, it was the achievement he was most proud of.

'This was where your mother lived?' Anna commented interestedly as he helped first Tia then her out of the boat. 'It's got to be one of the prettiest villas I've seen since I've been here.'

And it *was*, Dante silently acknowledged with pride, letting his gaze travel over the ancient olive trees and tubs of glorious red, white and pink bougainvillaea dotted all around. His loving glance strayed helplessly to his bewitching wife-to-be, with her dazzling copper hair, and his lovely daughter, with her sunlit blond curls, and he knew he was the luckiest man in the world.

He pocketed the motorboat key and reached for Anna's and Tia's hands. 'Let's go and take a look inside, shall we?'

'Do you have someone looking after the place?'

'Wait and see,' he answered mysteriously, urging them cheerfully onwards.

A young woman who looked like some avant garde artist, with wild dark hair, kohl-lined eyes and row of hooped gold earrings dangling from each ear, opened the door to them with a sweet-faced baby on her hip. A burst of animated Italian issued immediately when she recognised Dante, and she flung her arms around him with obvious affection and delight.

Fielding the little stab of jealousy that pricked her, Anna strove to hold on to the ready smile she'd adopted in anticipation of meeting whoever lived in the house now. Dante made the introductions, and the young woman who went by the enchanting name of Consolata hugged Anna and Tia in turn, making much of both Anna's and her daughter's eye-catching hair. Anna's anxiety dissipated.

'Come in…yes, you must come inside,' the girl urged in enthusiastic halting English.

They stepped into the most stunning glass-roofed vestibule. It reminded Anna of one of the greenhouses for exotic and tropical plants at Kew Gardens. It was so unique and beautiful that for a few moments she didn't know what to say. *What was this place? And who was Consolata?*

Glancing at Tia, whose hand was being firmly held by her handsome father, she smiled reassuringly. But her amazingly relaxed daughter was taking everything in her stride, glancing round the glass-roofed vestibule with wonder in her big blue-grey eyes, clearly loving every second of her visit already.

A warm kiss at the side of her cheek, an intoxicating drift of musky aftershave and Dante captured Anna's hand as well. 'My mother loved this place,' he explained softly. 'See that portrait over the marble fireplace? That's a picture of her that I had commissioned when she turned sixty. She was still very beautiful.'

'I can see that,' Anna murmured, gazing up at the stunning oil painting of a woman easily as bewitching as Sophia Loren—in fact, she didn't look dissimilar.

'When I returned to Italy, almost a year after her funeral, I had it in my mind to do something in memory of her—something that she would have been proud to be a part of. I spoke with Giovanna, and she told me of the problem of some of her daughter Ester's friends who are all single mothers. She then introduced me to Consolata, and some of the other young women who are struggling to raise children on their own. I donated the house to them, so that they could all live here and raise their babies knowing they were somewhere safe and secure that wouldn't be taken away from them. Giovanna manages the place, and the children and the mothers adore her. As well as five self-contained apartments in the building, there's a communal area and two large playrooms. All the women have access to local advisory and support services. Shall we go and meet some of them?'

All Anna could do was nod dumbly. Inside, she was deluged with so much pride and joy that she could scarcely contain it. She'd always suspected that the man she loved had the biggest heart, but nothing could have prepared her for *this*. What an amazing, wonderful and generous gift! What mother wouldn't be bursting with pride at having such a son? He had honoured his mother's memory in the most touching and incredible way.

Having experienced the challenges of single parenthood, Anna guessed how much such a place like this must mean to all those mothers. It also told her how deeply Dante must have been affected by his own experience of being the son of a mother who had struggled to raise him alone. But now the man had turned his childhood adversity into something positive and inspirational for the good of others.

Curling her hand more deeply into the curve of his palm, she knew what she was feeling blazed from her eyes as she gazed back at him. Instead of fearing that marriage might mean a loss of her independence and autonomy she was now actively looking forward to joining her life with this man. And when the time came to say her vows at their wedding she would utter them with absolute conviction and love…

* * *

Leaving the yacht in the harbour, the small group of well-wishers dressed in all their finery, including a couple of professional photographers, joyfully followed the bride-to-be and her groom on foot through a small network of cobbled streets to the plain whitewashed church on the hill, with its simple wooden cross.

Halfway there Anna laughingly took off her ludicrously expensive designer shoes, because the heels kept getting stuck between the cobblestones. But she didn't mind one bit. The sun was shining and the cloudless sky was a majestic azure blue—the kind of sky you dreamed of having on your wedding day. Everything was a good omen today. She couldn't have found a bad one if she'd tried.

With the straps of her cream-coloured shoes swinging from her fingers as they mounted the stone steps to the church, Anna glanced round at her daughter. Tia was holding on to the delicate tulle train of her mother's medieval-style ivory wedding dress as though guarding it from thieves or marauders intent on snatching it away from her. The expression on her angelic little face was one of intense concentration.

They stopped for a few moments on the steps as Dante gently but firmly pulled Anna into his side. On this, their wedding day, the mere sight of her husband-to-be stalled her heart. His suit was ivory-coloured linen, and beneath it his shirt was pristine white. Pushing aside some floppily perfect sun-kissed blond hair from his brow, Anna briefly bit down on her lip, then smiled.

Today his amazing eyes weren't the colour of winter. Instead they had the hue of a calm blue lake in midsummer, and here and there the glint of dazzling diamonds shone from their depths.

'You take my breath away, Dante Romano, and it's not just because you look good enough to eat.'

He brought her hand up to his lips and kissed it, avidly observing her from beneath his lashes. 'And I am in awe of your beauty and goodness, Anna mine. Today really *is* the best day of my life…so far—because from here on in it can only get better and better.'

A couple of camera flashes went off, and Grant Cathcart—bowled over by Anna's request for him to stand as father of the bride and give her away—called out, 'Hey, you two. The kissing's meant to happen *after* the wedding…not before it!'

'Yes, Mummy and Daddy—didn't you even know *that*?' Hand on hip, Tia let go of the train of Anna's dress for a moment and affected exasperation. As her parents and guests laughed, her look of exasperation was quickly replaced by one of horror as she saw the ivory train trailing over the stone steps. She grabbed it up again. 'I hope this hasn't got dirty—because if it has then I shall be *very* cross with both of you!' she declared.

'How on earth did we produce such a bossy child?' Dante laughed.

'It's got to come from *your* side.' Anna grinned. '*I*

was the personification of sweetness and light, growing up.'

His eyes narrowing, Dante tipped his head to the side, pretending to be doubtful. 'You sure about that, *innamorata*? Only I definitely recall one or two memorable occasions when the ability to be bossy seemed to come very naturally to you.'

'I'll make sure you pay for that remark later,' she whispered, her mouth trembling with humour as Dante once again pulled her towards him.

Hefting a noisy sigh, Tia turned round to the guests gathered at the base of the steps, in her ivory-coloured bridesmaid dress and pretty crown of delicate flowers, and threw up her hands. 'Everybody hurry up and go inside the church—before they kiss *again*!'

JOIN US ON SOCIAL MEDIA!

Stay up to date with our latest releases, author news and gossip, special offers and discounts, and all the behind-the-scenes action
from Mills & Boon...

 millsandboon

 millsandboonuk

 millsandboon

It might just be true love...

MILLS & BOON

THE HEART OF ROMANCE

A ROMANCE FOR EVERY KIND OF READER

MODERN

Prepare to be swept off your feet by sophisticated, sexy and seductive heroes, in some of the world's most glamourous and romantic locations, where power and passion collide.
8 stories per month.

HISTORICAL

Escape with historical heroes from time gone by. Whether your passion is for wicked Regency Rakes, muscled Vikings or rugged Highlanders, awaken the romance of the past.
6 stories per month.

MEDICAL

Set your pulse racing with dedicated, delectable doctors in the high-pressure world of medicine, where emotions run high and passion, comfort and love are the best medicine.
6 stories per month.

True Love

Celebrate true love with tender stories of heartfelt romance, from the rush of falling in love to the joy a new baby can bring, and a focus on the emotional heart of a relationship.
8 stories per month.

Desire

Indulge in secrets and scandal, intense drama and plenty of sizzling hot action with powerful and passionate heroes who have it all: wealth, status, good looks...everything but the right woman.
6 stories per month.

HEROES

Experience all the excitement of a gripping thriller, with an intense romance at its heart. Resourceful, true-to-life women and strong, fearless men face danger and desire - a killer combination!
8 stories per month.

DARE

Sensual love stories featuring smart, sassy heroines you'd want as a best friend, and compelling intense heroes who are worthy of them.
4 stories per month.

To see which titles are coming soon, please visit

millsandboon.co.uk/nextmonth

LET'S TALK

Romance

For exclusive extracts, competitions
and special offers, find us online: